Mistral Hearts

VALLEY OF SYLVEREN
BOOK THREE

JAIME RYANNE

WLL PUBLISHING

This is a work of fiction. All of the characters, organizations, places, and incidents portrayed in this novel are either products of the author's imagination or used fictitiously and are not to be construed as real.

Copyright © 2026 by Jaime Ryanne

All rights reserved.

No portion of this book may be reproduced in any form without written permission from the publisher or author, except as permitted by U.S. copyright law.

No content contained within this work was knowingly generated using artificial intelligence (AI). The content contained within this work may not be regenerated, repurposed, or processed using generative AI in any capacity.

Ebook ISBN: 978-1-965717-06-6

Paperback ISBN: 978-1-965717-08-0

Cover Illustration by Zureiil

Cover Typography by Jaime Ryanne

Map by Subtle Touch Creations

Editing by Isla Elrick

Proofreading by Adie Hart

www.jaimeryanne.com

For the unapologetically fierce women.

Content Note

This book contains mature themes, including explicit sexual content, aphrodisiacs (used consensually), and referenced toxic family behavior. For a full list of tropes and content notes, please visit the Books page of my website.

View the content guide here!

Chapter One

STIFLING A YAWN, Nocren Lowe made his way into the Sentinels' headquarters, nodding absently to the pair of clerks at the front desk. It had been three long days since the Storage Shed Debacle, as his fellow rangers and colleagues had taken to calling the newest kink in his current, disastrous mission.

He started toward the back room, thinking he'd grab one of the open desks and finish his report for the captain, when one of the clerks called out, "Hey, Lowe!"

Nocren slowed, turning his head to look back.

The clerk jerked her thumb toward the other side of the building. "Captain said to meet in the Big Room."

Confusion narrowed Nocren's eyes. "Did he say why?"

The so-called Big Room was the Sentinels' name for the conference room in the headquarters. It was rarely used aside from special occasions. Meetings took place in the captain's office, or sometimes one of the side areas if his office wasn't appropriate. But not the Big Room.

The clerk shrugged. "The Graelynd woman's already in there."

Before Nocren could ask more, a group of civilians came in, demanding every clerk's attention.

Exasperation audible only to himself, Nocren detoured toward the Big Room.

The Graelynd woman. Not terribly descriptive, but two faces immediately came to mind, though *why* either would be here for a meeting was unclear. Could it be Bioon Song, the Scourge of the Coalition, aiming for one last stab at clemency before they shipped her back south to Graelynd? He wouldn't mind seeing the captain deny her once again. It was the only bright spot for Nocren to come out of the Storage Shed Debacle.

Eternal Wind suffocate him—the ridiculous name had stuck.

Sure, the Debacle, or rather its result, was great for the community. A win for the Valley of Sylveren in general, and its university. Gods all break, it was especially fortunate for the neighboring kingdom of Rhell. The Storage Shed Debacle had exposed the treachery of Graelynd's Coalition of Trade. Without such an event, no one would know that an agent of the Coalition had nearly succeeded in stealing the plants required for the healing remedy needed in Rhell.

But gods all fucking break, why did it have to involve him?

It could be *her*, the other possibility in his mind for whom "the Graelynd woman" fit. Calya Helm. He struggled to think of her as just a woman from Graelynd. Just a name, about which he could remain objective. No, Nocren heard "Calya Helm" and could only picture the sharp-eyed, sharp-tongued brunette holding a rock. Leaning through the broken storage shed window and unlocking the door. Seizing a handful of desiccated leaves and waving at a crate bearing the logo of Sylveren University, her face lit up with smug triumph.

And Nocren? He'd been well and truly fucked with his trousers still on. Sentinels protected the Valley's interests, and the contents of the shed demanded an answer. Nocren hadn't had a choice but to act, and Calya had known it. Taken full advantage. She'd gotten what she wanted in disrupting the Coalition—to the detriment of Nocren and his mission—and kept them from sailing to the Song woman's aid.

But that had been important three days ago. It should've meant nothing to her now, so what reason would she have for coming here? As Nocren strode down the hall, the wind picked up, a soft whistle filtering through the glass windows. A breath of magic raced along his fingertips in response.

Nocren's mouth twisted. "Where were you when it mattered?" he asked the wind.

When he wasn't feeling so annoyed about the Debacle, Nocren knew he was being unfair. The wind carried as many truths as it did lies. Diviners learned quickly not to give the medium unconditional trust. Nocren knew of the risks inherent in his magic. Had fallen afoul of them as well, before he'd learned to read the wind with more care. Before he'd learned to keep his internal biases at bay. As much as one could, at least. The wind brought a flurry of vague impressions, wispy threads that blew through the mind one way and, depending on the diviner's intuition, came out differently the other. Every time he gave trust to the wind was like entering a bargain. An opportunity for insight, and for misconception.

But Calya. The wind had teased him with impressions of *her*, and he'd been a fool to listen. To indulge. How convenient that, in the glimpse of impressions he'd gleaned, the wind hadn't bothered to show her picking up the rock. He might've averted the Storage Shed Debacle if he'd seen how things would go. That the feeling of *Change* the magic had brought to him was exciting only for the wind because it didn't have to face any of the consequences.

When Nocren reached the conference room, the wind rose again as he grasped the doorknob. A thin current seeped through the window to twine around his fingers.

Brown eyes regarded him from a solemn face. "I'll never—"

Nocren blinked. He recognized those features. Remembered her voice. Rarely did the wind react so strongly without arcane encouragement from Nocren. It did so now. Made the words "I'll never" echo in his mind. Magic tickled at his fingertips, eager to be used. To call upon the wind and tease apart all the possibilities it offered.

He clenched his hand into a fist, his fingernails biting into his palm until the sensation of magic receded and the wind dissipated, the hallway's air becoming still once more. He had already been fooled by the wind once when it came to that woman; he wouldn't give into it again.

He knocked once on the door, then pushed it open without waiting for a response.

Calya Helm sat alone at the long table inside, a teacup set before her.

For a moment, Nocren contemplated leaving. A trickle of wind brushed the side of his face, a hint of both its apology and reproach flitting through his head.

His mouth opened, an inane excuse frozen, half-formed, on the tip of his tongue. Calya's brown eyes *were* regarding him from her solemn face.

But then she tilted her head ever so slightly to the side, a ghost of a smirk upon her lips.

"Mr. Lowe," she said. "Cutting it rather close, don't you think?"

Never before had he met someone whose voice was so perfectly suited to them. The low register and coolness with which she spoke, the neutrality in her tone. None of the bright, upbeat nature he associated with Graelynd speech patterns.

"I—" He hesitated. "What are you doing here?"

"I heard that the Sentinels were looking to charter a ship with clearance to sail Graelynd's waters. Helm Naval Engineering has some flexibility in its schedule." Calya spread her hands in front of her as she spoke. "Given what happened the other day, I thought Captain Malek'ko might be interested."

Nocren's gaze darted to the longcase clock at the front of the room. Its hands indicated there were still five minutes until the designated hour. "The meeting wasn't slated until—"

"In my world, you're already ten minutes late." Calya took a sip of her tea. "Is this the sort of professionalism I should expect of the Sentinels?"

Her world. Brash, entitled Graelynders. And she hailed from the capital, Grae Port. The heart of its Central District, a busy hub of politics and government and trade. Crowded, elitist; a place that believed worth and success were best measured in coin. He barely knew the woman and already Nocren could see how she was a product of an environment that grated on him at his very core.

He should have been repelled by her. As it was, he could barely look away.

His traitorous feet carried him into the room. "Says she who put a rock through the window of a storage shed."

Calya's smirk widened as he took a seat across from her. "The *Coalition's* storage shed, wherein we found evidence of their crimes at Sylveren University. Give me some credit. You can't make up more deserving parties—for or against."

If only she'd waited a few minutes before smashing it. Or explained anything with even a modicum of detail. If only she'd given him a godsdamned moment to find another Sentinel to secure the storage shed and let his business relationship with the Coalition remain intact. But no, she'd taken it upon herself to stop the Coalition delegates, and Nocren couldn't have let Renstown's constabulary take control if the stolen plants might have pertained to the Sentinels' case of possibly distressed researchers. Unfortunately, in the end, the plants had had nothing to do with his case, because of course that would be his luck.

Nocren scowled at her across the table. He saw a blend of nationalities in her features: brown eyes that tapered at the outer corner, and softness to her nose that suggested ancestry in the eastern Radiant Isles; a squared jaw framed by medium brown hair, not to mention her frank demeanor, spoke of her Graelynd roots. She looked around a decade his junior, somewhere in her late twenties, with skin still clear and smooth despite a ruddy complexion. That, paired with her hair, styled in a way that curled well clear of her slim shoulders, might've painted a picture of youthful sweetness. On a different person.

Not Calya Helm, with her sharp gaze and the imperious lift of her chin—the way she seemed to be assessing whatever she deigned to grant her attention. In her, there was nothing sweet to be found. Only a cold beauty and an air of thinly veiled impatience.

None of it should have appealed, yet Nocren found himself wondering what it would take for her to show patience.

"Excuses, from one making insinuations about professionalism," he said.

Calya shrugged. "Perhaps, but I instigate on the side of good."

"Or in the name of your self-interest."

"Am I so alone in that?" she asked, tone too sweet. "I seem to recall you growling about a year's worth of work undone."

Over a hundred active Sentinels of the Valley, probably half a dozen in Renstown at the same time, and *he'd* been the one caught up in the Debacle. Him, the only Sentinel negotiating a shared waterway deal with the Coalition so the rangers could gain access to the northeastern tip of Graelynd. Access they needed to investigate the odd communications they'd received from a group of Sylveren University researchers stationed out there.

Those negotiations had been dragging on, a year of patience and compromises, getting into the good graces of progressively influential people in the organization. Time he was never getting back.

"Because you wouldn't wait for— You didn't even *warn* me about what you were going to do," Nocren said, adding, "And I don't growl."

Her lips quirked in amusement, but she didn't correct him, instead saying, "You knew I was interested in the *Coalition's* storage shed. Clearly a conflict of interest, no? Need to think quicker on your feet, ranger." She straightened up, her hands folding primly in front of her. "Really, you should thank me."

"Whatever for?" Nocren said, regretting the words the moment they left his mouth.

"We basically saved Rhell, if indirectly. The real healing plants are alive and being... distilled or whatever. I'm not a grovetender."

"I'd never have guessed."

She ignored him. "The point is, the real plants are effective against the poison in Rhell. We kept the Coalition from going to Song's aid when she tried to destroy them, *and* we got the Coalition sanctioned. We're essentially heroes because of me. You're welcome."

Nocren squeezed his eyes shut as his brain shut down trying to follow her logic. It was true that in the seven years since the war with the empire of Eylle had ended, the kingdom of Rhell had still suffered. A cursed poison ravaged the lands and sickened those in proximity to the tainted ground. Losing the healing plants would've been devastating. Nocren understood that. And as someone who called the Valley of Sylveren home, he rejoiced whenever Graelynd's domineering trade organization got slapped with consequences. It happened so rarely.

He should've let that be the end of it, yet Nocren heard himself say, "Still, it's very convenient that your selfless actions had so many benefits, wouldn't you say?"

Another smile, this time with a wicked edge. "I said I'm on the side of good. Never said I do it for free."

The door opened again, this time admitting Captain Malek'ko. Nocren and Calya both stood, offering their hands in greeting before the older man took a seat at the head of the table.

"Lowe," the captain said in his gravelly voice. He nodded to Calya, shaking her hand as well before turning back to Nocren. "Everything handled across the lake?"

"Yes, just about," Nocren answered. "Though I had to promise the Renstown Watch's constable that you would send copies of the final report."

"Me," Malek'ko said, a thousand sighs held in the single word. He scraped a hand over his balding pate. He hadn't lost any more of his wiry hair kept shorn close to the scalp, despite the stress of the Storage Shed incident. But he had possibly gone grayer, his mustache now completely white. It stood out in stark contrast to his dark brown skin, lending no help whatsoever in masking the disgruntled look that crossed his face.

"It was the only way I could convince her to let me claim any rights to the contents," Nocren said. Then, with a wince, he added, "The Coalition delegates didn't take it well. They refused to meet with me after they'd been cleared."

"We've already received notice demanding your removal from any negotiations," Malek'ko said quietly. "That is, *if* they resume."

Guilt and frustration churned in Nocren's gut. He refused to look in Calya's direction. Didn't want to know what expression she wore. Indifference would only further annoy him, and anything like chagrin was unlikely.

Fortunately, Malek'ko continued on, turning to Calya as he said, "Which is why I asked Miss Helm to meet with us. We may have an alternative for getting to Desmond's Landing."

"What?" Nocren said in disbelief.

"Nevin is ready to test some prototypes of the healing tea," Malek'ko said, naming the ranger-turned-horticulture-professor at Sylveren University.

Ollas Nevin hadn't been an active Sentinel in half a dozen years. And, though he was a good sort, Nocren had always been of the opinion that the younger man was a better gardener than he was a ranger. Seemed to prefer it, too. He and his partner had grown a plant and, through a mix of luck and hard work, produced a remedy that could cleanse the poison devastating Rhell if caught before it became embedded in a body. It still wasn't a cure for the poison outright, couldn't reverse the blight where it had already taken hold in the ground. But it was *something*. Finally, Rhell had a way to contain the poison and keep its people alive.

"Will you have issues from the Rhellians?" Calya asked. "I imagine they aren't thrilled to be sharing a remedy that's still so scarce."

Nocren didn't admit to it out loud, but he agreed with Calya. It only made sense that the precious few batches of this miracle tea imbued with the strength of the Valley would go to Rhell. The Eyllic poison was singular in its purpose, seeking only the Rhellian wellspring of magic. Graelynd, being neither Rhell nor possessing a wellspring of its own, should have no use for it.

"Most of it will go north, but Nevin said they have a few leftovers to spare." Malek'ko unrolled a map covering the lower half of the Valley of Sylveren and upper Graelynd. He tapped his finger against a penciled circle surrounding the small dot that marked Desmond's Landing far out on Graelynd's northeastern coast. "Nevin said you did some checking up on the Coalition for him?"

Nocren nodded. "They were sending reports on his class to some project out in the Landing. It didn't amount to anything."

"Is there a chance they need the tea for a real threat?" Calya asked.

Malek'ko shrugged. "We haven't heard anything to suggest it, but whoever wanted Nevin's work out there might be interested in how the protection magic in the tea works. That's our excuse for getting to the Landing. We go under the stated reason of transporting the tea, since it's high value."

"I'll go," Nocren said. "I've researched the area plenty for the Coalition deal."

"And I plan to send you." Malek'ko's eyes went to Calya. "Which is where Miss Helm comes in. The enchantment in the tea is delicate and can't be refreshed at sea. It needs to get to the Landing as quickly as possible."

Calya clasped her hands in front of her. "Helm Naval's ships are in the area often enough. Adding an additional stop for one of our windrunners shouldn't be much trouble."

They began to negotiate, a discussion that required only intermittent comments from Nocren, affirmations of the routes and approximate schedules he'd been working on with the Coalition. When the conversation moved on to departure times and other logistics, Nocren's mind wandered.

He didn't know a lot about Calya's family's shipping company, Helm Naval Engineering, beyond it being one of the more prominent businesses in the maritime world. How fortunate for the Sentinels that the heir apparent to the Helm Naval enterprise would offer up space on one of her ships.

But at what price?

"I'll send word once I have a sailing date," Calya said, standing up. "We have ships large enough to accommodate a contingent of your rangers, but my father's trustee will push back against your inclusion without a solid reason warranting it."

"Our relationship with the university may help. I'll have the necessary details for you in time," Malek'ko vowed.

"I'll walk Miss Helm out," Nocren heard himself say.

Calya's eyes went to his, an unreadable expression brief upon her face before she smiled sweetly. "Very generous of you, Mr. Lowe."

She followed him out to the headquarters' front steps, pausing under the covered entryway as she pulled on her cloak. A furrow marred her otherwise unlined brow as she gave the gray sky a baleful look.

A trickle of wind licked around her, hardly enough to draw Calya's attention. But to Nocren, for a brief yet undeniable moment, it was a gale to his senses. An echoey feeling of *Important* and *Dramatic* and *Change* rattled around his head, the impressions carried by the wind as he stared at her and tried to ignore how his magic buzzed along his fingers. Calya might as well have been limned in gold for how unsubtle the wind was with its intent. Usually, it wasn't so forthcoming, giving him only snippets of possibilities and moving on, the epitome of temporality unless he leaned on the arcane to ask for more.

The urge to give in to his magic clamored against the bitterness of her recent conduct. So far, when the wind and Calya mixed, it brought nothing but complications to his life. Left his objectivity in tatters. He knew better than to go down that road.

Calya gave him a sidelong glance. "You seem to have something on your mind."

Everything about her pulled at him. Made Nocren want to know who she was and why the wind would show him visions of a virtual stranger. Made him want to know her. Learn what it took to make her give such a declarative statement. *I'll never.* The unspoken challenge in her gaze—in the brief image from the wind, in the way she looked at him now—it made him want to know if her words were meant for him.

"Why?" he finally said. "Why are you trying to help the Sentinels now?"

"I told you, Ollas mentioned that the Sentinels—"

"Feeling guilty?"

She scoffed. "This is business, ranger. I'm always looking to expand Helm Naval's partnerships, so when this opportunity arose, I took it."

Nocren crossed his arms. "Simple as that, eh? Because we're likely to do so much business together."

Calya's gaze fell away as she fussed with the hood on her cloak. "I don't regret my actions the other day, seeing as we averted a disaster involving my friends at the school. But I wasn't aware, you know, of your particular involvement with the Coalition at the time. So that is... unfortunate."

Nocren stared at her, amusement tugging at the corner of his mouth. "Are you— Is this your attempt at an apology?"

Another scoff, this one more pronounced, accompanied by

Calya flipping her cloak's hood up to cover her face. "Hardly. I'm expressing... empathy, or some shit."

"Word of advice," Nocren drawled, "the next time you're trying to fake empathy, don't follow it with 'or some shit' in the same breath."

"You're a fount of wisdom, Mr. Lowe." Calya squared her shoulders. "I prefer actions over words in all things, and penitence is no exception."

"I'm sure you do."

"Until next time, then," she said, tilting her face toward him.

Schooling his expression to neutral, Nocren made himself nod stiffly in response. The wind made her cloak billow out as she moved into the street. Nocren's magic sang beneath his skin, a tremor running through his fingers as it begged to be called upon. He ignored it, stuffing his hands into his pockets. But he stayed outside, watching until Calya's back disappeared from view.

I'll never.

The words, ones she hadn't spoken thus far, echoed in his head long after she was gone.

Chapter Two

As she passed by the Mighty Leaf's front windows, Calya Helm paused beneath the eaves to reorient herself before going inside. The sounds of merriment from the café's grand reopening spilled out into the street, words and laughter blurring together.

Under the guise of removing her cloak's hood, she snuck a glance at her reflection in the teashop's window. No sign of a pink tinge in her cheeks. Good. Not that the ranger had made her blush. It wasn't him but the briefly uncomfortable circumstances she'd found herself in, feeling pangs of... conscience, where he was concerned.

Lowe had seemed taken aback by her actions.

Calya's lips tensed with the tiniest of smiles. People underestimated her to their detriment. At only twenty-seven years of age and having grown up in her elder sister Anadae's seemingly perfect shadow, Calya was used to surprising people. Rudely. She delighted in it. Usually, her victims were fellow businesspeople or merchants in the maritime logistics trade. It wasn't often—or ever—that she had dealings with a Sentinel of the Valley.

Not that Lowe was a victim, or even a true adversary. More of a tool, and she'd used him accordingly, but that didn't mean Calya took pleasure in the ranger's own work being so negatively affected. She wasn't altogether heartless. Working on it, but not there yet. So, she felt a smidgen of guilt for causing him hardship. She'd have done it again, of course. But perhaps if she'd convinced Lowe to look into the Coalition's storage shed quicker, things would be different. They might've discovered the stolen plants with enough time for him to do whatever he'd planned to stop the Coalition while managing to keep himself on their good side. Still, the Coalition of Trade tended to know when someone was trying to exploit them—an activity the organization enjoyed so long as it was them doing the exploiting—so Calya didn't think much of Lowe's chances.

It was all moot now anyway. She'd come to Renstown to ensure that the Coalition didn't sail to the aid of their colleague, Bioon Song, as she'd tried to ruin a project at Sylveren University, and in that Calya had succeeded. With her help, Eunny Song had foiled her mother and defended their rare plant. In doing so, they'd secured the first remedy capable of healing someone sickened by the poison ravaging the small kingdom of Rhell.

It was a triumph for all. Of that, there was no doubt.

Peering through the window, Calya looked for any sign of Anadae, but her elder sister didn't appear to be part of the crowd inside the Mighty Leaf. Perhaps she'd gone next door to Eunny's repair café, Song's Scrap.

Calya thought about going in search of her, but weariness made up her mind. Even on a windrunner-class ship, it would take an hour to get back to the Helm Naval office in Renstown. She'd already crossed once today, at the crack of dawn, to help with the last finishing touches before Song's Scrap opened, and bed and HNE's latest trade logs called to her more than revelries.

With a final, mournful glance as a server walked past the window with a tray of winter-themed spiced teacakes, Calya made her way to the town of Sylvan's small harbor. She caught the last ship of the evening and settled in for the trip across the lake to Renstown.

Making herself as comfortable as a person prone to seasickness could be, Calya reached for her belt purse and the ginger candies she relied on to make the trip bearable.

Her fingers scraped the bottom, no organza bag of sugar and herbs to be found. All she managed to scrounge up was a single empty paper wrapper.

"Shit," Calya hissed. She'd been planning to spend the trip catching up on correspondence from her father's trustee, Wembly. Despite his dour manner, he was admittedly an efficient man, but their business relationship was tepid at best. Sometimes, Calya wondered if her father had instructed him not to oversee and advise her in the running of Helm Naval Engineering but to oppose and question every decision she made. Given that Andrin Helm had named Wembly to act in his stead rather than officially relinquish control of the company to her, whenever she found herself diametrically opposed to the trustee, she lost.

Wembly would want at least a brief discussion as setup for a longer meeting once she arrived at Helm Naval's office in Renstown. It would be unwise to go into any meeting without having reviewed the letters he'd couriered to her while she visited Anadae and friends in Sylvan.

Before she could disembark in hopes of finding a dockside vendor with the motion sickness candies, the ship's horn blared. Calya grimaced as the blend of active and passive spellwork that enabled the windrunner's great speed came alive. Her stomach protested the way the floor moved beneath her feet and the tingle of magic lacing the air.

Calya dropped back into her seat with a muttered, "Goddess fucking break me."

She'd put off Wembly until the morning. She wouldn't even be lying when she claimed sickness. The tea she'd had at the Sentinels' office was already threatening to reappear.

Closing her eyes, Calya let her mind drift, searching for anything but the nausea building at the back of her throat.

Lowe's scowling face came to mind. Those piercing eyes. Nice ones, Calya would give him that. Gray, like the storm clouds so often present in the Valley's skies. He always seemed to wear an expression that matched. Brow perpetually furrowed, jaw tight. There was a ruggedness to him, a bit of weathering in his face, a tousled quality to the dark hair that fell past his shoulders. It all made for a hard, imposing man. But then, Calya had never been interested in soft or sweet.

Lowe wasn't quite a barrel of a man, but his chest was broad enough to fill out his rangers' leathers. The forest green of the Sentinels' cloaks suited him well. He was a bit older than her usual partners. Gruffer and more growly, too. None of that bothered her. As distractions went, he'd do nicely.

Calya's lips twitched with a smile. There'd been something charged about their interaction at the meeting. Tension, but the antagonism had lessened more and more. She'd nearly made him smile, even if it was at her own expense. Their tension was a type that needed only a nudge of encouragement to go from wary to smoldering, unless she was mistaken about the look in Lowe's eyes, and rarely did Calya make those kinds of mistakes.

What secrets did the ranger keep locked behind his stoicism? She'd seen the barest hint before she left. A whisper of wicked humor. It left her hungry for—

"Caly?"

She jerked in her seat, eyes snapping open.

Her elder sister, Anadae, peered down at her.

"Ana... dae." Calya sat up, mentally chastising herself for relapsing into her sister's former, now discarded, nickname. "Dae. What are you doing here? I thought you'd be with Eunny and the others."

"I stepped out to say goodbye to a colleague heading back to Rhell." Anadae slid into the seat next to Calya. She dug in her cloak pocket and pulled out a small pouch of ginger candies, dropping it into Calya's lap. "You're already looking green around the edges."

Calya greedily stuffed two of the candies into her mouth. "I'd take offense, but I don't care." She breathed a sigh of relief as the queasiness in her stomach abated.

"I was planning to stop by the HNE office tomorrow, but then I saw you boarding," Anadae said, helping herself to a candy. She ignored Calya's squawk of protest. "What? I like how they taste."

"You should've mentioned you needed something at the office. I could've brought it over."

Anadae shook her head hard enough for her wavy, dark brown hair to bounce. "It's no trouble." She glanced around to make sure the other passengers were occupied before continuing in a lower voice, "Have you had any more issues with the joint protection deal you worked on with Brint and Avenor Guard?"

Calya's eyes narrowed, but she kept her tone as calm as her sister's. "There's still some accounting that needs to be straightened out, but nothing overly concerning as far as I know." She waited a moment, watching Anadae's face. "What don't I know, sister dearest?"

"It might be nothing," Anadae said. "The environmental resto project Brint drove into the ground out in Desmond's Landing—"

"The one that caused his fuckery with my route deal with AG," Calya said.

Anadae nodded. "Some of the mages who joined the remaining staff to get things in order are from SU. About a month ago, they wrote requesting some of the wards Ez and I made. Not prime stock, so we sent a few that were marked as seconds," she said, naming Ezzyn Sor'vahl, the youngest prince of Rhell as well as her partner in both love and work. Together, they'd devised the containment warding system keeping the poison from completely destroying his homeland.

"Why did they want them?" Calya asked.

"Apparently, to see if there were relevant applications of technique. But we never heard back." Anadae's expression turned grim. "I wanted to see if there was an error in the HNE logs when I made the request."

"The logs," Calya said slowly, wracking her brain for any memory of such a request.

"They were supplemented to a shipment following the new route with Avenor Guard," Anadae said. "There should be records and receipt of payment. Ez insisted on paying for the additional stop."

Of course Sor'vahl would insist. He'd have to, for Helm Naval would've offered to provide such a request as complementary. It was easy enough to arrange, seeing as a few wards didn't exactly take up tons of precious cargo space, and Anadae was the elder Helm daughter. Regardless, a stopover at Desmond's Landing was literally on the way; adding the package to one of the ships using the joint protection route Calya had arranged with Avenor Guard wouldn't overly upset shipping times. A quick update to the paperwork to ensure everything was logged and in order, and the change could slip into the regular schedule without issue.

But it was the kind of scheduling change Calya should've heard about. The logistics manager would've made a note of it since the request concerned her sister. Calya made a point of reading at least the summaries of Helm Naval's shipping logs every month. If her sister's name, or Sor'vahl's, for that matter, had appeared, she'd damned well remember. That she couldn't did not bode well.

"You didn't know," Anadae said, more a quiet realization than a question. There was nothing accusatory in her tone, yet it landed like a slap.

For years, Calya had been fighting to prove herself worthy of taking over Helm Naval. Had been forced to redouble her efforts when *Andrin* appointed a trustee instead of elevating his own godscursed daughter in his stead. Because she wasn't Anadae, the leveling presence to Calya's supposed hot head. But then, Anadae wouldn't have missed such an amendment to the logs. That Calya *had*... Perhaps she was slipping.

"It's possible something happened on the water," Anadae offered.

"The Bay of the Child is hardly the raging sea. Besides, it's a straight shot from Rhell's riverway to Desmond's Landing. None of our ships have taken damage or gone missing. No unreported changes in the delivery schedules. There's been... nothing. Nothing of this at all." Calya forced her lips into the shape of a tight smile. "I'll ask Wembly. He reviews all our records too, so maybe he'll remember."

Anadae gave her a look that said she saw through Calya's blasé tone, but she didn't press. "I'm surprised you're still here. You left Eunny's party a while ago."

"I had a meeting." Calya recounted her proposed business with the Sentinels, making sure to keep the details general. "Ollas told me about the complications I caused the Sentinels when I kept Bioon's cronies from sailing to her aid," she concluded. She didn't regret breaking into the Coalition's storage shed or helping to incite something of a citizen's detainment of the Coalition delegates. But the Sentinels did good work, and Calya didn't enjoy acquiring collateral damage.

"Caly has a heart," Anadae teased in a singsong tone.

"Never."

Anadae laughed, snagging another candy before Calya stuffed the pouch into her cloak pocket. "Are you planning to go to the Landing?"

"I wasn't." Calya gave her sister a shrewd look. "Should I?"

Anadae sucked on the candy, expression turning thoughtful. "I — Okay, this is all rumor, so don't read too much into it. But the colleague I met with earlier? She's coming off a consulting job with AG that had her in Central District a lot."

A sinking feeling settled in the pit of Calya's stomach, and this time she couldn't blame it on the motion of the ship.

"There are some rumors going around that Brint is maneuvering to get back on the Guard's board." Anadae placed a steadying hand on Calya's arm. "Small, very vague rumors. Not even enough to get the *Grae Port News* hounds sniffing. So, it might be nothing."

The periodical that circulated in Central District's capital thrived on such gossip, so for it to be quiet should've been a comfort. Yet suspicion lingered in Calya's mind.

"How is that even possible?" she asked, though she didn't expect a response. It was Brint. Censure by the Coalition of Trade and removal from his family's company's board for sabotaging the joint protection route deal *should have* been a career killer—Calya's father would have held it against her ever having a position of power in Helm Naval again—but Brint had a way of slithering out from under consequences.

Calya glanced at her sister. Concentration had turned Anadae's expression serious. Solemn, almost eerily like their mother, whom Anadae had always taken after more with her Hanyeok features than Calya and her square jaw ever could. They were half-Graelynder, but Anadae's hair would always be closer to their mother's shade of black than Calya's chestnut, her skin closer to the light brown with a golden undertone where Calya's was Graelynd pale and pink and burned like it, too. Not that the sun was anything to worry about in the dreary Valley.

"You've got Mother's thinking face on," Calya said.

Anadae's nose scrunched up.

"Well, not now. Wrinkles, sister dearest."

Anadae laughed, though there was a wryness to the sound. "I can reach out to some of my old AG contacts, see if any of them will share anything."

Calya waited a beat, made sure her voice held a concerned note instead of rampant eagerness when she asked, "Are you sure?"

Anadae likely was still friendly with people within Avenor Guard who might know more about the younger Avenor son and his motives. She had been unhappily affianced to the man for years and handled plenty of administrative tasks between the families' two companies. Her connections ran deeper than Calya's, but they were from a life Anadae had put behind herself with a vengeance when she'd chosen to break free of Brint. She'd left Helm Naval all to Calya to run so she could return to school and become the mage she'd always wanted to be. All she'd wanted was that life, and a man who'd actually love her in return.

"You don't have to," Calya said. As much as she might wish things were different, she knew she had to accept that Anadae wanted a life so different than previously envisioned.

"I know," Anadae said, gently. "I want to for you."

Calya never quite knew what to do with kind moments. Ones of gentle, earnest sincerity from someone she cared about. She cracked a smile before hiding behind her teacup.

"Besides, Ez wants to know what happened to our wards, too," Anadae continued. "But the kingdom can't get involved. Resources, diplomacy, you understand."

Calya rolled her eyes. "Of course."

"I'm staying with a friend in Renstown tonight, but I'll come by the HNE office tomorrow afternoon."

The thinned-down shards of the ginger candies crunched beneath Calya's teeth. She grimly plucked a fresh one from her small cache. A quick glance toward her sister revealed Anadae pulling a book from her bag and settling back to read. The very notion of reading was enough to make nausea rear its head.

Are you planning to go to the Landing?

Calya mulled over the prospect. The Sentinels needed the fastest windrunner HNE could provide—speed enchantments the mere thought of which had bile threatening to rise in her throat. Such a voyage would be tough to weather even with a chest full of the motion sickness candies.

But Lowe would be there. Not as a fantasy lingering in the corners of her mind, but in the flesh.

A flicker of heat stirred in Calya's belly. She let her eyes close once more, thoughts drifting back to the gruff ranger. Traveling by windrunner all the way to the Landing? Perhaps it wasn't so unappealing after all.

Chapter Three

Most of the lamps were turned down by the time Calya crept into Helm Naval Engineering's office building in Renstown. Only the front light still glowed, causing her to move slowly as she navigated through the dark to the stairwell leading to the residential floor.

She'd nearly made it, fingers outstretched to grip the handrail, when light flared at the end of the hallway. She bit back a curse as the tall, gaunt figure of Arthur Wembly cast a long shadow across the floor.

"Miss Helm. I thought you would take an earlier ship," the older man said.

"The festivities at Song's Scrap went longer than I'd anticipated." The small lie flowed smoothly off Calya's tongue as she forced a conciliatory smile to her face.

A disappointed exhale accompanied Wembly's frown. The man was the pinnacle of joyless. "I see. If you have a moment—"

"Sorry, Mr. Wembly, but it's been a long day, and the sail was unpleasant." Only a partial lie that time. Anadae's missing wards and the rumors about Brint lingered in Calya's mind. She wanted a chance to look over last month's shipping records before girding up for battle with the trustee. "If we could continue this in the morning, I'll—"

"I take it you did not read any of the messages I sent?"

Calya froze with one foot on the first stair. Smoothing her expression to neutral, she faced Wembly as he approached. "I'm afraid I didn't have a chance. But I met with the administration while I was at the university. Everything from the protection route with AG should be cleared up, and the final accounting will be sent next quarter."

She couldn't recall the specifics of Brint's failed research experiment, something about manufacturing a new type of armor that would've benefitted Avenor Guard. Only, the process was dangerous and toxic, and environmental cleanup very costly. Brint had used the longstanding relationship between his family's security company and Helm Naval to hide the evidence of his royal fuckup. Gods only knew how long he'd have managed the deception if not for the joint protection deal Calya had brokered between their two companies using a route that went too close to Brint's failure. In his efforts to keep it a secret, it had only unraveled further.

His mess, yet Andrin Helm saw only how it reflected poorly on *her*. She'd been the one to strike the deal, to not keep a closer eye on Brint and his erratic behavior. *Her* decisions that nearly embroiled Helm Naval Engineering in a scandal.

Eighteen months she'd been chafing under Wembly's thumb as she cleaned up every last bit of Brint's failure, excising every last hint of his taint. It was finally behind her.

Or so she'd thought.

"I've had letters from your father about your recent business arrangements made with the university," Wembly said, stopping in front of her.

"I sent thorough reports. The terms are favorable for us," Calya said, injecting false sweetness into her tone. "Not just monetarily, either. I've taken your lectures on building soft power and image to heart."

Which generally meant taking whatever Wembly advised and either doing the opposite or doubling her efforts, depending on what exactly he had suggested. He was always too conservative for Calya's taste.

"Miss Helm." Wembly sighed, eyes closing as if the words physically pained him. "Impulsive unilateral decision-making is what led to my position here. Such deals require discussion."

Calya had been patient. Mostly. Had worked her ass off even more. Put up with her parents' and Wembly's conservative approach, managing to secure deals and position HNE for growth despite the trustee's restraining hand. To her mind, Helm Naval needed less pearl-clutching and more boldness in its actions and plans. Entering into trade deals with Sylveren University and the Rhellian government to handle the transport of the new healing tea was a step in the right direction. The agreement she'd made while in the Valley was just one of the many plans she had for taking HNE into the future. Plans which required her having the authority to *take* the company anywhere.

"Speaking of discussions, that reminds me." Calya kept her tone light, but a wariness crossed over Wembly's face regardless. "I spoke with my sister while I was across the lake. She mentioned something about a shipment of the wards she and Prince Sor'vahl made for delivery in Desmond's Landing. I don't recall any such amendments to our shipping schedules, do you?"

"When was the request made?"

"A month ago."

Wembly inclined his head in an apologetic nod. "I'm afraid I can't recall such a request, either. We handle so many contracts. A supplement to an already established route, especially for goods we already transport quite often is"—his bony shoulders twitched in a shrug—"not something for which we would make special note."

A perfectly vague answer, nothing she could protest outright. How *Wembly* of him.

Calya mimicked his shrug. "I'll see if the Renstown port commissioner still has records." She raised a hand to stay Wembly's argument. "I need to speak with them anyway. I have another deal in progress with the Sentinels to get them one of our fastest ships out to the Landing. There's a lot to organize before we go, and not much time, so I'll be—"

"Go?" Wembly said, the lines on his brow deepening. "You intend to go with the Sentinels? To Desmond's Landing?" He spoke slowly, a mix of confusion and consternation in every word.

"Yes. This missing shipment business and it occurring on that particular route... Well, given all that's happened with that venture, I'd prefer to handle it. Personally." Calya feigned a yawn. "I'm very tired, Mr. Wembly. We'll continue this tomorrow."

The older man's mouth tightened into a thin line, but he didn't press. Backing away with a short bow, he murmured, "I've left your father's messages in your room. Please familiarize yourself with his arguments so we may discuss them in the morning."

"Of course," Calya said, her smile more of a polite grimace. "Goodnight, Mr. Wembly."

She turned away and climbed the stairs, his farewell floating up behind her. Once safely alone in her room, she sighed in the direction of her bed before eschewing it for the small desk in the corner. Several boxes of documents rested on the floor next to the chair.

Calya scoffed as she eyed the envelope Wembly had left on the desktop, recognizing her father's precise script—and how the letter was addressed to the Helm Naval office care of Wembly. Calya itched to rip the damned papers to shreds instead of read them.

But she was not a child. And, one day, she *would* run Helm Naval, turning it into the most successful maritime logistics company this side of the Great Sea, and everyone who'd snubbed her would fucking know it.

The letter from her father was no more than his usual moaning about her, to his mind, overzealous behavior. Too pushy and rash in the deals she sought. No respect for tradition and the way Helm Naval had handled transactions for decades. And by the Goddess, Wembly, couldn't he take her more in hand? Andrin Helm had his government image and contacts and asses to kiss down in Graelynd. His seat on one of the Council of Standards' boards was not guaranteed against his younger daughter's unruliness. The self-important twats in Central District couldn't abide forward thinking.

Blah, blah, blah, that was the gist of it, anyway. Calya tossed the letter aside. She turned instead to the boxes next to the desk. A fine layer of dust had settled over the tops, for Calya hadn't paid them any attention in months. Since she spent the majority of her time home in Grae Port, leaving the boxes in the Renstown office had kept them blissfully out of mind.

"At least you don't have to send for them from storage somewhere," Calya muttered to herself. The answers to the missing wards wouldn't lie within, but if Brint was wheedling his way back onto the Avenor Guard board, perhaps one of his conspirators was buried amongst the pages.

The boxes mostly contained copies of the agreement terms and scads of the useless correspondence Brint had sent, back when they'd been working on their joint deal. Pages and pages of nonsense and incorrect or missing figures—all by design to further his subterfuge, she now knew.

A splash of green caught her eye. She withdrew a mangled sheet of paper, mindful of its crumbly old wax seal. It was stamped with a snowcapped mountain over an open book. Sylveren University's seal once again. Green this time, for the earth magic department. The grovetenders, if she remembered correctly.

Between the poor condition of the paper and the cheap, faded ink that had been used, not to mention the cramped, slanted nature of the writing, Calya couldn't make out much of the contents. It was mostly names of things she didn't know, things like Rossala's Tears and glimmergum and blighted vervain. They sounded like herbs or something one would point out in a highbrow garden, except for maybe the blighted one, but then, Central *had* had a phase where dark flowers were in vogue.

Following the list of flora were sets of numbers rather than a personal letter, with a sign-off that was more scribble than name. All she recognized of it was the vague shape of the letter M. A postscript was scrawled at the bottom, though the only words Calya could make out were "fortnight" and "SUSink."

She sat back in her chair.

The joint protection deal and the specter of Brint Avenor. It just wouldn't die. A shipment of Anadae's wards requested by a distant team, neither recorded nor remembered, now *missing*, and no one knew why. And now this strange accounting from someone at Sylveren University hidden amongst frivolous paperwork.

Leaning forward again, Calya grabbed her pocket notebook and began scribbling a list of details to remember. Meeting with Wembly in the morning could wait. She wouldn't be screwed over by Brint fucking Avenor again.

Chapter Four

The Renstown commissioner's office was a bust. At least with regard to the amended shipping schedule and a box of errant wards, but Calya's trip to the port proved useful in other ways. Perhaps the deity Jin, the Everflow, She of the Golden Waters, smiled upon Calya's mission, for, late the evening before, a small but costly accident had occurred between some drunken Winterfest tourists up from Central District and one of the docked cargo ships. The port commissioner found himself with a number of time-sensitive shipments in need of new carriers, and Calya was happy to oblige. By late morning, she'd negotiated an extended berth for one of Helm Naval's smaller windrunners on the condition that the ship depart in the next two days with cargo destined for the Landing.

As she left the office, Calya spied the black-and-gold livery of Avenor Guard on the dock. It was a small unit of a dozen, and though Calya didn't recognize all of them, the last man off the ship noticed her and raised a hand in greeting.

"Lieutenant," Calya called out in greeting.

The brown-haired man dismissed his unit with a casual wave before turning to Calya. "Miss Helm. I didn't expect to see you here." His gaze flickered skyward to the heavy clouds and their promise of inevitable rain.

It was standard weather for the Valley of Sylveren, but the Valley and the lingering spirit of the Child embodied by the land had a way of making the environment feel welcoming—or not. It had never cared for her, never *claimed* Calya, and she wasn't ashamed to admit that the feeling was mutual. Renstown was a Valley town, but its size and location at the head of the river serving as the main route between the Valley and Graelynd made for a slightly less insular air.

"Seeing my sister," Calya said. "A bit of business, that sort of thing."

She'd known Orren Garr for most of their lives, he being only a few years her senior. They'd met several times over the years when he'd worked on joint contracts between their companies, though they'd never worked closely together. He came from humble means in Graelynd's North District but had gotten an offer after being noticed by Brint on a small job. Orren had worked his way up from the dregs of Avenor Guard, earning his rank and a small team before the age of thirty. He might've worked for another company, but Calya could appreciate his drive.

"I thought you were doing coastal work?" she said as they slowly made their way up the dock and toward the town proper.

"Been some smuggling activity out on the Hook," he said, referring to the tip of eastern Graelynd. "Got called in while we were working through the Bay. On leave until after Winterfest, then we'll probably have river duty on our way back to the capital."

They reached the head of the town square. Orren paused, glancing in the direction of the tavern before returning to Calya. "Would you care to join us, Miss Helm?"

He was good looking, in a very northern Graelynd sort of way. A little blockish, yet soft, with a big nose and brown hair that had a floppy quality for all that it was shorn short enough to curl around his ears. He had boyish charm. Not the type to hold her interest long-term, but perhaps...

Lowe's gray eyes flashed through her mind.

Calya kept her sigh internal. She gave Orren an apologetic smile, her tone regretful as she said, "I'm afraid I have a meeting. Enjoy your leave."

Orren nodded to her and they parted, him following his unit and Calya back toward the merchant offices. But the thought of verbally sparring with Wembly over her father's complaints—which would only be worsened by her forging ahead with her deal to secure a ship for the Sentinels—had her detouring into the dockside market instead. She meandered down the row, idly looking over the vendors' wares.

A windrunner had arrived while she and Orren spoke. As its passengers dispersed, some filtered through the market while others hurried down various streets. Burrowed into her fur-trimmed cloak as defense against the rising breeze, Calya's vision was narrowed to the stall in front of her. A man passing by bumped into her hard enough to knock her into the table. He didn't apologize, one hand fluttering in half-hearted acknowledgment as he strode on.

With a disgusted noise, Calya glared at his retreating back. She stamped after him. "Hey—"

His voice cut over her as he gestured to get the attention of another man lurking at the end of the market row. The newcomer had his cloak hood pulled up against the weather, but Calya thought she glimpsed hair that was the near-white blond common in Rhell. Not an uncommon sight, given that the kingdom of Rhell neighbored the Valley and many of its mages had studied at Sylveren.

"...we were meeting on the ship?"

Calya stilled. She knew that voice. Recognized its ability to carry, to cut through all manner of external noise. A quality that would've been fitting for a commander, or someone worth addressing a crowd.

Anyone but Calya's ex-business partner. Her sister's ex-fiancé.

Brint fucking Avenor. Here, in Renstown. In the *Valley*. Why? Frankly, Calya was surprised he was allowed to set foot in the Valley of Sylveren after the trouble he'd caused at the region's hallowed university.

"...had to... *in person*," the Rhellian man muttered, jerking his head to indicate they should leave. Calya heard only snippets of their conversation, the words tumbling amidst the ambient noise of the market crowd: "...letters can't put off... eval forever."

A Rhellian man in the Valley was nothing out of the ordinary, but one meeting with *Brint*? Highly suspect.

Keeping a respectful distance, she followed Brint and the other man. They strolled away from the market, following the stone road that skirted the edge of town. They climbed a short flight of steps to the main square, but instead of heading into the busy street, they paused at the railing overlooking the port.

Hovering at the bottom of the stairs was too far to hear more than snatches of their hushed conversation, so Calya nonchalantly walked by.

"It's fine," Brint grumbled, hands gripping the railing. "I have everything—"

"We're all fucked. It's just a question of how..." The other man lowered his voice even more until Calya had passed.

She ducked beneath the portico of a building across from where the men stood, keeping her hood pulled far forward. Tucking herself into the meager cover provided by the stone forming the side walls and open entrance, Calya closed her eyes to better focus on the men's conversation.

"...out of my hands. I couldn't lie to Saren's face!" The other man dragged a hand through his hair in frustration, knocking his hood back. Definitely Rhellian, and he lacked the polish Calya was used to seeing in his countrymen. Rhell culture tended toward staid and very put together. Nicer people would've called it timeless, classical; Calya tended to think of them as fussy and snobbish, where exceptions had more a tendency to prove the rule than flout it.

Given the Rhellian's tatty workman robes, which bore more than a few stains from dirt and who knew what else, Calya pegged him as a grovetender. One not so wholly loyal to Sylveren University, apparently. Or perhaps a broke grad student yielding to the burden of debts.

"What do you think we've been doing?" Brint said, scorn thick in his voice. "You should've warned me. I could've intercepted—"

"I wouldn't have had to if you kept your people on a tighter leash," the other man snapped back.

"Song's not here to save you," he hissed. "We can't fix it—"

"Save me? She got herself caught," Brint scoffed. "And because you couldn't stop a godsdamned letter, the fucking Sentinels are sniffing around about the fucking Landing. If *she* finds out, you can bet she'll stick her nose in. Anything to do with her precious company and—"

A hand grasped Calya by the forearm. "What are you doing?"

She reacted on instinct. Or rather, tried to. For several years, Calya had trained under a self-defense instructor, an expatriate from one of the islands far south of Graelynd. With umber skin and a voice like iron, the grizzled older woman hadn't minced words or encouraged Calya to form any delusions of attaining martial prowess. They'd drilled in a few basics—only what a young woman aggressively pursuing her business dreams in the meat grinder that was Graelynd's Central District should know.

Her instructor would've been disappointed to see her now.

Calya *did* manage to stomp on her assailant's instep, earning a grunt of pain. Rammed her elbow into his gut, too, though she scraped across what felt like a buckle and probably hurt herself more than her target. She knew she was supposed to flee; her instructor hadn't fooled around on that point. Make an opening and run. No pausing. A pause was an opportunity for thought to creep in. For Calya to think, and get mad, and want to win because she was a horribly graceless loser.

But she knew *that* voice, too. She paused, and instead of fleeing she found herself pressed up against the wall as Nocren Lowe loomed over her.

"Hello, ranger." Calya planted her hands on Lowe's chest and tried to move him. "You're kind of—"

He caught her by the wrists, holding her fast. In a mild tone, he asked, "Miss Helm. Why are you skulking in the temple entrance?"

"Because I didn't want to draw attention. Obviously," Calya said. "No thanks to you."

"I didn't realize espionage was one of Helm Naval's services."

"This is a personal—" Calya peeked under his arm. "Oh, shit."

She'd only turned her head a fraction, but out of the corner of her eye, she noted how Brint and his conspirator had gone quiet as they glanced over their shoulders. The other man nudged Brint, gesturing for them to leave. Brint only took a step after him, hanging back as he peered toward the spot where Calya and Lowe stood.

Another few steps and he'd be close enough to recognize her despite the scant cover of the portico and the big ranger standing over her.

At least one of those things could be put to better use.

Her hands were still splayed across Lowe's chest, her wrists still ensnared. She leaned into his hold, chin lifting as she met his gray eyes. "Kiss me."

Lowe's body didn't move, though his eyebrows rose. "Miss Helm, are you propositioning me?" he said, more amusement in his tone than suspicion.

She snorted. "You wish, ranger."

Lowe remained patient as a statue, something of a taunt in the bland smile he gave her.

"He can't see me," she whispered.

His gaze cut to the side, a furrow appearing in his brow as he noticed Brint. Lowe's attention returned to Calya. "Avenor?"

"Plotting something," Calya said.

"Pardon—" Brint started to call out.

"I don't want to spook him." Calya slid her hands up until she gripped Lowe's shoulders. "Help me put on a show. Kiss. Me," she ordered.

An amused huff sounded through his strong nose. But to Calya's relief, Lowe deigned to lean forward just enough for his lips to brush against hers. It was all very polite and unassuming, as perhaps should've been expected for a kiss between two relative strangers of a tepid previous acquaintance. But such bloodless intimacy did nothing for Calya's problem. A chaste little kiss was hardly the distraction she required.

Her fingers left Lowe's shoulders to twine through the long, dark hair at her disposal. "Indulge in a bit of theater," she murmured, pulling him closer and angling his head so he obscured more of hers from view.

It was an act, of course, but Calya could admit that she rather liked the idea of tasting the broody Sentinel. Wanted to see how the real thing stacked up against fantasy.

Lifting onto her tiptoes, Calya pressed her mouth to him, sucking his plush bottom lip in so she could lap at him with her tongue. The way Lowe went still, his surprise so overt she could feel it, made Calya smirk. A self-satisfied hum buzzed at the back of her throat as Lowe raised his hands to ghost across the sides of her face. His fingers shook. He'd gone taut, every lean, muscled inch of him firm beneath her touch, all but vibrating when Calya let her palm glide across his chest. He felt primed to explode at the mere suggestion of a spark.

"Oh, ranger, for shame." Calya had never been overly fussed about subtlety. Deepening their kiss, she caught his lower lip between her teeth again and bit down, letting a soft growl roll out of her throat. "Must I lead?"

Nocren wasn't the most devout, but when time allowed, he went to scatter salt and sand for the aspect of the air like a dutiful wind mage and farmer's son. The wind was often a bit frisky after such visits, so Nocren hadn't thought anything of how it had tugged him toward the harborside exit.

Until he'd seen Calya there, poorly hidden in the entryway. She was quick-witted and certainly full of pluck—but a spy, she was not. The curmudgeonly side of him had been tempted to walk away. From the little he knew of her so far, she was ambitious and reckless in equal measure. Where those two qualities went, in his experience, mess tended to follow. Gods all break, he'd pay money to *not* be involved with any of that.

The wind had no such qualms. Bursts of *importance* and *change* were loud in his head when he looked at the Helm girl. He gave in. But he'd meant to inquire of her motives just enough to sate the wind's curiosity.

And now this.

Must I lead?

Whatever resistance—or turmoil—Nocren had clung to, it evaporated in the face of Calya's teasing aggression. His answering growl was louder, maybe a tad exasperated. It also heralded a new level of enthusiasm. There were no polite, neutral touches to be found in the way he gripped her chin and tipped her head back. She didn't seem to mind, not with the way her lips molded to his as he claimed her mouth. When Calya opened for him, she made a pleased sound at how quickly, without a drop of hesitation, his tongue swept in.

She tasted like a mistake. The acknowledgment burst across his mind the same moment he put his tongue in her mouth. Or maybe it had already been there when she'd sucked on his lip... and *bit* him.

It didn't matter. While Calya Helm might taste like a mistake, Nocren could not find a drop of regret. Rather, his head and his cock wanted to see how far down the well he could go before hitting disappointment at the bottom. And he would—it was inevitable. Yet, it didn't stop the more feral part of himself from wanting to know more. To see if Calya could be tamed. If, instead of giving orders, she could be made to beg.

The breeze kicked up, causing his hair to whip around her face. Which was good; all the better to sell the illusion of two lovers taking advantage of any morsel of privacy. All just theater, as she called it.

But then Calya sucked on Nocren's tongue. His cock thickened in response, and she *noticed*, her mischievous hum echoing into his mouth.

It shouldn't have happened. He was unflappable. Indifferent. Captain Malek'ko had gone so far as to call Nocren *standoffish* on more than one occasion. Descriptors that, usually, Nocren agreed fit. To a fault, if one was inclined to consider said labels as negatives. He did not. He wore them like badges of honor, for rarely did disinterest and drama go hand in hand.

Drama, however, had found him in the form of Calya. And, against his better judgment, Nocren admitted his interest in her was more than a passing one.

He was gone, all thought of acting drowned out as lust roared through his head. When her hand drifted down, a single finger tracing his outline, Nocren groaned.

She smiled against his lips, her little puff of amusement tickling his skin. Her touch grew bolder, shifting to more of a caress. It teased, or threatened, to become a grip.

Couldn't have that. He might not be much of an actor, but Nocren had enough presence of mind left to know he was dangerously close to overselling their foolish ploy.

Calya pouted when he caught her roaming hand and pinned it next to her ear. Her knee bent, drifting slowly up as she pressed against his thigh. He shuddered, fighting the urge to lean against her.

A trickle of wind threaded between them. Calya's face flickered through Nocren's mind. Not as she was now, with a pink tinge to her cheeks, lips looking so thoroughly kissed. The wind's version of Calya, her brown eyes serious as she gazed at him, ghosted across his vision.

I'll never...

Common sense slowly filtered back into his brain. He knew better than to let himself be so caught up by the wind.

Nocren let himself savor her lips a final time, then pulled back until a hand's breadth separated them, breaking their kiss. He exhaled slowly, nostrils flaring.

Calya glanced to the side, and he followed her gaze. Neither Avenor nor the other man were anywhere to be seen.

"It worked." Calya straightened up, sliding away from him as she dusted off her cloak. "My thanks, ranger."

"What—" Nocren ran a hand across his mouth, fighting the urge to do something ridiculous and lick his fingers for a last taste of her. "What was that about?"

"I'm not sure." Calya shrugged, indifferent. "But Brint Avenor meeting I presume someone from the university for a hush-hush argument can't be good."

"That wasn't—"

A ship's horn sounded in the distance. Calya glanced toward the port, murmuring, "I've arranged a ship for— Oh, gods fucking break. *Wembly.*" She turned back to Nocren. "I have to go. Tell Captain Malek'ko I have a ship, but it has to sail within two days. Can you be ready?"

"Yes." Not much of a choice there. "The captain is working out the details with the university today."

"Bring the contract by as soon as it's ready," Calya said,

replacing her cloak hood to ward against a fresh round of rain. "It's a small ship. Can't take very many of you."

"I'll tell him." Nocren hesitated. "Miss Helm," he said, unsure of how to address what had happened between them.

Her eyes darted down. Nocren stood stock still, but her lips quirked into an arrogant smile all the same. "Don't make this awkward by getting sentimental on me now."

He managed a wry laugh in response. "Of course not."

She spun away, tossing back over her shoulder, "Name's Calya. Use it, since we're so acquainted."

Chapter Five

"What is he doing here?" Calya bit out, pointing at Brint Avenor's smirking face.

He sat in one of the plush upholstered chairs in front of Wembly's desk, looking completely at home in the Helm Naval office. Far too comfortable for a man who had tried to turn the company into a life ring to save himself from his personal failings.

"He brought a message regarding our business with his father." Wembly's voice was calm, as if such a weak excuse was perfectly reasonable.

"I would think anything he touches is tainted," Calya said.

Brint spread his hands in front of him, an affable smile on his handsome face. Her hand itched to punch him.

"Delivered the messages unopened, bearing my father's personal seal," Brint said. "I'm paying my dues again. Doing the grunt work." His face molded into a chastised expression. "I know I've got a long way to go to rebuild trust, but I'm trying, Calya. I know I fucked up, and I'm sorry for it."

Having worked closely with Calya for the last year and a half, Wembly must've seen the scathing reply gathering itself behind Calya's gritted teeth. Before she could let it free, he cleared his throat. "I took the liberty of pulling the shipping logs from our record archives," he said, opening a drawer on his desk and removing a thin folio. He offered it to Calya.

With a last frown in Brint's direction, she allowed herself to be distracted. As distractions went, it was short-lived. The entry for the trip that had presumably carried Anadae's wards showed no change. No request for a supplement at all. Which couldn't be right. If Anadae had delivered the wards to an HNE ship—and there was no reason to think her sister had lied—then there *had* to be a record. It was standard protocol.

And yet... nothing. The log bore their logistics manager's signature approving the submissions, and Calya's own initials showed she'd reviewed it.

"It's possible your sister sent her package on one of our partners' ships by mistake," Wembly said. "I can make inquiries and see if the paperwork can be found elsewhere."

"AG has been working a lot more on routes going through the Valley this past month," Brint added. "We do so much business together, maybe Ana put it on one of ours."

"*Dae* worked for Helm Naval for most of her life," Calya said. "She can tell our ships apart."

Brint held his hands up, his manner exaggerated. "Well, I'm sorry, Caly, I'm just trying to help."

"It's *Calya*. You and I aren't nearly so friendly. And I would love to be rid of you, if only your fuckups could be contained to your own interests."

Brint bristled. "What's that supposed—"

"Miss Helm," Wembly said, voice rising above them. "I note that you were late for our meeting. Did you have a chance to look over your father's correspondence?"

Calya dismissed his question with a wave of her hand. "That's not important right now. Mr. Wembly, I've made the arrangements for one of our ships currently at dock here to be available for my business with the Sentinels. I'll be gone at least a fortnight, given the distance to the Landing. My current schedule—"

Both men spoke up at once.

"You can't go—"

"Desmond's *Landing*? Why—" Brint leapt up from his chair, alarm on his face.

Calya glared at them. "I've made my decision, Mr. Wembly. End of discussion," she said, with as much grace as she could muster. Which wasn't terribly much, but she managed to keep her tone calm, albeit cold. Better than a shout. After all, Wembly wasn't her father—just a handler.

"You can't, Miss Helm," Wembly argued. "A young woman of your standing can't be playing errand girl on the outskirts of Graelynd. It simply isn't—"

"I'm not sixteen and about to debut before the upper crust of Central District." Calya threw up her hands. "Don't tell me this sort of thing *isn't done*. If I'd been born a man, you wouldn't be complaining."

Wembly carried on as if she hadn't spoken. "It isn't *safe*. It wouldn't be safe for the presumptive heir to a company of Helm Naval's stature regardless of gender. However, taking into account your father's role in the government, and that you *are* a young woman, there are too many risk factors. I am sorry, Miss Helm, but I must insist on opposing your wish to accompany the shipment."

Brint lurked in the background, leaning against the wall, arms folded across his chest. He watched the conflict unfold with a smirk on his face. Uncharacteristically for him, he didn't speak. No snide little comments from the sidelines.

If Calya had been in one of her rare charitable moods, she'd have taken Wembly's admission as something of a compliment. A recognition that she had some value to her family's company, and that the natural order of things implied it would one day be hers. But at the moment, Calya felt like she was losing, and that tended to make her feel even more obstinate.

"I've already signed the contract with the Sentinels and Sylveren University," she declared. A small lie, but the Coalition of Trade recognized verbal agreements as binding. Wembly could complain to her father all he wanted; it changed nothing. The trustee wouldn't risk tarnishing Helm Naval Engineering's reputation by reneging on a deal with as respected an institution as Sylveren.

"On what terms?" the older man snapped, a rare note of true anger leaking into his voice.

"The Sentinels are entrusted with the safe delivery of school property," Calya said. "It requires certain enchantments to maintain its efficacy, but refreshing them interferes with the spells required for by windrunners."

If they were lucky, the trip out to Desmond's Landing could be done in the better part of four days. Just enough for the tea's enchanted containers to last.

It was all pretense, Calya assumed. By her understanding, the tea was designed with the sole purpose of cleansing the sickness brought on by exposure to the poison that had been decimating Rhell. Regardless of what the research group in the Landing was working on, the Sentinels were essentially just escorting the ingredients for expensive, useless leaf water.

Not that her reasons for the trip were any better. *She* didn't need any convincing to hop aboard, but rather a plausible excuse. Following up on the missing wards and seeing the joint protection route with Avenor Guard that continued to have or be party to so many nagging little problems should've been reason enough. Calya's motivation and zeal for Helm Naval had seen her involved in numerous projects over the years—there was nothing outwardly surprising about her desire to go. Why her trustee would suddenly be antsy about safety made no sense.

"I am going, Arthur," Calya finally said, meeting his displeased look and refusing to look away. "What amendments to my travel plans would ease your concerns? And don't suggest canceling, because I will not."

Wembly and Brint exchanged looks. "Better security," the older man said.

Calya's brows slowly rose. "There will be multiple Sentinels on board, and it's a nonstop trip."

"Avenor Guard would be happy to work with you for this," Brint said. "I've been meaning to get out to the Landing myself to check on one of our projects. I could—"

"Absolutely not," Calya said, tone heated. "If you think I'd let you on this trip, one sailing *this particular* route, you've lost your godsdamned mind."

Brint sighed dramatically. "I said I was sorry, Calya! I made a mistake, okay? I can't do better—"

"A mistake?" she yelled. "You tried to ruin me, you fucking self-absorbed—"

"As a last resort! I was trying to fix things."

"Miss Helm," Wembly said, voice sharp. "Mr. Avenor. That's enough."

Calya rounded on the trustee, stabbing the air in Brint's direction. "We can't trust him. He's been—"

"What is going on in here?"

All three of them turned to face the office door, where Anadae stood with a surprised look on her face.

Brint recovered first, head whipping back toward Calya. "What have I been doing, Calya?"

Anadae's appearance was enough to dampen some of Calya's fire. It made her pause long enough to realize the trap in Brint's words.

She ignored the men, instead going toward her sister. "Anadae, what are you doing here?"

"I was looking for you." Anadae's gaze flitted between Calya and the men. "What are you arguing about?"

"They think I need a babysitter to go to the Landing with the Sentinels."

"We don't know the Sentinels," Wembly clarified.

"I have business out there, too." Brint's chin jutted out, a mulish look on his face.

"I see," Anadae said calmly. "I'm sure we can come to an arrangement." She held Calya's gaze. "Even if that means some compromises."

Compromise. Twenty-seven years in the world, and the word had yet to grow on Calya. But Anadae took her hand and gave it a reassuring squeeze. Or maybe it was a warning. Either way, it asked silently for trust.

Begrudgingly, Calya relented. "Fine. What did you have in mind?"

Two hours later, Calya walked with her sister to the door of Helm Naval's headquarters.

"I can't believe you talked me into letting that fucking doorknob come," Calya muttered.

Anadae snorted. "You can't stop Brint from traveling everywhere."

"No, but I could've at least not let him on my fucking ship."

"I don't like it, either," Anadae admitted. "And I'm surprised Mr. Wembly is so forgiving, though if Brint's telling the truth and his father really is letting him start at the bottom..." She shrugged.

"He's worked with Daddy Avenor often enough over the years. I suppose seniority rules." Calya wrinkled her nose.

For all her griping, it could've been worse. Anadae had mediated the compromise, helping convince Wembly that Calya had the authority to travel pursuant to Helm Naval interests. He was able to pull rank and insist on heightened security measures, though Calya disagreed with there being an actual need. She'd have to break the news to Malek'ko that only one Sentinel would be allowed as a representative for Sylveren, which she imagined would go over poorly. But, though she had to allow a contingent from Avenor Guard for security, she'd been successful in lobbying for Lieutenant Orren's squad to be the chosen ones.

Which suited her much better than having some Wembly-appointed babysitter or a pack of hounds loyal to Brint. Orren wouldn't try to micromanage her, so Calya would be free to investigate why Brint continued to be such a thorn in her side. And oh, how she intended to. She couldn't take over Helm Naval if their disastrous joint protection deal kept popping up.

"I had better pay Malek'ko a visit," Calya said. She could've sent word with a page, but the changes to their travel itinerary were not suggestions, and she wasn't one to hide behind paper to convey disappointments.

"I'll do it. I need to finish making arrangements at the school, anyway." Anadae pulled Calya into a hug. "We're not letting them win. Be ready to go at the dawn sail."

"We? The dawn... What?" Calya blinked. "Sister dearest, what are you plotting?"

"Yes." Anadae winked at her before stepping out into the rain. "The dawn sail. Don't be late."

Calya watched until her sister disappeared around a curve in the road. A smile twitched across her lips. She couldn't remember the last time she'd felt this kind of excitement—the last time Anadae had felt like a partner in business. Temporary business; Calya held no illusion that Anadae would come back to HNE. But the heady feeling rushing through her was welcome nonetheless.

No, Brint and Wembly hadn't won. Far from it.

Closing the door, Calya went back up to her room to pack.

Chapter Six

CALYA STOOD under the dock's covered waiting area, watching as the last of the supplies for the trip were loaded onto the ship. Anadae was already aboard, checking over a set of trunks, each emblazoned with the Sylveren University crest of a snowcapped mountain above an open book. Her partner, Ezzyn Sor'vahl, third-born prince of Rhell and a man Calya had known in a vague sense since she was a shitty tween, stood beside her.

Ezzyn's head was tilted toward Anadae as he listened to her speak, but his gaze kept flitting farther down the ship.

Orren's squad of Avenor Guard personnel were already on board, and she watched as they disappeared below deck to stow their gear. Only Brint and the lieutenant remained above, standing at the railing and surveying the dock activity as they conversed. A sour look marred Brint's otherwise handsome face.

And there's nothing you can do about it, Calya thought, smug satisfaction filling her with warmth despite the chill air. Brint's protesting Anadae and Ezzyn's presence on the trip had been in vain. The university wanted them to handle delivery of a resupply for one of the research teams out in the Landing, and Avenor Guard had no grounds to take on the work. Plus, as Anadae had suspected, no one aside from Brint was interested in the diplomatic ramifications of denying a prince.

Calya's lips twitched with a barely concealed smirk. Had Anadae always been so crafty, or did the freedom of pursuing her mage work bring it out? Brint might be charming his way back into his family's good graces, but the Helm sisters had his measure. Anadae was willing to be polite with him—she was nice like that—but Calya relished a grudge. To her mind, there was no more worthy a subject than Brint fucking Avenor.

Although, her trustee was a close second. Wembly wanted her to "check in" with Orren regularly during the trip. Which she had no intention of doing. What would it matter, anyway? Whether Wembly remained in Renstown or returned home to Grae Port during her absence, half of the country would separate them in either direction. Even if Orren tattled on her and reported that Calya had ignored her trustee's request, Wembly wouldn't know until they'd already returned.

Besides, Arthur Wembly's days of authority were numbered. Calya wouldn't leave Desmond's Landing until she had every answer she desired so far as it even tangentially related to her business. Her father would have not a single reason, no hint of plausibility or excuse, to deny her right to ascension. If Brint wanted to interfere, he'd have to physically drag her back home.

As if he had the balls to try it.

Movement along the water drew Calya's eye as one of the smaller boats that ferried between Sylvan and Renstown pulled up to the dock. It was a passenger-only vessel—not as fast as a windrunner, but without freight it was able to traverse the width of the lake in four or five hours, other conditions permitting.

Which meant her friends had been up for a while. Eunny Song's dark hair on its own would've blended in with the crowd, but next to her partner Ollas Nevin's brown curls and Zhenya Lee's pearl-white bun, the trio stood out. Ollas trailed just behind the two women, towing a light handcart laden with a single, large box.

Something like relief washed over Calya. Which was disconcerting, for she didn't like to think that she'd been *worried* about Brint or Wembly's machinations. She was made of sterner stuff than that. It was too close to sentimentality, the gladness she felt at seeing those familiar faces and knowing they were coming with her.

Calya waved, allowing herself a tiny smile when Eunny waved back. She was Anadae's best friend, but Calya had known her for most of their lives. Despite the four years separating them, they enjoyed a pleasant friendship. Of a sort. Not the same level of closeness Eunny and her sister shared, but considerably more than Calya had with anyone else. Which was probably telling of something, but she didn't have time for maintaining emotional connections when she had a company to take over.

Eunny was her ally. If anyone could despise Brint as much as Calya, and be unrestrained in showing it, it was her. Well, Ezzyn, too, but that was more of a dick-waving contest.

Calya eyed the cart as the group came to a stop beneath the shelter. "Is that the blessed tea?"

Hard to believe that a container the size of a house cat, albeit a large one, could be of such significance. Especially considering how its contents, while valuable nearly beyond measure only a few days' travel north of here, were useless where she was going. But the expensive leaf water made the ship sail, so Calya could pretend to care about it. At least until they got underway.

"The benefactor of all your travels," Eunny said with a flourish. "We come bearing gifts."

"I saw." Calya nodded toward the box.

Eunny tutted. "Real gifts." She turned to Ollas, shooing him away. "Remember, the *copper* scoop. Three *heaping* spoonfuls. Don't let these Renstownies try and use the plated one. I know who does their metalwork around here. The *cop*—"

Ollas kissed her. "I know, love. One of us is actually from the Valley, remember?" Ignoring the way Eunny's cheeks puffed out in mock annoyance, he glanced at Calya and Zhenya. "Since I'm being relegated to the coffee and tea run, would you like anything from the roastery?"

Calya demurred, and with a wave, Ollas departed for the market.

Zhenya settled next to Calya, who looked her over surreptitiously, mind churning with what she could remember from the handful of days they'd known each other.

"You're a grovetender, too, right?" Calya asked. "How'd you convince the school to send all three of you?"

"I'm mainly inkmaking and inscription work," Zhenya replied.

"Nev and I can make the tea, and even grow some if there's actually a need," Eunny added. "Zhen's the best for freshening enchants."

The short, Hanyeok-descent woman bore the pearl-white hair that marked her as hailing from the Deiju region of Hanyeok. They were of similar age, though the Deiju white hair and softened Hanyeok features would probably make Zhenya appear in her indeterminate late twenties long after she left them behind. Calya, with her hard jaw and fair skin, would wear the effects of time with unflinching honesty. Zhenya was a senior assistant to one of the professors at Sylveren, and she hadn't hesitated to throw her lot in with Eunny and stand against the Coalition's meddling. Calya didn't know her well, but she was a quick judge of character. Zhenya had proved her worth many times over already.

Anadae and Ezzyn walked down the gangplank to join them under the shelter. "We're almost ready up there."

"Still waiting on a few," Calya said. "And I need to sign off on the extra cargo with the dockmaster."

Anadae looked over her shoulder back toward the ship. "I haven't seen Malek'ko's Sentinel yet, either."

"He'll be here," Calya said.

"Hopefully soon. Brint is getting antsy, and he'd love to use Ollas's history as a Sentinel as an excuse to leave."

Ezzyn muttered under his breath about useless nepotistic bastards.

Calya cracked a smile in agreement before looking at Eunny. "You mentioned gifts?" A hopeful note crept into her voice.

Eunny grinned, producing a bag of motion sickness candies. A big bag, stamped with the Sylveren University seal, the blue ribbon fastening it indicating it had been made by one of the higher-level graduate students.

"Oh, thank fuck." Calya greedily took the bag, raising it to her nose for a sniff. A mix of ginger spice and mellow sweetness, with a tingle of magic for good measure, made her shiver.

"Don't get all carried away. These might not be enough for your delicate constitution." Eunny offered a vial with scummy green liquid inside. It had a consistency like syrup, and just looking at it was enough to make Calya's gorge rise.

"Whatever that is, no. But thanks?"

Eunny forced it into her hand. "To reach the Landing in under a week, the ship is going to be burning its mages at both ends." She nodded at the vial. "That tastes about as good as it looks, but it'll put you out no matter how rough the water gets. Goddess, I'm making even myself feel a bit sick just thinking about it. Maybe we'll need a third plan."

"I'll consider it," Calya said. She kept quiet about how she'd have to be absolutely desperate before reaching that point. She planned to study the information she'd gathered on the town of Desmond's Landing during the voyage and make any additions to her small notebook of vital details. She couldn't get anything done from a medically induced coma, even if it was a more comfortable way to endure the trip.

"I have something for you, too." Anadae held a small velvet pouch, a nervous smile on her face.

Calya offered her palm out, blinking in surprise when her sister upended the pouch and a bar-shaped silver pendant on a matching chain spilled out. Etched into the metal was the outline of a wave, and even with her mundane senses, Calya felt the soft hum of magic warming her skin.

Holding the pendant between thumb and forefinger, she gave her sister a questioning look.

"It has a frost protection enchantment I've been working on," Anadae said.

"Frost protection?" Calya held the clasp ends of the chain up in offering. "Are you becoming a battle mage?"

Anadae settled the chain around Calya's neck. "Hardly. So, be careful about how you use it. Just snap the bottom—"

"Your confidence gives me such confidence."

Anadae mussed Calya's hair, laughing as she sidestepped her answering swat. But the mirth dimmed as her gaze landed on the pendant. "Just... be careful, Calya. Brint's, well, we all know he's useless. But you're trying to expose him." She hesitated, voice growing softer, more distant. "It's rare that he ever has to face consequences. When he does... he's not the Brint we knew when we were young."

Ezzyn slid his arm around Anadae's shoulders, his lips grazing the top of her head. To Calya, he said, "If you'd like a fire charm as well, you need only ask."

"I can probably whip up an emetic," Eunny offered. "It's been a while, though, so you'll really need to time that one right. Don't want to end up in the splash zone."

"I'm touched, all of you," Calya said dryly, "but no."

"Coward," Eunny said.

Calya examined the pendant. "So, I break it if I need to use it. What exactly does *it* do?"

"It should send out a freezing blast. Kind of like a wave you can direct."

Her eyebrows went up. "*Should*?"

"You'll be fine. Just... only use it if you have to." Anadae hugged her. "Since we're waiting, I've never visited the lake from this side. I'll be back!"

Calya crossed her arms. "Ah, I see. So that's why you really wanted to come early."

"No," Anadae said, drawing out the word. "Happy coincidence. Zhen, did you want samples, too?"

The pair hurried off to descend toward the lakeshore, ignoring Calya's exclaimed, "It's the same water as on the other side."

Eunny clapped her on the shoulder. "It's a mage thing." She waved, strolling back toward the market. "I'm going to see what's taking Nev so long."

Calya and Ezzyn stood in silence as they watched Anadae and Zhenya kneel at the water's edge. Anadae laid her palms against the gently lapping waves, faint shimmers of golden light gathering at her fingers.

"She worries about you," Ezzyn murmured. "About HNE. Not your handling of it, but how your father and that trustee are acting. About Avenor." His lip curled at the name of Anadae's ex.

"They're not making things easy," Calya admitted. "But once I find out what Brint's done, once I clean up his mess, HNE is mine. They won't have any reasons left to deny it."

"You've always been committed," he agreed. "For as long as I've known you, the goal's never changed."

Though Calya had only been a budding teenager when Ezzyn became Anadae's magic tutor, she'd loudly declared her life's ambitions to anyone. Whether they asked her about it or not. "I do know what I want."

A small smile accompanied her words, but it wavered as she watched her sister. Anadae played with the water, magic dancing along her fingertips as she directed a thin stream to jump around the air before finally landing in a specimen jar Zhenya held out. Their laughter reached Calya's ears, making her heart clench. She couldn't remember the last time she'd seen her sister reveling in her magic at all, let alone with fellow mage friends. Sure, Calya had seen her perform some magic since she'd returned to school, but it had been small, or instinctive. Never purely for fun.

Anadae had been so serious, a perfect Helm daughter, when they were kids. Even when Ezzyn had tutored her as a teen, her magic use had been strictly academic. Calya had never known her sister harbored a secret desire to pursue her magical education. She'd never known the kind of mage Anadae could be. In her tunnel vision of a Helm Naval where the sisters ruled the company in tandem, Calya had assumed that, since Anadae had never mentioned wanting something different, a different outcome didn't exist.

Anadae had changed, and Calya could finally see how it was for the better. See that her sister was happy, more truly herself. Now, it was Calya alone who remained the same. Who still wanted the same thing, despite the costs. The humiliation, the fucking sting of being assigned a trustee. Yet in spite of it all, she stayed the course. Remained unfailingly committed, as Ezzyn said. *Fixated*, others might assert, but what was so wrong about remaining steadfast in her wants?

"I still fuck up sometimes," Calya whispered. "Call her Ana. In my head." She glanced at Ezzyn. "Do you?"

He watched as Anadae bid goodbye to the lake and trailed her fingers through the shallows. "It's different for you. Harder. You weren't there to see how she found her way." He spoke gently, without rebuke, yet the words nipped at Calya's skin all the same. "You had to be told how 'Ana' no longer fit, whereas the rest of us lived it. It'll feel more natural with time."

Calya didn't begrudge her sister's happiness, but envy lingered. That Anadae's happiness was so... simple. Not uncomplicated, not without work, but in the end, her happiness could be found in magic and a man. She didn't have to choose, and both could be attained. Kept. Calya had always known her path, yet it felt like she hadn't come any closer to achieving anything. She had no magic, and though in essence a man was at the heart of the crux of her happiness, he was not a prize but a gatekeeper. Anadae had realized what she truly wanted and transformed her life to get it. Calya didn't know if she could do the same. If capitulating to her father's stated whims would ever be enough.

She refused to bend instead. Would grind away until even Andrin Helm's stubborn mind was made to change. Until he was forced to acknowledge her tenacity.

Eunny, with Ollas and a bulging market bag in tow, rejoined Anadae and Zhenya as they trooped back to where Calya and Ezzyn waited. A flurry of activity on the deck resulted in Anadae and Ezzyn moving on to discuss a report with the windrunner captain. As the weather shifted, bringing a biting wind and frigid rain, Calya was about to suggest moving somewhere warmer when Lowe appeared on the dock.

"Hey, he looks familiar." Eunny nudged Calya's shoulder. "Isn't that the guy you had a staredown with outside my shop?"

"The very same, but we've come to... an understanding." Understatement, but not necessarily untrue. "He's the one Sentinel allowed on the trip."

"Oh, really," Eunny said in a gleeful tone. She mimed cupping her ear. "What's that? Do I hear destiny calling?"

"Don't get ahead of yourself." Calya raised her chin in greeting as Lowe spotted them. "He's coming along in a work capacity only."

"I believe the kids would call this a *slow burn*, Caly."

"I believe it's called *unrequited*, Eunji."

Ollas laughed at Eunny's mock outrage at the use of her full name. Looping his arm through hers, he motioned toward the cargo loading area. "We'll meet you by the hold, Zhen." That said, he tugged Eunny toward the side entrance into the lower levels of the ship.

Calya rolled her eyes and turned to Zhenya. "Do you have to put up with her matchmaking nonsense all the time?"

Zhenya chuckled, though there was something melancholic in

the sound. Shaking her head, she glanced around, noting the distance between Lowe and where they stood under the shelter. In a voice so quiet Calya had to lean closer to hear, Zhenya said, "I have a friend living in Desmond's Landing. Froley. They run the inn, and their wife has a bakery attached. The whole thing's kind of a general meeting place for the locals."

"Sounds like a nice arrangement," Calya said, a question in her tone.

"Froley is... they're good people. A little, um, a little *unconventional*, but they do good work. They're honorable."

"Why are you telling me this?"

Zhenya bit her lip. "Just so you're not—not surprised when we get there."

"I'm still not sure what I'm being warned of. I'd rather you were blunt than subtle. My feelings won't be hurt, I promise."

"Careful. That sounds like sentiment, Miss Helm." Lowe stopped in front of the two women.

"You're late, ranger," Calya said. "Five more minutes and I'd have ordered we leave you behind."

"Heartless."

She smiled sweetly at him. "You flatter me."

Zhenya's eyes darted between them, lips pinching together to lessen her smile. "Maybe I should—"

Wind joined the fray, a short flurry swirling around them before dying away. A trail of yellow sparks lingered over Lowe's hands before dissipating in another gust of wind.

None of them spoke, but Zhenya immediately looked to Lowe, a question in her eyes.

"I don't have any answers for you," he said to her, his tone going soft. It had a note of gentleness Calya had never heard before. Of sympathy. "The choices you'll have to make... they haven't changed."

Zhenya said nothing, her head bobbing in a small nod, more to herself than in answer to the Sentinel's words.

"If you aren't ready to face some of those decisions," Lowe continued, his tone becoming more measured, "then you should be on your way."

Zhenya blinked rapidly, comprehension dawning on her face. "I—I'll go see if Eunny and Ollas need any help with the tea crate." She hurried off.

Calya faced Lowe, suspicion narrowing her eyes. "What was that?"

"What?" His face remained impassive.

"Are you a—"

"Nocren?" someone cut in.

In unison, Calya and Lowe turned to the newcomer. He was another Sentinel, as evidenced by his ranger leathers and the bow-and-arrow sigil engraved onto his cloak pin. The cloak itself wasn't the standard forest green but a deep crimson. Though his boots were more for comfort than fashion, the black leather worn and creased from use, the dark shirt and trousers beneath the leather guards spoke of high quality.

Amber eyes peered out from beneath a strong brow. His white skin was tan enough to suggest some time spent outdoors. Something about his straw blond hair, long enough to be pulled back into a half-tail, suggested Rhellian origins, but the red undertone cast doubt on such heritage. A few stray locks framed a serious face, though his expression was neutral enough as he regarded them.

"Kelse," Lowe said, chin dipping in greeting.

The blond Sentinel offered his hand to Calya. "Rhydian Kelse."

She returned the handshake. "Kelse, of the Kelse Emporium?"

He smiled politely. "Indeed. Though I'm here in more of a split role today."

The Kelse Emporium, headquartered in Rhell's capital, was one of the finest perfumeries in the Empyrean Territories. Their signature scents sold for hundreds to thousands of gold crowns per bottle.

"Calya Helm," she murmured.

"Of Helm Naval Engineering?"

"The very same." She tried not to preen at his recognition. "I believe we handle the logistics for your Graelynd distribution."

Rhydian nodded. "Yes, several accounts."

"Are you here playing the ambassador?" Lowe asked.

A humorless laugh came in answer. "Unfortunately. I heard Ezzyn was around here?"

"He's already on the ship," Calya said, motioning to where Ezzyn could be seen on deck, consulting with the captain and Anadae over some sort of list.

"I should speak to him before you need to leave." Rhydian hesitated, glancing at Lowe, then toward the ship. "Did I see Zhenya here?"

There was a long pause broken only when Lowe murmured, "She's already left."

Rhydian's smile was more akin to a grimace. He nodded farewell to them both before leaving to hail Ezzyn.

Calya watched him go, then gave Lowe a sidelong look. "Not just an air mage. You're a diviner." Not a question but a statement.

He nodded once, the motion short, almost terse.

A diviner.

Calya frowned. "I don't put much stock in auguries."

She'd run across a few mages claiming to have such gifts. The hacks peddled no more than guesswork with sparkles, and the serious ones couched their forecasting in caveats. Based on the wary look Lowe gave her, Calya was willing to consider him one of the latter. Serious. But for something that was supposedly so predictive, diviner's wisdom came with too much uncertainty for her taste.

A singular current of wind swirled quietly around them. Just them; no excessive flapping of the shelter's canvas awning. Intangible, yet it felt like a hint of a caress.

Calya met Lowe's gaze, raising one hand as if she could cup the sliver of air circling them. "Can you see what waits for us in the Landing?"

Lowe didn't move. For the longest time, he didn't even blink, his gray eyes boring into her as the air turned briefly electric. A flash of gold drew her attention to his hands, but then it was gone, his fingers curling into fists. His eyes pressed closed, his shoulders tensing.

Lowe exhaled, the wind quieting as if dispersed by his breath.

"Change," he said softly. "If we go, things will never be the same."

Calya frowned. "How cryptic." She crossed her arms. "You can't be any more specific?"

"Never ask the wind for specifics." A huff of wry laughter escaped him. His hand flexed, but then he turned away. "Unless you want to risk my bias."

She gave him a considering look. "And if I did, would you indulge me?"

"Haven't I indulged you enough, Lady Heartless?"

Calya stepped closer to him. "I wouldn't say—"

"Caly!" Brint's obnoxious tone carried across the dock.

"Goddess damning... mother*fuck*," she muttered under her breath, turning to see Brint striding toward her. At least he appeared to have the shipping manifest in hand for her to sign and leave with the dockmaster.

"Is this the Sentinel rep?" he asked, jerking a thumb at Lowe.

"Yes, this is—"

"Brint Avenor. Calya's business partner," Brint said, offering his hand to Lowe.

Calya scowled. "We aren't partners."

"Nocren Lowe," the ranger said with an admirably neutral look on his face as he gripped Brint's hand.

"The others are already on board if you wanted to check in with them," Calya said to Lowe. He hesitated, as if unsure about leaving her with Brint, so she added, "I'm right behind you."

"Isn't he a little old for you to be flirting with?" Brint said as Lowe walked away. Probably loud enough for the other man to hear, though he gave no indication of it.

Ignoring him, Calya took the shipping manifest and moved to find the dockmaster.

Brint caught her by the arm before she could pass him. "Caly—"

"It's Calya," she said in her iciest tone, jerking free of his hand.

He held his palms up, all dramatic innocence. "I'm worried for you."

"I'm sure it won't surprise you to hear that I don't give a fuck about—"

Brint spoke over her. "This is your last chance, Caly—Calya. To get out. With the workload you have already for HNE shit. When I was talking to Wembly, it didn't sound like he'd be writing happy thoughts to your dad. You can't take this trip back once we're on it."

Things would never be the same, just as...

Gods all break. This was why she didn't entertain divination; it tainted everything with the notion of prophecy. She'd already made up her mind. Neither man's words would stop her.

Brint gave her arm what he must've thought was a friendly nudge. "I'm just looking out for you."

"Kindly don't."

Spotting the dockmaster talking with the captain of a neighboring ship, Calya started off in his direction. Brint followed, and when she glared at him, he did another of his exaggerated placatory gestures. "We're just going the same way. I need to talk to him, too."

The sail couldn't get underway fast enough.

Chapter Seven

THE SAIL COULD NOT END FAST ENOUGH.

Nocren lay on his bunk, trying to read the notes he'd taken in preparation for the trip. His handwriting skittered in front of his eyes as the ship heaved itself over a wave. He turned a page, pleading with his brain to focus on the mission. On the words, names, places, and descriptions that he'd written with his own damned hand. Yet his eyes passed over the ink, uncomprehending. They were just meaningless lines, doing little to keep his mind from drifting, unerringly, back to her.

Calya Helm, the memory of her, haunted him. The way she'd felt under his hands, her taste. The sparkle in her eyes when she'd challenged him. The way she'd been unimpressed by his wind.

Would you indulge me?

It was more than foolish, how tempted he was to do just that. It was dangerous. He knew what it meant to go down that road. Where it led. How it ended, because it could only ever be the same.

Nocren had retreated to his cabin almost immediately upon them setting sail. With the wind finding ways to filter in, to whisper in his ears whenever he saw Calya around the ship, removing himself from temptation seemed the smart thing to do.

Once they arrived at the Landing, he would have distance. He'd have work to occupy his mind, and so would she. His wind's fixation with her would dwindle when whatever business she was pursuing in the Landing had her full attention. Nocren already knew how single-minded she could get when it came to her own goals, and what she would sacrifice to achieve them. He'd been the victim of such ruthless actions, and the rational part of his mind still remembered.

He turned another page, and this time, a handful of words leapt out at him. *CH-Ambitious. Reckless. Do not trust—*

Nocren tried to skip past, but his fingers remained stubbornly clutching the small steno pad—keeping it open to the page, his eyes glued to the sentence he couldn't finish. A true statement, but a warning of her or a reminder for him?

Nocren relied on his instincts, had always trusted in them, in himself. Under most circumstances, he had a good head on his shoulders, and not just as a diviner. Trusting his gut had saved him a time or two, in Sentinel work and beyond. When it came to Calya, he knew trust was a dangerous thing. Worse than hope. But instead of looking deeper, forcing himself to answer the *why* of his tumultuous feelings when it came to her, what they meant, he faltered.

Nocren tossed the pad aside before slumping onto the bed again. He allowed himself a melodramatic exhale. A few more days and they'd make land, and he could bury himself in work and everything would be fine.

But they weren't at the Landing yet. Isolated in his blessedly, or cursedly, small but private cabin, Nocren was stuck with his thoughts and the constant nagging of the wind. It was relentless with its needling at him, plucking at his skin as it tried to tempt his magic to the surface. An invitation, a *flirtation,* was the attention from the wind. A promise to give him some insight for free.

She'd asked him what awaited at the end of their trip, and though he'd only allowed himself a glimpse, the impression the wind gave him remained. Stuck in the back of his mind, just beyond thought, begging him to look again. To look closer.

Arm thrown across his eyes, Nocren gave in.

A prickle of magic skittered across his fingertips as he bowed to the wind and his own curiosity, letting a few dots of golden light bloom outward until they buzzed across his skin.

"I didn't lie to you before."

Her voice echoed in his mind, distorted as if spoken from a distance, with the wind snatching fragments of the sounds as it whipped around him. The now-familiar impressions of *Important* and *Dramatic* and *Change* shone bright, but they weren't the only ones. There was still much potential in this reading from the wind. Notions like *Pain* and *Relief* and *Anger*. *Desperation*. That last flickered like a dying flame, at times bright and at others so weak as to be practically nothing.

When Nocren looked inward, he could envision the wind rendered in curls of silvery smoke and gold-tinged white mist. It was a story waiting to be unraveled, so little yet told. In this form, so much was still possible.

The sensation of *Change* felt the brightest to his mind, calling just a touch louder for his magic. Or was he too craven to touch on *Desperation* and see where it led? Had he been burned one time too many in chasing those kinds of feelings, to the point where he subconsciously assumed it ended with loss instead of victory?

No, *no*. This was the bargain diviners made. Putting their faith in intuition.

Mentally loosening his hold, Nocren pulled more magic from the sphere at his center and let it free. Asked the wind for *Change*.

The impression of *Change* flared warm. The picture of the smoky wind in his head swirled, a pulling sensation building behind his eyes. One by one, the other impressions, the emotions still so vague and capable of becoming anything, vanished as Nocren committed to one interpretation.

Let the gamble begin.

"I didn't lie to you before."

A feeling of melancholy suffused him. Bitterness and disappointment, but above all, a weariness. The sensation of hope all broken to pieces and ground to dust.

Brown eyes met his. Calya. Her expression was solemn, a mix of wistfulness and the same bitter weariness.

"I'll never love you..."

Nocren opened his eyes. The wind no longer hummed through his mind. The only noise was the creaking of the ship as it soldiered on through the turbulent sea.

Muttering a curse, Nocren got up. This was why he didn't do that kind of reading anymore. The personal kind. Why the wind had fixated on that specific scenario, of Calya's vow against love...

Against *him*.

Nocren shook his head. He sat up, stuffing his feet back into his boots and reaching for his cloak. It didn't matter why the wind wanted to build on this one vision. He knew the wind could lead him astray if he wasn't careful. In the end, it only showed what was possible. So long as Nocren kept his wits about him, Calya's words would never amount to more than what could've been. She couldn't deny him her love if he never gave her the chance to begin with.

Not particularly eager for company but certain he'd lose his mind if he stayed in his cabin any longer, he headed out, letting the door slam behind him.

I'll never love her, either, he thought. To the wind. To himself. *I can't.*

At least thirty-six hours stood between Calya and solid, unmoving land, and she was counting each and every one of them.

As much as it pained her to admit it, Anadae had been right. Less so, at first. Calya's coveted anti-seasickness candies worked moderately well for the first two days of the voyage. Yes, she spent her waking hours in a mild state of nausea, but she could work through a little discomfort. Spend part of her day up in the deckhouse reading the dossier she'd assembled for the trip, distilling down the names and places most likely to yield answers about the joint protection route and whatever this bullshit was that continued to plague it. The evenings were for relaxing. Socializing with her friends and fending off Anadae's attempts to mother her, make her drink more water.

Ship life was easy—keep out of the windrunner mages' way, eat enough of the ginger candies to mitigate the stomach-turning effects of the mages' magic, and avoid Brint as much as humanly possible. She wouldn't have minded some idle time with Lowe, but he'd spent most of the voyage thus far holed up in his cabin.

She hadn't even been able to ask more about whatever message the wind had brought for him. Not that she *believed*, but something about the way he'd looked at her piqued her interest.

At least, it had at the time. They'd hit rougher seas the morning of the third day, and not even the Sylveren candies were a match for it. Not when the ship was traveling at speed, magnifying the effects of every wave or crest or swell or... whatever maritime word fit. The godsdamned ship made sure to hit every one of them.

She'd abandoned her cabin, hoping that fresh air and an unobstructed view of the horizon would work miracles.

They had not. Calya hunkered down, shoulders up around her ears, teeth gritted as the ship bounced over the waves and what little food she'd managed to choke down threatened to come back up. One arm was wrapped around her front, while her free hand clutched the bench frame bolted to the deck.

Doing any work was out of the question. Not even thoughts of Lowe were much help. Her mood was as sour as her stomach.

"Divination's a crock of shit," she muttered to herself.

If we go, things will never be the same. Well, she could've told him as much. There would be answers in the Landing. Maybe not ones she wanted. Not ones she *liked*, but she'd know if Anadae's wards had arrived or not. If they'd even truly been requested. And the Sentinels would know... whatever the fuck it was they wanted to know. So, of course they'd be changed. Wasn't that how time worked? Who she was today wasn't who she'd be a month from now.

Lowe had sounded all mysterious when he'd said the words, but really, it was a generalization, just vague enough that it could always be true by technicality. The wind didn't know shit.

Such thoughts, while perhaps a touch morbidly satisfying, were hardly a lasting distraction. Which left Calya with Eunny's vial of last resort. The foul motion sickness remedy had been a constant companion in Calya's pocket. A "just in case" for when the most desperate of times were upon her.

She withdrew the vial from her cloak pocket and held it up in front of her face. The slow sloshing of the thick, sticky liquid proved to be especially unappetizing to look at. Her fingers wrapped around the narrow flask, hiding it from view and her easily susceptible stomach.

Calya had taken that kind of anti-nausea draught only once before. It *would* ease her current woes, at the expense of consciousness. Taking it this late into the trip, even with the delay the weather had caused, she'd be lethargic to the point of uselessness for at least another day upon arriving at the Landing.

She couldn't afford to be so hindered. If Brint was using the remoteness of Desmond's Landing to hide his attempts to worm his way back on the Avenor Guard board, she had to be ready to take up the hunt the moment they landed. Giving Brint fucking Avenor, with his obnoxiously effective charm and his underhanded ways, a head start on any sort of coverup was asking for failure.

Calya would eat glass before she willingly let him thwart her again. Would sit up there in the deckhouse, miserable and cold, stomach empty and twisted upon itself. Would court dehydration and death before she let another mediocre man go unchallenged in trying to wrest HNE from her.

The door leading to the ship's salon opened, and Eunny strolled out. Her gaze immediately went to Calya, a sympathetic smile forming on her lips. "Thought you might be up here."

"As if I'd be anywhere else," she groaned. "No promises I won't vomit on you."

Eunny kept Calya's bucket on the bench between them as security before she took a seat, indicating the vial still clutched between Calya's fingers with a jerk of her chin. "Before you go the extreme route, I have a proposition for you that doesn't include being in a coma for days."

"I'm listening." If nothing else, Eunny was providing a momentary distraction.

Eunny dug in her pocket, holding up a slender glass bottle blown in the shape of a feminine body. A detailed one, with the suggestion of hands pressed over her mound. Generous curves, erect nipples, head tipped back so the delicate lines of her hair cascaded down her back, creating enough texture so one could easily grip the bottle. The figure's head faced up, mouth shaped to form the opening for the cork stopper.

The design was distinctive, and the deckled paper label wrapped around the glass even more so. It bore the flourished script of House Oleander, a well-known apothecary in Graelynd's capital whose wares catered to intimate pleasures. *Erotic enhancements*—that was what the line of aphrodisiacs like the one Eunny currently held was called. Calya knew of it, though she'd never experimented with the one offered to her now. The glass was a dark ruby red, the most potent the company offered. The highest of quality, and with a price to match.

"You're traveling with a Scarlett Kiss?" Calya said.

"What can I say, I like to be prepared." Eunny grinned and gave the bottle a gentle shake. The liquid swirled freely within the glass, golden shimmers flaring in reminder that it was a magic-laced potion. Not merely a sweet-scented contraceptive, but the promise of a good time.

A very good time. After all, it was a product from House Oleander; quality was assured. A Scarlett Kiss *would* take away her nausea. In a sense. Eunny wasn't wrong on that part. But rather than simply resolving her problem, the philter would replace it with a different set of feelings. Urges. Much more pleasant, to be sure, but also equally demanding in their own way. Inescapable, only instead of queasiness she'd be consumed with hunger.

Calya gave Eunny a suspicious look. "You don't need it?"

Eunny scoffed. "It was going to be for Nev. This—" She flapped her wrist to indicate the rough sea. "I mean, I'm not as affected as you, but getting tossed into the wall every other wave isn't exactly conducive to my rest. Might as well do something else with the time if I'm going to be awake."

"Ollas isn't seasick?"

"Hardly." Eunny shook her head. "Says it feels like being rocked to sleep."

Calya fought down a fresh bout of nausea at the notion of *rocking*.

"What do you say?" Eunny asked. "This dose should last through tomorrow. At least get you to calmer water."

With some quick maths, Calya confirmed her assessment. The wares from House Oleander were fast-acting, the effects kicking in after several minutes at most. Given her empty stomach, it might happen even faster, with more intensity. Which would be a nice change of pace after a day spent clutching a bucket.

Though, for the numbers to matter, there was a missing variable to address.

"Does that come with an invitation?"

"Ha," Eunny said dryly. "Normally, I'd be game to try anything once, but you're like my baby sister, and we don't do that here. Find your own."

"Where?" Calya whined.

"What kind of an understanding did you come to with that ranger?" Eunny asked.

Lowe. If she were to ask him, what would he say? He hadn't exactly complained about their kiss. She might've instigated, but his response, the way his blunt fingers had gripped her chin and raised her lips for him... she'd ended up being the one surprised. She didn't usually care about that particular act. *Kissing.* Eh. Calya saw it more as a pleasantry, a pretense of civility before devolving into more enjoyable, carnal endeavors.

Instead of freezing her ass off up here, what would it be like to be warm in his bed, surrounded by the scent of leather and salt and, inexplicably, the wind? To taste his kiss again?

Calya dismissed the errant thought. Lowe wasn't here.

"Not that kind," she said, a sulky edge to her voice. "I think he's been avoiding me. At least, he was before I shackled myself to the sick-bench."

Eunny pursed her lips. "Boo. Okay, what about the AG guy you're friendly with?"

"Lieutenant Orren?"

She snapped her fingers. "That one. Saw him down in the salon."

Orren. He was conventionally handsome, if burlier than Calya's personal preference. She liked a slightly leaner physique, nicely muscled shoulders, toned rather than so built up that she saw only a hunk of meat. But of her limited options on board, he was the most appealing candidate. Of those possibly available, anyway.

Besides, if Orren did a passable job at getting her through the worst of the storm, poor boy would be all tuckered out after. Leaving Calya free to have a look through his cabin without distraction. She liked the lieutenant well enough, but he was still Avenor Guard. She'd been the one to insist on his assignment to her security detail, but who knew what orders he'd been given? She intended to find out.

"Good enough for me." Calya plucked the glass bottle from Eunny's hand.

The older woman went with her so far as the ship's salon. She gave Calya a kick in the butt, murmuring, "Go get him!" under her breath before heading off in the direction of her cabin.

Down in the salon, the rocking of the ship felt worse. A group of Avenor Guardsmen, Orren amongst them, sat at a table in the back corner. Objectively not a large distance, but in her current state, Calya knew she'd never make it to the group without retching.

Desperate times.

Willing her stomach to behave, Calya leaned against the bulkhead and uncapped the Scarlett Kiss, pulling the cork free with her teeth and spitting it off to the side. She emptied the contents in two swallows. It had a mild sweetness that reminded her of the fruits from the southeastern Radiant Isles, with a finish tart enough to make her wince.

Calya took a few slow, grounding breaths as a tingling sensation zipped through her body. She shivered, and the strange feeling faded as quickly as it had appeared. In its place, an ember of heat flickered to life at her core as the Scarlett Kiss settled in. The nausea that had been her constant companion began to fade, leaving her emboldened in its absence.

The walk to the back of the salon didn't seem nearly so fraught anymore. She pushed off from the bulkhead, but hadn't taken more than a few steps before Brint blocked her way.

He held up the discarded cork. "You dropped—" His eyes widened at the sight of the bottle still clutched between her fingers.

He snagged it, and though she held on, he dragged her hand up to eye level. "Caly," he said, and gods all break had she never hated more the way his voice carried. "Is this what I think it is? What's a girl like you doing with—"

"Get fucked, Brint," she snapped.

In such tight quarters, and without the crisp outside air as a buffer, the layers of his cologne had her suppressing a gag. Clearly, Brint had stocked up on the trendiest scents in Central District and layered them without any sense for moderation. Or separation. The man reeked like a candle shop that had put all its Winterfest shit on clearance.

He leered at her. "I'm not saying no if—"

"You're disgusting." Calya gagged. "I don't fuck my sister's castoffs."

"Cast— You can't be serious? I was fucking other—"

"Think very carefully before you brag about your infidelities."

Brint's mouth snapped shut. It didn't remain so for long, as a snide expression filled his face. He wiggled the empty Scarlett Kiss still clutched between them. "So, who were you planning on sharing this with?"

"Me," came Lowe's voice from behind her.

Brint dropped his hold on the bottle, causing Calya to stumble back a step without the extra resistance. Lowe steadied her, his arm snaking around her shoulders.

"Him?" Brint said, expression torn between disbelief and suspicion. "Really?"

"Yes. Specially negotiated, of course." She sneered at Brint before turning to face Lowe. "Let's be clear on a few things. This is a temporary, mutually beneficial arrangement."

"Noted," Lowe said. Though he spoke calmly, a benign curve shaping his lips, his gray eyes remained unreadable.

Whether it was the pressure of improvising or the nudging of the Kiss working through her veins, Calya embraced the way it freed her tongue.

She poked Lowe in the chest, a playful haughtiness in her tone as she declared, "You're contractually obligated to give me at least two orgasms before I even consider sucking your cock."

Brint laughed nervously. "Oh, Caly, you're so blunt. I've always liked that—"

"Understood." Lowe's fingers grazed her cheek. "Any other demands?"

"Yes. We will not be kissing or cuddling under any circumstances." Not that the latter had ever held much temptation for her, but best not to take chances when it came to the ranger. Not if she was about to spend the rest of the day and night in a magic-induced heat with the man.

Her eyes slid to Brint, who was staring at them. A touch horrified, but also jealous. She fluttered her fingers at him. "Do you mind? We need to discuss the finer points of our fucking."

"Gods all— You don't have to be such a frigid bitch about it," Brint groused.

Calya smirked. "Why deny my true nature?"

Brint swore again before slinking away. Neither Calya nor Lowe paid him any attention, their eyes locked on each other.

"So, are we agreed?" she said, the few words taking an alarming amount of willpower to come out nonchalant.

The knot of his throat rose and fell. Calya had the sudden urge to lick it. Wondered if he'd let her. What would the ranger smell like after fucking all night?

Calya wet her lips, a zing of pleasure arcing straight to her clit at the way his gaze locked on her mouth. A small, prideful part of her brain warned against him. Against the pull that had already started to form between them, one that would only grow stronger.

Only because you're denying yourself, the hungry side of her mind supplied. *Building the idea of him up in your head. The truth always disappoints. This'll make it easier to forget him later.*

Calya was inclined to agree with her carnal self. This wasn't fishing for anything serious. Relationships were something she'd done away with years ago. When she wanted a change of pace from her own ministrations, she had a few partners of similar mind that she could call upon. But seeing as none of them were at hand, and a sexy ranger *was*, why not indulge in what was essentially nothing more than a pleasant way to pass the time?

"Agreed, and I'll bet I can change your mind."

"On?"

"Kissing me. Again." Lowe ran his thumb across her bottom lip. "You seemed to—"

Calya bit his thumb. Briefly, but hard. "Doubtful." She smirked up at him. "But you're welcome to try."

Lowe's hand went to the small of her back, and he guided her out of the salon.

Chapter Eight

HE'D LOST HIS MIND. Nocren could think of no other explanation for his actions. Divining magic could do that to a person; he certainly wouldn't be the first. The wind and his magic had been obsessed with Calya since the moment their paths crossed. But every time he thought he understood the wind's intention, reality slapped him in the face.

Showing her into his cabin, Nocren closed the door and leaned against it. Jaw set, he willed himself not to move. Avenor may have been all too eager to benefit from the woman's reckless actions, but Nocren had a few scruples left.

Calya frowned at him. "What are you doing?"

He had to give her a final out. Even if his more base nature rebelled against the notion, urging him to take her.

"We don't—" His voice came out hoarse. He cleared his throat. "We don't have to do this. I just, when I saw Avenor, I... I don't want you to feel—"

Calya removed her cloak and tossed it over the foot of his bed. When he didn't react beyond silence, she rested her ass against the narrow bunk. With slow, deliberate movements, she dragged one boot off. For a moment, Calya held it up, a question and a taunt.

Nocren remained like stone. Unmoving. Definitely, *noticeably* hard, if the pressure at the front of his trousers was any indication. But he didn't flinch when Calya let her boot drop to the floor. The second followed. All the while, her eyes never left him. Then she sauntered toward him, swaying slightly with the movement of the ship. In his tiny cabin, it didn't take long for her to be in front of him again. She reached out, one slim hand trailing over his crossed arms.

"I'm not some naïve debutante. This isn't my maiden voyage," she murmured, fingers traveling up to graze his chin. "I can separate business from pleasure. Can you?"

Nocren's brow twitched. Disgruntlement rose within him at her words.

The corner of her mouth curved, rounding her cheek. "You disapprove?"

He stopped her wandering hand, catching her wrist as she palmed his erection. "Are you always this trusting? You hardly know me."

An emotion passed over her face, there and gone so fast he couldn't be sure what he'd seen. If it had even been real. He couldn't even ask after it, for Calya's cool fingers pressed against his lips.

"This is just sex. I'm giving you my body for a night, that's all. Our implied contract doesn't require trust."

"Always thinking of business."

"Always," Calya agreed. She gave him a frank look. "I didn't just find that bottle on the ground and drink it on a lark. I know what I'm doing. I wanted this. No sentiment, remember?"

Nocren stared down at her, watching as a shiver ran through her frame. He felt the hairs on her arm stand up, her skin briefly turning to gooseflesh as the full effects of the aphrodisiac hit. The tiny bumps receded, a warm flush spreading across her body in its stead. Her eyes closed in a long, slow blink, and when she finally met his gaze, he could make out his reflection in her blown pupils.

"Have you considered how you might be hindered by your... condition?" Nocren made himself say.

Calya groaned. "I was counting on it, but if your delicate sensibilities aren't so inclined, I'll take care of myself." She made a crude motion with two of her fingers.

When he remained frozen in place, brain and cock screaming contradictions at him, she made an exasperated sound. Turned to retrieve her shed clothes. Prepared to leave.

"Wait." Eternal Wind damn him for sounding so fucking hoarse.

Calya slowly spun again to face him, head tilting to the side in question.

Nocren reached behind his back, hand fumbling to find the door's heavy lock. "Last chance, sweetheart. I don't do one and done. If you stay, you're locked in here until morning."

She scoffed, twining her arms around his neck. "You don't scare me, ranger."

"I don't want your fear, Calya." He threw the deadbolt. "But I will make you scream."

She smiled hungrily. "Is that a promise? Even with the Kiss in my blood, I won't be so easily impressed."

"We'll see."

Taking her by the shoulders, Nocren reversed their positions, pressing Calya's back against the door. He undid the laces at the front of her bodice, carefully drawing the cord through the eyelets. The buttons of her shirt went in equally slow fashion, but evidently, the pace was too lackadaisical for Calya and the enhanced hormones running through her. She shrugged out of her shirt impatiently, dropping it on the floor. She reached for the placket at the front of his trousers, growling when he caught her hands and pinned them above her head.

"Lowe!" she complained.

Nocren tsked at her. A lace-trimmed ivory band covered her breasts, a silver pendant with a wave etched in blue hanging between them on a long chain. He lifted the necklace with one finger. "Pretty, but I wouldn't have thought it your style."

"A gift from my sister."

"On or off?"

"On. It has a protection charm. To keep men honest for her baby sister." Calya tugged against his restraining hand.

Nocren smirked. "I doubt you have such troubles." He pushed her breastband up, but instead of adding it to the growing pile of clothes, he left the garment tangled around her elbows.

"Patience," he drawled, fingers skimming over her exposed breasts. He cupped one, luxuriating in how it spilled over his hand. The gentle weight nestled against his palm, her nipple already beginning to pebble at the slightest attention. Arousal added a delectable pink flush to her fair skin, heightened sensitivity causing her to shiver when he tweaked her nipple.

With one hand, he kept her wrists anchored in place while the other continued its slow trek down her body. He traced the modest nip of her waist, followed the line of her form as it flared into her hips. It was an easy thing to push her trousers down, letting them snare her shifting legs.

Her panties followed suit. Nocren's finger pressed along the juncture of her thighs and pelvis. Feathered across the chestnut curls guarding her entrance. Started to tease at her lips. But when she tried to cuddle into his touch and draw him in, Nocren pulled away. At her exasperated sound, he smirked. What fun it would be, to have her in such play. Use his body to cage her in, use his fingers and mouth to bring her to the edge—and leave her there. Repeat the sensually vicious cycle until she was malleable in his hands. Until she tucked her face into his neck and begged for release.

Nocren's cock bobbed in agreement, the fantasy playing out in his mind driving his arousal even higher.

Calya gave him a haughty glare, a pointed tug against his hand emphasizing her annoyance. "For someone who's supposed to be fucking me through a storm, you're doing a shit job of it."

He leaned in, mouth stopping next to her ear. "We've hardly begun. Be nicer to me"—his free hand drifted lower until it hovered above her entrance again—"or you'll be waiting all night."

Her thighs parted for him. "You wouldn't dare," she said, a moan escaping as he traced along her seam, the flesh already wet with desire.

Nocren only chuckled darkly in response, enjoying the way her eyes closed, her head tipping back as he let one finger slip between her folds. In truth, she was right. At least for tonight. As enjoyable as it would be to edge her until dawn, especially with the Kiss influencing her every reaction, Nocren's own will wouldn't hold out that long. The desire to bend her over the bed and rut into her like an animal was intense to the point of aching.

Besides, there was more than one way to make the imperious little minx beg.

Calya tried to grind against his hand. Her breath caught when he finally let his finger breach her entrance, her exhalation long and ragged.

"Prove to me that I wouldn't have been better off by myself," she said, hips angling up into his touch.

She was already soaked, her pussy so pliable. So fucking ready for him. The addition of a second finger elicited another moan of pleasure, her hands twitching against his hold. Her inner walls clenched around him, dragging his fingers the slightest bit deeper.

"We both know I already have." He curled his fingers as he rubbed along her front. "Look at how hungry you are. Your little hands aren't enough to please you."

"But yours can?" The snark in her tone was undermined by a gasp as his fingers found the spot that made her back arch.

"I know it." Nocren's thrusting picked up. "This is just a taste, sweetheart."

He shifted so his knee could keep one of her legs open, his hand still pinning her arms above her head. He was immovable even as she began to squirm.

"This will be enough for you to come, but it's not what you want." Nocren's teeth grazed her ear. "Not what *I* want."

"Which is?" she hissed out, her pussy's rhythmic clenching beginning to stutter.

"I'd have you on your hands and knees, your ass up in the air for me, your hair wrapped around my fist. I'd finger-fuck you until your pussy was nice and swollen. I'd have you coming all over the floor until you begged me to stop." Nocren pressed the heel of his hand against her clit and crooked the fingers he had buried inside her. With a nip at her ear, he murmured, "And then I'd give you my cock."

Calya spasmed, breath escaping as short, sharp puffs as she came. Nocren grunted as her liquid heat drenched his hand, her pussy rippling around his fingers. Her hips bucked lightly with each wave of pleasure, drawn out by his long, slow strokes against the tender spot on her front.

Gradually, the quivers faded, and she exhaled a hoarse, "Fuck."

Nocren eased his fingers free, holding them up so she could see how they glistened in the lamplight.

"Good girl." He smirked, stepping back. Put his fingers in his mouth, making an appreciative sound. "So sweet."

Calya snorted. "Don't think so highly of yourself, ranger." She extricated herself from the rest of her clothes. "I'd say this speaks more to the abilities of House Oleander than you."

"Is that so?" Nocren cupped her chin between his fingers, tilting her head back. A rosiness warmed her cheeks. In the meager lighting of his cabin, her lips appeared plumper and darker. So pillowy soft.

He dipped his head to see where looks and reality met, but before he could capture her mouth, Calya's hand came up to block him.

"Have you forgotten the ground rules?" she said, pushing his face back.

He met her words with an indignant huff. But he let her usher him toward the bed, saying in a mocking tone, "I don't recall any qualms the other day."

She shrugged, a fussy *hmph* sounding behind closed lips. "That was a ruse." She plucked at his shirt. "Don't make me use my imagination."

He obliged, dragging his shirt and cloak over his head, his trousers and shoes coming off in a tangle to be dealt with later. His cock, finally free to jut up toward his stomach, had a bead of pre-come shining at the tip.

Calya eyed him—it—her teeth pressing into her lower lip.

Nocren reached for her again, the pad of his index finger tapping against her mouth. "A ruse? No." He jerked his hand back to avoid her bite. "I think you liked it."

"I think"—she pushed against his cheek until he dropped onto the bed—"mouths can be put to better use."

Calya scrambled on top until she straddled his face, her thighs holding him still, knee nudging his cheek. She tilted her head, eyes bright as she grinned down at him.

Then she canted her hips, hovering an inch above his mouth, so close that the damp heat of her core caressed his skin. Her sweet musk filled his nose, had his cock bobbing in anticipation. He all but salivated like a damned dog.

Nocren grabbed Calya's waist and pulled down, his mouth opening to meet her. A soft cry reached his ears as his tongue licked along her seam. She wriggled in his hands as he teased between her folds, reveling in her taste. He lapped up the honeyed come that had pooled at her entrance, swallowing down her addictive blend of sweet with a hint of tang—delved inside for more, deep as he could, intent on the source.

Calya's thighs quivered, gripping and releasing her hold on his face as she rode his mouth. Soft moans blurred into harsh breaths as Nocren dutifully ate her out. When she sank down onto him, snuffing out all chance for breath, straining to take his tongue even farther in, Nocren did his part. Tipped his chin what small amount he could to grant a better angle and waited for her to rise again so he could snatch a quick breath.

Being a diviner, morbid curiosity about one's end came with the gift. Add in a rough-and-tumble job, and Nocren knew that there were a number of unpleasant, violent ways his life might end. He tried not to have an opinion one way or another, for the alternative was to slowly go mad.

Tonight was an exception. Let death come for him, buried between Calya's thighs. It was a much more peaceful way than he'd envisioned he'd go.

She leaned back, her pelvis shifting enough for Nocren to breathe again. He groaned into her flesh when her hand closed around his shaft. She gave him a slow, firm pump, smearing his pre-come around his cockhead, then slid her hand down, exposing his crown to the cabin's cool air. Her pace increased, grip tightening as she gave a short twist with each stroke.

She slapped his hand away when he tried to slow her down, giving him a particularly forceful squeeze. It didn't take long for Calya to have him wound tight, pressure mounting until his tipping over felt imminent. But then she'd loosen her fingers, hand pausing enough for him to reset the smallest amount as she wiggled her hips and ground against his mouth.

A sweet torture, and one he would've gladly endured any other night. Any but this one—the only they would likely ever have. An anomaly, courtesy of her bout of motion sickness and her very unconventional way of dealing with it.

Tonight, he wouldn't waste his come by blowing it all over his stomach. If the wind thought Calya was so damned important, then Nocren would ensure that she remembered her time with him, too.

Laving her pussy from back to front, Nocren sucked her clit into his mouth. Rolled it between his lips, tugging enough to make her tremble and contract. Her grip on his cock weakened as another orgasm built.

Nocren's hand slithered up her chest, palming one of her breasts. Calya arched into his touch, into his mouth, her breath catching as he pinched her nipple. He repeated the motion, this time sucking on her clit at the same time. Pressed it against his teeth.

Calya's entire frame shook. She cried out, hips rising as the sensations became too much, more of her sweetness flooding across Nocren's tongue.

He let her escape upward, dragging the back of his hand across his mouth. Then he grabbed her by the waist again and lifted her enough so he could immediately rise to a sitting position.

"What are y-you—" Calya yelped as Nocren slid his fingers roughly through her folds, coating himself in her arousal.

He slicked his cock, already wet from her efforts, and positioned the tip at her entrance.

Calya gripped his shoulders. "Lo-Lowe. I—I just—"

He cradled the back of her skull in his palm. "You wanted to get fucked through a storm, sweetheart. Take it."

He pulled her onto him as his pelvis bucked up, not stopping until he was buried to the hilt. She opened for him so nicely, crying out against his neck, her inner walls tight yet deliciously yielding. Calya Helm might've called herself a cold-hearted bitch, but she burned hot at the center.

She bounced on his cock, tits heaving, fingernails digging crescent-shaped gouges into his skin. He didn't care. He ignored her panting cries, his hand still molded around the back of her head, angling her so their lips met. She struggled, tried to avert her face, but it was futile. It wasn't a kiss so much as a claiming. An act and reminder of possession, at least while she was in this space with him. A reminder that she'd agreed to put herself in his care, and gentleness had never been on offer.

Nocren licked into her mouth as he crushed her body to his—made her taste the tang of her come while he experienced the way her sweetness mixed with the lingering berry flavor of the Scarlett Kiss.

Trembles rippled across her body, her cries growing more desperate, muffled against his lips. He'd never given her pussy a chance to adjust to his intrusion, and so close on the heels of her second orgasm, her sensitivity was at its peak. Nocren cared about that least of all. Or rather, he'd been counting on it.

A dull, wet slap sounded each time their bodies met. Calya's ass thumped against the tops of his thighs, and she struggled weakly as he rolled his hips, rubbing against her engorged clit. She didn't fight the kiss anymore, either, her lips fumbling against him as she wound tighter. The effects of the aphrodisiac had her flushed again, glorious heat radiating off her skin and embracing his cock.

Perhaps Nocren wasn't so far removed from Avenor, for he was happy to take advantage of Calya's vulnerability, too. A state she'd offered up to him so freely, knowing so little about him. Brash and fearless, and still so young. Self-assured. He imagined that she was rarely, if ever, so exposed in the bedroom. No, his Lady Heartless was sure of her control.

His lady? A troubling thought, but true enough for the time being. The Scarlett Kiss laid her bare, left her open and tender, able to take everything he gave her in such quick succession.

Calya tensed, her hands shaking even as her pussy went impossibly tight. She whimpered into his mouth as she came, her contractions tipping his aching cock over the edge. At his first pulse, her pussy squeezed him, grabbing on and doing its damnedest to suck him in. The suction drew from him an extra spurt of come as he splashed across her walls.

With another small whimper, she sagged against him, sporadic quivers making her limbs twitch. Nocren dragged his hand across her sweat-soaked hair, pressing a kiss to her temple. And smiled to himself when she grumbled.

Once he'd caught his breath, Nocren gently laid her on the

bed. Calya mumbled something as he cleaned her up, but her eyes never opened. Within moments, her breathing had deepened with sleep.

Nocren considered waking her to insist she hydrate. "Calya."

No response. He set a waterskin on the floor next to her and carefully slid onto his side of the bed. Fighting the ridiculous urge to pull her snug against his side, he instead rolled onto his back.

He must've been affected by the Kiss, too. No other explanation for it. An alluring woman who he was, regrettably, attracted to had showed up and demanded sex with him. So what if he'd acquiesced? It meant nothing. He hadn't forgotten the wind's warning, for all that it was silent now.

They'd arrive in the Landing tomorrow and go their separate ways. Simple as that.

Calya woke with a dry mouth and a steady thrum of need pulsing at her core. Gingerly, she pressed her inner thighs together. A hint of soreness filtered through the haze of lust that remained, the Scarlett Kiss still alive in her blood.

But its presence had abated—somewhat. Its roar dulled, and though a part of her brain was wholly dissatisfied when she clenched and came up empty, it was not so loud that she couldn't set her mind to other tasks. Ulterior motives, one might say.

Nothing *nefarious;* she had no intention of screwing over her current allies. Calya had loyalty, but it followed a hierarchy. Seeing what the Sentinels were up to in the Landing, if such information was to be had, wasn't meant to make things difficult for them. But she had to be certain their business didn't interfere with Helm Naval.

Careful not to jostle Lowe, who lay beside her, Calya sat up. The tiny porthole in his cabin was covered in salt spray, but what little she could see through the smudged glass told her it was still night. Late, given the darkness and the quiet.

Noticing the waterskin next to the bed, Calya grabbed it. A content sigh hummed at the back of her throat with her first swallow. Water had never tasted so good.

Belatedly realizing the noise she made, Calya glanced at Lowe. He didn't react, his chest rising and falling with a steadiness that seemed too natural to be faked.

"Ranger," she whispered. No response. "Lowe."

He slept on.

Carefully, Calya slipped away from the bed. She peered down at him, trying to spot any change, to see if he became too still. Nothing. Good enough for her, so she hastened on. The ship felt more stable now, but she knew anything could come along at an instant to rouse him and ruin her plans.

She took another sip from the skin before replacing it on the ground. And dismissing the thought of what the gesture said of him, and what it evoked in her. Shied away from introspection, because as long as those feelings remained unexamined, she could pretend their existence was nothing more than flights of fancy. Once they were admitted, they were real, and real things generally had to be dealt with, which was... unwanted, at this time.

Lowe's pile of clothes was nearest to the bed. Calya dug through it, unsurprised when she found nothing of note. They'd been stuck on the ship for four days, so why bother toting anything interesting about? She pulled his cloak around her shoulders to ward off the chill air, ignoring how the Kiss tried to nudge her mind back toward the six feet of ranger who could keep her warm.

She prowled through the cabin. Given it could be covered in just a handful of strides, it didn't take long. Lowe's cabin was smaller and less furnished than her own. No drawers or cabinets to rifle through. Scant shelving was tucked into the odd angles created by the door leading to a shared washroom.

Lowe hadn't unpacked at all, and Calya found his sole bag wedged next to the frame at the foot of the bed, half buried by a cast-off blanket. Inside, she found a few spare clothes, an extra knife, and some kind of tool wrap made of oiled leather. After a quick debate, she left it and its potentially noisy buckles alone. Whatever his mission in the Landing was, perhaps the details were carried in his head rather than a bag.

As Calya replaced the blanket, something small slipped from where it had been caught in a fold. She grabbed it before it could fall to the floor, and the object bent under the force of her touch.

It was a steno pad similar to the one she carried, only this was even smaller, no larger than her palm.

After another quick glance Lowe's way, Calya flipped the pad open and began skimming the pages. Deciphering them was a chore. The lamp had burned down to embers, and Lowe seemed to think handwriting consisted of short, cramped lines, and the less shape to a letter the better. Calya had started to think the notes were written in code until she spied familiar wording.

AG + SU res – site share?
AG sus invlvmt. HNE prob cover.

CH- Ambitious, reckless. Do not trust—

Calya knew the Sentinels were looking into suspicious messages from a Sylveren research group stationed at the Landing. It was a small comfort to know that Helm Naval wasn't suspected of nefarious dealings, presuming she'd interpreted his scrawl correctly. Less a comfort to know that they might be being used by Brint.

The words about Calya herself were... true. She'd have said the same. Yet, to know they came from Lowe's hand left a bitterness in her mouth.

Tucking the pad back into the blanket, she returned to the bed, hesitating at its edge. Lowe lay on his back, one hand resting atop his ribs. Even in sleep, his features held on to the remnants of a scowl.

Ambitious, reckless. Do not trust.

He was right not to. She knew it, and still, Calya wished, just a little, that she could prove to him... not that he was wrong, but that she was more than those words. A small part of her saw this gruff ranger whose path kept crossing her life and wanted to take it as a sign. Wanted to let him in. Wanted him to see through her thorns.

Disgust with herself rose up. Calya nearly voiced it before remembering to stay quiet. Gods all break, clearly the aphrodisiac was wreaking havoc on her hormones for her to be entertaining such sentimental drivel. Lowe was nice to look at, and equally nice to ride. He might be a joyless grump, but he wasn't a stingy partner. Quite the opposite. Definitely a better choice for the storm than Orren.

Calya tugged down the blanket draped over his bottom half, exposing his groin.

Yep. Very nice, in looks and feel.

The Kiss reminded her that there were other senses yet to be assessed. Plenty of nighttime left, and actually, no longer a need for silence.

Calya slid back onto the bed. She drew her finger along the length of his shaft, smirking to herself when Lowe stirred.

Easing down next to him, she took his cock into her mouth. Slowly sucked her way down until her nose just started to tickle the trail of hairs leading to his groin. She hummed as his cock began to harden, forcing her lips farther apart.

Lowe jerked awake, groping along the sheets. One hand caught in her hair, but she brushed him away, giving him another lazy suck.

"Calya, what are..." Lowe mumbled, groggy with sleep.

Nice to know he hadn't been faking it, the secret of her nocturnal adventures safe.

She released his cock with a wet pop. "Do you remember my ground rules?" she asked, tongue tracing the head of his cock. "I asked for two orgasms."

Calya met his gaze as her lips reached out to kiss away the bead of arousal forming at his slit.

"You gave me three."

Chapter Nine

IN GENERAL, goodbyes weren't Calya's style. As for the first morning following a passionate but ultimately meaningless evening— absolutely tedious. She loathed navigating someone else's awkward feelings as they came to terms with their actions and determined their new comfort. Or lack thereof. Best to avoid it altogether. Would Lowe be clingy or aghast or have some inflated belief that he now owned a share of her time? Calya would happily never know. How silly of her, to have entertained *sentiment* last night. Self-pity, wanting him to see the real her. Thank the Goddess she hadn't given voice to such weakness.

She eased out of his bed once more as the blue light of predawn fought its way through the clouded porthole. Lowe didn't move, one arm resting above his head.

Calya lingered, allowing herself a final moment to enjoy the sight of him, unimpeded. It would have to be her last. She had work to do, and didn't have the time or inclination to convince him of the merits of a casual arrangement. A shame, because once Lowe had gotten on board last night, he'd proven Calya's worry of him being a prude quite false.

She hadn't even been able to properly suck him off before he'd bent her over the bed and finished himself inside her. Not that she was complaining, since he'd made sure she came, too. Twice. And sure, some of that was motivated by his own pleasure, as he'd growled nonsense into her ear about how it felt to have her come undone all over his cock. Still, he was a conscientious lover. Possibly her best. One of. No point in putting him on a pedestal. Even if his body deserved such placement and he had the skills to match. Calya could appreciate his rugged approximation of handsomeness.

Such a pity that the timing didn't work out. Or the location. Or his profession... Really, nothing about their circumstances was favorable to further dealings.

Quietly donning her clothes, Calya inched the deadbolt on the cabin door open and made her escape.

By the time the windrunner received its docking orders for the Landing's small but surprisingly busy port, Calya was ready to face the day.

Washed up and in a fresh set of clothes, she stood on the deck to watch their approach. The effects of the Scarlett Kiss dwindled, helped along by the crisp winter air and the first real, solid food she'd been able to keep down in days.

When Lowe emerged from below deck, she gave him a polite nod before returning to the list she'd made of immediate tasks to run down upon disembarking. The action was a simple, undramatic message, a signal of moving on. Both for him and the twinge of desire that bloomed in her chest at the sight of him. A last vestige of her enchanted hormones, nothing more.

"Miss Helm." Orren joined her at the deck rail. "We should review the itinerary for our movements on—"

"Lieutenant, we both have priorities for our companies. I don't require an escort."

He shifted uneasily, his agreement in conflict with whatever missive Wembly and Brint had put in his head. "Have you ever been to the Landing?" he asked.

"No, is that a problem?" Calya replied. "I wouldn't have thought you'd try to micromanage my affairs."

Orren had the good grace to appear chastised as he admitted, "No, miss. But Mr. Avenor mentioned that your coming on this trip required, ah, extra attention."

Brint fucking Avenor. Orren might've been willing to relent if his orders came from anyone else, but if the ask came from Brint, that was harder to dislodge. Whether because of Brint's supposed status in the family company or his hand in getting Orren his position, if the meddling was ordered by Brint, she would need to tread with a little more care.

Calya forced a touch of softness into her tone as she said, "I intend to check in with HNE's operations in town. Should I need to leave the central area, I will let you know. As a courtesy, you understand."

"I'd appreciate that," Orren said, all business, but there was a hint of relief in his expression as he nodded to her before moving on.

Calya glanced over her list. She'd need to arrange for her belongings to be stored at the inn, then coordinate with her sister and friends in delivering the tea and tracking down the wards. If said wards had ever arrived—and the source of the request, if they'd ever existed.

She'd need to familiarize herself with the main hub, too, but it was a small town and shouldn't take overly long to tour. There were only so many places for the offices of Avenor Guard and Sylveren University to be set up. Involving herself in those affairs wasn't technically part of the joint protection deal Helm Naval had with AG, but she'd be damned before she left this desolate rock without seeing the never-ending source of so many troubles. Even if they were only adjacent to her business on paper.

Plenty to keep her occupied, so her memories of the voyage could become dust.

"Calya." Lowe approached, voice only loud enough for her to hear as the windrunner crew bustled about in preparation to dock.

"Lowe," she said, a neutral expression on her face.

His mouth tensed—whether with indecision or dread, she couldn't say, but it all added up to the same thing. He thought they needed to have one of the awkward conversations she'd been so determined to avoid.

"I'm rather busy," she said, indicating the small notebook in her hands. "Worry not, I plan to give Captain Malek'ko a report on anything of note."

"That's not—" Lowe sighed. "Look, about what happened."

Calya raised her hands as if to ward him off. "It was a fuck and chuck, nothing more. Don't concern yourself over my tender feelings. I assure you they don't exist."

"Right. Because this is all business to you." His lips formed a smile, but there was no humor in his face.

"Yes, but that was more a way to pass the time." Calya moved to brush past him.

He caught her arm. "You act like people are all fungible." He leaned toward her, voice softening even more. "I know that's what it is. An act."

"Do you?" A pang of hurt, of wanting, struck in her chest in the cold pit where a heart should be. Calya ignored it. Reminded herself that she had no time for such tenderness and the emotion it would bring, even if brief. Even if she was tempted by him. A little. She could admit the ranger sparked a sense of temptation in her that had been absent for so long she'd forgotten what it felt like.

She couldn't allow it. No feelings, not until Helm Naval was fully hers. Anything that didn't directly support her acquisition of the business was either a distraction or a weapon that could be used against her. If she let herself believe anything other than that...

No. Calya hadn't come this far by allowing exceptions.

Her fingers covered Lowe's hand. "Your first impression was the right one. Don't let yourself be fooled, ranger." She slowly pulled free from his grasp. "Ambitious. You say reckless, I prefer ruthless."

Confusion marred his face before realization set in. His jaw tightened, and Calya forced her hands to her sides instead of brushing away the tension she'd caused.

"But you're right not to trust me," she murmured, allowing a wistful smile to flicker across her lips.

Over his shoulder, Anadae emerged from below deck.

"Calya," Lowe said, but nothing followed, his mouth working as he tried to find the right response.

She didn't wait for him, stepping around and going to meet her sister instead. "You can't trust me, ranger. Never forget that."

Once the enchantments on the tea had been refreshed, Zhenya led the group to the inn, An Honorable Pelf. It was nestled toward the end of the main road, on a bluff overlooking the harbor. The innkeeper, Froley, was large and formidable looking, with short, iron-colored hair and brown eyes more prone to sharpness than warmth. They seemed an odd choice for an innkeeper, as Calya didn't get a sense of hospitality from them, but they got her settled on the upper floor on the far side of the inn, away from the noise of the common room on the ground level.

Glancing out the window in her room, Calya pointed at the other buildings scattered around the town square. "Where might I find the offices for the university and Avenor Guard research teams?"

Froley gestured farther up the main street to a nondescript building. "Used to be for storage before Mayor Krowe built a new set closer to the docks. That was back near the end of the war.

Converted the old sheds to suit the university folk better when they're not in the field."

Calya thanked them, suppressing a frown as she saw Lowe already on his way into the building. "The field?"

Froley nodded. "Depending on the research, there are other sites outside of town. Always a few of the mages around here. You can find them in the common room or the bakery most nights."

"Good to know."

Calya looked around the room. Her belongings were stowed if not unpacked. Good enough for now.

She went downstairs, where the entire Sylveren group met up and made their way to the office building Froley had pointed out. It wasn't too far off from the town's square—not that the town was big enough for being on or off the main drag to matter much. The road curved slightly down as it led away from the inn at its peak, but Calya guessed it wouldn't take more than a quarter of an hour to walk from end to end and see the majority of businesses. A community of this size wouldn't take long to understand. If all went well, she'd be on her way home in a day or two.

Leading the way, Calya let herself in through the same door she'd seen Lowe use, following the sounds of voices to an open room with several desks situated in the center. Lowe stood next to a harried-looking younger woman of eastern Radiant Isles descent, probably an Initiate Three or Four by Calya's guess. She quickly scribbled notes as another man spoke to Lowe, nodding along every few words. An extern, perhaps.

Aside from Lowe, two men, another woman, and the extern completed the group. All Graelynders, and one of the men and the woman wore gray robes with the sigil of Sylveren University stitched along the right front.

Despite their attire, Calya got more of a Central District impression from them, based on their more coiffed appearances. Trim, sleek haircuts and demure but tailored shirts and trousers beneath the robes. Expensive leather shoes that weren't polished to a shine but didn't show signs of regular wear, either. Too clean for the winter weather. Of course, they could be the most conscientious mages when it came to personal appearances that Calya had ever seen, but on a random weekday when they were supposedly in the midst of a project?

The other man was undoubtedly the mayor of Desmond's Landing, Krowe. Fur-trimmed cloak over finespun wool. Speaking in an unctuous tone, and far too smiley.

"You must be Miss Helm," he said, noticing Calya's approach and abandoning the conversation to offer a limp handshake. "I was just telling the Sentinel that—" His eyes widened as he took in Calya's companions. "Er, everything's in order," he finished, voice weakening. "Lot of you to be making the trip out to our fine little town."

Calya watched the mayor as the rest of the group introduced themselves. Was it her imagination, or did he seem to pale at hearing Ezzyn's name?

"Prince Sor'vahl, we had no word you would be coming." Krowe rallied, his politician's smile back in place as he gestured widely, though if he meant the office or the people was unclear. "We'd have been more prepared."

"There have been some communication issues," Ezzyn said. Though his tone was polite, the Graelynd mages and the mayor all seemed to become a tad more guarded. "The opportunity to follow up in person came about late."

"I was just saying, Galwynd's team is top notch. We were about to show the correspondence records to—"

"Galwynd? Eren Galwynd?" Ezzyn said. "He's here?"

"Oh, no, not right now," the mayor chuckled. "He's off checking on another site. Should be back any day."

"We should get this properly stored," Ollas said, indicating the crate of tea.

"Preferably in a place with humidity enchantments for the entire room," Zhenya added.

The extern looked at her superiors. "There's workspace in the other building, but the enchantment runes need refreshing."

"I might be able to help with that," Zhenya said.

"Lily, show them," the woman mage said, indicating the door with her chin. "Show the Sentinel our correspondence logs while you're at it."

"This way please." The extern, Lily, motioned for them to follow.

Lowe's gaze flicked to Calya, his expression unreadable, before he and the others departed, leaving Calya, Anadae, and Ezzyn behind.

"I have some questions regarding my company and the needs of the research efforts here," Calya said, nodding shortly to the Graelynd mages. "I'm concerned we have a shipment missing. Could you point me in the direction of whom I should speak—"

"No, no, not at all," Mayor Krowe said at once. "As I was telling our Sentinel friend, everything's been going fine here."

"Yet we have a request for some of their wards," Calya said, tone mild as she nodded at her sister and Ezzyn. "They were sent on one of my ships. Did they arrive?"

The woman mage waved dismissively. "That was a mistaken request. We've already cleared it up with them. You probably haven't heard yet because of the travel times."

"We're very happy with the routes provided by both companies," Krowe added. "Been working a treat for years."

"Can you confirm receipt of the shipment?" Anadae asked.

The two university mages exchanged looks. "I believe the request came from Matthias," the man said. "I don't recall if he got the shipment or not, but it's likely. He took most of his things when he left."

"Left," Calya repeated.

Another silent exchange of looks occurred between the mages. Mayor Krowe glanced at them, his easy smile still fixed firmly in place. "I can ask the dockmaster about this, see if he remembers. I'll let you know what—"

"*I'll* ask your dockmaster later, thank you," Calya cut in. "I'm a bit paranoid after so many mishaps. My apologies."

The mayor made a blustery amalgam of understanding and wheedling attempt to change her mind. Calya ignored him, her attention returning to the mages. "Who is Matthias?"

"A Magister Two doing work toward his Magister Three level," the woman replied. "I'm Treen and that's Aylton. We're all working on experiments for the university, but our reporting has been consistent, as we told the Sentinel."

"University work?" Anadae said. "I thought this was a Graelynd job. Unaffiliated."

"I misspoke. It's technically outside work, but we've received approval to use some of the data here for our Mag Threes once the work here is done."

Aylton sniffed. "Easier to simplify for explaining to non-Sylveren University folks."

"Which we aren't," Ezzyn said. Hard to say which was more brittle, his tone or his smile.

Regardless, it put the other mages' hackles up, which didn't serve Calya's purpose. "Makes it easier for me," she said. "What was Matthias working on?"

Treen shrugged. "Growing some type of plant for textile use in South District. I'm not an earth mage, so I don't know the particulars."

"Why did he leave after receiving his shipment? Isn't that odd?"

"Not necessarily," Aylton said. "He might've gotten tired of the grind and left for a different project. All the earth funding has been going toward eco resto work in Rhell. Understandably," he added with a nod toward Ezzyn.

"He never mentioned this to you?" Calya struggled to keep her skepticism in check. "He simply vanished one day."

"We weren't close," Treen said. "We aren't always in here every day, or at the same time."

"What are the rest of you working on?"

Treen gave Calya a polite, regretful smile. "I'm sorry, Miss Helm, but your company isn't part of our contract, and the work is classified."

Before Calya could argue, Brint came through the door.

"Avenor!" the mayor cried. "I was wondering when you'd stop by."

Calya watched the men greet each other heartily. "You two are acquainted?"

An understatement, obviously, but she enjoyed how uncomfortable the mayor looked. She knew Brint had *had* some kind of private project here, though whether it was truly a thing of the past or not was growing more suspect by the moment. Still, it stood to reason the mayor would've gone out of his way to make himself known to a member of as influential a family as the Avenors. But there was business friendliness, and then there was the smarmy level on display.

"We, uh..." Krowe glanced at Brint.

"I've made a few trips on AG's behalf," Brint said, shoulders lifting in a careless shrug. "Would you excuse us? I have business I need to discuss." Though his tone had an affable charm, his lip curled with the sneer she knew was truer to his nature.

"One last question," Anadae said. "Is this your primary office?"

Calya glanced around the room. Tables and papers and filing cabinets. There was a workstation toward the back with some sort of crystal model-projection system, and she glimpsed storage racks on the rear wall, but her sister had a point; it wasn't nearly the level of equipment they'd expected to find. Song's Scrap had more testing paraphernalia than this supposed research office.

"Yes, I was given the impression there was a larger team

present," Calya said. "Doing... I'm not sure of the proper phrasing, but more active research?"

"Much of our research is theoretical," Aylton said. "Funding issues, as I've mentioned."

"You're welcome to look over Matthias's desk." Treen gestured toward a table toward the back of the room. "We haven't had a chance to pack up what's left."

Calya kept a bland smile on her face as she murmured her thanks before going with Anadae and Ezzyn to investigate the desk. It didn't escape her notice that the mayor was able to stay for the classified meeting, but then, Krowe and Brint seemed cozy.

Matthias's desk didn't have much, whether because he'd truly taken most of his things during his departure or because his colleagues had already picked it over. All that remained were irrelevant forms and what appeared to be some old task lists that hadn't been thrown out.

Calya was about to slam one of the desk drawers in frustration over the dead end, but she checked her childish impulse at the last moment. She could punch a pillow when she got back to the inn.

Her abrupt motion caused something to rustle at the back of the drawer. A slight scrape of paper on wood. Reaching to the back, she found the crumpled remains of an unfinished letter. More of a list, really, for aside from the salutation of *Lady S*, there were a few lines that resembled code more than sentences. It was signed with a simple *M*.

Pushing the drawer shut, she declared, "Nothing useful here," as she surreptitiously pocketed the note. "Any luck with you?"

"Doesn't appear so," Anadae said, her gaze lingering on Calya's before she straightened up. "Let's find the others."

Brint and company watched them leave, but no one seemed to suspect Calya's petty theft.

"There's another cohort from Sylveren stationed here. A real one," Ezzyn added. "We should try to find them."

Lowe exited the building from a side door. Calya waved. He

hesitated at the sight of her, but instead of coming over, he turned away and strode off toward the town.

"I'll catch up with you later at the inn," Calya muttered to her sister.

"Just don't do anything reckless."

"I would never." She tossed her head. "We don't share the same risk assessment—that's different."

Anadae blew a laugh through her nose, but she didn't comment further. While she and Ezzyn headed toward the docks, Calya went after Lowe.

Chapter Ten

SHE CAUGHT up with him within seconds. "You're ignoring me."

"I'm working," he replied.

"As am I." Calya kept pace with him. "We both agree that something is wrong here."

Lowe grunted, which she took as concurrence.

"It's all too neat," she continued. "Brint and the mayor are far too friendly, and those supposed mages?"

Lowe's gaze flicked toward her and then as quickly away, but now his head was inclined the slightest bit in her direction.

The corner of Calya's mouth curved up. "Definitely not from Sylveren."

"Because you know the school so well?" Lowe said, though there was no bite behind the words.

"I know Grae Port," she replied, naming Graelynd's capital. "I know Central District. Those mages, Treen and Aylton? I can believe they're here conducting research on something, somewhere, but they're not reporting to anyone at the university. Any university, for that matter. Not first, at least."

"Who do you think they are?"

"What did you find when you delivered the tea?"

"Not much." Lowe remained impassive, his face a mask of neutrality. "The assistant showed us around, and then Nevin and Zhenya found what was left of a greenhouse setup, so I left."

"You don't find that odd?" Calya asked, her exasperation plain. "That office was practically empty. If research has been conducted here for years, shouldn't there be more people? More—more... stuff?"

Lowe stopped and faced her. "What are you asking of me, Miss Helm? I'm here on Sentinel business."

"Oh, am I Miss Helm again?"

"A few hours ago, you were ready to jump off the boat to put distance between us."

"That's a bit dramat—"

"You backed away," he said quietly. "You told me not to trust you. Already change your mind?"

"It's called pivoting." Heat rose in her cheeks. She turned away and resumed walking.

Fortunately, he fell into step beside her.

"I said what I said," she continued. "But in this, our business interests align."

Lowe shook his head. "And you'll work with me up until they don't anymore, at which point you'll act in whatever way serves you and your company, isn't that right?"

"My duty is to HNE first, that's true." She ignored his wry smile. "But HNE isn't in the habit of treating its partners poorly."

"How good of you."

"It's good business practice." Calya spread her hands before her. "A gesture of goodwill. A shipment of the wards my sister makes were supposedly requested and *supposedly* delivered here. But the man who requested the shipment has conveniently up and quit the entire field of study. When I spoke of my intention to question the dockmaster, Mayor Krowe tried to intervene."

He nodded at her to continue.

"There should still be records of goods received at the port, especially in one this small."

"Maybe," Lowe said cautiously.

"And Brint. His old project out here that he fucked up is supposed to be under new direction. How is he allowed to just, just *be* here and those mages are okay with it?" Calya gestured emphatically, hands cutting through the air. "Something, *many* somethings, are wrong here!"

Lowe stopped again, frustration writ large across his face. "What do you want me to say, Calya?"

"Work with me to fix it," she said at once. "I'm not asking you to forsake your duty to the Sentinels, but our reasons for being here, there's a connection."

Lowe continued to stare at her, his frown solidly in place.

"You're scowling," she said.

"My face has a tendency to do that when it comes to you."

She lifted her shoulders in a dainty shrug. "I do have that effect on people."

He ducked his head, one hand coming up to press against his jaw. Not quick enough to hide his smile.

A gust of wind set the edges of their cloaks flapping, and a lock of hair was blown across Lowe's face. A crackle of golden sparks swirled between them before fading.

Their eyes met.

"Tell me," Calya murmured, fingers waving gently through the air, "what does the wind say?"

"I thought you didn't believe in auguries," he said.

"I'll make an exception."

He sighed.

"Why are you so opposed to working together?" she asked, genuine curiosity in her voice. "We both benefit."

"The wind is... It's not *the* future. It's possibilities. Keep asking after the same thing, keep chasing one path out of many, it influences the outcome."

"Risks your bias," she said quietly.

He nodded once.

"Your wind, does it keep telling you about..." *Us?* But she couldn't ask about that. Wouldn't let herself start to care about what his answer might be. "This?" she whispered.

"Like you said, something is wrong here. A lot of connections." There was something pained in his smile. "I don't like to use my magic this way. Calling on the wind so much for the same thing. It's... It doesn't go well." He cleared his throat, any hint of vulnerability banished. "There's enough going wrong here as it is, don't you agree?"

Calya considered his words. His reticence. His... fear? No, wariness. Caution, well-justified. She wondered what had happened to make him so guarded. Wondered if she could coax the answers from him.

But that was too much like sentiment. Like asking for trust. Which he would never give without asking the same from her in turn. And that, she could never do, even if nascent threads of temptation were beginning to form.

It's only business, she reminded herself.

"Then forget the wind." Calya took a step closer, sliding her fingers along the edge of his cloak, but not closely enough that she touched him outright. "You don't want to be rid of me so easily." She hummed softly to herself as he stilled. "Not when we seem to have a rapport."

A ragged puff of laughter escaped through his teeth. "Do we?"

She tapped his chest. "Unruffle your feathers, ranger. What will it take to soothe your bruised ego?"

"My bruised—" He shook his head.

"Let us bargain," Calya said. "Name your price. But don't you dare try to cheat me."

The corner of his mouth curled up, a sly gleam in his eyes. He leaned toward her. "All right. By the end of the day, I want a compliment from you—"

Calya scoffed.

"—*and* you have to mean it."

"Bold of you to presume such a thing exists."

"You have to mean it. No faking."

"It's cute that you think you could tell the difference." She sidestepped him, fingers fluttering. "Come on, we've a dockmaster to—"

Lowe caught her by the arm, swinging her so she faced him again, and cupped her chin, lifting her gaze to meet his.

"Oh, I know I got the real thing out of you." He stroked one finger down her cheek. "I felt it."

A frisson of energy ran from where his fingers held her skin straight to her clit, an involuntary shiver running down her spine. Which, of course, he noticed. The smug bastard.

"Start practicing your delivery, sweetheart." Lowe released her and strolled onward.

Calya stared after him for a moment, then gave herself a mental slap. Stopped herself from gawking like a godscursed fool. What the fuck was wrong with her, getting all aflutter over some arrogant ranger?

"Going to make you grovel," she muttered.

The sound of his laugh trailed back to her. "By the end of the day, Lady Heartless."

Dockmaster Gormund was firmly in Mayor Krowe—and thus Brint's—pocket, but he couldn't outright deny Calya access to the shipping manifests for her own damn company. He did, however, insist on accompanying her to review the documents, citing port security.

A bullshit excuse, but Calya determined it wasn't a battle worth picking. Not yet, at any rate.

"I can only spare a few minutes. Busy day, you understand," the dockmaster groused. "Be quick, please."

"I'll do my best," Calya said, flashing him a bland smile. She sat on the opposite side of his desk and picked up the sheaf of papers he offered, ignoring the way he consulted his pocket watch.

It didn't take long to thumb through the shipment receipts. At this point in the season, Helm Naval didn't have many routes going up the coast, preferring their rivercraft for northern transport. She found the page that matched up to the date Anadae had supplied her wards. And there, added at the bottom, was the line noting the crate as cargo. Not an amendment, but written like it had been an original entry, bearing the logistics manager's signature—and the initials *CH* in pointed letters.

Calya stifled a gasp, but her hands shook. Seated next to her, Lowe glanced over. "Find it?"

"Yes," she replied, forcing herself to slide the papers back across the desk. "It matches what we have back at the Renstown office as well. I'm so sorry for wasting your time, Mr. Gormund."

"Yes, well, I told you we keep our paperwork in order," he muttered, showing them out.

Lowe waited until they were halfway back to the inn before asking, "What did you really find?"

"It's a forgery," Calya growled, mind flashing back over her logistics manager's precise lettering. The sharp lines comprising the C and H of her supposed initials. "Or rather, the document is real enough. My sign off is not." She dragged a hand through her hair, thoughts careening. "I knew Anadae couldn't have made a mistake. Someone drafted a new manifest after she made her request and sent that with the shipment. With my initials."

Lowe mulled over her words. "Who has the authority to write up and file a new order?"

"Me," she said. "And Wembly."

Chapter Eleven

As they walked back toward the inn, an upper floor window on the adjacent building slid open. Eunny poked her head out, waving to get Calya and Lowe's attention. "Up here!" she called before disappearing back inside.

"The Foggy Window," Lowe read off a carved wooden sign. A fresh breeze rose up, prompting him to sniff the air. "Smells good."

"The wind's seal of approval?" Calya deadpanned as she moved toward the door.

"Sometimes it's just the wind."

The bakery was oddly shaped, long and tall with at least three stories worth of height, yet the entire space was one large, open room. Though there was an upper level for more seating and a lift built into the far corner, it was more of a mezzanine than a fully separate floor. The ground floor's seating area extended out to the edge of the bluff, the large glass windows giving spectacular views of the water.

A bell tinkled above Calya's head, signaling her arrival. As she closed the door, a low voice sounded behind her.

"Returned already," Froley said, standing in the short hallway that connected the inn and the bakery. "Your friends are upstairs.

Bakery's that way if you're hungry. My wife'll see you're taken care of. Roxy!" they called in a louder voice. "Special guest."

"Just guests," Lowe said.

"I was being polite," they replied. "The future director of Helm Naval Engineering, who sailed in on a windrunner full of Avenor Guardsmen, Sylveren folk, and a lone Sentinel? You're trouble, I just don't know what kind yet."

"Oh, that," Calya said. "Limited travel options."

Froley turned away, a mutter of, "Sure," tossed over their shoulder before they walked back into the inn.

Calya went to the bakery's front counter. It was the smallest part of the building, with a few kettles stowed up against a stack of assorted plates, all fighting for limited rear counter space. A good chunk of the wall was taken up by a two-basin sink. A single, long shelf held over a dozen tea tins, labels facing out, the varieties written in a clear, easily readable print. The effect was somewhat spoiled by most of the labels' remaining empty space being filled with drawings of flowers and hearts and other little sketches relating to the tea.

Countertop seating offered a few spaces next to a pastry case. The glass was clean and clear, lit well from a lightstone cleverly installed in the top. Offerings of sweet and savory baked goods were divided neatly in their respective halves, making a most inviting display.

A winding staircase led to the upper floor, which was empty save for where Calya's friends had taken over a table at the back. More tables and chairs of varying sizes were set up around the dining area. A couple dressed in worn work clothes occupied one of the window-side tables on the upper floor. They glanced at Calya before continuing with their chatter.

A few other tables on the main floor were filled. A man sat at a table large enough for six, a pot of tea and a triple-tiered stand of half-eaten treats vying for space with a mass of papers spread out across the tabletop. He hunched over the paper he was working on, scribbling furiously. Farther on, a table of university-age girls eyed Calya and Lowe over their cups. Their gazes lingered on the ranger. Calya scoffed, fighting back an irrational desire to lean against him.

Lowe noticed her stiffness. He glanced the source of her annoyance, and his lips twitched in what must be smugness. "Not feeling jealous, are you, Lady Heartless?" he murmured.

"It's ingrained selfishness." She pointedly slipped her arm through his. "Sharing is against my nature for all things. No matter how... trivial."

"Really going to have to stretch yourself to think of something nice about me, aren't you?"

Calya's acidic reply was cut off as the proprietress arrived. A plump woman with the cheeriest countenance Calya had possibly ever seen greeted her as she popped behind the pastry case. "Hello! I'm Roxana."

"Calya Helm," Calya replied.

"Nocren Lowe." He offered his hand and received a floury shake.

"What can I get for you?" Roxana asked, grabbing a plate. "On the house for a special guest. Any friends of Zhenya are friends of ours."

"Whatever the house recommends," Lowe said.

Calya allowed herself one longing gaze at a flaky pastry stuffed and drizzled with chocolate. She gave Roxana a tight smile. "I'm afraid sea travel doesn't agree with me, especially at the speed of a windrunner. What do you suggest for a recovering stomach?"

The baker clucked sympathetically. "Let's see how you do with the herb bread and butter." She cut a hearty slice from a loaf speckled with dried herbs. "I've got a tea that'll keep you soothed. Any reactions to anti-nausea magicks?"

"Only good ones."

With Lowe carrying a tray of two personal-sized teapots and cups, and Calya bearing more bread and a fruit-filled hand pie for Lowe wrapped up in cloth, they made their way upstairs to join the others. A wooden canopy frame enclosed the nook where their table was placed.

Though the bakery never filled, it was also never empty. A steady stream of people came through, either to make use of the inn's mailing services or to have a quick bite from the pastry case. A number of sailors stopped by with their own large flasks, filling from a large pot of the "brew of the day" before heading back to the docks.

For a town that was even smaller than Sylvan so far as a permanent population was concerned, both the bakery and An Honorable Pelf saw a hearty amount of traffic. Calya quietly observed from her upper-level vantage, sipping her tea, the bread having been quickly demolished. Roxana was kindly, greeting most everyone by name with good cheer—even the few Avenor Guardsmen who came by, though they were among some of the briefest visits.

A sizeable amount of business seemed to take place via the port. Few large ships stopped, but smaller ones, both merchant vessels and the lighter craft used to ferry small goods or messages, came and went with regularity. Far more than the records at any of Helm Naval's offices would suggest, considering how much of the shipping they handled for Graelynd.

More than the Coalition ledgers would reflect, too, if she were to guess.

Setting aside her empty teacup, Calya looked around at her friends. "So, who's going first?"

"Wait." Zhenya leaned over to tug on a braided cord of brown rope next to her seat by the wall, and it released the ties holding up gauzy, cream-colored hangings that draped over the wooden canopy frame and down to the floor. Woven in amongst the ordinary threads were thin strands that intermittently glowed a soft gold, forming a series of runes Calya didn't recognize. The ambient noise of the bakery warped for a moment, a strange heaviness to the air inside the canopy, before it normalized again. Only this time, the outside sounds were the slightest bit muted.

"Fancy. When did you make these?" Eunny asked, running a finger across the glowing thread.

"On the trip over. They still need some work." Zhenya squinted at the curtain closest to her seat. "Inscription work through thread isn't my strong suit."

"It's safe to talk in this, then?" Calya asked.

"Enough. Just don't shout."

"This place sees far more activity than I would've thought." She looked at Zhenya. "Froley's a smuggler. That's what you meant by 'unconventional.'"

The inkmaker blushed, shoulders hunching up around her ears. "Yes, but they're on our side!"

"Did you find out about our wards?" Anadae asked, gesturing to herself and Ezzyn.

"They arrived. I saw the proof of receipt myself, complete with my fucking name attached. Courtesy of Wembly, I've no doubt," Calya snapped.

Anadae muttered a curse.

"We know Brint had a failed side project here that was shut down and handed off to someone else. But those offices down the street are practically empty." Calya's voice rose as her frustrations gained steam. "Those were Coalition mages in Sylveren robes we met, I'd bet HNE on it. And they're blaming everything on a man who conveniently decided to disappear."

"The Sentinels had a message from him," Lowe said. "Matthias. He wrote last year, asking about how scope of authority might be handled in the event of malfeasance. We were looking into it, but then we got a follow-up message saying everything was fine. All communication since has been minimal, dodging our questions. With the distance, the border, no direct complaints... there wasn't a lot we could do until now."

Calya gave him an incredulous look.

Lowe held his hands up in defense. "I was going to tell you."

"We have some answers about the side project. Kind of," Eunny said with a grimace. "The Coalition bailed out Brint's fuckup and took over the project through a proxy. Brought in some Sylveren grads on contract."

"Who's overseeing it on the Coalition side?" Calya asked.

"It was my mother," Eunny said quietly.

"But she's been..."

"Yeah." Eunny ran a hand across her mouth. "Which might explain why shit's gone sideways without her here to run it."

Bioon Song was certainly a force to be reckoned with, and Calya didn't doubt that Eunny's now-disgraced mother had likely been the glue holding together the mysterious project out here in the Landing. But Bioon had only been caught and ousted from power within the last few weeks. Was Brint's fuckery out here truly so quick to collapse without her to steer it, or had it already been going wrong and he was too inept to handle it? Neither scenario boded well for them.

Except they were going to fix it. Calya had sworn she wouldn't leave until she had answers. Solutions. Proving Wembly's deception would be difficult, for she imagined the crafty old man had taken steps to cover his tracks. But if she could expose more of the Coalition's wrongdoing, if they were engaged in even more illicit activity than had been previously shown by Eunny and Ollas's victory against Bioon Song, Calya would be... well, not a *hero,* but it would be newsworthy. Helm Naval's reputation would gain favor amongst Graelynd's fickle upper crust.

Her father would have no excuse to deny her ability to lead the company. She could fire Wembly herself.

Her daydream was interrupted by Anadae's groan. "The Coalition. Wonderful. We should've brought an army."

"And instead, we have one Sentinel of the Valley," Calya said, then glanced at Ollas. "One and a half."

"Hey!" Eunny cried at the same time Ollas smiled and said, "Fair enough."

"Are all of the mages left here Coalition plants?" Calya asked, hands forming fists on the table.

"Not all," Ollas said. "Some of the assistants are from the university, and there are a few grad students around here doing real work. But Treen and Aylton, no. We don't know how many are under the Coalition's thumb, by choice or force."

"Why haven't they gone to the authorities? Involved Central?" Calya asked.

"Lot of ships coming in not flying flags," Zhenya said, an uncharacteristically hard edge coming into her voice. "The capital's been dead to the Landing for a century at least. They operate... differently, out here."

A reality the Coalition would happily exploit as it suited them.

"How do you know Froley?" Calya asked.

Zhenya ducked her head. "I studied abroad out here during Initiate levels, and helped them with some... stuff."

Eunny snapped her fingers at Calya. "Focus. What do we do next?"

Anadae leaned forward, gaze intent. "What did you find in the desk?"

Calya withdrew the discarded note from her cloak pocket and spread it on the table.

"'Lady S' is probably my mother," Eunny said.

Lowe held the paper close to his face, eyes narrowing.

"What is it?" Calya asked.

"The mage who contacted us was named Matthias."

"Same handwriting?"

Lowe shrugged. "It's been a long time, and I only saw the letters once or twice, but it seems likely."

"Okay, so we try to find out more on this Matthias guy," Eunny said.

"Lily, the assistant that showed us around when we were

storing the tea," Ollas murmured, setting another scrap of paper on the table next to Calya's find, "she mentioned previous trials done at the different sites. Drew me a map."

"When?" Eunny asked. "I didn't—"

"She waited until you were helping Zhen," Ollas said soothingly. "I think she was spooked by your relation—"

"Yeah, I get it." Eunny slumped back in her chair, lip curling. "We should split up again."

"Froley said there's a village south, toward the southern forest," Zhenya said. "They've had a bad time lately with illnesses. Asked if we could look in on them."

"Sounds like our thing," Eunny said, nudging Ollas. "We won't need to refresh the tea container charms for a few days."

Anadae examined the map, fingers roving over the dots indicating sites in the surrounding area. She pointed at one to Ezzyn, who nodded. "We'll take this one," he said, tapping a spot farther out toward Graelynd's Hook. "There's another SU cohort stationed out that way, doing restorative work on the coast. I know the team lead."

Calya pointed out another dot on the map. "This one looks close. I'll— We'll ask around." She nodded at Lowe.

As they stood up, preparing to go their separate ways, Ezzyn added in a low voice, "Be vigilant, everyone. Eren Galwynd is a Rhellian grovetender who's spent the years since the war doing restorative work back home." He looked around at all of them, expression grave. "He shouldn't be here at all, much less helping to run a Coalition project."

"For the mundane among us, which I suppose is only me," Calya said grumpily, "what exactly should I be looking for?"

"You'll know," Ezzyn said, tone dark. "If you do, find me. No discussion."

The group separated, Anadae tugging her dour-faced prince back toward the patisserie case while Eunny, Ollas, and Zhenya went back outside. Snippets of conversation floated back to Calya as she and Lowe strolled after them, with words like "greenhouse" and "dirt" and "it's *soil*, love" punctuated by Eunny's long-suffering groan.

Despite it being early evening, the dark of winter had settled while the group met. Lamps lit the street, and Calya smothered a yawn behind her hand as exhaustion crept up on her.

"Find him, he says. So he can burn everything to a crisp." She yawned again. "Not to sound like an old lady, but—"

"Calya," Lowe said, fingers gentle upon her shoulder as he steered her back across the street toward the inn.

She stopped at the base of the front porch, eyebrows rising in question.

A dimple formed in Lowe's cheek as the corner of his mouth curved up. "It's the end of the day."

She scrunched her nose in a pout. "Is it—"

"Caly!" Brint's loud voice drew their attention. "I've been looking for you."

"Brint," Calya said, doing her best to keep the animosity from her tone.

"Hey, about what happened earlier with Morris—er, I mean, Mayor Krowe. I feel awful about it." Brint dragged his hand through his dark blond hair, a contrite smile on his face. "Let me make it up to you over dinner."

"Apologies, Brint, but I have business to discuss with Mr. Lowe," Calya said sweetly. "You know how it is."

Brint eyed Lowe, expression frosty. "I see." When neither said anything more, he sighed. "I won't keep you, then, but find me later, please? It's important."

She doubted that last part very much, for it was the kind of thing Brint would add on to ensure he got whatever it was he wanted.

He stomped up the few steps to the inn's porch and disappeared inside, letting the outer door close heavily behind him.

"We need to do something about him," Calya muttered. "He's

going to be a problem if we don't preoccupy him with something else."

"Agreed. However—" A smile teased at the corners of Lowe's normally serious mouth. "I believe we had a deal."

"I don't recall."

"Show some grace, Calya."

"I have none."

"I believe in you." The teasing smile grew into a smirk. "A compliment. Something nice."

She made a face at him. "You don't strike me as the type to want a *nice* woman."

"I don't, and you're not. However, we had a bargain, and I think I'll find this enjoyable."

"Yes, well... all right." Calya squared her shoulders, giving Lowe a lofty stare, eyes raking over him from head to toe. "I like that you're not handsome."

He blinked. "That I'm not— How is that a compliment?"

"It is from me." Calya gave him a falsely coy smile. "So many of the men in Central are just walking rectangles. Pretty enough, but bland."

I feel like I can be free with you and still be me, unchanged, and you seem to want it.

But she was teetering dangerously close to the edge of liking that feeling too much. To the point where she might give the feeling a chance to grow, or, Goddess break, speak the words aloud. Speak them into being. Because even if the words and feelings were honest in the moment, what of when she changed her mind, as surely Calya would? She didn't have the time and certainly not the desire to deal with the messy fallout that would inevitably come after.

"You're... refreshing," Calya murmured instead.

She brushed past him and up the steps. "I'll deal with Brint in the morning."

Chapter Twelve

A COMFORTABLE BED on solid ground did Calya wonders. Her room faced out toward the water and a small cove where the locals moored their boats. Thanks to an enchantment on the glass, the cries of seabirds and dock-goers were muted to gentle background noise. It was akin to the apartment she rented in Grae Port, situated near the pier where Helm Naval kept its main office and workshop. How many weeks had it been since she was last home? Three at least, for she'd been up in the Valley to see Anadae, and then there'd been Eunny's conflict with the Coalition, which Calya had happily joined.

Homesickness was a foreign concept to Calya. She didn't feel a sense of belonging in the capital, not in the same way that her sister spoke of her connection to the Valley. For Calya, Grae Port was where her company lived, and there was work to be done. It wasn't nostalgia forming in her chest but resolve. As she watched a small craft head out, the captain raising a hand toward the dockmaster's station and receiving a wave of acknowledgment, an idea formed in her mind.

After refreshing herself, she made her way downstairs in search of breakfast—and Brint. Courtesy of the Pelf's excellent staff, she soon found herself with a cup of strong black tea in hand and her target in sight.

He'd claimed a large table all to himself in front of the main room's best view of the harbor. The location didn't surprise her, given his penchant for luxury in all things. That he was likewise solo was unusual, for she'd have expected him to be holding court over the less-seasoned men who'd signed on with the Guard. Or perhaps having breakfast with the mayor at his manor on the opposite side of town.

As she approached, Calya noticed the papers Brint had flared out around his plate. He frowned down at them, a pencil in hand as he struck a line through several words before scribbling a note of his own, his wandering scrawl in stark contrast to the cramped, slanted letters of the original writing. "Higher than last time," he muttered to himself.

Calya slowed her footsteps, but too late. As if sensing her interest, Brint looked up, his hands reflexively scooping the papers together. His guarded expression didn't soften upon recognizing her but rather slid from suspicion to annoyance. Surly, like an overgrown man-child dead set on holding a grudge.

"Calya," he said, clearing away his papers before she could get a proper look.

"Brint." Assuming a nonchalant manner, she drew out a chair and settled in it sideways, ready to pop up the moment he became absolutely unbearable. "You asked me to find you."

"I meant last night."

"You said later." Calya lifted her chin toward the papers he'd stowed in his bag. "Work?"

"Nothing important." An easy smile bloomed across his face, his tone going treacly, cajoling, as he leaned toward her to say, "About yesterday—why don't you come with me and my boys to visit our north site? I'll show you around, see if we can figure out the reporting mix up."

Calya matched his meaningless smile. "I'd appreciate that.

Tomorrow, perhaps? As I told Mayor Krowe, I have several items of business to discuss with the dockmaster. HNE's logs are paramount to our reputation, so I intend to crosscheck the copies that should be on record here. I've some tasks from Wembly, too, so I'm afraid I'm rather busy for today."

"Oh, I... Yes. I'm sure Dockmaster Gormund will get you all settled." Brint's smile never wavered, but the strain at the corners of his eyes and the tension in his brow told Calya everything she needed to know. When she visited the dockmaster's registrar, doubtless they'd have copies of Helm Naval's last three months of logs already waiting.

A new person entered the main room: Lowe. He paused, searching the room. When he saw Calya, his neutral expression hardly flickered. He gestured toward a table at the farthest corner of the room, away from Brint.

Calya waved, shooing him on. "In a moment," she called out.

Brint glowered at Lowe's back, then turned his reproachful gaze on Calya. "So. You're fucking him now?"

She tsked as she sipped her tea. "So what if I am?"

"You should be more careful, Caly. He's using you. A Sentinel of the Valley? They don't care about anything to do with Graelynd."

"Mutually beneficial usage. Is it really so different than what you would've done?"

Brint's acting was improving; he managed to appear semi-convincing with his affronted look. "I would not. We have *business* together. I mean, really, since we're both here, we could look at revisiting the partnership on that joint protection—"

"I already have a partner for my business here in the Landing," Calya said. "And considering how our last agreement worked out, I'm not exactly eager to revisit anything with you."

Brint laughed, loud and false and with an excess of effort to sound unoffended. "I suppose I deserved that."

Calya took another sip of tea.

"Can't believe you went with him, though," he grumbled, his performance short-lived. "Gods all break, Caly, he's *old*. I thought you had standards. You're more like a baby sister than—"

"And yet I basically was yours, for years." Calya stood up. "That didn't stop you earlier."

She sauntered away to join Lowe at his table.

"What was that about?" Lowe poured her more tea, setting Ollas's map next to her cup. "They gave it to us, since the others already know where they're going."

"I've gotten rid of him for the day." Calya nodded at the map. "The northern site is a bust. Shall we explore this one after he leaves?" She tapped a different spot toward the base of some scrawled *river's edge mtns*.

Lowe gave her a dubious look. "It's a bit of a hike."

"I brought my walking boots."

The great outdoors was being added to the list of Calya's enemies. Her boots were perfectly suited to walking along the trail to the western research site. Her feet, however, not so much. The uneven streets of Grae Port were nothing compared to the rock-and-root-laden path they traversed now.

After Lowe had outpaced her for the umpteenth time, he dropped behind her on the trail.

"Haven't we been out here long enough for you to surmise that I don't have a fucking clue where I'm going?" Calya snapped, blotting sweat from her forehead. She'd been chilled when they first set out on their adventure, but after what felt like half a day spent bushwhacking, the wintry air was all too warm.

"Just follow the trail," Lowe said, sounding like he was enjoying himself far too much. "It's better to let the weakest member of the group set the pace."

"Weak." She sniffed. "Excuse me for having been ill for most of the voyage here and now being asked to climb veritable mountains for hours."

"We've barely been out here for *one* hour, walking around the base of what is, at most, a hill." She could practically hear Lowe rolling his eyes. "Which you could jump off the very top of and have to work to sprain your ankle."

"Lies." Calya smacked a branch out of the way with the staff he'd given her after she'd tripped for the hundredth time. *Hours* ago. "It's midday at least."

"An hour and a half if I count you dawdling at the inn," he said, nimbly sidestepping when she poked the staff at him. "I did warn you that it was a hike."

"I've gone for plenty of walks outside." She stopped. "Are you sure we're going the right way?"

"Let me consult the nearest street sign," Lowe said dryly. "There should only be one path out here, Calya."

She looked around but saw only a thicket of frustratingly evergreen shrubs on all sides. A true path had given way to a few breaks in the greenery, narrow and twisty as they disappeared from view. "I'd say the local wildlife decided otherwise."

Lowe glanced around, chin lifting as a breeze rustled the leaves. He squinted at the roughly sketched map the extern had provided. After turning to face the water, which could be glimpsed through bare patches in the spindly trees around them, he said, "Go left. We should be getting close."

Calya turned in the instructed direction. A faint line of worn, dead grass suggested a hint of a trail, and the shrubs grew smaller as they led away.

"Good plan. At least we get to go downhill—"

Too vigorous a step combined with her lack of attention as she turned her head to call back to Lowe, and Calya slipped as a loose rock beneath her foot gave way. *Downhill* turned out to describe a sharper incline than she'd bargained for as she lost her balance and fell.

She shrieked, the sound cutting off as she bounced off something large, hard, and with much less give than her side. Lowe shouted behind her, but she didn't register anything beyond her own pained gasp.

Mercifully, the hill was short, and she tumbled into a clearing, narrowly avoiding impaling herself on an old marker stick at the end of an overgrown field.

Groaning weakly, Calya pushed herself up to a sitting position. She wiggled her fingers, then her toes, relief coursing through her when everything moved as it should. Her cloak sported a few new rips, her sleeves and trousers torn in multiple places. Already, the burgundy fabric of her right sleeve darkened as she bled freely. An ache built in her side, the pain growing as her wits came back.

"Calya!"

"Here, I'm fine," she wheezed, and looked around. "I found the site."

What was left of it. A dozen marker sticks were placed around the edges of the desolate field, breaking it into quadrants. Although, enough time had passed that, if not for the markers, there wouldn't be any distinguishing features to indicate separations at all. A barren patch of hard-packed dirt suggested the placement of multiple structures, but only one long shack and the skeleton of another remained.

Lowe leapt clear of the shrubs, landing with enviable grace on the clearing's level ground and springing over. He knelt in front of her, his hands deftly running over her scalp, her chest, checking front and back as he assessed her damage from stem to stern.

"I'll live," she said, wincing as he peeled the stained fabric from her right side.

"By the grace of Carram's breath," he muttered, naming the aspect of the wind. "Let's get you inside and see if they've left any med kits around."

"I can walk," Calya said, taking his hand and hauling herself upright.

"Sure you can." He stooped, one arm hooking under her legs, the other steadying her back as he lifted her off the ground. "But we're not risking you trying and managing to break your leg."

"Lowe!"

The corner of his mouth lifted with the hint of a smirk. "Don't fight me, sweetheart."

She hmphed, though more for her pride than anything else. Lowe was refreshingly solid, and now that she'd been off them for a moment, her feet added themselves to the tally of aches and pains. "So you'd prefer me docile instead?"

She liked the way his chest shook with a laugh. "We both know you don't have it in you." Much softer, murmured almost like an afterthought, he added, "But, no."

The site looked as if it had been abandoned some time ago. The remaining buildings, temporary construction that must've been deemed not worth the trouble of salvaging, were beginning to fall apart. The shack's sod-and-pole roof had developed holes, but it was mostly dry inside. A few rudimentary desks and chairs were left behind, though all the chairs were broken.

Lowe set Calya down on the sturdiest of the remaining tables, then went off to rifle through drawers.

"Guess they haven't used this place in a while," she said, giving the building a critical look.

"See how the ground all around here is still bare? No weeds, nothing, even though there's all that open space," Lowe said as he picked through the remains of a medical kit.

"Enchantments still in the ground?"

"Maybe. For the size of this place, there must've been more equipment. People. They saved most of it instead of abandoning it like this thing." He nodded at the shack.

Finding an old roll of bandages and cleaning lint, Lowe came back to where Calya rested. There was nothing but the water in the skin he carried for cleaning her wounds, but only the one on her side was somewhat deep. Nothing a mender back in town couldn't right... once Calya managed to hobble back.

She didn't fuss as he tended to her, quietly grateful to just sit and try not to flinch as he worked on her side.

"Thank you," she said softly, looking down rather than meeting his eyes. "I'm not sure I'd have known how best to do this myself."

"Always," he murmured. "You never have to ask."

There was a sincerity in his voice, in the way he spoke, that evoked a sense of yearning in her. It made her want to fall into him and the inherent promise in those words with a reckless abandon that should've unnerved her. They were feelings too much like sentiment, yet the part of her that was usually repelled by such things stayed quiet.

Lowe mashed a few herbs he'd taken from a pocket on his shoulder harness with some of the water, the pommel of his knife serving as a crude pestle. "Tell me something about yourself."

Calya shook her head, chasing away the inexplicable feelings that had jumped on her moment of weakness. She raised an eyebrow at him. "I'm not a child. I don't need to be distracted from the pain."

"Humor me," he said. "A piece of Calya Helm beyond the thorns."

"Ah, a secret, then. One of my little-known facts." She leaned toward him. "I admit, I'm not exactly what you would call outdoorsy."

Lowe snorted. "I'd've never guessed."

"Tell me something of you, then," she said. "Your origins. You're Valley-born?"

He shook his head. "The Fahr Squall, a long time ago. My family managed the pollination of particular stands of trees in the taiga for generations."

"You have family in the Valley?"

Another shake of his head. "The Eyllic Empire would've taken a tacit interest in us, since the Emperor tracks all mages as potential threats. But a diviner? Remaining in the Fahr Squall all but guarantees conscription. I've been in the Valley over twenty years. My family were living in the mountains near the border with Rhell, last I heard."

He spoke of the separation easily enough, as if it didn't bother him. As if the Eyllic emperor's obsession with others' magic hadn't forever altered the course of Lowe's life.

Freedom or servitude—hardly a choice at all. A cruel twist for one whose gift was reading possibilities.

"Do you miss them?" she asked.

His hands stilled, and Calya wondered if she'd overstepped. Broken some unspoken rule between them, asking something so personal when she'd hardly given him an equal-value answer. They'd shared in each other's bodies by mutual, unsentimental accord. But now she asked for a piece of heart, and she found she cared more than she should for his answer.

"It's easier this way," he replied after a moment. "Divining... it's hard enough for me to read the wind. It gives, but not unconditionally. Not without cost. And the more you push about an outcome—you remember how I mentioned bias? You risk not reading the wind anymore but your own head. Your own wants and worries, and that leads you astray. But that's a... difficult... concept even for a diviner to grasp, much less someone who only wants the benefits. It can be hard to break from the wind, once you've had a glimpse of what it can do. It's hard to be content with only that."

"Sounds like you're speaking from experience," she said.

He looked at her, and though he didn't speak, Calya could feel the turmoil stuck behind his clenched teeth. The hesitation struggling against a long-held wariness. Burdens and grief her gruff ranger hid behind an aloof stare.

She said nothing, either. But when she placed her palm against his cheek, he leaned into her touch, eyes closing.

"When we were still young, my little sister asked for my wind. I was in my teens then, and old enough to know better, but she kept nagging me. I was young and stupid. I caved."

"Was she hurt?"

Lowe shook his head against her palm. "No, it was something good. Helped her win a silly bet against her friend, I think. I don't really remember the start anymore, just how it went after. Pain would've been better. It might've taught her something. Been a warning for all of us. But no, a little win, it felt good. Got her fixated. It hooked my whole family. That's the thing about the wind—it feels so good to be right. To hold that power. Even if it's for some small, stupid thing, it makes you feel invincible."

Calya's fingers tensed at the anger that leached into his voice. Lowe's hand came up to cover hers, holding it against his cheek as he met her eyes.

"They kept asking. For little things, of course. Predict the weather, best spot for work, which path would be fastest. People started noticing. Eyllic mage corps heard whispers, so we moved. I started saying no, but they'd ask for new things instead. They were my family. Always small things, but it was never enough, and I started to fuck those up, too. Couldn't trust the wind anymore." The bitterest smile in the world crossed his face. "You asked if I miss them, but I..."

"Leaving was the right choice," Calya murmured. "I'm sorry you had to do it."

His body shook with his exhale. "Long time ago."

She leaned back on her hands, playfulness coming back into her tone as she said, "Of course, my advice is somewhat suspect, it coming from one without a heart."

Lowe snorted, the somberness that had overtaken him receding. He scraped up a bit of the paste he'd made, which was now an icy blue color. "Breathe out when I apply this and try to relax."

Calya watched him, her mind a tangle of thoughts she might say in response to what he'd shared. A shadow of sadness remained in his gray eyes. His pain was still so real, and that, she could respect.

She pointed her chin at the paste. "Is it going to hurt?"

"To quote the mender who taught me this, 'you might feel some discomfort.'"

Calya hissed through clenched teeth as the paste touched her skin. It burned, though she couldn't decide if it was hot or cold. She gripped Lowe's shoulder, her breaths shaky though she tried to make them as measured as she could.

"Good girl," he murmured. "Tougher than you— No, definitely as tough as you look."

The burning sensation lessened, taking the deep ache along with it and leaving a numbness in its wake.

"Surprised?" Calya panted.

"I'll admit, I don't know what to make of you," he replied, wrapping a bandage around her abdomen.

She eyed him warily. "Meaning what?"

"Oh, you are ambitious and reckless, that's not up for debate." His lips quirked with a small smile. "Hard to trust a woman who goes through your shit while you sleep. Who's borderline obsessed with her work. For a company that doesn't deserve how much she wants it. But..."

"But?"

"I don't understand you." His hands stayed at her waist, gripping her gently. "But I want to."

Goddess, but she wanted it, too. So much that it wasn't merely unnerving but a sliver of dread at her core. A hint of terror, lurking in the emptiness where she'd banished her heart and feelings and the weaknesses that came with having such things. His words, the vulnerability he'd shared with her, plucked at the intertwined fear and desire she hid in the dark hoping they would die.

She'd wanted something to call her own. That proved her place in the world—that it was at the top. That the world needed her contribution, too. Since she was a small girl staring up at the beautiful ships her parents crafted, ships that enabled travel and commerce across all of the Empyrean Territories, Calya had known that Helm Naval was her answer. The company would be her vessel, if not literally—and what a cruel twist of fate it was to find she couldn't stomach being on one—to achieve the belonging she craved.

"I..." The confession lodged in her throat.

It had seemed like fate. A perfect setup. Her parents had crafted the Sea Runner enchantment, and even if it was their only magical creation of note, it still endured. They built a reputation for designing and building reliable ships. Calya knew she could direct innovation to greater heights once she gained some respect in the industry. And Anadae, with her diplomatic grace and her water magic, so reminiscent of their mother in looks and abilities, they'd complement each other so well. The future was theirs.

Except, then Andrin had gone into politics, and Mina Helm had supported him. They'd traded their business for a minor position. The Transportation Board, a subset of the Council of Standards. That was it. Not *bad*, exactly, but her father would be just another councilmember's name among dozens. Might as well be anonymous.

Calya could've weathered that. The end goal she'd envisioned, which her parents had implied was a sure thing, it was always for the company to go to her and Ana anyway. But then Ana had left, too. Chased after magic and fallen in love and made a home so far away from what their lives should've been. Now, Calya was the only one left who seemed to care about what the Helm name meant. Who wanted the company at all.

"I've wanted HNE all my life," she said at last. "To rule it, yes, but not so I could sit behind my father's desk. I could make it a true force in the industry. The best. *I* could do that, if they'd let me. If they'd listen." She let go, just a little, of her tightly collared vulnerability as she murmured, "Andrin doesn't deserve me, but the company does. *I* deserve it. I'm so close, though it should've been mine already.

"I want that. I'll work for it. That's the extent of the story." She nodded once, though for whose benefit she couldn't truly say.

"Is it that simple?" he asked. "You want something, and you don't stop until you get it?"

"It is for me." She let her hand rest lightly against his chest. "But I've been fighting for the company my whole life and only rewarded with meaningless titles to show for it."

"Does that mean you'll stop?"

"And let them win? Never." Calya eyed him, the slightest tremor running through her fingers as she said, "Ambition that's never borne fruit. Is that really a trait you want in a woman?"

Lowe pressed his palm against her waist, mindful of her injury. "I think you could conquer the world."

"And yet you don't run away," she murmured.

"No," he replied, voice so soft he all but mouthed the word.

Calya's legs slowly hooked around his sides. Lowe didn't resist when her ankles clasped together behind him. He bent toward her, his free hand bracing against the tabletop.

She grasped his shirt and pulled him to her, and he came willingly, his mouth covering hers. She moaned appreciatively, lips parting for him. His tongue swept into her mouth, stroking over hers again and again. When Calya let her head tip back, he rained kisses down her throat. Sucked gently at her pulse point until she shivered. Smiled against her skin.

When she dragged him up for another kiss, he leaned into her, cradling her face with his palms.

The table creaked in warning. Lowe removed his weight, forehead resting against hers. "When you fell, I thought—I thought..."

Calya hummed softly. "Worried about me, ranger?"

"Yes," he replied, tone solemn. "Too damned much, and I don't know why. I don't form attachments, either, Lady Heartless, not anymore. We hardly know each other, but you... you scare the fuck out of me."

The wind whistled through the broken doorway.

Calya stared at her reflection in his eyes. "What does the wind tell you?"

"I'd rather hear it from you. What is this?"

"We might not know the minutiae of each other, but you know me to my core," she said.

Calya was single-minded in her drive. Determined not to be derailed as the rest of her family had. Distractions had never stood a chance against the prize that was her company.

Until him. Until she'd bumped into a Sentinel and thought of him only as a conveniently placed tool for her use. How wrong she had been. Fighting the whispers that had started as mere intrigue and flirtation and a superficial attraction. Convinced herself that was all the silly feelings were. Nothing more than a product of her own impulsive desires. But they weren't, couldn't be, because impulsive things didn't linger, let alone build.

But he had shared with her, and she with him. They'd let themselves be vulnerable with each other. Never before had Calya felt confidence in a lover. Not like this. True feelings that had only continued to grow, even if she'd tried to ignore them. She couldn't claim ignorance any longer, to herself or to him. Lowe could be her mortal peril, the thing to finally knock her off her chosen path.

Only if she let him. If she spoke the words into being.

"I want Helm Naval. And... I want you. For a time," she said, tone playful even as her heart thundered in her chest.

"Diviners aren't meant for romance. For relationships," Lowe whispered. "And I won't use my wind for people. Not like in the past. Not if it could do damage."

He was the first with such a gift that Calya had ever met. Though she didn't know the pain of it, his confession left no doubt as to how it could poison love between people.

But this wasn't love between them, only a mutual interest.

Relationships had never held much appeal for her, and Lowe's mouth, delectable as it was, didn't expel HNE from her mind. Didn't make the hole in her chest where a heart should reside suddenly feel any less cold. Lady Heartless she would remain. As for his other concerns...

"I said I wanted you, not your wind. And it's not a relationship." She nudged him back so she could stand. "It's enjoying each other's company while we're stuck out here at the edge of civilization."

"What happens once we're back in civilization?" A smile tugged at the corners of his mouth, though a note of wariness remained in his tone.

"We reevaluate. Perhaps it's your turn to proposition me this time." Calya smirked at him before picking her way through the mess left behind in the building. "Come on. If I fell down a mountain, it had better be for a reason."

Lowe snorted but held his tongue. They split up, digging through the scraps, emptying desk drawers that were little more than the slats of crates nailed together. Though the site had clearly once been heavily used, little in the way of identifiable material remained to suggest what work had been done. Some broken glassware, an old ledger missing most of its pages. There were several rotten stakes left in the field that cordoned off an abnormal, circular bit of swampland. The ground was murky and stinky, but it didn't match the descriptions of the Eyllic poison so far as Calya could tell. She took a sample, using a shard of glass to scrape a bit of the dirt into a bandage remnant and storing it in her cloak pocket.

After having retrieved his staff, Lowe came back in, a scrap of fabric in his hand. "Look at this." It had been torn from one of the marker stakes, the weathered cloth faded and stiff. "I found the real road, too. It's at the end of the field. A few more steps to the left and you'd have gotten there."

Calya held the scrap up to the light, trying to make out the faded words written on one side. It was a list. Numbers and ingredients, mostly, and what might be a date, though the writing was too washed out for her to be sure. The hand was slanted, the lines cramped like having any space between them was the enemy. Rossala's Tears. Glimmergum. Blight of Vervain. She'd seen a list like that before. The handwriting, too.

Fortunately, the contents of her cloak's pockets hadn't been lost in her fall. She flipped open her pocket notebook to the crumpled paper found in Matthias's desk, which was tucked next to the faded list she'd taken from the box of Brint's old documents back in Renstown. Potions, and the same written ingredients, though the numbers were different.

Which was interesting and all, but Calya was far more intrigued by the similarities in the handwriting. Matthias wrote with tiny letters that had a distinct lean. The words weren't complete, some faded away to nothing on the scrap of fabric, but enough remained for conviction to harden in her mind.

"What do you think?" she asked, giving the papers to Lowe.

His brow furrowed as he compared the writing. "Our missing mage?"

Calya nodded. "Looks like it." She carefully tucked her notebook back into her cloak pocket, then added the stake marker as well. "He's been writing to Brint."

The memory of Brint hunched over those papers at breakfast flashed through her head. She'd seen such penmanship yet again, just that morning, while he mentioned a discrepancy and wrote over the top of someone else's report. *Higher than last time*. Something he'd only know if he was receiving figures regularly.

"I need to search Brint's room."

"You say you want me and are already talking about getting into another man's room," Lowe teased, offering her his arm.

Calya leaned into his support as they began to walk back to town. "No, he's far too handsome," she said with a sly smile. "I think I've gotten a taste for ranger."

Chapter Thirteen

WITH ANADAE and Ezzyn traveling to the other site and Eunny and the others still at the neighboring village, Lowe suggested consulting Froley for help. They had a trusted mender on call at the Pelf, and within an hour Calya was, mostly, good as new. An imbued salve would make short work of her scrapes and bruises; by tomorrow morning, they'd be healed over, and after another day or two, nothing but a distant memory.

Her ribs weren't as easily fixed, the bruising worse than she'd initially thought. A deeper healing was more than the mender Froley employed could do without drawing attention Calya wasn't willing to risk. As Lowe went off to find her some food, Calya settled for an extra thick bandage and an imbued ointment that managed to stick to—and stain—everything it touched. After extracting a promise to reapply it thrice daily until her bruising faded, the mender left.

"The rooms here aren't that big, not even the fanciest the inn has. Not by Central standards, anyway. It shouldn't take too long for me to search—"

"This is a bad idea," Lowe said, not for the first time since she'd mentioned it.

"It's not broken." Calya wolfed down a cheese-stuffed pastry Lowe had acquired for her. "You've never worked through an injury?"

"My job is different, and you know it."

Calya tapped her side, no sign of tension on her face. "I could wrestle a bear and not feel it through this. I'll be fine."

"You should rest." Lowe stole a piece of biscuit from her plate. "I'll keep you company."

A tempting proposition. After a day tromping through the woods, the notion of curling up in bed, with Lowe to wait on her hand and foot, was enough to send a lick of heat through her core. Her stomach tensed, and when the motion caused only a mild twinge of discomfort, Calya's mind jumped to all the possibilities opened by such a finding. Being on top was a given. After all, they couldn't have him crushing her delicate ribs. If he wanted her flat on her back, well, didn't Sentinels need to problem solve on a regular basis? Calya accepted that she would never be one of the more creative types, but she could encourage it in others. Especially if she was the recipient of such ingenuity.

She snatched up the biscuit before he could steal another bite. "That will be our reward."

"For?" Froley said, suspicion drawing out the word.

Calya met the innkeeper's unflinching stare. "Are you with us?"

They shrugged. "I'll help, if I can."

"Good. I need to expose Brint."

Lowe pinched the bridge of his nose. "Calya."

"It's your turn to distract him."

"If only I could match your feminine wiles."

"Appeal to his vanity," Calya said. "He does so love to feel superior. Doubly so after you swept me out from under him—so to speak—on the ship."

Lowe wasn't deterred. "If anyone's going to be searching his room, it'll be me."

"Oh? Because the Sentinels do so much training in breaking and entering?"

"Because one of us is currently injured and has the agility of a brick."

"I may not be a trained spy, but neither is he." She looked at Froley. "Do the rooms at the inn have any kind of defensive warding?"

"Just for flooding and fire."

"Don't, Calya. Let me handle this part, please."

"Don't be ridiculous," Calya exclaimed. Noting how several other patrons glanced their way, she lowered her voice. "If, *if*, it all went to shit, what do you think would happen if he found you there?"

They might technically be in Graelynd, but if the Coalition had its hooks in the town, Calya imagined they would carry out their own brand of justice. If a group of Sylveren researchers could be hidden away, what chance did a lone Sentinel have of escaping a similar fate, or worse? She didn't believe the researchers dead— most days she didn't, anyway. The Coalition's ruthlessness reached heights to which Calya could only aspire, but even so powerful an organization wouldn't risk the Order of Sylveren's ire. Not so soon after being caught meddling at the university. And those actions had been nonviolent. *Killing* a group of mages? That was a step too far, even for the Coalition.

Now, holding the people against their will and forcing them to finish whatever work the Coalition was carrying out here, *that* she could believe. Undoubtedly there'd be another lawsuit, another public censure, and massive fines to pay by the end of all this. Maybe even complete cessation of all dealings with the Valley unless Graelynd's Upper Council meted out a serious punishment as well. But what did the Coalition care in the meantime? For them, few consequences couldn't be softened with ever more money, and they had that in abundance.

Lowe was frowning at her, as usual, but with concern rather

than irritation this time. "What do you think will happen if he catches *you?*"

Her mouth opened, but the blithe retort wouldn't come out. What *would* Brint do? Blustery, arrogant Brint. Oh, sure, he was a fool, but not so foolish that she'd likely be able to talk her way out of being caught. He'd love to have something over her. Would use her predicament to his advantage, and that wasn't a slippery slope but a hellish downhill slide to put her earlier tumble to shame. If she capitulated to his demands even once, it would be never ending.

The worry on Lowe's face suggested more. A fear for her safety... but from *Brint?* Brint being *violent?* Even when his last scheme had been crumbling around him and Anadae had refused to be his lifeline, Brint hadn't tried violence. He'd damn near shit his pants when she'd responded to his lies and manipulations with a bit of violence of her own. No reason to think he'd suddenly found his spine.

"Best we not find out," she said, her confident air only a touch forced.

"Don't go without me, Calya." A certain urgency tinged the quiet words.

She looked at him over the rim of her teacup, draining the last of it instead of answering.

"This is madness." Lowe turned to Froley. "How did it get this bad? You run this town, allow the Coalition to—"

"We're not working with them," Froley said, not pleading but fierce. "But they hold the cards. So long as we don't interfere, they leave us alone. They watch." A shrug. "So do we. But information's only worth so much if you can't use it. The folks in Central haven't exactly filled us with confidence that we wouldn't be trading one shitty master for another."

"Sylveren has had mages out here for years," Lowe said. "When did the Coalition get in?"

"The Coalition's only been here, five, maybe six years. After the war, but just. Things were fine at first." A bitter smile curled Froley's lips. "We didn't realize how entrenched they were until it was too late. Then we were stuck with Avenor coming here for months at a time."

"Brint? Doing what?" Calya asked.

Another shrug. "Not running a hybridization program for plant armor or whatever shit they keep reporting to the capital and the Valley."

"The Coalition had paperwork forwarded to their people here from Sylveren," Lowe said. "Do you remember them?"

"Eren's team is the main one here. Been a lot of mail for them all winter."

"Do you remember a Matthias?"

Froley nodded. "One of the Sylveren mages. A real one, not a Coalition plant. One of the good ones."

"The Coalition mages say he got sick of the work and disappeared."

Froley's eyebrows went up. "They're saying they don't know where he went?"

Calya shook her head. Lowe's gaze darted from one to the other before settling on Froley. "You didn't know he left?"

"No," they said slowly. "He hasn't been by in... in a few months. But sometimes he's gone for a bit."

"They say gone for good."

"He didn't—I'm sure of it," Froley said, a stubborn set to their mouth. "He'd have said something if he was really moving on."

Calya filed that information away for later. So, he really was missing without a trace, and probably not of his own volition.

It should've been a sobering thought. The kind of thing to instill despair at the enormity of what she was up against. It *was* serious, no doubt about that. But every word, every way in which she was being outmaneuvered, every move to reduce her to nothing but a pawn to be handled by any other will than her own...

She seethed. Every fucking affront was an ember in her, and she was building to a burn.

"You said Brint's been here for months at a time," she said. "Since when?"

"Couple of years," Froley said. "Things have been off ever since he came around. We used to see the mages around town more. Then they started staying holed up in their labs. Transferred to other areas. There's a few left in town, but the only ones you see regularly are Eren and those Coalition mages."

"Could they have been smuggled out?" Lowe asked.

Froley snorted. "I'd know. Ol' Gormund may think the docks are his, but..." They clicked their tongue, then looked at Calya, their face grave once more. "He's trouble. Avenor. He's got the mayor and the dockmaster in his pocket, too."

"Who can we trust around here?" Lowe asked.

"Leave my people out of whatever you're here to do. The locals. They got to live here after you go back to your Valley."

"I won't cause you or your town any trouble I can't fix," Lowe promised.

Froley's smile held more pity than anything else. "One Sentinel against the Coalition's pockets. I don't like your odds."

"The Coalition's days here are numbered," Calya said through gritted teeth. "Brint Avenor's been playing with fire and getting away with it for too long."

Froley gave her an appraising look. "Zhenny mentioned you were determined."

"Ambitious. Reckless, even." Calya glanced at Lowe before grinning darkly at Froley. "If you can trust one thing about me, it's that Helm Naval is mine, and I am so fucking tired of Brint and the Coalition getting in my way. I'm not leaving this place until I'm satisfied."

Froley's delighted cackle rent the air. "I like your spirit. Maybe not your chances, but I'll back you as I can." They nodded at Lowe. "Luck to you ranger, keeping up."

"Don't I know it," he grumbled.

Further conversation was interrupted by the door opening and Eunny, Ollas, and Zhenya trudging in. They joined Calya's table, Eunny pouring the last of the tea into Calya's cup and draining it in one go.

"I'll get us more drinks," Ollas said, heading for the counter.

"Where have you been?" Calya asked.

"What's wrong at the village?" Froley said at the same time.

Eunny's golden brown skin was sallow. She laid her arms on the table to cushion her head, mumbling, "Zhen?"

"They're sick," Zhenya said quietly. "Eunny's been imbuing infusions all day."

Lowe's face drew tight. "The Eyllic poison?"

Zhenya chewed on her lip, her eyes pinching shut for a moment before she shook her head. "No. But there are similarities." Worry tinged her words. "We're going to take our healing tea back tonight and see if it can help."

Ollas returned with a fresh pot of tea and biscuits and gave Eunny's shoulder a gentle shake. "Eat, love."

"What did you find?" Zhenya asked.

Calya gave an abbreviated version of their adventure, omitting her intention to search Brint's room. Her friends had enough on their plates without adding undue anxiety over her plans. Finally, she showed Ollas the dirt sample they'd taken from the site. The gardener examined it closely, calling up a small golden spark that flickered twice at his fingertip before it went out.

Ollas held the fabric scrap out to Zhenya, who did her own quick assessment, her magic remaining a steady glow as she passed her hand over the dirt.

"It feels kind of like the corrupted soil in Rhell," she said. "Not the same, though. It *is* contaminated, but it feels different. Not as aggressive."

Froley's shoulders relaxed. Slightly.

"We've got to send word to Ezzyn," Ollas said. "He has the

most experience with it, *if* it is related at all to what's in Rhell. We need them back here."

"Write fast," Froley said, eyeing a clock hanging on the wall behind the bakery's counter. "If you can get it to the dock before the hour, I've a boat that'll take it."

"We'll deliver it," Calya said when Eunny started to rise. "You need to rest, and we're not as useful as you lot are to a sick village."

Maybe Lowe could be, but Calya selfishly didn't want him to leave. Given the way he'd been hovering around her, she liked to think he wouldn't want to be separated, either.

With a hastily penned letter in hand, they hurried down to the dock in search of Froley's fastest messenger boat. Lowe had to sprint down the dock to catch it before it left, but they managed.

"How long do you think it'll take to reach Anadae?" Calya asked him as they watched the dark horizon swallow up the boat. It was an impossible question, she knew it, but worry and hope were clawing their way up her chest, wrestling and trampling each other in turn. She didn't like it, how helpless she felt. This was why she didn't let herself care about things she couldn't control.

"Not soon enough," Lowe remarked.

The trip back to the Pelf went slower, Calya's feet beginning to drag as weariness set in. Between trekking through the mountains, falling down them, and the incomplete mending, sleep beckoned.

Dulled as she was, Calya perked up when the sound of Brint's voice was carried to them by the wind. She looked around, spotting two figures going toward the mages' office across the street. Brint was trying to speak quietly, which, from him, only made the conversation sound more suspicious.

Though Calya tried to slow down, Lowe kept her walking. "Don't draw attention," he murmured. "But look at who he's with."

Brint and his companion stopped outside the office door, directly under its lamp. Calya couldn't hear their parting words, but before the other man went inside, she had a clear view of his profile. Rhellian, wearing a tatty cloak.

Excitement flared to life in her chest, burning off any lingering exhaustion. It was the same Rhellian man she'd seen meeting with Brint back in Renstown. The same man who was supposedly just off "checking on another site" for the Coalition's planted mages posing as Sylveren folk.

Eren Galwynd had returned.

Chapter Fourteen

"I DEFINITELY NEED to search Brint's room," Calya said with poorly contained glee.

As he followed Calya back into the inn, Nocren didn't try to hide his dismay, but she ignored it all the same. For all her insistence to the contrary, the beginnings of fatigue were starting to show, and not even the return of the Rhellian mage could truly cure it. He'd get her back to his room. Maybe have food sent up instead of letting her go back out and do something foolish. Like breaking into Avenor's fucking room, or spying on the mage, or... who knew when it came to Calya and her plans.

She needed a distraction, and if that meant putting her in his bed, so be it. He'd remind her that she wanted him. For a time. For now. Careful phrasing to hedge bets against their unlikely future. Nocren didn't care. A primal urge in him suggested that once he had Calya upstairs, he wouldn't be inclined to have either of them going back out this night. If a clear-minded Calya was half as ravenous as the one fueled by the Scarlett Kiss had been, then he doubted she'd have any interest in leaving, either.

"I'm going to have a chat with Froley," Calya murmured as they entered the inn's main room.

Nocren eyed her, making no attempt to hide his skepticism.

She nudged him toward the bakery. "Get us some food to take up. I'll be right back." Then she left, chasing after Froley as they went down the hall.

Nocren filled a bag with the last of the pastry case's goods, then went back in search of Calya. He looked over the inn's moderately full main room, not yet accustomed to how the Pelf also served as housing for most of the scholars and graduate students doing research in the Landing. It wasn't nearly so crowded as the Mighty Leaf on any given day, but almost a dozen or so people were seated at various tables around the large room.

"Hey, ranger. Lowe."

Nocren registered the voice only after he'd turned at the sound of his name. Avenor had returned from his shadowy meeting and tucked himself into a lonely corner table.

Nocren cast a last, desperate glance around for Calya, but she was nowhere to be found. He couldn't snub Avenor, who was waving to get his attention, so publicly.

Swallowing his contempt for the man, Nocren pasted what would have to pass for a neutral expression on his face and went to join him.

At the man's emphatic gesture, Nocren dropped into a seat across from Avenor, even though it put his back to most of the room and left him feeling exposed.

"You called?" he said, dipping his head in a small nod of greeting.

"Seen Calya lately?" Avenor asked, folding a copy of *Grae Port News*, the periodical from the capital city, and setting it beside him.

"Earlier, at the dock." No point hiding it, especially if Gormund had reported their visit like a good little lackey.

"I didn't think the Sentinels would stoop to work with the likes of Graelynders." Avenor laughed, the sound loud and too practiced to Nocren's ears.

"It's not a formal partnership," Nocren said with a shrug. "Our interests happened to align, that's all."

"A word of advice, ranger..." Avenor wagged a finger at him. "She can't be trusted."

Nocren forced himself to remain still, for all that Avenor's declaration made him inwardly bristle. "Your company partners with Miss Helm's often. Do you not trust your business partners?"

Avenor's lips formed a smile, but his eyes remained hard. "We're in the business of making money. If your work here has a fraction of warmth to it, Caly will ice it out. She's ruthless when it comes to HNE, and she'll pick it over anything else." He settled back in his chair, legs invading Nocren's space. "She turned her back on her own sister when her dreams went against Caly's vision for HNE."

Nocren said nothing. It wasn't anything Calya hadn't already said—warned him of—herself, though in different words. The sourness in Avenor's tone was likely as manufactured and false as the rest of him.

I'll never love you...

A whisper of wind seeped through a crack in the window. Nocren's hands balled into fists beneath the table. Avenor was trying to needle him. Nocren knew it, and yet...

"...warn you, since you don't know her like I do. So you always know where you stand with her," Avenor was saying. "Never first."

The wind picked up, whistling through the glass, stirring Nocren's hair and calling a twinge of magic to ripple through his fingers. As it did when it wanted something.

Out of the corner of his eye, Nocren saw Calya peek into the room. She found him—and his table companion. A mischievous grin spread across her face. "Help me," she mouthed.

Dread swept through Nocren's gut. Though from his position Avenor could see the main room, he didn't have an immediate eyeline to the front desk, but all it would take was a turn of his head. Already, his eyes narrowed the slightest bit as he realized

Nocren's attention had strayed. He moved to look over his shoulder—

Nocren's arm jerked as he called the wind. A few crackles of Nocren's magic lit the air, and it swirled around the pair of them, rustling the paper folded at Avenor's side.

Avenor startled, his attention whipping back to Nocren. He stared at the golden motes of light as they landed on the table and twinkled before fading.

Slowly, he looked up, a covetous gleam in his eyes. "I'd forgotten. Is it true, then, you're a fortune teller?"

"A diviner," Nocren said, keeping his internal disgust in check. "It's not an absolute magic."

Avenor dismissed the warning with a careless wave of his hand. "What's the price to tell my future?"

Calya had disappeared. Off to carry out her reckless plan, he presumed. "Help her" indeed. If he was going to extract payment from anyone for this farce, he knew who would be at the top of the list.

Motioning for a server to bring tea, Nocren inclined his head toward Avenor, saying, "A gesture of good faith after our shitty start."

Elated by her stroke of luck, it took all Calya's self-control to keep her gait unhurried. She nodded to a maid as she strolled in the direction of her room, then paused at the end of the corridor. A swift look confirmed that it was empty. With light steps, she went to the opposite end, away from her own lodging and instead to Brint's large corner room.

In a nod to Desmond's Landing's small-town feel, the inn used simply wrought metal keys, and the handles lacked magic-reinforced lock mechanisms. Though there was a fortified lockbox in the backroom on the main floor for valuables, only Froley held that key, and Brint wouldn't have constrained himself to waiting on the innkeeper's convenience.

Froley also had a master key for the entire inn, and had been willing to give Calya a handful of minutes to use it at liberty.

The door creaked as Calya let herself into Brint's room. He'd turned the lamps down, or a maid had done so for him—he wasn't the type to be mindful about burning someone else's fuel.

She maneuvered around a trunk Brint had left open on the ground with clothes spilling from it. Picking her way around his mess, she turned up the lamp on the writing desk in the corner, just enough so she wouldn't trip over anything. Brint had the largest single room in the entirety of the inn, and appeared to have done his level best to scatter his belongings everywhere. She couldn't begin to fathom how he'd managed to pack so much of his personal shit for the trip.

She prowled around the edges of the room, leery of casting any shadows that might be seen through the many windows set into the rear and side walls. For all Brint's mess, it seemed to be just that: frippery. If she'd been hoping to find a gleaming document penned in golden letters and detailing his collusion with Bioon Song, such a childish fantasy was thoroughly doused. Given his cozy relationship with the mayor, any such documents and the convenient box of missing wards were probably displayed within Krowe's manor.

Conscious of her precious few minutes dwindling with every moment, Calya turned out the desk drawers as quietly as she could. Nothing of interest, the few papers on top benign letters to his father and the Avenor Guard board with general updates.

Annoyed at her brilliant plan's disappointing outcome, Calya moved back toward the door. Perhaps another round with the Coalition mages was in order. Could she leverage her having seen Eren meet with Brint into something more?

Lost in thought, she nearly crept past the small stove against the wall without sparing it a second look. She'd have continued right past if not for her foot slipping as something beneath her shoe fluttered away. She caught herself on the wall, wincing as her ribs protested the erratic movement.

One hand pressed to her side, Calya knelt to retrieve the offending item. She squinted at it in the dim light. A scrap of paper? No, an envelope. A torn piece, to be precise, with only a few broken-off lines of the handwriting remaining.

Calya's eyes went to the stove's small door, and she reached for the handle.

The tea was just a prop. A touch of the theatrical employed because gormless worms like Avenor would only give Nocren's magic credence if they saw something with their own eyes. Even when what their eyes saw was completely unconnected shit.

A curl of steam floated up as Nocren poured a cup for Avenor. The weather had decided to play along with his show, a storm sweeping in from the sea to blanket the town with heavy rain. The wind sent sporadic gusts to rattle the windows, and it took hardly any effort to find the right current for his plan.

"Do I need to drink this?" Avenor asked, a shadow of disgust on his face. "I thought you worked the wind. Or do you need to grease your—"

"It's for your benefit, but you don't need to drink it."

Nocren touched on his magic, letting it unspool from his fingers to intertwine with the steam rising off the cup. It glistened like a golden thread, spiraling up and fading just above the level of their heads, breaking into pieces and coalescing anew in a steady stream of light. A few pinpricks of gold broke away, floating like bubbles and popping at random, but the miniature combustion was no larger than a fingernail.

Nocren inhaled slowly, his gaze going unfocused as the wind caressed his face.

Trouble, the wind impressed upon him. Danger in all forms. Avenor as the cause, the victim, at the heart of the concept. *Change* whispered around the edges of Nocren's mind, but it held a discordant note, unlike when the word accompanied thoughts of Calya.

Reaching for the brighter spot in his mind, Nocren chose to follow danger.

Avenor, hunched over a desk, writing a letter addressed to his father. A sheet of numbers lay next to him, the figures not matching those he put in the letter.

The scene dissolved, reassembling to show Mayor Krowe toasting Avenor. "Settled! And for a third less than we predicted."

Another fade to darkness, the vision blurring until clarity unfurled once more.

A man stepped out of a room, pulling a heavy door braced with iron shut behind him. The clang of metal against metal filled the air as the man dropped a bar into place, locking the door from the outside. Another clank sound followed as the man fussed with the door. He turned around, one hand leaving his pocket. Avenor. Then he walked away, the glow of runes etched into the door fading in the background.

"Well?" present-day Avenor prompted, the impatience in his voice dragging Nocren out of the wind's touch. "How does my future look?"

Bleak, he wanted to say. *But for everyone else most of all.*

"You've nearly reached the end of your trials," Nocren made himself say. "Successfully, I might add, but not without effort or conflict."

Hunger filled Avenor's face, but also a flicker of doubt. "I'd like how that sounds, if you had specifics. You just used some pretty words and a light show to cover how general that fortune was."

"It's not a fortune," Nocren said through gritted teeth. "It's... possibilities, not the definitive future."

"Sounds like an excuse to me."

Truly, the Goddess Syvrine must've smiled on Avenor. It was the only explanation for how he'd made it all these years without a broken nose.

Rain pelted the glass as the wind surged. Nocren's magic pulsed beneath his skin, eager to taste the thin stream seeping through the windowpane.

He hesitated. It had been so long since he'd done such personal readings. What he did for the Sentinels was always small. Open questions, like what could he expect if he cleared that trail? What were the warning signs for each Coalition delegate? How should he approach them? A touch of the wind here and there, more like consulting an almanac. Most days, he didn't consult the wind at all. Just an ordinary man relying on his wits.

He'd forgotten the slippery feeling of the wind when it was eager like this. Hungry to show him everything. Anything. This was the wind at its most dangerous, the potentialities it would show most colored, whether by Nocren's own desires or Avenor's.

Change whispered through his skull—still inharmonious, but this time with an unmistakable similarity to how it felt with Calya.

No, not similar. Connected. If she was in trouble...

Nocren closed his eyes once more.

A slim figure rifled through a desk, tossing all manner of papers and random writing paraphernalia aside. The woman paused, picking up a thin notebook held together with twine. She started to unwrap it, then froze, her head whipping around to look over her shoulder, bringing her face into view.

Calya.

Change, *the wind pressed into Nocren's mind, but this time with a sense of foreboding. He didn't remember feeding the wind more of his magic, but the scene dissolved just as it had during the last sequence of visions, slowly coming back into focus in a dimmer light.*

A dark room devoid of any furnishings aside from a plain sconce on the wall, its torch unlit. The feeble light came from above, slivers of it creeping in through the slats of the ceiling. Not a roof but floorboards. A basement cell.

More light flooded the room as a door at the top of a short flight of stairs opened. A silhouette filled the doorway—Avenor. He gazed down at the bottom of the cell. Sensations rolled from him, dread and hope coalescing into panic-infused relief.

Calya was on the floor, hands bound in front of her.

Nocren's eyes opened, the sticky feeling of Avenor's rejoicing still burning in his mind. Avenor's emotion in the visions had not been a kindly release but that of frayed nerves—the shaky exhale of a man who knew he'd escaped harsh judgment by the skin of his teeth. Guilt and glee rolled into one.

It set off something dark and defensive in Nocren's chest.

"Why is Calya a threat to you?" he asked.

Avenor stared at him as if digesting the words. Then, abruptly, he sprang up—"Thanks for the reading"—and strode quickly toward the stairs. He didn't seem to hear Nocren calling after him.

Nocren was forced to watch helplessly, his mind churning, as he walked away.

"Fuck."

~

One of the papers Calya had seen Brint reading earlier that morning was in the tinderbox. What was left of it, anyway. A corner of the paper, though scorched, was still intact enough for her to make out entire words.

...tion steady, but ward prot is
  ...50% at best. W/o Song <u>you must</u>
  ...ur lies. Help us, or I

The letter was signed simply *M*.

Calya's fingers shook. The slanted handwriting matched that of the other notes she'd found. The scribbly 'M' of Matthias. Reporting to Brint. Making *demands* of him. The mention of wards. Could it be Anadae's missing ones? And *Song* could only mean Bioon.

Calya chewed her lip. Matthias had been the one to contact the Sentinels—before he'd suddenly changed his tune. If Froley believed Matthias to be "one of the good ones," perhaps the tonal shift had been against his will.

And now he was gone. Hidden away wherever Bioon's-now-Brint's secret project was held?

Pocketing the fragment, Calya dug through the tiny stove for any more clues but came up with nothing. Still, her find was huge. It was confirmation that Brint and the Coalition's mages were lying. The wards had arrived, were being used in some manner.

Calya frowned. Memories of the contaminated dirt she'd found with Lowe and Zhenya's reluctant acknowledgment of "similarities" to the Eyllic poison rose up. But no matter; she'd theorize with the others later. Her time with the master key was long since up, and she'd promised that nothing—

Heavy, urgent footsteps grew louder as they marched up the corridor. Toward Brint's door. They were already upon her. No chance of escaping without notice, the room being the last one in the hall.

At least, if she went out the same way she'd come in.

His room was situated such that it looked out on the pier on one side and the forested hills on the other. Calya chose the hill-facing window; it wouldn't do for her to have an audience to her rooftop escapades.

She hurried to the window and pushed it open, grateful that the storm covered the groan of the hinges, and even more grateful for its dormer-style design. She scrambled through, easing it shut and pressing herself into the crevice behind the shutters.

Not a moment too soon. Brint's door opened, light flaring as he turned up the lamps. The door closed with a slam Calya felt in her bones.

But she'd made it outside, with the noise of the storm providing needed cover. Less welcome was the onslaught of rain. The roof wasn't meant to be used as a pathway, and Calya's progress mincing along the gutter was painfully slow.

Faintly, she heard Brint's footsteps as he stomped across the floor. She inched farther along, heart racing. Another window sat between her and freedom. Gods all break, what if the room was occupied?

Focus, she ordered her spinning mind. Her clothes clung to her skin, her fingers going numb as she clung to the shingles. The sound of Brint throwing open his harbor-side window so hard that it banged against the inn's siding nearly made her slip.

Faster, Calya!

She was nearly past the awning of the adjacent room's window. If she could get to the other side, she could find cover around the frame so Brint wouldn't see her if he gave his forest-facing window the same treatment.

Almost there.

The gutter creaked as she took another step, wobbling and beginning to crumple as her weight settled. Calya leaned forward as far as she could, fingers outstretched for the shutter.

The gutter's complaint went from a creak to a groan. She'd

have to jump. Launch herself the remaining few feet and hope she could grab hold of the shutter—*not* plummet to her death or, at best, grievous injury. She had a bitter feeling that, when it came to landings, she'd used up all her luck for the day.

The window beside her slid open. Calya startled, feet slipping on the unstable gutter. She began to fall, the only sound she could make a small, horrified gasp.

Steely fingers wrapped around her flailing arm and dragged her in through the window.

Chapter Fifteen

"You little fool. Develop a fear of heights."

The words were hot in Calya's ear. Never before had she been so glad to hear Lowe's growling voice.

Relief and shock blurred together as the reality of her narrow escape took hold. A good thing he had an arm wrapped around her to keep her held against his chest, because her legs shook, threatening to give out. She'd be in danger of tumbling back out the window if not for his grip.

She nearly *did*, startling when Brint threw open his other window with a crash. On this side of the inn, unless she'd grown wings and managed to spirit herself safely out of view, a simple glance left and Brint would've seen her. Caught her mid-escape—if she hadn't splattered herself across the ground first.

Lowe swept his hand to the side, golden light spiraling up from his fingers before winking out. The wind howled, sending a torrent of rain to lash the building.

Over the roaring weather, Calya heard Brint's muffled cry, followed by the dull thump of the window swinging back to hit him. The sound of his cursing faded before cutting off altogether as his window was pulled shut.

Carefully, Lowe eased their own window shut with one hand, the other still holding Calya close. Only after they'd retreated farther into the room and Calya was stable on her own feet did he release her.

"You couldn't just wave your hands to magic me down?" Her voice wavered as she teetered on the edge of hysterics.

"I don't have the gift of flight." Despite his dry tone, his shaky exhale suggested Calya wasn't the only one grappling with a sudden spike of adrenaline.

"How did you..." She gestured at everything, as if the broad motion could make meaning of the myriad half-finished thoughts swirling in her head.

A faint smile was briefly visible before Lowe ran a hand over his face. "Luck. He left the main room in a hurry, and I couldn't go after him for any plausible reason. I went outside to try and warn you when I saw this woman with a death wish traipsing about on the roof in the middle of a fucking storm."

"Not traipsing. Escaping hastily and with no plan."

"Fortunate for us, then, that this room is vacant. Can't say the same for the trellis outside. Remind me to settle up with Froley later."

"I've a key to return, too." Calya held up the master key.

She shivered, the chill of her damp clothes making itself known now that there was no fear of impending doom to serve as distraction. She had to clamp her fingers around the key to keep from dropping it.

In the hallway, footsteps from the direction of Brint's room thumped past. Lowe pulled Calya to him again, retreating to the wall on light feet. They waited, breaths held, until the sound of Brint's passing faded and he didn't immediately return.

"He's probably gone to look for me," Calya whispered.

"Then we should keep you where you can't be found."

Though his gaze was pointed straight ahead, Lowe must have felt the arch of her brow. The corner of his mouth twitched. He ushered her quietly to the door, peeking out to make sure the hall remained clear. They took the narrow servants' stairway down to Lowe's room on the main floor, located at the rear of the building.

His was a modestly sized room, the furnishings a single bed and small desk. Nothing as lavish as Brint's suite, but there was a small hearth, an orange glow visible through the front vent. A low stool was placed next to it, with a blanket folded neatly on top.

Though the impulse to pitch face first into the warm air was strong, Calya held herself in check. "Careful, ranger, or I'm going to start thinking you're a gentleman after all."

"I can disabuse you of that notion," he murmured in her ear. Plucking the master key from her fingers, he gave her a gentle nudge toward the fire. "Think on it while I return this to Froley."

Her mind was already a few steps ahead.

"If my room is clear, some dry clothes would be nice," she called after him. "And my belt bag. It has a few personal items I could use."

"At your service." With a mocking bow, Lowe left.

Calya required no further encouragement. She left her clothes in a sodden heap on the floor. Her bandages had come loose, soaked through with rain and sweat. They joined the pile of clothes as she wrapped herself in the blanket. She settled onto the stool, content to let warmth seep into her bones. It was hardly a plush seat, but in that moment, battered after the jaunt in the woods and rain-soaked from her rooftop escape, the stool and fire-warmed blanket were the pinnacle of luxury.

She examined one of the scrapes on her arm, fingertips pressing lightly around the newly healed flesh. A dull pain emanated from her ribs if she aggravated her bruised side, but short of any jarring impact, the injury was nothing of concern. Certainly not the kind of thing that would hold her back from any of the activities she might engage in tonight.

Might. Calya smiled to herself. She had every intention of letting her ranger prove just how wild he could be.

Her ranger? What a ridiculous, impulsive, completely nonsensical notion.

But was it? Calya burrowed deeper into the blanket, thoughts turning over and over in her head. Her ranger. Unanticipated, yes, but could she truly call it illogical? Her past partners had merely been business of another sort—terms and conditions agreeably met, and exclusivity had never been one of them. On the list of things she'd wanted out of those casual arrangements, monogamy hadn't made the cut. Discretion, adequate skills, no drama, those were the qualities she'd cared about. Absolutely no sentimentality.

Yet, the thought of sharing Lowe made her jaw clench. He was *hers*. For a time, as she'd said, but for said time, she wanted all of him. Which wasn't so out of character for her in the end. Possessive and fierce defense of what she staked out as hers, was that not Calya Helm at her core? Only, instead of a business contract, she sought it in a personal agreement.

Even if she never uttered the words aloud, Lowe was *her* ranger. But was she his, and in what capacity? Calya couldn't remember the last time she'd contemplated such distinctions, if ever.

There was a soft knock at the door before Lowe let himself back in. He stayed there, back pressed against the wood. Calya looked over her shoulder, a half-smile on her lips.

"Planning to stay there forever?"

"Depends," he murmured. "What do you want, Calya?"

She let the blanket slip from one shoulder. "Isn't it obvious?"

"I want to hear you say it."

Slowly, she stood up. She let the blanket fall to the floor, her eyes never leaving him, one hand settled against her hip. "Come, ranger. Change my mind about all these gentlemanly notions I have of you."

Lowe bolted the door, then sauntered toward her, setting the clothes he'd brought from her room on the vacant stool. He shed his cloak and the shoulder harness, leaving them where they fell.

His shirt came off in one fluid motion, but instead of discarding it, he used it to blot the still-damp ends of her hair.

"How sweet of you," Calya teased.

She smothered a yelp as he abruptly swept her up and carried her the few steps to his bed. The shirt fell to the ground, but Lowe didn't seem to notice. Or care. He tossed her onto the bed, freeing his hands to shuck off the rest of his clothes.

When he moved to climb on top of her, Calya sat up, splaying one hand across his naked chest. His muscles twitched beneath her touch, causing a hot streak of pleasure to run through her. It made her pussy clench, anticipation ratcheting up.

"Careful, ranger," she said, rising onto her knees, her hands moving to rest on top of his shoulders. "My poor ribs, you know."

She pushed Lowe onto his back, straddling his hips. His hardening cock nudged the cleft of her ass, and a grin spread across her face as she peered down at him.

"That's better," she purred. "Can't have anything pressing too hard on me."

"Because you're so delicate," Lowe said, his hands settling around her waist. "Had this all planned out, didn't you?"

She shrugged. "I know what I want." Her hand slid behind her back to grasp his cock. "I do what it takes to get it."

"Reckless." His breath caught when she dipped lower to fondle his balls. "Matters of business and the heart, they're all the same to you."

"The same?" Calya wrapped her fingers around his shaft again, giving it a slow pump. "I'll never…"

His hands tensed around her waist.

Calya gazed down into his gray eyes. Took in his solemn expression. Or was it apprehension? His body gone perfectly still, he stared back at her, waiting on her words. There was a heaviness to the silence between them. They'd come to a precipice, only Calya didn't understand the cause of such gravity.

A strange sense of expectation stirred thoughts and words

Calya had always considered forbidden. *Never hurt me,* she almost said. But no, that wasn't what she meant. Hurt only happened to those with hearts. With feelings and sentimentality and a belief in attachments. *Never break my faith in you. Never let me down.*

If only he could promise her that. He probably would, if she asked. Would say the words, make those pledges here in the moment. He'd probably even mean them.

Yet the gesture would be useless. Lowe could say the words and still break every promise in the end. Life hardly cared for intentions. He'd realize the futility in making sentimental vows to a woman who only knew how to love her work.

Best to never give him the chance of finding out. Even if a small, stubborn part of her had awoken and wished for something else. Wished for her to change, even just a little.

"The heart is never first," she made herself say, renewing her methodical stroking of his cock. "You and I, this is business of the most pleasant type."

Let their infatuation be like a falling star. Bright and hot. Short. Lasting only long enough for them to form hazy memories that could be recalled with vague fondness. Pleasant, because neither of them would stick around long enough for it to go bad.

"Business," Lowe echoed back at her.

"That's right," Calya said, letting her thumb circle his slickened head.

"Then I think it's time I set new terms."

∽

Never first. The heart is never first.

The words jangled in Nocren's head, Avenor's and Calya's both. Thin air currents flowed through the room, the wind omnipresent as ever. Yet it was silent now. He could feel its presence, but it didn't offer any impressions. No warnings, no encouragement.

Whatever consequences awaited him in the morning, Nocren would incur them all on his own.

Despite Calya's casual demeanor, something had changed. Not in her words or her voice, but in her eyes. The way she looked at him with a hint of wistfulness. She was quick to hide it away, donning her armor—her act of viewing everything through the dispassionate lens of business. Trying to distract him with her sly hands and self-assured touch.

Nocren gave in. If the wind could abandon caution, then so could he. He could live as simply as Calya did. He wanted her, and neither the fickle wind nor the gloriously naked minx straddling him gave any indication that he should stop.

But their positions? No, that wouldn't do. If Calya claimed to want him, Nocren would educate her on what it meant to be his.

Before his murmured words of setting new terms were finished, he spun Calya around in his lap so her back pressed into his chest. His legs wound around hers, holding her open for his hand to trail across her pelvis. When she tried to struggle, he pulled her arms behind her back, looping his own longer one above her elbows to keep her restrained.

Letting his free hand resume its lazy journey across her mound, Nocren brought his lips to her ear. "My terms, Calya. You come twice for me. That's reasonable, isn't it? Only then do you get to ride."

"How gentlemanly of you," she said, wriggling against his hold.

"You didn't want a gentleman, remember?" He gave her pussy a light slap, just enough for her to start in surprise, an indignant gasp escaping her lips. He slipped his fingers between her folds, and smirked against her neck to find her already wet with desire. "Take your orgasms and thank me after."

"Thank you?" she scoffed, struggles renewed as she tried to angle her hips away. "You want my gratitude. My *submission*."

"I'll have it, too." Nocren's legs kept her from moving far, not that she was trying to escape. More just being contrary, fighting him because she *could*. Gods all break before Calya Helm made anything easy.

Gods all break *him* the day he wanted her to.

"My submission is a gift, and not one freely given," she said. "You want it, you have to earn it."

She turned her face away from his lips with a haughty sigh. Nocren took her bared throat as an invitation, latching on, sucking hard enough to leave a mark. Let his tongue feel her pulse, the beat rapid beneath his mouth.

His fingers traced around her entrance. She was slick with her arousal, and he parted her, savoring the tremor that ran through her frame.

"Earn?" He tugged at her ear with his teeth. "Is that the mistake whatever boys you've fucked in the past have made?"

"Prove you're a better lover then, ranger," Calya said, all breathless impatience as her hips tried to sink down on his teasing fingertips.

"Are you going to ask me nicely?"

Hands scrabbling behind her back, Calya raked her fingernails across his abs. "Never."

Nocren's dark chuckle ruffled her hair. "Then you won't mind if I'm not gentle."

He put two fingers in her, rumbling with pleasure when her inner walls squeezed tight as if trying to break him. Her back arched, hips rolling with his rapid thrusting. Each motion made her tits bounce, nipples forming little points that tempted his mouth. Her head tipped back, hair brushing against his shoulder, a soft moan buzzing in her throat. He painted wet kisses down her velvety skin, inhaling her innate musky scent, memorizing it.

Nocren's thumb swiped over her clit, eliciting another moan. Another clench. He repeated the motion, sometimes only flicking over the sensitive bundle of nerves, other times making slow, firm circles. When she whined, he ground the heel of his hand against her, his fingers curling, pressing. He found the spot that made her hips buck against the cage of his legs and focused on it.

"So cute of you to try and resist." He nuzzled at her ear. "My Heartless, such a fighter."

"You think this is resistance?" Calya panted, face turning toward him, mouth offered up.

"Definitely not a challenge." Nocren's lips sealed over hers, tongue licking in to taste her mouth. Her pussy was tightening around his fingers, her hips no longer straining to take him but rather moving as if of two minds, one still hungry for him and the other growing too sensitive as she neared her peak.

But there was nowhere for her to escape. When she bit at his lower lip, it only sealed her fate.

Nocren deepened the bend of his wrist, rubbing across the sweet spot on her front wall. Kept his fingers buried, his pressure and pace unrelenting even as she began to writhe in his grasp. Her back arched again, her breaths a series of cries as her pussy bore down.

He brushed his lips against her ear. "That's it. Come for me, sweetheart."

Calya's arms twitched, her pelvis stuttering against him as the climax rolled over her. Soft moans punctuated every grip and release of his fingers, every deliberate stroke he made. She shivered when his palm caressed her clit, and the possessive beast in his chest clamored for more. Wanted to feel her perfectly wrecked beneath him. She who laughed in the face of anything gentle or tender. That suited him just fine. Ideal, really. There was no Scarlett Kiss fueling her blood tonight, no liquid magic to soften her up. She'd take his cock all on her own, like the good girl he knew was in her. If he had to work for it, well, he'd make it worth both their time.

Nocren released her, and Calya slithered forward until she lay on her side, her body still shivering at odd moments as she came down from her present high. He made a show of examining his fingers and the way her desire clung to his skin. Made sure she watched as he sucked each digit clean.

She propped her chin on her hands. "What do I taste like, ranger?"

"Heartbreak."

Her nose scrunched up as she laughed. "Maybe don't give up forestry to become a poet."

Reaching past her, Nocren opened the nightstand drawer and pulled out the bottle of lubricant he'd procured earlier, just in case. Next to it, he placed a sheath.

"More?" he asked.

Calya flicked the sheath onto the floor. "You've only managed one orgasm, Lowe. If you're going to supplant the *boys* of my past, you'll need to do better than that."

He glanced at the rejected sheath. "There something I should know?"

She pointed at the small bag he'd retrieved from her room. When he tossed it onto the bed, she pulled out a thin bottle. It bore the same elegant label of House Oleander as the Scarlett Kiss but was otherwise drab in comparison. Clear glass, gently molded into the shape of a rose stem, with the opening carved to resemble the bloom.

Pulling the cork out with her teeth and spitting it onto the ground, Calya swallowed the tiny bottle's contents. She set the glass aside with more care than the cork, pointing her chin at the sheath. "We won't be needing any of those."

Not a philter, then, but a regular contraceptive potion.

"Want to feel me that badly, eh?"

A hint of color appeared in her cheeks. "Last time was... With the Kiss, it—it *tinted* everything. Nicely, of course, but"—she waved a hand to dismiss any concerns before he could give voice to them—"I'd rather nothing in the way. I want you as you are."

Nocren stared at her, unable to form words. His cock had no such compunction, bobbing in agreement with her.

Calya smirked. "At least this once. Who knows, maybe I'll prefer a barrier—"

"Not fucking likely."

Nocren gripped her by the waist, pulling her back until she was bent over the bed, her belly pressed against the mattress. He ignored her squawked protest, grabbing a pillow and tucking it under her with a short, "For your precious ribs."

A benefit of the cushion was in how it lifted her pert ass up off the bed. Presented her for him. A slice of moonlight came in through the window, so bright after the dark of the storm, slanting perfectly across her backside.

Nocren's cock throbbed as he palmed her ass. He resisted—barely—the urge to give her soft, fair skin a slap. To see it turn rosy from his hand.

His gaze drifted lower, homed in on the dollop of creamy whiteness gathered at her entrance. He breathed in hard through his nose, jaw clenching. It was a struggle to think over the roar of blood pounding in his ears, and what little thinking his brain was doing revolved around making Calya leak with his seed next.

She was being mouthy again, riling him up with sly comments about his manhandling of her, how controlling he was, all while wiggling her gorgeous ass in his face.

Nocren ran a fingertip up her spine as he let his cock nudge against her entrance. Calya shivered with anticipation. But he only teased her, the head of his cock nosing in before he pulled it out again. He drizzled lubricant onto his fingers, slathering it over his cock and taking the time to make sure her pussy was coated.

His cock slid through her wet folds, the length of him impressed upon her. But not in.

Calya ground against him, her impatience plain. "Get on with it. Or do you enjoy being cruel?"

"Why, do you suddenly want a nice man?"

"Do you know any?" she shot back. "I might be interested if they'd rather fuck than play games."

Nocren wrapped her hair around his fingers, pulling her head back. "Let's see how sweet and fuckable you can be."

He swallowed down her indignant growl, reveling in how it transitioned to a moan as he thrust into her, burying his cock in one swift, unyielding motion.

True to his word, he didn't show her any gentleness. He could have; he was capable of such things. Could've gone with softer touches. Let her dictate the pace, his depth. Instead of having her hair in his fist, the wet slap of her ass hitting his thighs and mingling with her rising cries, they could've made love. Not this lust-fueled fucking. When he felt her stiffen, her climax imminent, in a different life, Nocren might've slowed down. Taken the time to watch her come undone all over him. Claimed her mouth, tasted the pretty little sounds she made thanks to his cock.

Maybe one day. If they had more time, as he hoped they would. If they didn't wake in the morning and remember all the ways their lives were incompatible. How *they* shouldn't fit.

But at present, they fit all too well. Like she was made for him. The prickly, heartless woman who didn't want a gentleman. Who didn't ask for a reprieve when he continued to fuck her through an orgasm, slowing but never stopping. Even that concession was short-lived. Nocren pounded on toward his own release, hands moving to Calya's waist to pull her back, making her meet each slam of his hips. Every breath from her was a cry muffled against the bed.

When he finally emptied into her, she trembled beneath his weight. His cock pulsed, squeezed eagerly by her inner walls. She sucked him farther in, so hungry for every inch. Repeatedly clenched around him, as if she could never have her fill even as she milked him dry.

He reached for her clit, grunting in dismay when she knocked his hand aside. She nudged him off, freeing herself enough to push him onto his back, and kept her hand on his chest even as it began to shake with exhaustion.

"Calya," he tried to protest, to point out how the rigors of the day were catching up.

She ignored him and clambered to sit astride him, their combined fluids leaving a trail across his hip. She stuffed his softening cock back inside and, through sheer force of will, rode him until she brought herself to the edge.

Watching her lovely tits bounce with each determined roll of her hips was enough to give Nocren his second wind. Calya's head fell back as he stiffened inside her, the extra girth no doubt providing welcome friction. She didn't fight him again when he took her clit between his fingers—squeezed him in response to the circles he made over her nub. She coiled tighter and tighter.

A light pinch of her clit in time to a thrust was enough to make her snap. She came hard, body shaking as she drooped over him. A frenzy of short thrusts, and Nocren managed to paint her insides with a last spurt.

They both flopped onto the bed, utterly spent.

Nocren turned toward her, brushing a sweat-darkened lock of hair from her eyes. "Calya," he murmured, hesitation creeping in. "Did I..."

Her exasperated sigh put an end to any nascent trepidation he might've felt. "Don't ruin a good thing by getting sentimental on me now."

Nocren laughed and leaned over to kiss her, ignoring her half-hearted grumble to fully savor her swollen lips. "A good thing? That was only the start. I'll have you begging next time."

Her only response was a pillow shoved into his face. Nocren wrestled it away, placing it under her head. He slipped out of bed, hunting down a clean cloth and wetting it from the dregs of the pitcher before returning to clean her up.

A trickle of wind blew through the room, swirling around the sole lamp and snuffing it out with a small gesture from him.

"Did the wind foresee all of this?" she asked in a drowsy voice.

Nocren got back into bed. They lay on their sides facing one another, though Calya's eyes were already closed. "In a way," he replied softly.

Her lips twitched with a smile. "Won't that be useful, having a diviner on call."

A chill ran through him, robbing him of any response. The implication of her words, so casually spoken—as if she'd already forgotten his bleak confession of how a gift like his was poison to relationships.

After all, theirs wasn't a relationship. Not a real one.

But her words landed like rocks.

Because even if she'd spoken in jest, his own dread colored each word. The seductive pull of the wind, how readily it filled his hands, eager to gel with his magic and produce a reading for her. Of her. Anything that had to do with Calya, the wind rose in him. Dangerous, for how subtly it tried to turn his mind. Tried to erode the defenses he'd put up, that had served him for years. Decades. All of it threatened to crumble at the mere thought of her asking. All his life, Nocren had had to keep others from being reliant on his magic. So long that he'd never properly considered himself being affected the same way.

If she asked for his wind, he didn't know how long he could deny her. *You scare the fuck out of me,* he'd said, without truly understanding the depth of that statement. How true it was, or how much that realization could hurt.

Calya didn't notice his silence, her breath deepening with sleep. The wind brushed across her hair, but she didn't stir. It didn't offer any insight to him, either, remaining starkly quiet. Not that it mattered. His mind filled the empty space.

I'll never love you back.

But he didn't love Calya. He hardly knew her, as he'd said before. Yet now, like then, it seemed a feeble excuse. Untrue.

Nocren almost reached out to stroke her cheek. Almost. Instead, he rolled over and contemplated the ceiling.

When sleep continued to elude him, he carefully left the bed, shrugging back into his clothes as he padded to the door. He paused on the threshold, glancing back to where Calya lay, still fast asleep.

Calya Helm, in his bed. The woman who had wormed her way into his life. Made it feel like something other than torpor.

Quietly, he left her behind.

Chapter Sixteen

Avoiding the inn's main room—although it sounded deserted at this late hour—Nocren went out through the back. He struck off down the road, his mind wandering as much as his feet. There was a briskness in the air now that the storm had abated. He'd hoped it would wake him up. Clear his head of the old doubts lingering at the edges.

A chill wind wrapped around him, offering nothing in the way of enlightenment. When he reached out, the soft glow of magic at his fingertips, the wind flurried away, recalcitrant as only the fucking wind could be. His annoyance came out as a puff of condensation. No use trying to get the wind to cooperate; he'd burn through magic for a scattering of images and even more confused impressions than he already had. Maybe other air mages could wrestle the element into submission, but Nocren could not.

My submission is a gift.

Calya. He'd thought the wind had meant for him to be wary of her, but then it kept throwing them together. Tempting him with the possibility of her. Never before had he met a woman whose acquaintance necessitated a set of fucking directions. Repeatedly, she threatened his staid, painstakingly curated life, yet every time he recognized her danger, he wanted to fall in.

Worse, hadn't she been frank with him? All business, no heart. He'd identified her moral directive early on: ambitious. Reckless. Do not trust,—well, that was a sentiment shared. He couldn't trust her. She'd confirmed it, by word and action. Snooping through his room. Through Avenor's. Her quip of having a diviner on call.

He couldn't trust himself with her. That last remark had been a joke, but the reaction on his part, it was a warning. He knew better than to ignore it.

But Nocren had known better than to do so many things when it came to Calya. She'd opened up enough with him to let a sliver of vulnerability see daylight. He wanted to do the same, to dare to hope that he'd found a kindred spirit. Conventional wisdom might have warned against diviners forming attachments, but there was nothing conventional about Calya.

The wind didn't contradict him on that part.

Nocren comforted himself with those thoughts as he plodded toward the bakery side of An Honorable Pelf. A flicker of lamplight shone in the window on the upper floor, drawing him in.

The front door was locked, but unwilling to admit defeat, Nocren went around the back. It was curiosity driving him, he told himself, not a vague sense of unease at the thought of returning to the inn. Not Avenor's smug words of always knowing where one stood with Calya and the wind's whisper of *Change* spiraling through his head. He wouldn't forsake the scant amount of peace he'd won for himself.

The back door was locked, too, but the shadow of figures sitting at a table above it was visible through the window. Froley noticed his presence, descending the stairs with something silvery glinting in their hand.

A knife, and they held it in a way that implied they possessed not only the knowledge but the will to use it.

"It's me," Nocren murmured when their face peeked through a curtain next to the door.

Froley's hard stare didn't waver, and for a long moment Nocren thought they'd refuse him entry. But then they stepped away. He heard a snippet of their voice calling up the stairs—"the Sentinel"—before the door creaked open.

"Out for a midnight stroll?" Froley closed and locked the door behind him.

"Something like that." Nocren nodded toward the blade in their hand. "Expecting someone else?"

"Something like that." Froley led the way back up the stairs. "I don't believe you've met Magister Eren."

A cloaked man sat beside Zhenya at the small table. He looked up, his eyes narrowing as he tried to place Nocren. Then he sat up, recognition dawning on his face.

"Not formally," Nocren said.

"You. You and that Graelynd woman were spying on us." Eren's shoulders hunched, elbows coming to rest on the tabletop. His eyes met Nocren's for less than a second before darting away.

The Rhellian was the picture of exhaustion, the lines around his eyes and mouth more pronounced than most men in their midfifties. His unshaven jaw had gone past the point of scruff and into beard territory, poorly maintained. Lack of sleep bruised his eyes, his pale hair limp and beginning to look greasy.

Yet, for all that the older man looked in desperate need of rest and hygiene, there was nothing strained about him. No peace, either, but a sense of subdued resignation. The Sylveren University robe was gone, replaced by a nondescript shirt, trousers, and brown cloak. A battered haversack rested on the floor next to his seat.

"Going somewhere?" Nocren asked.

Eren glanced at Froley, who sighed and waved their hand as if to say *carry on*.

"Away," the Rhellian man said, his tone careful. "The project here is... There's nothing more I can do."

"For what?"

Eren shook his head, his palms coming up to press into his eyes.

"He's going to find out," Froley said.

Eren shook his head again, voice muffled by his hands. "Not before I'm away. We had a deal."

"What?" Nocren started forward, unease twisting in his gut. "What is it?"

Froley put their hand out to placate him. To Eren, they said, "Tell him. You owe it to—"

"What do I owe a Sentinel?" Eren snapped.

"You owe it to all of us if what you've said is true." It was Zhenya who spoke up, with a fierceness Nocren hadn't known she possessed.

Froley thumped Eren on the back. "We've already made our bargain, and I'll honor it. Now talk."

Nocren looked back and forth between them, fighting the urge to grab the other man by the collar and shake until answers fell out.

Several seconds passed where Eren didn't speak. He simply stared down at the table, at his hands, as if seeing beyond their emptiness.

"Your researchers. The wards the Helm girl is looking for. Matthias. All of it," he said at last. "It was us. But they said they had it under control!" He looked up, a feverish gleam in his eyes as he searched Nocren's face. "It was. We were so close to finding a cure. We would've, if we'd just had more time. If Song hadn't gotten herself caught. Left us with *Avenor*. He had to run his fucking mouth..."

"What are you talking about?" Nocren asked.

Eren ran a hand through his hair, making the thin strands clump. "We were so close. I was going to save Rhell, you have to believe that. To hell with Avenor and the Coalition. I did it for my kingdom. I would've..."

"You're talking about the Eyllic poison." When Eren didn't answer, Nocren grabbed his shoulder. "Hey. The researchers from Sylveren. They're alive?"

He nodded absently. "Alive. Working on our experiment. Containing it."

"You're certain?" Zhenya asked, in a way that suggested he'd made such assertions before but she still needed to hear the words.

"Yes," he hissed. "For now, I am certain."

"The poison," Nocren said, revulsion rising. "Here?"

"It's... complicated. But I'm not lying—it *is* contained."

"For now," Zhenya said bitterly.

"What the fuck were you thinking?" Nocren snarled. "A fucking Rhellian. You should know—"

"What does a Sentinel of the Valley know of Rhell?" Eren was on his feet, rage making splotches of color bloom on his pale face. "Your home is safe! Your people aren't living—*dying*—under a curse. Years of this and no end in sight! I don't care what paltry steps the Restorers of the Alliance claim to have made. A victory means nothing if it *does* nothing to change what the war has wrought."

Nocren got a vague sense he was witnessing a man on the verge of a breakdown. He raised his hands in a placating gesture. "Just tell me where to find them."

"West of the site you've already found. Toward the mountains." Eren hung his head. "Go. Don't go. You will make no difference. It's going to run its course. You can't stop it, only pick up the pieces once it's done."

A series of taps sounded against the door. Froley peered out the window. "Your boat's here, mage. They won't wait."

Eren picked up his bag, then faced the others. "Song had her reasons. I have mine. But with Avenor's incompetence..." The fight drained out of him. Only a tired, defeated shell of a man remained. "I thought I could save Rhell. I failed."

He left without a backward glance. Nocren turned to Froley, gesturing incredulously after the Rhellian. They only shook their head, closing the door once more and leading Nocren and Zhenya into the bakery's empty front room.

"Does he go to face judgment from his king?" Nocren demanded.

"I'm sure he will one day." Froley dug through one of the upper shelves and pulled down three glasses and a bottle of clear liquid. "Our deal was that he send word to Rhell. Ensure that we're freed from the Coalition's chokehold."

"He swore with blood that whatever is wrong here, it's not the same as the poison in Rhell," Zhenya said, raising anguished eyes to Nocren. "We have to believe that."

Believing something and it being the truth, those weren't always the same. But Nocren didn't have the heart to give the young woman more anxiety. What else could they do?

He watched Eren through the window until the mage was swallowed by the night. "He commits treason and gets away with it. You agreed to that?"

"Lesser of two evils." Froley shrugged. "We have to live differently out here, Sentinel. And we'll be here long after you've gone back home." They poured liquid into the glasses and held one out to Nocren. "I don't know where he'll end up, but he doesn't get to go back home."

Nocren stared at the glass. A part of him screamed to find a map, to charge back out into the night and... and what? There'd been something fatalistic in Eren's eyes, and even if Nocren stooped to very un-Sentinel ways to glean answers, he wasn't sure the Rhellian could give them.

The other side of him, the wearied, rational part, knew it was futile. And not only because he imagined Froley would intervene if he meddled in their business.

Froley gave him a knowing look. "Tread carefully, Lowe. It won't take long for the Coalition's mages to realize the good Magister is gone."

Nocren sat heavily in a chair and knocked back the drink. He coughed as it burned all the way down. "This is shit."

Froley snorted. "Not a celebration. I don't break out the good stuff for moral victories."

He looked at Zhenya. "Do you want to come with us to find the site?"

She shook her head, worry creasing her brow. "I can't. We need to take the healing tea back to the village in the morning." She glanced at the clock on the wall. "We're trying to let Eunny sleep as long as she can."

They lapsed into silence, each wallowing in their thoughts.

Froley took a measured sip, eyes on Nocren. "You going to tell your Helm girl, or shall I?"

"She's not mine."

"Sure."

Nocren declined any more of the foul brew. "I'll tell her."

"Hang on." Froley grimaced. "I'm sure she'll want to go haring off first thing."

Nocren said nothing. Answers were finally within reach. His Sentinels' mission and her company's interests, intertwined. But if only one could succeed, how would he choose? And would Calya even wait long enough to consider anything beyond her own goals?

Sentinels or Helm Naval, Nocren or the company she was determined to rule. Would it even be a choice?

Chapter Seventeen

WAKING up alone was nothing unusual for Calya. The norm, really. Her other casual arrangements knew better than to stay overnight, and that was her preference. At least, usually. Opening her eyes to find the space next to her empty, Calya felt a pang of emotion alarmingly like sadness. An intolerable notion, one which she quickly dismissed.

"This is why *you* never stay the night," she muttered to herself.

She sat up, casting about the room for any sign of Lowe. A fresh waterskin that hadn't been there when they fell into bed stood on the nightstand. So, he had ventured out to obtain creature comforts and then vanished again. Unless perhaps he'd gone out to hunt down food. Provide for her. The thought held a certain appeal. Not domesticity, but pampering.

He was thoughtful, her ranger.

Her ranger. The notion was still a strange one, but the vehement rejection she'd felt before didn't materialize. Instead, she was filled with... consideration. Maybe. A cautious playing out of what such a scenario would look like. Surely she would tire of it within a week. Days. Nothing so formal as a relationship. Mutually agreed exclusivity. It was a topic she wouldn't mind broaching.

But first, clothes. She went to the pile he'd left on the stool the night before and hastily dressed. Judging by the quality of the light peeking through the window, it was still early morning, though a steady drizzle of rain kept the sky gray.

Calya was slowly buttoning her shirt, contemplating the relative merits of leaving on her own versus waiting like a sad, hopeful puppy for Lowe to return, when a soft knock sounded on the door.

Before she could determine if it was appropriate to bid someone enter when it wasn't her own room, the door opened and Lowe stuck his head in. "You're awake."

"Well spotted." Calya took a sip of water. "My thanks for this."

He barely cracked a smile.

She peered at him, taking in the shadows beneath his eyes, the tired set of his shoulders. "Did you sleep?"

"A few hours." His gaze wavered, dipping to her partially exposed chest before he made himself look away.

Calya raised her arms, indulging in a lazy stretch that let the fronts of her shirt fall open. When he turned away, ignoring her and going to his travel bag on the ground, she frowned.

"Having morning regrets?" Her tone came out sharper than she'd intended. *Foolish, Calya. Don't let him think you care.*

His hands jerked, her words landing too harshly for his quick "No" to be believed.

A good thing, then, that she hadn't been impulsive enough to voice any of her thoughts for exclusivity. For something more.

"I see." Calya finished doing up her shirt. "Then I'll be on my way."

No fussing. She'd extricated herself from similar situations a time or two. Maybe not quite the same, where if she'd had any feelings they might be in danger of being... not *hurt,* but bruised. Like her poor ribs that he'd been happy to exploit the night before.

She silenced a sigh. Of course the moment she found a man who could handle her at night, he turned out to be moody and fragile in the morning. She had the will to defuse touchy situations in business. To make herself amenable. But Goddess fucking break her before she tiptoed around the bedroom.

"Wait." Lowe held his hand to stop her. "Sorry. Calya, it's just..."

"I'm going to need more than that."

A ghost of a smile flitted across his lips. "A lot happened last night. I'll explain more later, but I've got a general location for where Avenor moved his side project. There's another site west of the one we found yesterday."

Calya's irritation vanished as excitement took its place. "What happened?" she demanded, stuffing her feet back into her boots.

"Eren Galwynd fled late last night. Some kind of deal made with Froley. He gave up some info on what's happening here in exchange for a boat out."

"Why didn't you wake me?" Calya asked. "We could've been—"

"You were practically dead on your feet. Rolled down a hill—"

"A very steep one."

"—almost fell off a roof..."

"Yes, yes, and took a tumble with a ranger. Multiple." She waved her hand dismissively. "This is bigger than all of that."

"Galwynd also confirmed the Coalition's involvement," Lowe said. "We need to be careful. The sick villagers Ollas and the others are treating, and the dirt we found... it's like the poison in Rhell."

Calya stared at him, the enormity of his words evaporating whatever blithe humor she'd felt. "We need to find the other site." She went back to buttoning her shirt, turning away as she cast about for the rest of her clothes. "You have to use the wind. Find the fastest way— I need to talk to Eunny. See if Froley can..."

Her mind leapt from one thought to another. She gathered her old clothes from the floor, grimacing at how they'd dried stiff and crunchy on top but were still damp where they'd lain against the ground. At least her cloak was decent, though its weather resistance charm was badly in need of freshening.

Noise outside the window drew her attention. Staying to the side, she glanced through the semi-sheer curtains to see the Avenor Guard contingent milling about in front of the inn. Lieutenant Orren spoke to a stablehand, their conversation inaudible from Calya's vantage point. The lad trotted off soon enough, and the gist of the conversation was clear: Avenor Guard was getting ready to ride out. But to where?

"It looks like Orren's boys—" Calya glanced toward Lowe, realizing a beat late that he hadn't responded to her last comment.

He'd gone rigid, eyes wary as he stared at her.

"Don't. I can't ask the wind for this," he murmured. "I've been calling it too much already."

There was no heat in the words. They were cold. Cold and carefully said, with a guardedness that lanced through her. That seared across something still in the vulnerable stages of new growth, cutting deep. How quickly he assumed the worst of her. That she was no different from the family who'd used him for their trivial wants.

Lowe didn't trust her. Or didn't trust himself with her. The distinction mattered little in the end.

Somewhere along the way, despite her best intentions, Calya had let a few threads of trust form. Thin as frog hair, and thus as easily broken, but spun into being all the same. A minor investment, but a true one, the kind she so rarely allowed herself. Given the wariness in Lowe's face, almost yet not quite masking a glimmer of pain, he must've reached a similar conclusion. The both of them, surrendering to a touch of sentiment.

She couldn't let that stand. Not when Helm Naval was within reach.

"Don't be so serious, ranger," she said, with as much haughty indifference as she could muster. She jerked her head to indicate the window. "AG is gearing up for something. Think they know about the runaway mage?"

Lowe frowned at her. Wavered, as if he might press. Might demand that whatever was off between them be cleared up, to whatever end. It was unknown territory for Calya, being with someone who cared enough to take that time. *To discuss.* She wasn't sure if she wanted it or not, and wasn't that an alarming thought?

But he merely shook his head, grabbing his shoulder harness and buckling it into place instead. "I don't think Froley would've told them, but I don't know what else Galwynd did before he bolted. He's confessed everything to his king already."

So, it was to be strictly business between them. She could do that.

"When?" Calya asked.

A shrug came in response. "A few days ago at least, I think." Lowe eyed the activity on the ground, standing on the other side of the window from her. "Can we trust the lieutenant?"

Calya went toward the door. "I like Orren well enough, but he's still a Guardsman, and if Brint contradicts their orders, I don't know where his loyalty falls. Trust no one."

Their eyes met across the room. A silence fell between them, so loud with the unspoken thoughts clearly on both of their minds that it was all but visible. Palpable.

Not even me. Especially me.

Calya left, her strides purposeful. Measured. She wadded up the tangle of emotions he caused in her and threw them down the hole in her chest where her heart should be.

Only once this was all over, when she sat behind the grand director's desk at Helm Naval's head office—only then would she let herself feel something over her few erstwhile days with the ranger.

Chapter Eighteen

FROLEY HADN'T TIPPED off the Avenor Guard contingent that something was amiss: the Coalition had done it themselves. Not directly, but upping and vanishing, leaving the office on the main street a mess, didn't scream of subtlety.

Calya had dealt with the Coalition enough to know that when they wished, they could be inconspicuous, using a delicate touch instead of a deliberate blow. Abandoning their main base in town and doing nothing to mask their departure had been a choice. Less obvious to her was their motivation. Did they simply not care, thinking themselves untouchable... or were they running as surely as Eren had?

Calya scarfed down a quick breakfast of buttered toast as she went to meet Lowe on the inn's front porch. He glanced at her as she approached, mouth working as if he might say something, but then he closed it. She pretended not to have noticed his momentary indecision. It was better this way, for the both of them. No opportunity for the wrong thing to be said, and they wouldn't have to slog through the tedium of undoing any harm done later. Things were already fucked between them. Time to put her walls back in place after she'd foolishly let them down. Thorns out, and no allowing herself to think about the disappointment that tried to well up.

She gave a small, disgusted shake of her head that some part of herself still entertained such feelings. No sentimentality, for or from either of them.

The Avenor Guard men spilled out from the stable's small courtyard. Roughly half already had their mounts, while several more trickled in and out of the mages' office building. A small huddle formed around Orren where he stood in front of the office's front door.

"Notice anyone missing?" Calya asked, stopping beside Lowe.

He scanned the group. "No Avenor."

Calya hummed in agreement. "Where are we searching?"

"Somewhere west of the other site. Toward the mountains."

Another groom emerged from the stables, three already tacked-up horses in tow. Ollas and Zhenya emerged from the mages' office building, both carrying sturdy saddlebags.

"We're going back to the village."

Calya startled as Eunny's voice came from over her shoulder.

"Sorry." A grin briefly lit Eunny's still-wan face. "Zhen told you?"

"I've gotten the short notes," Calya said, jerking her thumb at Lowe. "We're going after Brint. We'll stop him, and whatever this is. Any word on Anadae?"

"No, and the storm last night didn't help things."

"I'm sure she—"

Eunny gripped Calya's arm. "The Coalition wanted to make a wellspring. That's what my mother's deal with the Eyllics was supposed to be. The poison for a wellspring." She released Calya, nodding grimly to both her and Lowe. "Be careful. Bioon said it never got that far. That it was always *for* Graelynd, but intentions don't mean shit."

"*You* be careful," Calya said. "We're not the ones putting our hands on poison." She hoped. And the villagers weren't poisoned, not in the same way. Or, at least, that was what she'd been told.

With a final nod, Eunny went to mount up.

As Calya watched her friends ride off, a soft hiss from behind caught both her and Lowe's attention. Froley indicated over their shoulder to a table at the back of the room. The young research assistant, Lily, who had given Lowe the hand-drawn map on the first day sat alone, looking pale and worried.

"Found her hiding in the root cellar this morning. Gently now," Froley murmured as they went to join the young woman. "The kid's scared, and none of this is her fault."

Lowe went first, pulling out a chair next to the young woman while Calya sat across. "Lily," he said softly. "Do you remember Miss Helm? I mentioned that we came over together to look into the project you're working on."

Lily gave Calya a suspicious look before turning to Lowe. "She's not from the Valley. She's with Avenor Guard. I won't—"

"I've worked with the Guard," Calya said, tone firm but even and polite, "and I've done business with Sylveren University. I'm here at the behest of my sister, Anadae Helm, and Prince Ezzyn Sor'vahl."

It wasn't exactly a lie, just a massaging of the truth. Name dropping, but names that signaled the morality of her cause. The particulars didn't really matter except to make clear, "As far as I'm concerned, my main objective is opposing whatever the Coalition is doing here, regardless of who my previous business partners have been."

The girl glanced at Lowe for confirmation, and when he gave an infinitesimal nod, she relaxed with a shaky exhale. "I already told Froley I didn't know it was going to happen. They just came in the middle of the night and ordered everyone out. Took some papers and things, but they left in a hurry."

"Who's they?" Lowe asked.

"Treen and Aylton. They're not from Sylveren. Treen got one

of her Adept levels there, but they're both from Grae U. Work for the Coalition." Lily rubbed her eyes, voice bleak. "They sent most of us working here to the other site the same day you arrived. It was only me and Juni and Wisk left. Aylton came last night and used magic to make them go."

"How did you escape?"

"Mr. Eren... he tried to save me. In his own way. I saw him leaving. The assistants all live on the floor above the workshop, and I heard him in his office late, so I went to look." Lily bit back a sob, eyes glistening. "Followed him to the Pelf. He said I could go with him, but this, this is my home. I said no, and he told me to hide. Said he was sorry."

"So you hid. Smart," Calya said. "We wouldn't know what happened otherwise."

"I tried to go back for the others, but Treen and Aylton were already there with more people. I didn't recognize them. I didn't know what to do, so I came back here. The Coalition don't fuck with Froley if they don't have to."

"Have you told any of this to Lieutenant Orren?" Lowe asked, and got another mulish shrug from Lily in response.

Calya frowned, mind skating back over what the young assistant had said. "You mentioned another site. Where?"

"We have a couple. I've only been to—"

"East of the abandoned site we already found, toward the mountains," Lowe said.

Lily swallowed hard and nodded once.

"Can you tell—"

Calya cut herself off as Lily vigorously shook her head. The younger woman pulled aside the collar of her shirt, exposing a fading tattoo of the Coalition's crest. "It'll be gone in a few days if it's not refreshed. But I can't— They made sure to gag all of the assistants."

Lowe's expression darkened. He pulled Lily's sketched map

from his pocket and set it on the table. "Can you mark where it is?"

With a shaking finger, she traced a line from where the inn was marked with a simple dot to the edge of a grouping of squiggly lines. The boundary between the Valley of Sylveren and Graelynd; the Valley had unofficially ceded the northeastern coastal tip to Graelynd instead of following the natural line formed by the Grae-Run mountains. The spot Lily pointed to lay at the northeastern-most edge.

"There's bigger maps in the workshop, if they didn't take them," she mumbled. "Sorry I can't do better."

"You did great," Lowe said. "Thank you."

Calya nodded her agreement.

Froley came back over, giving Lily a soft tap on the shoulder. "Go on over to the bakery. Roxy is making you something fresh."

The young woman sagged with relief, hurrying away in case anyone thought of something else to ask of her.

Froley eyed the map still on the table as Lowe dug out a stub of pencil and roughed in the marks Lily had indicated. "There's an old service road that runs up that way. Most of... part of the way," they said. "Could save you some time."

"Take whatever we can get," Lowe said.

Calya only half-listened, her gaze caught on Orren's men still hanging around in front of the Pelf. "None of that's going to matter if we can't get rid of them," she said, heading for the door.

Lowe caught up before she was halfway across the road. "Do you have a plan?"

"Working on it." She went straight past Orren, intent on the workshop.

The lieutenant noticed, breaking off conferring with his men. "Miss Helm."

She stopped, motioning for Lowe to go on without her. She waited for Orren to approach. "I hope you're not going to try and insist on leaving me an escort now." She looked over his men. "I don't think you have any to spare. Especially considering it looks like you've lost one."

Orren regarded her, his brows drawing together.

"Where's Brint?"

He ignored the question, simply sighing. "What are you doing?"

"Attending to my company's business. I presume you've already searched in there, but I'll let you know if I find something you missed."

"What are you looking for? We could—"

"Where do your loyalties lie, Orren?" Calya gave him a pointed look. "Brint's gone, and so are the Coalition mages he was so friendly with."

Orren's mouth firmed into a thin line.

"He's an Avenor in name, but he isn't the Guard," Calya said. "Man or mission, lieutenant? I think you're going to have to choose."

Orren shifted from foot to foot, but he didn't try to stop Calya when she continued into the mages' workshop. It was a mess inside, drawers turned out, paper scattered all over the tables. Not ransacked, but it was clear the Coalition mages had known they wouldn't be returning and thus there was no point in retaining orderliness.

Lowe looked up as she came in. "Did you mention Avenor?"

"Yes. Orren gave me nothing. But I daresay Brint is acting on his own." Calya looked around the office's main area. "We need to find the map."

They split up, digging through heaps of paper left by both the fleeing mages and hired mercenaries who had come after them. Minutes passed, the only sounds those of pages rustling or the creak of wood as a stubborn—or damaged—drawer was wrestled open.

Patience not being one of her virtues, Calya inhaled, words at the ready. But she paused. Sighed. Another inhale, breath held as she stewed over the right way to broach the subject.

Lowe noticed. "What?" he said, exasperation creeping in.

"Let the record reflect that I am being serious and asking this in good faith." Calya spread her hands before her. "Can you ask the wind for help in this?"

"No." Lowe went back to scanning a handful of folded pieces of paper tucked into a book Eren had left behind.

Calya glared at him. It was a reasonable question, and he knew it, yet that didn't stop the reflexive walls he raised.

"I wouldn't have asked it of you if it wasn't important," she said quietly. "I hope you realize that."

She wandered away to peruse the back counter. A few larger rolls of paper were tucked into the corner, their ends crinkled and smushed from rough handling. She set about opening them up, scanning the contents. Layout for the workshop. Another layout for some kind of research site—an old one, judging by the many crossed-out sections and notes to "refer to Roll v.4" and other such scribbles.

Behind her, Lowe sighed heavily. "Sorry, Calya. It's— The wind doesn't—"

Her hands shook as she unfurled the third roll of paper. She interrupted him, remembering at the last moment to keep her voice down. "I don't care! Lowe, look at this." She kept the roll of paper—the *map*—flattened with one hand while she dug in her cloak pocket for her small notebook.

He joined her, taking over the map. "What is..." His eyes widened as he looked down.

"Sink." Calya tapped a point on the map. "The Sink, and the University people! Not SUSink, gods all break, I'm— The Sink!" she repeated. "I found a list in Brint's documents that mentioned it, but I thought—never mind. We originally considered a berth here for the joint protection route. Brint was against it. Against Desmond's Landing entirely, because of the Coalition's project at the other site. What if this is where Lily meant? That the whole project was moved here?"

Lowe squinted at a black dot scribbled onto the map. "It *is* east of the other site." He looked at Lily's sketch. "More in the foothills than the mountains, though I guess she couldn't get specific."

Calya leaned closer to examine the map, her finger tracing over the lines demarcating land... and sea. "This is more detailed than the maps the Empyrean Territories use. They don't show an inlet here."

Lowe frowned. "The surveys I did with the Coalition didn't show it, either. Should we take a look?"

She shook her head. "Too much attention, and we can't investigate them both." She looked up, eyes alighting as, outside, Orren gestured at something to one of his men. "I have a better idea."

Setting the map against the edge of the counter, she carefully tore it apart, downsizing it to a scrap that included the narrow channel and inlet just north of their intended destination.

"What are you doing?" Lowe asked.

"*We* can't be in two places at once, and we know the site isn't on the water," Calya replied, drawing a circle around the inlet. "Unless we don't believe the traumatized assistant?"

He followed her back to the front of the workshop. "I thought we couldn't trust..."

She tilted her head at him. Lowe only closed his eyes, pinching the bridge of his nose as he muttered, "Them. You said not to trust them."

"I don't know that we can," Calya murmured. Pausing outside the door she met Lowe's gaze, her lips forming a small, sad smile. "Faith, ranger. We're going on faith."

Then she marched over to Orren, taking him by the arm and tugging him a few steps away from his men. He followed, eyes darting down to where she pulled at his arm, then up to her face. "Found something?"

"Maybe." Calya gave him the map fragment, pointing at her

circle. "This doesn't exist on any official map. I wonder why that is."

Orren stared at the lines, a furrow forming in his brow. "Why are you giving this to me?"

"Consider this a gesture of... Oh, fuck it. How long have we known each other, Orren?" she asked. "I'm ambitious, but not stupid, I would like to think. If the Coalition are involved, and I think we agree that they are, then I can admit you have the superior manpower. Do not let them get away with this."

Orren's fingers tightened around the map. He nodded, turning toward his men, but he paused to look back at Calya. "Would you like to come with us?"

She smiled. "My thanks, but I have matters to attend to down here. Good luck to you, lieutenant."

"And you, Miss Helm." Orren strode back to the stable.

As Calya watched him go, she hoped she wasn't seeing another friend ride off for the last time.

Chapter Nineteen

They borrowed horses from Froley. Nocren debated having Calya ride behind him, but she insisted she could manage on her own. He set the pace, trying to balance mindfulness of her stamina with a sense of foreboding that grew every minute that slipped by.

For her part, Calya kept up with minimal complaint, but the lack of griping did nothing to settle Nocren's nerves. They rode single file down the neglected backroad in terse silence. An occasional curse when her horse jolted her in the saddle or a branch scratched at her face was the only sound she made.

The tension lingering between them wasn't helped by his mediocre attempt—singular—to have a conversation. When she gave only a monotone, short reply with nothing in the way of continuation, he gave up. He was a shit conversationalist, anyway, accustomed to having small talk die out around him. Never mind that silences between them hadn't been so ugly before.

Maybe Calya was simply preoccupied with the task before them. When he'd chanced a look over his shoulder, she hadn't paid him any attention. A furrow creased her otherwise smooth brow, her gaze not vacant but her mind elsewhere.

They bypassed the turnoff to the old site, the road growing even more overgrown and dilapidated as they followed a course going toward the point Lily had indicated. After another hour of gradual climbing, the horses pushed through a thicket to stumble onto a new road. Not one of uniform cobbles, but hardpacked dirt and gravel, wide enough to fit a horsedrawn cart.

They halted, Calya's horse pawing at the ground. Even with a shod hoof, it barely scraped the surface.

"This didn't get here by accident."

"No, it didn't," Nocren agreed grimly. He motioned for them to move off the road, following it from the overgrowth on the side.

It didn't take long for them to reach a small clearing, the road leading to the foothills of the eastern mountains. A few structures had been erected within the clearing, though two weren't buildings so much as large shipping containers that had been repurposed. A spindly tower rose up at the far edge, bracketed by trees, though for what purpose Nocren didn't know. The tower was hardly more than layers of scaffolding, the few platforms too thin and paltry to hold much weight. A single person, maybe, but he wouldn't dare climb it in any weather but the lightest breeze.

Aside from marked paths through the clearing, the remaining bare ground was sectioned off into strips, wards marking each corner. They reminded Nocren of garden plots, in a way. Plots of bare dirt, the air distorted around the perimeter by the heavy containment spells in the wards.

Calya dismounted to crouch beside a plot, tilting her head to see the ward's sides. "It's similar to the ones Anadae designed, but not the same."

He joined her on the ground. Each ward was capped by a chunk of clear quartz, with several more chips set into the wooden shaft. The amalgamation of different strains of magic exuded was enough to make Nocren feel ill after less than a minute of close proximity.

Calya was similarly affected. She backed away, her mouth

working as if to rid herself of a foul taste. "Goddess. I'm not even magical and I can feel the pulse of these things."

A wisp of light swirled within each ward's stone cap. It emitted a faint glow, more gray than the golden-yellow Nocren was accustomed to seeing when one called on their magic. Squinting through the rippling barrier created around each plot, he focused on the ground. "Does that look wrong to you?"

"It's dirt. I've never seen Eylle's poison, so I wouldn't know what it looked like. However"—Calya waved her hand to indicate their surroundings—"considering the context, I'd say everything about this place is very fucking wrong."

Nocren grimaced. He looked around, but there was no one in sight. No movement. Even the wind had gone dead still. Yet, unlike the previous site, the silence here carried an eerie quality. Not one of abandonment, but as if everyone had simply vanished. There was a sense of life to the emptiness, as if all the people had merely been plucked out of the setting, like pieces from a board while the game was still in play.

"Come on," Calya murmured, heading toward the closest of the shipping containers.

Loosening his knives in the sheaths at his waist and chest, Nocren followed close behind. Tensed for danger, he held himself ready for anything as Calya pushed open the door.

The container was as empty as the rest of the site. Empty of people, but signs of activity—*recent* activity—abounded. Tables pulling double duty as both desks and workstations filled every inch of the interior. The surfaces were covered with storage crate shelving holding logbooks and all manner of papers, cups of pencils and pens, inkwells and corked bottles. Someone had even managed to cram a teapot on a warmer stand into a corner.

Nocren gingerly touched the side of the vessel only to find it cold, the warmer's candle long since gone out. But the contents of the pot itself weren't that old. Cold, yes, but not evaporated to nothing. The liquid that remained was unspoiled.

The tables told a similar story: ink dried on the nibs of neglected dip pens, but the inkwells themselves were still mostly wet. The lamps on the walls burned, oil levels low in their reservoirs.

Nocren moved to examine a large technical drawing on a scroll that spanned the full width of the back table. "It's like everyone just... stepped out."

"But to where?" Calya muttered. "And why? No, wait, I think I can answer that one."

He looked her way. She had her notebook out again, flipping through pages as she compared her notes to a logbook on the table in front of her.

"They're all records of earth magic trials. Containment... and breaches." She opened another heavy ledger, scattering loose papers that were tucked at the front. "Expense reports. Brint, you shit-for-brains, lying weasel. I'd be impressed if I wasn't so pissed." She met Nocren's eyes. "I guess we know where the people from his old project went. Mostly know," she amended, looking at the container devoid of anyone besides them.

Nocren traced the lines of the drawing in front of him. It was somewhere between a concept and a blueprint, detailing a series of excavated rooms and tunnels in the hills abutting the clearing, all built around a pool underground. More lines and arrows indicated a pattern of flow into and out of the pool, though he couldn't read the symbols written at various parts along the cycle.

A smaller sheet of paper, letter-sized and bearing the Coalition crest—a scale and coins— embossed at the top bore a quick sketch of a grassy-looking plant on one side, and one of the same plant transitioning to grow blade-shaped leaves interspersed with large, frilly flowers, on the other.

Reacts to contaminated ground. Preventative to curative under right conditions—needs high concentration.

The note was signed simply *S*. Unease burrowed beneath Nocren's skin as he backed away from the table.

Calya was going through each of the logbooks on the table. She tapped a chart pushed to one corner. "Some kind of schedule, though it's hard to say exactly what the parameters are. Seems to cycle through on a weekly period, minus the ones scratched out." She motioned next to a small tray containing several polished stones, each etched with a single rune. "These seem to be some kind of safety mechanism. They've got their own paperwork and everything."

Nocren ran his thumb across the rune, testing it with a spark of his magic. The etching flashed gold before fading. "It's a neutralizing agent. These are enchanted for earth magic." He picked one up. "Probably for those plots outside."

He went back out, Calya in tow, and tossed the stone into the closest bed of dirt. The stone blazed with golden light as it passed through the barrier. It landed on the ground and burst apart with a loud pop, faint curls of steam billowing up. A sizzle filled the air along with an acrid smell, and fine grains of soil shifted along the surface. The light in the ward's stones flared, then went out, the invisible barrier dropping away.

Using the butt of a ward, Nocren brushed it through the dirt. It felt dry and gritty, more like sand than anything else.

"Huh." Calya considered the plot. "Guess the Coalition weren't being completely careless."

"Aside from trying to make something like Eylle's poison here, you mean." Nocren looked toward the hills rising at the back of the clearing. Despite the apparent efficacy of the neutralizing stones, his sense of foreboding wasn't comforted. If anything, it grew worse. "This way. I think they're dug into the rock."

Leaving the horses to their own devices, they found a door set into a natural crevice. Nocren held it open as he ushered Calya through, his fingers brushing the side of her arm. She glanced sideways at him, her expression unreadable. But she didn't flinch away, and as they crept through the tunnel, she followed a step closer to him than she had when they'd first set out.

The tunnel opened into a deep cavern. A mixture of light sources kept the space somewhat illuminated. They hadn't traveled very far, and bright spots higher up on the walls and ceiling suggested breaks in the stone. More scaffolding was littered throughout the cave, with torches and lamps betraying the construction's scant, temporary nature. A pair of torches across the way marked a ramp up to a room built into the wall.

But the main source of light came from the floor itself and a shallow pool of water that had formed in a bowl-like divot in the stone. The water seemed to be lit from within, though as they approached, Nocren saw that it wasn't magic in the water but another piece of quartz. A much larger one than those capping the wards, and there through the designs of human hands rather than nature. The bowl in the floor also felt off, too perfect. Likely made with the help of an earth mage versed in stone shaping.

"Is that... the wellspring?" Calya asked, walking around the edge of the bowl.

Calya only had a surface level interest in magic, caring more about what it could do for Helm Naval than its greater role in the world. She wasn't particularly well-versed in the subject, but she'd never gotten the impression that her home was running short on magic. A ley line ran through Central District, and the magic-born citizens of Graelynd seemed to draw just fine from what energy was inherent in the land. The country served as a natural basin for the excess that flowed down from the Valley, and Calya had never heard rumors, substantiated or otherwise, of the threat of a drought. If they were to have *more* magic, she didn't know what a new surplus would mean.

"A poor imitation of one." Nocren gazed around the cavern, visualizing the drawing he'd seen in the container and the space before him.

Calya gasped softly. She spun away from him, walking quickly toward the ramp on the other side of the cave.

"Calya." She didn't slow. Nocren cursed under his breath. "Calya, wait."

She hurried up the ramp. By the time Nocren caught up, she stood before a long table set against the wall overlooking the cavern, where a window spanned the distance to allow full visibility. The glass held a faint aura of power, enchanted to withstand who knew what kind of damage.

"They did it," Calya murmured, perusing yet another logbook, this one with clearly missing pages. The one she held between her fingers had the bottom half torn away. "I can't believe they really tried to— Those arrogant assholes."

But couched in her annoyance was a hint of excitement.

"What are you talking about?" Nocren asked. "*Who* are you talking about?"

"The Coalition." Calya looked up briefly, a grim smile on her face. "They must know we're close, that's why... It doesn't matter. I'll nail them to the wall with this. HNE will be... Father *can't* deny it this time."

Alarm rang through Nocren's head. There was something chilling in Calya's words. No, not just the words but her tone. She sounded vindicated. And hungry. Oh, so hungry.

The warning intensified, and in his growing dread over Calya's manner it took him a moment to realize it was the wind assailing him. Once sure of his attention, it whirled through the room, scattering loose papers left and right. Calya looked up, confusion narrowing her eyes.

Nocren didn't let himself dwell over how *right* it felt, how sweetly his magic called to him when it came to her. How easily his defenses fell, his personal rules blown away like they were made of dandelion fluff, when the wind rose for her.

He stopped fighting it, allowing the magic to flow into his hands. *What happens?* he asked of the wind. *Will she be safe?*

He let his questions go, inwardly bracing for the wind's message.

. . .

The pool surged. The water level was higher than when he'd seen it before, arcs of light breaking the surface like jumping fish. The water crackled as light flowed in through channels carved in the walls, the floors.

Unnatural, *the wind whispered.* Wrong.

Before Nocren could try and follow the potential fates tied up in those words, the image of the pool melted away. It refocused, bringing a vision of Avenor standing on the deck of a ship, hands clasped in front of him. He shook his head, the picture of shallow regret. "I tried," he murmured, voice distorted by the wind.

Coward, *the wind seethed. Or was it Nocren himself?*

Again, the scene changed without giving him the option of intuiting more from the vision. The garden plots outside came into focus. This time, the wards were dark, their quartz stones shattered. The ground in the plots was not sandy and matte but dusty and gray. As Nocren watched, a dully glowing line of moldy green crept beyond the confines of the bed, the ground for several feet on either side of the wood leaching of all color.

Change, *the wind screamed at him. This time, the scene lingered as the wind let the impression of* Change *flare so bright in Nocren's mind it burned. He blinked, as if clearing sunspots from his eyes.*

Calya appeared in the scene, rushing toward the garden bed. She held several glass jars in her hands, and they tumbled to the earth in her haste as she knelt beside the bed's wooden wall, ignoring how the wood was grayed and rotten. Perhaps she didn't notice it at all.

Nocren couldn't move, couldn't speak. Was forced to stand and bear silent witness as she scooped the contaminated dirt into the jars with her bare hands. All the while, she muttered under her breath, "Evidence. Need evidence or they'll never believe me."

A presence loomed at his back, causing Nocren's hackles to rise. He tried to turn his head, but the vision belonged more to the wind than to him, and it kept him still. He felt Avenor's approach before finally seeing him as the other man stalked past on silent feet.

Calya gave no sign of noticing. A stack of ledgers had appeared at her side. She had her pocket notebook in hand, writing a note as her gaze went from the jars she'd filled to the page and back. Her lips moved, but Nocren couldn't hear her words. Only the sound of his own heart thundering in his ears.

She scribbled away, oblivious as Avenor kept coming. She didn't see the rope that materialized in his hands.

The scene blurred once more. Calya and Avenor reduced to silhouettes, grappling with one another. Nocren thought he heard a scream, but then the sound of Avenor's laughter filled his head. The vision began to fade, everything going black as all sound became one long, discordant note in his mind.

Change, the wind whispered a final time, its voice weak.

Eyes snapping open, Nocren staggered against the table, dimly aware of Calya's hand shaking his shoulder.

"Lowe? Lowe! What happ—"

He shoved himself upright. "We're leaving, now."

"Leaving?" Calya repeated, incredulous. "But we just—"

"We can't wait for Sor'vahl. We're getting Orren's men, the other mages in town, anyone. Everyone! We're burning this entire site to the godsdamned ground before—" Nocren paused, halfway down the ramp before he realized Calya wasn't with him. He beckoned to her. "Come on."

She stood in the doorway, rigid with tension. Slowly, she shook her head. "No. No, I can't, Lowe. I'm sorry."

He stared at her, uncomprehending. "What are you talking about?"

"The Coalition is involved here. Involved in *treason*. I can't leave before I have evidence."

"Evidence?" he said, voice cracking on the word. "Calya, there's a fucked-up wellspring having a meltdown, and all you can think of is your fucking career?"

"This is more than that," she snapped back. "You're not from Graelynd, you wouldn't understand. But I have a chance, here. It's the Coalition! Do you have any idea what it would mean— I can take them down, but only if I can tie them to everything—"

"I know plenty about them." Nocren's hands balled into fists. But he made himself loosen his fingers, though they shook with the effort. "I'll be your witness, okay? Let's go."

"Your word won't mean anything. You're a Senti— Listen, their ties run deep. But if I can preserve some—"

"I saw what happens here if we stay, Calya." Nocren slashed a hand through the air, leaving a faint trail of sparks. "Avenor. He gets away. You... he... If we don't destroy this place, it—"

"Brint?" She sounded more confused than doubtful. But she shook her head, dispelling the flicker of hesitation. "You said they're only possibilities," she said quietly. Calmly. Without a hint that she'd given what he said the fucking care it deserved.

"No. No, are you listening? The wind's been trying to warn me about this. About you, me, Avenor. About that!" He pointed at the fake wellspring. "I don't know how to make you understand, but Calya, please, trust me. You have to come with me right now. I asked the wind, Calya, so would you—"

"I didn't ask you to do it, Lowe. Not this time. You didn't have to use the wind that way." Her arms were folded across her chest, her gaze flinty. "And I don't *have* to do anything. I'm staying, and I'm going to prove they're behind this. Alone, if I must."

"Listen to yourself. You're one woman, Calya! You don't have magic. I know the Coalition better than you think, and *I know* that they'll just sabotage whatever you find. Your evidence won't mean shit. It'll be compromised, or they'll have bought experts to discredit it. You can't win."

She stared at him. A shadow crossed her face. Disappointment. Maybe even true hurt. But soon, a cold mask settled into place. Disdain colored her voice when she murmured, "So much for believing I'd conquer the world."

"Calya..."

She turned around and walked back into the observation room, slamming the door behind her. Nocren reached it just as he heard the heavy scrape of metal and the clang of a bar settling into place. He tried the door anyway, and was unsurprised when it didn't budge. He went back to the ramp to find Calya at the window, her face impassive.

"Calya, don't do this. Please, come with me."

"Go. You're wasting precious time, according to the wind."

He climbed over the ramp, wedging himself onto the narrow strip of rock in front of the window. "Calya, it isn't safe. Avenor catches you, do you understand?" He pressed his palm to the window. "He's going to fucking get you, and I can't—"

"This is why we didn't form attachments, ranger." Her lips formed a sad smile. "So we wouldn't care."

"You care, I know you do," he pleaded. "You care about *me*. We... We were—"

"We?" Her eyes closed for a moment. When she finally looked at him again, there was pain in their depths, but her tone was coarse. "There is no *we*. Did you think I let you in?"

"You and I"—Nocren's fingers bit into the glass—"we've only just begun. You have a heart, Calya, and it's mine, and mine is yours. Open the door. I'll stand with you against the Coalition if that's what you want, just—"

"My lack of a heart was never from loss," she said quietly. "You think we've become something? That you matter? Your words cannot change me into what you've wished me to be."

"Calya," Nocren rasped, desperation becoming fear becoming a wild blend of anger. "Don't be so fucking reckless. He'll catch you and then—"

"You almost had me figured out right from the start, you know. The parts that mattered. Ambitious. Do not trust." She placed her hand against his, the glass warming between them. "But reckless? No. I've done the calculations, ranger. It's not recklessness, it's personal risk, and I'm not afraid of it. I'll take my chances against Brint."

"I won't," he whispered. "Calya, please."

Her fingers bent in the tiniest of waves. "We both said no sentimentality. I, at least, meant it. I'll never love you back. Do you get that? We had a nice fuck, but the heart is never first."

With that, Calya walked away, vanishing through a door in the back of the room. Nocren pounded his fists against the window. Kept going, yelling for her, until the enchantment in the glass came to life. A loud hiss sounded, and sparks crackled along the surface, burning his skin and forcing him to stumble back over the railing.

Nocren fell to his knees on the ramp.

Calya never returned.

Chapter Twenty

Her back pressed against the wall, Calya closed her eyes. Against the sound of Lowe calling after her. The pounding of his fists against the window. Each landed like a blade through her heart, or whatever tenderness she'd allowed to grow in its place.

Safely out of view, Calya finally let fall the cold detachment she'd mustered to stand against him.

She'd thought she'd hardened herself off. Been toughened by past failures. Learned not to feel so that other people's actions never mattered enough to reach this level of *hurt*. Anadae's running off to Sylveren and how she'd hidden the decision from Calya for so long. Their father's repeated opposition and rejection and denials of every attempt Calya made to grow the company, and all with Mother's blessing. Gods, the hiring of Wembly, because apparently Calya couldn't be trusted to manage Helm Naval even though she'd demonstrated her competence and commitment over and over again.

Each time, those bitter disappointments had felt like betrayals. After all, what could be worse than family's lack of faith?

Lowe.

Nothing in her life had ever hurt like him. Everything else, *everyone* else, had been little more than Calya's stung pride. But he...

She'd lied in turning him away. He'd found the cracks in her stone heart and let some light in. Carved a little space. But he couldn't claim it for himself, not in the end. She couldn't let him. Not if it meant letting this opportunity—HNE, defeating the Coalition—slip through her fingers. She chose the emptiness of denying him instead.

The sharp crackle of the window's defensive enchantment activating made her recoil. Lowe's hiss of pain pierced her even from across the room, had her reaching out—

Calya closed her fingers, making a fist. She remained in the hall, the doorway mere inches from her fingertips. It would be nothing to go to it, to look out and see him and try again. Two steps. He was still there, waiting for her.

What have we done to each other?

Slowly, Calya faced the doorway. Let her fingertips brush the edge of the crudely shaped frame, just out of sight.

Then, exhaling roughly, she forced herself to walk away. He'd be back. He'd return with whatever firepower he could muster and put the entire site to the torch. She had no intention of going down with the Coalition's sinking ship, but she hadn't chosen this path for fucking giggles, either. A one-woman army, if needs must. She'd get what she needed, and Lowe...

They'd have to see where they fell after. See if there was anything left.

The hallway grew darker as Calya moved farther from the observation room. There were no torches here, only chill stone as she followed the pathway. It felt like she was moving gradually down, eventually rounding a corner. The hall ended at another door, but this one was slightly ajar, emitting light from within.

Calya softened her footsteps and quieted her breath, taking measured inhales and soundless, open-mouthed exhales despite her rapidly beating pulse. She crept up to the door and peeked in.

Empty. It was an office, or as close to one as she was likely to find in this cobbled-together site. The furnishings were as plain as those of the containers out in the clearing, but there were more of them. More supplies and equipment—though all showed signs of having been searched. Organizers toppled, spilling writing instruments and random other tools across the desk. Books left open with pages falling out; others had been tossed onto the floor.

Calya pushed the door open wider and sidled into the room, ears straining for any sound of company. None came, the office's previous occupant seemingly long gone.

She approached the desk and began picking through what was left. The desk itself was still plain, barely more than rudimentary boards and nails slapped together with milk crates for shelves and drawers. But the recordkeeping materials were of quality. Notebooks with finer papers, stab-bound but with stronger waxed thread and many neatly sewn signatures. The ones out in the container "offices" were more like clumsily made pamphlets in comparison.

A toppled jar that had served as a bookend betrayed the fact that many of the notebooks on the shelf were missing. So, too, did the crate drawers that had been left out of place. Calya leafed through the notebook still on the desktop. It was newer, only a few pages filled, and those had been ripped out. What scraps remained held numbers that meant nothing to her without context.

She picked up the jar, intending to set it upright before moving on. The jar itself was unremarkable, heavy and not very uniform in a manner that suggested poor skill rather than deliberate artistic choice. A few pieces of gravel had spilled out, but when she gave the jar a shake, the remaining stones within rattled with muted thumps.

Upending the jar over the table, Calya poured out the last of the gravel. A single wax seal fell out as well.

She stared at it, at the sterling silver color, the lustrous finish the likes of which only one institution was allowed to use. Rumor had it that the mage who'd made the formula had been... discouraged from ever speaking of the process, and any attempts to recreate it were silenced.

Calya didn't need to see the sigil to know that it was from the Coalition, but beyond the scales and coins, a third element was embedded in the mix: a key. Only a member of the Coalition's seven ruling councilmembers used the tripartite seal.

With a shaking hand, she picked up the seal, her fingertips brushing against irregularities on what should've been smooth wax on the back. Flipping it over, she found a date from three months ago scratched into the surface.

She peered into the jar and dug out a dozen more seals. Only one other was from the Coalition's council, the rest a mix of colors but all bearing the Avenor family crest. Every seal had a date etched onto it, going back to shortly after the war. There was no consistency to the frequency of the seals. The oldest was from a few years back, then there were several starting eighteen months ago, spanning the time when Anadae had broken off her engagement to Brint and gone back to school. The frequency dipped again, with only two since the summer.

Calya sat on a stool beside the desk, lining up all the seals in chronological order. None of the dates meant anything to her, no matter how she wracked her brain. Not holidays or anything newsworthy, at least not that stuck out in her mind. She believed the seals could link Brint to the Coalition, but without something more concrete, it was hardly conclusive. One didn't just find a Coalition councilmember's seal lying around, but short of discovering correspondence from Brint or records to shed light on the dates, she was shit out of luck.

Huffing with annoyance, Calya kicked the nearest crate. It rocked back before tipping forward to right itself, landing with a thump that sounded too heavy for a few slats of wood. Something shifted inside it, bumping against the inside walls.

Leaning forward to examine the crate more closely, she realized the interior space was too shallow for its external dimensions. The slats were closer together at the bottom quarter of the crate, obscuring the view through the otherwise railing-like pieces. Calya had presumed it was for more strength or stability, but what if...?

The crate had a false bottom. The wood panel was thin, and whatever trick had been used to fit it seamlessly in place yet still make the damned thing removable eluded her. She snapped one of the corners in trying to pry the bottom up and, glaring at the splintered piece of wood, tossed it on the ground to join the rest of the debris.

There wasn't much space in the hidden compartment, only room enough for a pair of thin journals and a few loose papers. A quick scan revealed that one journal was being used as a mix between a calendar and a logbook. She looked up the first Coalition seal date and found a short entry:

Starter culture received, transported by Av & CM A. Containment protocols in place. Ley line tap tmrw while CM A on hand to assist.

"CM A" had to mean one of the Coalition councilmembers, and diverting energy from the ley lines supported Lowe's theory that the site's purpose seemed to be creating a wellspring.

She half-turned, her mouth opening to tell him of what she'd found... and then her brain caught up. How quickly she'd grown accustomed to the idea of sharing things with him. Having a partner in this endeavor. A twinge in her chest arose at the thought. How long would it take him to get back to town? He'd be faster without her there to slow him down. And when he arrived, what then? Once his duty here was done, he would return home. As would she. There was nothing that bound them together.

You care, I know you do. You care about me.

Silly, sweet ranger. Thinking the best of her. That it was in her to be good, to be *happy*. To be content with the kinds of things everyone else seemed to care about. To be one of those people who could be happy in the now instead of always striving for something more. Calya, always so ambitious and reckless and untrustworthy, she didn't know how to enjoy the little things. She didn't even know how to define them. Hadn't known such things since she was a child, if then. It was sad, really, the speed and ease with which the memory of simple pleasures had left her, replaced by the drive to matter, to leave some mark on the world.

Insatiable... and alone. It hadn't bothered her before, but now?

Calya shook her head. There'd be time to indulge in a proper wallow later. Was it truly even wallowing if she was right, too?

Whoever had kept these hidden notes must've known what they were doing at the site was deeply illegal. Perhaps even criminal, for she read on and found logs of correspondence with Brint, as she'd dearly hoped she would. Estimates for cleanup of tainted ground. Brief mentions of people—only initials—falling sick.

The loose papers were Anadae and Ezzyn's joint paper on the design and use of their containment wards. In the margin, a scrawled note read *ES/ON plant = preventative. Curative in concentrated blight. E trying to obtain.*

Her breath caught. This was it. Her incontrovertible proof. The makings of it, anyway. If she could find the author, even better. But the log would lead her to the experiments, the sickened —*poisoned*—people. The Coalition had admitted to entertaining the idea of working with the Eyllic Empire to adapt the poison, but they'd denied ever going through with it. The Empire had reneged on the deal, refusing to share their secret of how to make a wellspring, and so the Coalition had balked at dabbling with poison.

Perhaps they'd simply decided to forge ahead on their own.

Engrossed in her thoughts, Calya didn't hear the approaching footsteps until they were close.

Too soon to be Lowe returning with help. Grabbing the journal log and a handful of the seals, Calya bolted for the door on the other side of the office. She burst through it—

—straight into an ironclad grip. She struggled, kicking at her assailant's legs, her head whipping forward and up in an attempt to gain any advantage.

She was swung against the wall. Twice. Hard enough to leave her stunned, her legs buckling.

"Easy there, Erv. She's even more trouble for me if she's dead."

A hand reached for her face, fingers glowing with gold light. Darkness crept into Calya's vision as the fingers pressed against her forehead.

The last thing she saw was Brint fucking Avenor frowning down at her.

"You should've left it alone, Caly. I warned you not to pry."

Chapter Twenty-One

No matter how hard he tried, Nocren couldn't convince his legs to move faster. He trudged away from the underground cave, the wellspring project... Calya.

She'd made her choice. It wasn't him. She would never choose him over her career, her company—the only thing she'd ever deemed fit for love. He'd never stood a chance, and the wind had shown him as much. Warned him over and over again of the change Calya would bring. The change she'd bring about in him, slowly lowering his guard. Worming her way in, even though he'd always known better than to open himself up for such pain. He'd thought he could keep any attachments at bay.

He was wrong.

The bitter realization did nothing to stem the sense of failure that plagued him, that slowed his feet, urging him to go back. He hadn't tried hard enough to convince her. Hadn't explained well enough how the wind worked, or the extent of the danger it had imparted to him. If he had, Calya would've seen how reckless her vendetta against the Coalition and Avenor was. How flawed her risk assessment had been.

Or was he wrong to have thought he could? That what he'd

seen was true? Had he fallen into old traps again, succumbed to guilt and stress like a novice diviner—let his bias turn to fear and not seen how tainted the images were in turn?

It wouldn't have mattered, his bitter mind supplied. *Her ambition was always going to trump your words.*

Natural light shone up ahead, heralding the entrance to the cavern. Nocren slogged onward; he just needed to get above ground and hope the horses hadn't wandered off too far. The open air would slap sense into him, and he desperately needed it. There were messages to be sent. No doubt the Rhellian king would dispatch ships to investigate right away. Ezzyn Sor'vahl was likely setting the ocean on fire at that very moment in his haste to reach the Landing.

Nocren needed to inform Captain Malek'ko of his findings. The Sentinels and the Order of Sylveren would need to move quickly if they were going to claim authority over the site. What remained of it. Nocren had every intention of destroying it, just as he'd said. But he would need backup in securing what remained and to keep the Coalition at bay. They were already in flight, perhaps to set up in yet another location. He couldn't let them get too entrenched.

At least his mission could be considered a success. The murky circumstances and lack of communication regarding the Sylveren researchers had only been the start. Even if they never found Matthias and got his confirmation, there was the attempted wellspring. The abandoned site. The village where the others were treating the victims, no doubt sickened from runoff or some other evil seeping out of the Coalition's experiments here.

The Sentinels had more than enough cause to assert dominion over the Landing, bringing it back into the Valley's boundaries. He'd need to get word to his superiors as quickly as possible so they could get the declaration in motion before any Graelynd authorities mounted a defense. The Order would put their weight behind the Sentinels' claim, and Graelynd would be hard-pressed to refute it, considering what had gone on under their nose.

Maybe Froley would help. Nocren couldn't make them any guarantees, but the Sentinels would likely be able to come to an agreement with the mildly questionable smuggler. Certainly something better than the implied knife to the throat that was the Coalition.

Victories, yet they rang hollow for him. He'd never considered that the cost would be a personal one. He might still be struggling with the decision of whether or not he could bring himself to pay it if Calya had not decided for him. For them both.

Nocren went into the container office and grabbed the box of neutralizing stones. He tossed them one by one into the remaining test plots, grim satisfaction rising up as each flashed and went inert.

Pocketing the leftover stones, his gaze swept across the clearing a final time. He lingered over the faded mark on the outside of the closest container, the initials of Avenor Guard barely visible in the fading light. Could Orren and his men be counted on to stand against Avenor and the mayor now? Maybe, but Nocren's shallow well of trust had run dry. Another thing he'd have to beg from Froley—the town's own militia, or whatever passed for it. Enough backing to force Orren's compliance if necessary.

The wind swirled around Nocren, plucking at his sleeves as he went in search of the horses.

He ignored it.

It persisted, shifting from a breeze to a personal gust, tugging at his cloak, whipping his hair about his face.

"No, I've heard enough from you today."

He raised his hand up in defense, attempting to bat it away. A futile endeavor, considering how with the wind there was nothing to hit, and it fucking knew it. It blew again, directly in his ear.

"Enough," he growled, brushing hair from his eyes. "I don't want to hear—"

He blinked, focus sharpening on a point above him. A beam of light flashed three times in rapid succession, illuminating the top of the strange, delicate tower at the far end of the clearing. It was reminiscent of the lighthouse farther out on the Landing's point, though the brief pattern of light seemed more like a signal than a guide. A different type of warning, perhaps?

Going to the base of the tower, Nocren looked up. Another triple burst of light, then all was dark. But in the short span between eye-searing brightness and nothing, he thought he saw a gem of some kind at the top of the structure.

With a gentler but still insistent buffet, the wind gave him a nudge closer to the tower. It continued to curl around his hands, calling to his magic until his palms tingled.

Nocren closed his eyes and allowed himself a frustrated scream behind sealed lips. Then, with an aggrieved exhale, he opened his eyes and began to climb.

Not up the structure itself—he didn't have a death wish—but up the closest tree. He was nearly level with the gem when it lit again. At closer range, Nocren saw that the gem was housed in a box-like container with only the front panel left off. It concentrated the direction of the light so it was visible only to the north. If he hadn't been practically underneath the tower, he'd never have seen it. Not a protective tower, then, for they were too far from the water for it to serve the role of a proper lighthouse.

Craning his neck to look in the direction the gem's light faced, Nocren squinted into the evening gloom. Trees and mountains were plentiful in the region. If it had been daylight, maybe he could have spied some of the coast between breaks in the tree, but now...

Except, there *was* something in the distance below him. A small dot of light. Not a flash but steady, maybe a touch flickery like a lamp. Not just flickering, either, but weaving slightly from side to side.

Like the light was on a boat.

"Gods all break," Nocren muttered. The inlet from the map. It was real. A hidden, narrow cove lay in front of him, though its exact distance was hard to estimate given the darkness. Definitely not on any of the maps he'd seen while working on his ill-fated deal with the Coalition.

The wind tore through the trees, shrieking around Nocren, making the branch upon which he perched shake. It called for his magic, more insistent than he'd ever seen it. For it to be offering him possibilities with such fervor rather than playing hard to get, it was more than annoying or a bit of fun—it unnerved him. Especially after the last time. His faith in himself, shaken.

"Fine, fine. Calm down," he mumbled, letting a drop of his light float up to be caught by the wind. Only one impression came to him, bright like a star. *Change.*

Nocren's chest went tight, but he made himself follow the feeling. "What is it?"

Calya stood a few feet from him, her body turned partially away as she looked off somewhere else.

"I didn't lie to you before."

There was a weariness in her words, in her voice. An echo of the bitter disappointment he felt. The anger, at her, but more so at himself for daring to hope.

She slowly raised her eyes to his, letting her carefully neutral mask fall, her sadness bared for him to see.

"I'll never love you back."

Nocren flinched, his hands digging into the tree's bark. He didn't need to put himself through this again.

"Not the way you deserve."

He blinked. The wind whistled in his ears, *Change* pressing at the edges of his mind.

It was... different.

A different outcome. The outcome the wind had been teasing him with for weeks. While not without pain, it was *different*. And, for the wind to still be so insistent, did that mean it was still a possibility? Rarely did the wind spend time on what had been, and when it had, it always showed him true memories.

But this, this alternate meeting with Calya, had not yet come to pass.

Could still be.

The sounds of a door being shoved open and voices nearby had Nocren shrinking back against the tree's trunk. Carefully, he looked down—and nearly lost his grip.

Three men moved swiftly down a path, headed for the cove. One was Avenor, and he spoke in low, urgent tones to a burly man carrying something over his shoulder: "...with the others."

The burly man grunted a question, but Nocren couldn't make out the words.

Avenor shook his head. "...yet. I'm checking... others."

Avenor and the third man split off, keeping on toward the water and leaving the big man to take a different path winding back into the underground base. As he passed beneath a torch, Nocren gasped, shock robbing him of common sense. Fortunately, the wind blew the sound away, and the man carried on, ignorant to Nocren hidden above.

Slung over his shoulder like a sack of flour was Calya. She flopped limply with his every step, no sound or struggle from her. The sight was ice through Nocren's heart. Made his mind come to a standstill as it tried to process what his eyes saw. She couldn't be...

No. Her wrists were bound. They wouldn't bother to bind a corpse.

The burly man was nearly out of sight, his path leading through another door in the rock.

Nocren didn't hesitate. Didn't think about warnings or consequences or lessons from the past. Didn't consider whether what he did was safe or inviting true catastrophe.

Golden sparks jumped from his fingertips, caught up in a rush of wind that raced away toward the ground. Toward Calya, as she disappeared before his eyes.

"Help her. Let her see. *Make* her," he whispered, pushing his last drops of magic into the wind. "Whatever it takes."

He tore out of the tree, taking the last dozen feet in a slide-fall the consequences of which reminded him he wasn't quite so young anymore. He didn't care.

All other thoughts and plans abandoned, Nocren ran back into the mountain.

Chapter Twenty-Two

SOMEONE WAS SHAKING HER. It started out gentle, with a light touch on her shoulder and soft words murmured into her ear. A civilized approach, as if she'd fallen asleep in a coach. But, gods all, she was so tired. Her mind resisted the nudge to wake from the dark. Calya had never understood the appeal of sleeping in, seeing it as a waste of perfectly good working hours. Until now. Cocooned in the peace of darkness, with nothing to make demands of her in time or energy, she saw the merits. Would've continued enjoying them, too, if not for the progressively more determined hand on her shoulder.

If the original attempt had been one of courtesy, the rough jolt she received now was akin to the way she'd kicked the side of Anadae's bed to wake her when they were children. As wakefulness was forced upon her, Calya felt a touch of compassion for her sister's past disgruntlement.

"What?" she grumbled. Or, rather, meant to, as she shrugged off the offending hand. The croak that emerged from her dry throat was closer to a sound of protest than an intelligible word.

"Got to wake up, girl," a deep voice said above her. "They're coming back soon."

Calya forced her eyes open, wincing as she struggled to adjust to the room's light, weak as it was. She was lying on her back, and when she moved to sit up, she found that her wrists were tied. She stared at the thin rope, her brain sluggish as she tried to recall previous events.

Strong hands helped her upright. A dark-skinned man, his coal-colored hair shot through with gray and coiling to his shoulders, peered into her eyes. Satisfied with whatever he saw, he gave a brisk nod. "Avenor put you out, miss. Anything broke?"

"It's Calya," she replied, coaxing moisture back into her papery mouth. "I'll live. Who're you?"

"Matthias," he replied. "Why's Avenor so interested in you?"

"My winning personality." Calya rubbed the side of her head. "I feel like shit."

He met her words with an amused grunt. "Ervin gave you a knock, too."

She took in their surroundings. Three others huddled at the back of the cramped room. There were no windows, the sole light source a small lamp and whatever brightness filtered through the door above a short set of stairs. She squinted upward. So, they were in some sort of basement.

Calya refocused on her fellow cellmates. Two were women of Radiant Isles descent. Vresha, she guessed, one of the southern regions, given how the lamp's meager glow deepened their golden-brown skin and dark hair, the metallic lines etched into their almond-shaped earrings winking in the light.

The last member was a white man with dark red hair and a beard that hadn't seen shears in a while. He wore a long gray coat with the initials for Grae University embroidered on the right breast, though the stitching had seen better days.

The same could be said of the whole group, all of them looking as worn as Calya felt. But that was the extent of their similarities. Her eyes lingered more on the differences. One in particular.

Though they were all bound, the others were restrained by

manacles rather than simple rope. While the Grae U man was the only one in official attire, the rest had a mix of robust, practical clothing and just a general... air about them that gave the impression of mages, even though none wore robes or anything identifying.

She looked at the man who'd woken her, her mind slogging back through their conversation thus far.

"Matt—*Matthias.* You're the one who wrote to the Sentinels. That was your office I found down in the cave."

"Are you with the Sentinels?" the older Vreshan woman asked, hope in her voice. "Are they coming?"

"Yes," Calya said with more conviction than she felt. "I came with a Sentinel, and word has been sent back to the Valley and to Rhell."

"Galwynd?" Matthias asked, apprehension pinching the corners of his eyes.

"Gone. He made a deal with—"

"That spineless fucker," the Grae U man snarled, the lilt of his accent and short vowels rendering the rest of his ire too hard for Calya's still magic-addled brain to follow.

"I met two other mages," she said instead. "Treen and Aylton. They were Coalition?"

More nods and angry muttering came in answer.

"Where are they? Why are you—" Calya scrubbed her hands over her eyes. "What—Just, what. Why, how, all of it."

The mages exchanged hesitant glances.

Calya shook her bound hands for emphasis. "Since we're all down here, I'd say we're well enough on the same side. I found your secret journals," she said, nodding at Matthias. "You were gathering evidence. Why didn't you tell the Sentinels the truth?"

"We didn't know, not at first," the younger Vreshan woman said. "Sylveren sent us to do bioremediation work after Avenor's failed project was discovered. We thought it was toxic overflow cleanup."

"So, the garden beds of poison dirt I saw outside were...?"

"Not a choice," Matthias said, voice hard. "The Coalition didn't give us one. I *did* send word when we started to suspect something was off, but Song got suspicious and started screening our mail. Had to be careful after that."

"Some of us fell sick. Then we knew," the Grae U man said with a bitter laugh. "They threatened to withhold what few remedies we had if we didn't cooperate."

"More like *obey*," the older Vreshan woman said.

"We've friends still here. Somewhere," the Grae U man said. "Can't leave them. And the work... it almost... well, worked."

"Making a poison?" Calya thought back to the dirt in the beds. The exhausted look on Eunny's face as she prepared to ride back to the Landing's neighboring village. "I think you succeeded."

"A cure," he snapped. "Before our defenses broke. You're not a mage, so what are you doing here?"

Gods, there were so many reasons she was here, but this wasn't the time or place to get into them with a magic elitist. She had a headache as it was already without trying to condense her life story for strangers.

"I'm here to stop Brint fucking Avenor," she said. "The what and the why together. Working on the how."

Matthias huffed with a grim laugh. "On that, we're all aligned."

"They're already clearing this place out. Why?"

The Grae U man's shoulders slumped. "Our containment for the poison. It keeps breaking. The poison keeps changing, and we don't have enough people to share the load. They know we can't stop it from getting through. Not this time. Song might've had a plan, but she's gone, and Avenor's useless."

The defeat in his voice made Calya's blood run cold. She wasn't a mage or a scholar or a journalist. The closest she'd ever been to the Eyllic poison was what she'd read about in the papers during the war, and that had ended years ago. She and Anadae had never discussed her more recent work with specifics, and besides, it took place up in the Valley. Calya's personal dislike of the place aside, it had a way of conveying a feeling of safety. She only really knew of the poison from a business perspective, the danger and cost measured in aid provided by Helm Naval ships. For something like the poison and its aftermath to take root in Graelynd... it was too horrible for her to fully comprehend. Calya had always assumed the Coalition was at least *a little* corrupt, but never to this degree. Greedy, sure, but not reckless. Dangerous.

"Is there anything you can do?" she asked.

"The Coalition has the source," Matthias said. "We might be able to slow the spread, but not forever."

"Not without getting poisoned ourselves," the older Vreshan woman whispered.

"That's been their plan all along," her younger countrywoman said. "Make this look like our fault and leave us here to rot."

"My sister knows we're here. Anadae Helm. She'll come, and my Sentinel is here, and he's already getting help as we speak."

The others didn't appear to share her confidence, but the words buoyed Calya. Anadae and Ezzyn would be sailing toward them already, and they knew far better than Calya what it took to stop the poison.

As for *her* Sentinel, the sentiment might not hold true anymore, but there was no doubting that Lowe would help. Even if he didn't care for Graelynd, his morals had never been in question. Calya and the Sylveren mages wouldn't be abandoned. She wouldn't let herself entertain any other thought.

Further discussion was cut short by the sound of footsteps approaching the door. A scrape of metal against rock, and then the door groaned open, revealing Brint silhouetted in the doorframe. He clomped down the stairs, followed by a big, barrel-chested, unsmiling Graelynder who was the physical manifestation of everything Calya found repellent in men. What had Matthias called him? Ervin?

"Brint." Calya struggled to her feet, ignoring the wave of nausea that came with the motion. Her pride revolted at the thought of letting him sneer over her, and if she managed to vomit on him, all the better.

"Oh, Caly. It doesn't have to be this way," Brint said, stopping in front of her.

Ervin glared at the mages, planting himself between Calya and the others.

She held up her bound hands to Brint. "I agree. Be a dear and do something about this."

Brint laughed, the sound false and grating. "I've always liked your spirit, Caly. Now, be a good girl and tell me what I want to know, and I'll see about making you more comfortable. Where is the ranger?"

"No idea. We aren't partners."

"Don't waste my time. I know you've been poking around my business together."

"I don't know what you're talking about. I'm here for HNE."

Brint leaned in, an ugly smile curling his lips. "Liar. You're not much of a spy, Caly. I found you with Matthias's notes, remember?"

She somehow managed to keep her face blank, though on the inside she winced.

"That was a nice trick with the window in my room, though. How'd you manage it? The ranger, I presume."

Calya shrugged. "Maybe I'm better at spy shit than you think."

Brint snorted. "Next time, don't leave ash all over my floor."

Well, fuck. Calya scowled at him.

"I'll ask again. Where is the ranger?"

"I told you, I don't know."

"Don't lie to me. I know Eren sold us out. He'll be dealt with. What did the ranger do? Where is Ana and her pet prince? Who else knows about this place?"

Calya didn't speak. It wasn't even about refusal and being

obstinate—there were only so many ways to say "I don't know," and Brint didn't seem to be in a headspace to hear any of them. She was merely contemplating word choice when he took her by the shoulders and gave her a shake.

"Who fucking knows—!"

Brint's bellowing was accentuated by progressively more violent shakes, snapping Calya's head back. Something cool and solid thumped against her chest, sliding up her skin until it popped up above the collar of her shirt.

Anadae's pendant. Though it had lain against Calya's skin, warmed by her body and practically weightless to the point she'd forgotten its existence, now a whisper of ice suffused the metal. It leapt at the end of its chain as if it had a mind of its own. An intent and a target instilled in the magic.

The movement didn't go unnoticed, Brint's hand jumping up to grab the pendant. "What is—"

Anadae had said all she needed to do was snap the end.

Calya swung her bound hands upward like a club, but Ervin reacted fast enough to jerk her back a step. Whether Brint's hold was tight enough or the pendant simply wanted an excuse to break was impossible to say.

Be careful about how you use it turned out to be rather vague as far as directions and setting expectations went. Irrelevant, too, for the resulting concussive blast sent Brint flying back into the wall.

Calya's trajectory was cut short by Ervin at her back, and her impact equally padded by his bulk, which left her disoriented rather than unconscious as the blast of icy air faded. She sat up, shaking frost from her hair.

"Everyone still alive?" she asked, crawling off Ervin's prone body.

The other mages, having retreated to the back of the small room, had escaped the powerful, concentrated radius of Anadae's pendant.

Matthias knelt next to Brint, feeling for a pulse. "Not dead," he said gruffly, moving on to go through the unconscious man's pockets.

"Neither is he," the older Vreshan woman said, crouched by Ervin's head.

"For now." The Grae U man glared down at Brint's henchman, hands flexing.

Further violence was forgotten as Matthias uttered a soft, joyous grunt. He pulled a stamp-like key from one of Brint's pockets and pressed the flat, square end against his manacles. The key glowed white, causing a series of symbols to flare on the band of each cuff before they opened with a metallic click and fell to the ground.

Matthias quickly went about freeing his colleagues while Calya appropriated the belt knife hanging from Ervin's waist for her own purposes. He had nothing else useful on him, but on Brint she recovered her pocket notebook.

She faced the others. "Let's go. If your friends are still here, they can't have finished scrapping the place."

"What about them?" the Grae U man said, jerking his head at the Graelynders as they all filed out up the stairs.

Matthias pulled the door shut, dropping the bar back into place. "Leave them. We need to get the others."

"Do you know where they are?" Calya asked as they hurried away.

"You've seen the spring we were trying to make?"

Calya nodded.

"Below it," Matthias said. "That's where they've kept the sick. Avenor's office. The source. It's all below."

"Isolation, to keep it from spreading," one of the Vreshans muttered behind Calya, every word bitter.

They paused at the end of a hallway. They were on a different side of the underground cavern than the one Calya had entered with Lowe. Half a dozen people moved across the floor, carrying crates of supplies toward another passage at the back of the cave.

"Any friends left up here?" Calya murmured.

"Those AG boys will stand with us," Matthias said.

She looked back at the people ferrying supplies out on the floor. Brint had turned his own people into captives?

At the Grae U man's skeptical hiss, Matthias glared back at the group, meeting each of their eyes. "They will. Especially without Avenor here. The Coalition fucked them as much as they did us."

He didn't put it up for discussion, instead striding forward, his hands glowing with golden light. Then, dropping to his knees, Matthias slapped both palms against the floor. Veins in the stone burned bright, racing in a line toward a man standing slightly apart from the rest. The stone melted around his feet, rising to mold around his legs before hardening at the knees. He wobbled, off balance, but the stone kept him from completely toppling over.

Calya hovered at the edge of the hallway, breath held as Matthias straightened. He held up the strange key taken off Brint, his voice too low for Calya to hear what he said to the men gathering around him. The other mages filed past Calya to flank Matthias.

The Grae U man went to the one restrained in stone—a Coalition guard, judging by the way the rest seemed so ready to turn on him. A flare of light in the Grae U man's hand shone as he made a slashing motion, and the captive man swayed. His eyes closed, his body went limp, and he crumpled to the ground with a snap, his lower legs still held upright by the stone.

Calya swallowed hard. A grovetender and a mender. She'd seen mages of those affinities before, and she wasn't exactly a stranger to seeing magic performed. But the small remedies Eunny made, Ollas's gentle coaxing of the blooms in his beloved greenhouse, even her sister's ice spells... none of them had prepared Calya for the reality of magic wielded for violence.

One of the Avenor Guard men stepped up to Matthias and offered him his arm. Matthias raised the key, and only then did

Calya realize that each of the Guard had thin bands around either their upper arms or wrists.

The sight and sound of the band being unlocked, of their colleague being freed, galvanized the rest into action. The Grae U man and the Vreshan women were already headed toward a different wall in the cavern, disappearing down a cleverly hidden path that blended into the rest of the rock.

As each member of Avenor Guard was freed from whatever controlling magic had been imbued into the bands, they followed the others. When only Matthias was left, he gestured to Calya. She'd started toward him, noting how the Coalition agent still breathed, when a gust of wind came howling through the cave. It whirled around her, filling her ears, her lungs, until a whisper of the wind even seemed to touch inside her head.

A doorway filled her mind. Similar to Matthias's underground office, but her mind knew this wasn't the same. The door blurred, the image resolving inside the office. Brint stood across from her on the other side of a desk. A real one, not hastily slapped together scrap lumber and rocks forced by magic to become nails. A small lockbox, barely larger than the thin journal tucked inside of it, lay open on the desk. A half-folded letter sat on top, the contents blurry but the signature at the bottom crisp. Atria, one of the seven councilmembers for the Coalition. A silver wax seal still clung to the top of the letter, the scales and coins and key in sharp relief to the rest of the obscured scene.

Brint added the wax seals Matthias had saved, tossing them in before closing the box's lid. It didn't have a conventional keyhole but a flat tab that slotted into place on the front. Brint touched it with a glowing fingertip, and a loud, ominous click echoed in Calya's head.

Her hand came into focus as it reached for the lockbox. As her fingers brushed the surface, the lid sprang open, and fire came out. Flames everywhere, filling her vision until she couldn't see or think of anything except the crackle and hiss of fire. She could taste the smoke in her mouth, feel it clogging her airways as she inhaled. But she didn't choke. Didn't cough. The smoke kept coming, relentless, and though a distant part of her mind clocked the danger, her body wouldn't respond.

A voice filtered through the roaring blaze. She couldn't discern words, but it sounded achingly familiar.

Lowe. Her heart constricted at the thought.

Through her pain, a new sound broke through. Not Lowe. Hers. Calya's own voice, clear despite the sensation of smoke in her throat, and she was screaming.

"Stop!"

Calya blinked, stumbling as the wind loosened its grip.

"Lowe?" she whispered.

He wasn't there. The wind unraveled from her, a faint trail of yellow-white light fading before her eyes. She turned, following the trail. It arced back toward the ramp leading to the observation room before disappearing completely.

"Calya," Matthias called.

She glanced back to where he stood at the mouth of the hidden path. A road that held no flames, and though there would be signs of devastation below, if she went with him, at least she wouldn't go alone.

If only she could take that path in good conscience.

Shaking her head, Calya turned back toward the ramp and followed the wind.

Chapter Twenty-Three

CALYA HAD NEVER BEEN one for thinking much about death or the myriad ways a person could die. It had always seemed a pointless exercise to her. If her headstone should read anything other than her name and the title of Director of Helm Naval Engineering, followed by dates spanning multiple decades, then hers had been a life wasted.

Yet, as she retraced her steps toward Matthias's office, she could admit that death by fire sounded like a bad way to go. What had Lowe said of the wind and his divinatory magic? It represented possibilities, what could be. But was it a warning of what would happen if she stayed her current course? Or had it been urging her to go with Matthias and the other mages to escape a fiery fate?

"Why the fuck does anyone seek out divination?" she grumbled.

The office door loomed in front of her. Steeling herself, Calya held her breath and reached for the handle.

A wry laugh escaped as she surveyed the room. Little had changed since the last time she'd been there. How long ago had it been, a couple of hours at the most? Aside from Matthias's secret journals and stash of wax seals—which were missing—everything else was as she remembered. But then, the vision of her maybe-but-maybe-not future had left her with the impression of another door. Similar in appearance, so it had to be around here somewhere, but not Matthias's office.

The damning journals were gone, but neither Brint nor Ervin had had anything of the like on them. The Avenor Guard men hadn't, either, their labor spent on hauling out equipment and supplies. Anyway, Brint wouldn't have trusted them with such sensitive materials. Incriminating.

Calya walked back out of the room and continued down the hall. It narrowed, spiraling down, the air growing colder and... odd. Almost charged, a strange, intangible current becoming stronger as she continued deeper into the mountain. The hallway ended with another door looming before her, but this one was already ajar. She nudged it farther open with her foot. Her lips parted with a small gasp.

It was undoubtedly the office that the wind had shown her, and undoubtedly Brint's. Unlike Matthias's office, which had appeared hastily scooped out of the existing rock, Brint's was comprised of large, tidy bricks. Whether they were individual stones or just nicer interior detailing, Calya didn't know, but the semi-circular room certainly had the fanciest touches of anything she'd seen at the site, above or below. Multiple bookshelves of different sizes. Wall hangings, some artistic and others that were concept drawings for the site. He even had throw rugs to soften up the rock floors.

Finally, along its back wall stood a large window overlooking a pit. Calya went past Brint's desk and out to the short balcony and tight staircase that led down to the floor.

Here, she realized "pit" was too crude a word. The crater made in the stone below was a perfect circle molded from the rock. What Calya had at first glance thought were cracks in the otherwise smooth surface were actually channels—as purposefully wrought as everything else about the indentation, the channels flowing from multiple directions across the floor, running up and out of the crater to the cavern's walls.

These channels weren't empty, either. Light flowed through the narrow troughs fed by lines crawling down from the ceiling. Or did the channels send the light up along the walls?

Calya gazed upward, unable to pinpoint where the glowing lines disappeared in the inky darkness over her head. The winding path down from Matthias's office had done nothing for her sense of direction, but she guessed that she was below the attempted man-made wellspring.

The center of the crater was dominated by a large glass sphere. At least, that was how it appeared to Calya's distinctly unmagical mind. It was twice her height and several strides across.

Big enough to hold more than the two people suspended inside.

Two silhouettes were visible against the glow of the ball. Calya slowly moved closer for a better look. A path had been carved around the inside of the crater, saving her from having to slide to the bottom. As she approached, an odd, unsettling hum, similar to what had been around the garden plots, assailed her. She stopped a few paces back from the glass, starting in surprise when she recognized the people within.

The Coalition mages, Treen and Aylton, floated within the sphere. Their hair and clothes drifted in a weightless way, as if suspended in water, but without being soaked through. Tendrils of magic, burning so intensely that they appeared more white than gold, streamed from their hands. The light swirled together, forming a braided cord that collected at the center of the ball and flowed into a quartz stone like the one in the wellspring above.

Hesitantly, Calya tapped on the glass. A jolt ran up her arm, and she yanked her hand back before it could spread farther. Neither of the people in the sphere gave any sign of noticing her, their eyes closed, their bodies upright yet limp. Faint wisps of yellowish smoke, or perhaps mist, wafted within the glass, broken up by intermittent sparks of white.

The image was almost mystical, almost haunting in a way that Calya would've called magey, artsy, weird. Almost, but not quite. Really, it was more cursed than enchanting; the white sparks didn't glimmer or crackle. They popped, splattering the glass as if they were made of liquid rather than light before slowly evaporating...

Except not fully evaporating, either. A residue was left behind, drying down to barely more than dust as it joined the mist.

Both of the mages enclosed within the ball appeared alive yet lifeless. Signs of ill health were visible, their cheeks sunken, their hair lank and thinning as if some had fallen out. Calya had met them only days ago, and already they were so diminished.

She searched for a way into the sphere, but the structure was eerily seamless. Thick, jagged lines glazed the surface along one curve of the sphere where it reached the ground, but nothing like a door appeared. It defied her knowledge of construction, which admittedly was basic and more applicable to wood than glass.

At a loss, she retreated to Brint's office. There she found the journals and a few of the seals Matthias had saved stuffed into a small leather pack alongside another ledger. A tiny hearth was set into the side wall, a plain brazier nestled at the center, embers glowing orange-red.

The wind's message of fire still prevalent in her mind, Calya approached the hearth with trepidation. It burned gently, the coals seemingly well contained. Runes glowed at the base of the flue as the air magic imbued in the stone directed the smoke up and away instead of letting any spill into the main room. However, a pile of books thrown on top of the brazier was forcing the enchantment to work overtime. Most had already turned to ash, falling apart when Calya tried to salvage the remnants with a poker left on the floor.

Only the top-most book—another journal, palm-sized, the same as her pocket notebook but with fewer pages—was somewhat legible. The thin leather cover, though blackened and cracked, had kept the contents from being a complete loss. Yet, as she gingerly flipped the cover open onto Brint's desk, her heart sank. The little journal's pages had been old and delicate even before their time in the fire. Portions of every page bore damage. Some had lost only the corners, but many had been reduced to half their original size, if not less. Writing in a language Calya didn't recognize accompanied sketches, and she wasn't entirely sure what they were sketches of, either. In all honesty, *sketches* might've been a leap of an assumption. One page seemed to depict a contraption similar to the glass sphere. The writing was sparse, a few lines here and there, more like notes or captions than thorough documentation.

Calya smothered a last ember with the edge of her cloak, her nose wrinkling against the smell of burnt leather that wafted up now that the journal was removed from the flue enchantment. She had flipped through a few more pages, unsure if it was worth trying to save the unreadable book, when the pounding footsteps of someone racing toward the office echoed down the hallway.

She stuffed the little notebook into her cloak pocket, grimacing as she heard a stitch tear. The footsteps were nearly upon her. Fight or flight? But if the latter, then to where? There could be a dozen more tunnels for her to get lost in if she ran out into the crater room. Or none. Perhaps this was the end of the line, and the only way out lay through the same hallway she'd already passed through. The same hallway bringing whomever barreled toward her, panic and desperation fueling their steps.

Calya snatched the poker from the ground. She could hear her old training master's aggrieved sigh in her head, and a wry smile curled her lips at the thought.

Brint stormed into the room. Because of course it would be him, the cockroach of her life. He looked like shit. *Ragged* barely began to describe him, and a new gash across his temple—from her ice pendant, perhaps?—painted the side of his face and hair with crusted blood.

"Calya," he panted, staring at her as if he couldn't decide whether to be glad or pissed.

"Brint." She raised the poker in a way she hoped was menacing. Weapons handling hadn't been a focus area for her. "You've been a busy boy."

"It's not what you think," he said. "I can—"

"I *think* you're growing the fucking Eyllic poison in *Graelynd* for the Coalition. I *think* you're committing treason," she hissed. "I just can't imagine why."

"Patriotism. This is *for* Graelynd, Calya."

"*For* Graelynd? I didn't get that impression, what with you poisoning mages and keeping people in magic shackles and"—she jerked her head in the direction of the pit—"your nightmare bubble. How many people have you fed to that—"

"No one has died. We haven't had any casualties." An ugly pause followed as his mouth worked but no sound emerged, the *yet* held back on the tip of his tongue. "Not one," he finished weakly.

"What happened? Things have been going bad here for months, Brint. Gods, or has it reached years? If this is for Graelynd, why didn't you fix—"

"What do you think I've been trying to do?" Brint snapped. He took a step closer, raising his hands in a placating manner when she waved the poker. "The containment measures Eylle promised weren't enough. People got sick. I tried to get restoration efforts here."

"What efforts? You mean, when you were trying to scam Sylveren grovetenders into consulting on your 'harmless' project"—she sneered the word—"or do you mean how you've graduated to just kidnapping people and forcing them to salvage your fuckups?"

"It's not my fault!" he cried. "If that paranoid bitch had just told me more of her plan, I would've known the next step. I would've known how she meant to fix this."

"You're incompetent." Calya gave a bitter laugh. "What were you going to do, throw me in the hold while you escaped? Or just leave us in that cell and hope maybe someone found us before we died?"

"It was never meant to be lasting harm."

"Was that before or after your goon threw me into a wall and you *magicked* me, you asshole?"

"You're one to talk." Brint indicated the gash on his head. "I *tried*, Calya. I tried to talk to you, to see if I could trust you, and then we could've worked together."

"To do what? There's no fixing this mess."

"Try again. We were so close here, and the Coalition is committed, even without Bioon," Brint said. "We'll have better protections. Think of what it'll mean!"

Calya pointed at the Coalition mages caught in creepy stasis in the glass ball. "All the mages here think the project is fucked."

"The Coalition has resources everywhere. They have lines in at Sylveren, in the Restorers. We're going to be more prepared this time."

His eyes gleamed in the firelight, something zealous and imploring blurring together in the way he looked at her. Anadae had only scratched the surface with her warning of the changes in Brint. Calya saw not the arrogant, mostly harmless dipshit she'd always known but a Coalition fanatic.

A prickle of fear ran down her spine.

She tightened her grip on the poker, trying to draw comfort from its weight in her hand. "Why, Brint? Why would you get involved in this? You're stupid, but I didn't think you were *this* stupid. You've got to know this can't end well."

The last vestiges of anything friendly between them faded from his expression. He dropped his cajoling tone, meeting her words with a disdainful scoff. "Graelynd will have a wellspring, and we don't need the Eyllic Empire to get it," he growled. "They thought they were the only ones, but we've already begun. And who's the stupid one, Calya? We've been tapping the ley lines from the Valley runoff for years. Years! They've never even noticed."

"If you're making a wellspring, what do you need *poison* for?" Calya shouted. "Isn't that what's trying to kill Rhell? That's all the poison does, and you want to grow them side-by-side."

"No, no! They lied to us, to the delegation," Brint said, his head whipping back and forth with the vehemence of his denial. "You need the power from the poison. You need enough to seed the well."

Calya's eyebrows rose toward her scalp. "You've been huffing too much of your own poison."

Brint let out an exasperated sigh, some of the annoying, shitty weasel she remembered creeping back in. "You're not a mage. What do you know?" he said, dismissing her with a wave of his hand.

"Yeah, I keep hearing that. But I don't need magic to see that you've lost it." Calya gestured at the brazier. "You see it, too. Destroying evidence? You're fucked. The Sentinels know what you've done here. Rhell knows. You're going to be lucky if Sor'vahl doesn't chop you into little pieces of meat and cook you."

A spasm of emotion twitched across his face. Uncertainty, maybe even a good dose of fear.

"I'm immaterial at this point, Brint. Give it up."

The apprehension on his face faded, pushed away by conviction. By a sureness edged by panic and tinged with pity. He smiled at Calya, his expression a mix of regret and resignation that had her instinct to run shrieking past her reckless bravado.

"Immaterial," Brint said. "You don't have to be. You can be a part of this." He went to the desk, raising his hands in a non-threatening manner when Calya brandished the poker. She took a step back, not letting him narrow the distance between them.

He pushed the half-filled leather pack containing Matthias's journals aside and revealed what looked like a clear stone brick that had been propping the bag up. She'd thought it some kind of paperweight or similar frippery. An odd choice for a desk ornament, but there was no accounting for Brint's lack of taste. But with the bag out of the way, Calya saw the brick held a small, vaguely cube-shaped object suspended in its center. The brick appeared more like a block of ice than the glass sphere down in the pit, but the same opaque yellowish curls of smoke wafted within. The cube at the heart, no larger than a grape, had an oily look, like it was comprised of thousands of tiny grains of wet sand. Though overall gray in color, some spots were a patchier white; thin veins of moldy green appeared, spread, and then faded in a cyclical manner.

The starter culture the other mages had mentioned. Calya didn't need Brint to confirm; even standing several feet away—and a mundane, to boot—she sensed the blob's oppressive aura.

"We can start over, and this time we'll finish the wellspring," Brint said. "Help us, and HNE can—"

"Can what? It's a wellspring. You don't transport magic in buckets," Calya said in a scathing tone.

"The Coalition will be your friend. Think of the business they can send your way. The deals. Your father wouldn't be able to ignore that. No more Wembly getting the final say over your plans. HNE would finally be fully yours."

"It will be anyway." She gave him a grim smile. "I've found the root of all my problems. Daddy Avenor is finally going to cut you out of the family."

His face darkened. "You're making a mistake."

Calya shook her head, chest stuttering with her wry laughter. "My mistake was—"

Brint dove at her. It was a rookie slip-up on her part, one for which Calya's old training master would've berated her for hours. Letting her guard down, getting drawn into pointless arguments, distracted by the block of poison while Brint slowly angled closer.

She *did* manage to crack him across the shoulder with the poker, but his momentum had him crashing into her anyway, despite his bellow of pain. She might not have been able to stop him even if she'd managed to stab him with the poker, such was his bulk.

They fell to the floor, snarling and scrabbling at one another. Brint grabbed the poker, and instead of getting into a futile wrestling match, she let it go, jamming her elbow into his throat during the opening her lack of resistance created.

He recoiled, choking for breath. Calya shoved off him and struggled to her feet. She stamped on his hand to make him drop the poker, but her feet were faster than her hands—she kicked it away in her panicked haste, snatching at air.

No matter. Her old training master had been onto something about running.

Calya took a few wobbling steps, adrenaline surging, but her brain lagged behind. Out to the pit, or back into the hallway? The pit room might be a dead end, but what if she ran into Brint's Coalition cronies? If he was still here, surely, he must have co-conspirators hanging around to help him escape to wherever the supposed Wellspring Plan B was.

Brint took the decision out of her hands. Light streaked past her, hitting the window and shattering the glass. Calya screamed, her arms raised to ward off the falling glass as she ran for the door. Gods fucking— She'd forgotten that, though he wasn't a particularly good mage, Brint wielded light and had played at learning some of the combat moves of a lightwrath.

Another bolt of white-hot light smashed into the open doorway, making her hesitate. The moment of indecision was enough for Brint to catch up, tackle her, and send them both to the ground again. As Calya scrambled to get up, she hissed in pain, broken shards of glass biting into her hands. The previous injury to her ribs roared back to life, making her gasp for breath.

More pain erupted along her scalp as Brint hauled her up by the hair. He dragged her back to the desk, grabbing one of her bloody hands.

"Sorry, Calya, but you've left me no choice," Brint said through gritted teeth. "You get to be material now."

He forced her palm against the poison's brick enclosure. Calya screamed again as searing heat raced across her skin. A blinding light flashed up from the brick, and it felt like fiery needles stabbing into her hand.

When Brint finally released her, Calya ripped her hand back, expecting to leave a layer of skin behind. She heaved herself backward, only stopping when her shoulders thumped against the wall. She stared down at her palm cradled against her chest, preparing herself to see raw, burned flesh.

Her mind whirled, trying to reconcile the very real pain she'd just felt with the relatively normal skin of her palm. Sure, she had some cuts from the glass, but no extra damage.

Almost. Almost no extra damage. The last of the needle-like pain concentrated at the middle of her hand, fading—but not without leaving a thick, jagged line bisecting her palm. More than a simple scar. A brand, a marking like that on the glass sphere, only in miniature.

"What the fuck did you do to me?" The words fell from her lips in a horrified whisper.

"You asked me why. Why I got involved with this. Does it even matter anymore?" The fervor was gone from his tone. He sounded... sad, with a bitterness not entirely directed at her anymore but inward. "Money. Prestige to match my brother. Power. This far in, does it even matter?" He offered her a broken smile. "Like you said, it can't end well, not anymore. For either of us."

"Brint."

"Unless you help me. Help yourself." He nodded at her branded palm, holding a hand up to show he had one to match. "The Coalition would never let us out. Eylle's bargain binds. Even if I got away, what then? You called this treason—do you really think the Upper Council at home would see it differently? Would the *Valley*?"

"Am I poisoned now?" Calya demanded, ignoring his attempt to play the victim.

"Yes. No." Brint shrugged. "You're with me now either way." He came toward her, his hand outstretched to help her up. An offer that felt like it would seal her fate.

The wind screamed through the room, whipping loose papers and lighter bits of broken glass into a frenzy.

Calya grabbed a shard of glass and swiped at Brint's hand. He jerked back in time to avoid being shredded, but she still managed to catch a few fingers. He staggered away, cursing as he clutched his hand.

"You hateful bitch," he snarled.

"You forget, Brint dearest," Calya said, summoning her most heartless smile. "I already chose a partner for this business venture, and it was never going to be you."

He started toward her—

But *wind* tore between them, crackling spots of blazing gold in the air keeping him at bay.

Calya looked to the office's door in time to see Lowe come crashing through.

Chapter Twenty-Four

Calya was utterly uncharmed by anything, always. But Lowe storming right up to her, his wind snapping at his hair, sorely tested her resolve. He cupped her face between his hands, his eyes searching hers, bright and intense, as if he had to convince himself she was truly there.

His lips parted, the beginning of a sound emerging when his head whipped to the side. He pulled Calya against him, using his body as a shield between her and Brint's wildly fired magic.

Brint fucking Avenor. Calya glared at him, stepping around Lowe. Her ranger tried to block her, his arm raised in defense. She nudged it aside, giving him a reassuring squeeze before she faced Brint unimpeded.

The golden boy of the illustrious Avenor family was looking positively rumpled. His handsome features, already marred by Anadae's frost protection spell, had picked up several more scratches from their struggle. A bruise was beginning to bloom on his cheek, creeping above his beard. He was starting to look winded, too, chest heaving, mouth agape, which gave Calya a touch of smug satisfaction. Nice to know she wasn't the only one not conditioned for fighting. He obviously wasn't accustomed to such explosive magic use, if the sweat staining his brow and the slight shaking of his hands were anything to go by.

"It's over, Brint," Calya said. "Roll on the Coalition and maybe the Upper Council will—"

Light flared around Brint's hands, and he bellowed, not so much words as the sound of rage and desperation blurring together.

Lowe pushed Calya behind the desk for cover and grabbed the chair, throwing it at Brint. It exploded as Brint's magic hit it, scattering wood and magic as the force sent Brint staggering back.

A stray chunk of wood hit the brazier, spilling embers across the floor. The rug beneath the desk caught fire.

Calya scrambled back, slapping out a few sparks that landed on Lowe's clothes. Brint stared at them from across the room, his eyes widening as the fire eagerly spread onto the nearest books.

The books. The evidence. All the physical ties she needed to prove his and the Coalition's treachery.

Brint seemed to realize it at the same time—and, apparently, decided that stymying her was worth having less reference material for the new site he still believed was within his grasp. He lunged for a bookshelf near the outer wall and scattered more papers onto the flames. Then he bolted outside, half running and half falling down the stairs, heading for the pit.

"Stop him!" Calya cried, arm flung out after him. "He can't open that thing."

She had nothing to go on but a hunch, a sense of foreboding that Brint putting a hole in the sphere, intentionally or not, was tantamount to releasing the poison.

Lowe hesitated, visibly torn between wanting to chase Brint and take Calya to safety.

"Go," she said, giving him a push. "I'm right behind you."

"Get out of here, Calya." He gave her a severe look before he charged down the stairs.

It was advice she fully intended to take. But not empty-handed.

Calya dropped to the ground, crawling on the floor as the flames crackled above her and licked along every surface. For a room underground, made entirely from stone, it sure was filled with flammable shit. Logbooks burned on the shelves, the map on the wall reduced to ash that joined the smoke in the air. Brint's treachery, the Coalition's plans, and the resources at their disposal—the full extent might never be known now that so much was lost.

But she could salvage a piece. That would be a start.

She had to grab something useful, get Lowe—*then* she could dwell and have hysterics and shock and a bodily shutdown. Not a moment before.

The small lockbox she'd seen in her vision from the wind. It was somewhere on Brint's desk. It *had* to be, and within were the seals Matthias had saved, correspondence with the Coalition.

Box. Lowe. Out. Calya repeated the thoughts in her head as she crawled toward Brint's desk. *Box. Lowe. Out.* That was it. Three things. She could handle three things.

More bolts of Brint's errant magic shot through the air. One hit the narrow, spiraling staircase outside, and a harsh shriek of metal tearing and the resultant crash told Calya her exit options had just narrowed.

Another small jet of white-hot light came through the broken window, ricocheting off the ceiling to smash into the corner of Brint's desk. The wood, already weakened from the fire steadily eating through its legs, collapsed with a groan and showered Calya with sparks. She yelped, raising her arm to protect herself.

A thump sounded, audible even over the building flames, as something heavy landed next to her.

Calya stared for a moment, unable to make sense of what she saw. The poison culture lay on the ground, its ice brick container now covered in crazed lines. Lines that resembled—

A crack sounded, a new fracture nearly as long as Calya's thumb forming along one corner. Though still fixed in the center, the blob of poison was slowly beginning to move, shifting a minute amount as though breaking out of stasis.

Calya reached for the brick, fingertips hesitating for a split second as intention and memory clashed. She'd already been branded by the thing. It couldn't do it again, right?

With a hasty prayer to the Goddess, she made herself grab the block.

It *was* hot, but not the same searing pain as when Brint had forced her bloodied hand against the ice-glass. More surprising was the weight, the way the block *resisted* her efforts to drag it closer.

"Why are you so heavy?" Calya hissed, straining to slide it across the floor a few feet to the wall. Casting about for anything that could help, she saw the bag Brint had been stuffing with Matthias's notes—and there, beneath a journal, was the lockbox.

She lunged, snagging the bag's strap and yanking it toward her as the bookshelf next to it gave way in a cascade of sparks and books turned burning orange by flame.

The lockbox skittered away, not having been fully secured within the bag. Calya dumped what remained of the bag's contents, most of which was on its way to becoming ash. Her fingers screamed in protest as she seized the poison brick and forced it into the narrow confines of the bag. Pain blared up as her nails tore from the pressure, but she didn't let up. Gritted her teeth, a hoarse cry ragged in her throat, as she *made* the stiffened leather stretch the last little bit.

The bag was so impossibly heavy with the poison brick inside, yet still she heaved herself and it over the broken window ledge. Flopping onto the other side, she leaned against the wall, gasping in the slightly cleaner air. New points of pain spread all over her body. Calya was certain she'd cut herself on the window. She was probably sitting on glass right now, but she couldn't find it in herself to care.

Below, Lowe wrestled with Brint, whose hands blazed with his light... but in a haphazard, guttering way, like a candle on the verge of being snuffed out. He moved with desperation fueled by exhaustion, as if he knew death awaited the moment he let up.

Lowe looked worse for wear, too. Though the wind screamed around them, even from Calya's vantage point it was clear that the element didn't deal the same physical damage as Brint's magic. Maybe if Lowe's gifts had been more for storm-calling or wind-shaping than divining he could have used his magic for a direct kind of violence.

Those shortcomings aside, it didn't seem like it particularly mattered. Where the wind lacked, knuckles made up the difference.

Lowe punched Brint, and he fell heavily, head cracking against the stone floor. His light magic flickered, a few weak sparks floating up from his fingers before they went out.

Staggering forward, Lowe dropped to a crouch, his knee slamming into Brint's chest. The ranger grabbed Brint by the collar and raised his fist.

Calya flinched, forcing herself to stand. Glass shifted beneath her and scattered as she did. By averting her eyes, her gaze went back into the burning office—and landed on the lockbox. It was several strides away, partially buried in burning rubble, but maybe, just maybe, she could get to it. If she went now.

The sound of Lowe's fist against Brint's face reached her ears. It made her look down... and her eyes caught on the leather bag, the strap still clutched between her fingers.

The bag was already full to bursting with the block of poison. She could never fit both it and the lockbox.

Lowe drew his fist back for another strike.

Calya squeezed her eyes shut. She *could* reach the lockbox. She'd seen herself reaching for it.

She'd also seen that choice ending in flames.

But how could she turn away? The lockbox was what tied the

site, the poison, all of it, to the Coalition. Yes, Brint had been willing to sacrifice Graelynd, and who knew how many lives had been ruined in the process—the only sentence befitting his crimes was death—but what did bringing him down matter compared to bringing down the Coalition?

Brint wasn't enough. He'd carried on with the Coalition's horrific plan out of fear of defying them. He'd as much as admitted it, right after trying to seal her into the same fate. He wasn't evidence; he'd be the Coalition's scapegoat. And even if Calya got out with the poison, there was no explicit link between it and the Coalition. Besides circumstantial evidence, all she'd have was Brint's word, maybe the Sylveren mages'. She'd have witnesses, but witnesses lied. People could be bought, could be turned. People failed. The Coalition were the masters at finding the fractures in people and pressing until they broke.

The lockbox was her last—her *only*—chance at having incontrovertible proof of the Coalition's involvement. She was certain of it. Hers would be a household name if she exposed their treason.

Her mark on the world.

All of it could be hers if she put her hand, her life, into the fire.

She forced herself to take a first step toward the door, wavering as a blast of heat hit her face.

Box. Lowe. Out. It could only ever be in that order.

Before she reached the doorway, her name rose above the blaze of the flames.

"Calya!"

She looked over the broken stairway to find Lowe standing at the bottom.

There was roaring in his ears. The fire, his wind, maybe just the adrenaline surging through his veins. Nocren didn't care. Didn't pay it any attention. His mind was too full of the many scenarios the wind had shown him. Avenor, with Calya as his captive. Avenor, escaping on a ship. Avenor, standing in front of a different wellspring as a ring of corruption spread across the ground.

Nocren would die before he let any of it come to pass. Before he'd let this piece-of-shit coward get away. Even as his skin erupted in agony beneath Avenor's glowing hands, his resolve never wavered. No, it grew with every blow he landed, rejuvenated as Avenor weakened.

"Carram leave you gasping," he snarled, casting Avenor to the ground.

As he knelt over the pathetic wannabe lightwrath, the wind tore at Nocren's face, his clothes, howling in his ears.

His tunnel vision was such that the wind couldn't penetrate. Not at first. He punched Avenor, vicious satisfaction flowing through him when the bigger man merely flopped like a ragdoll.

But the wind persisted—and as Nocren raised his fist to deliver his final blow, his hand faltered.

Calya's face filled his mind. *Change,* the wind pressed upon him. The word carried hope and despair in equal measure.

Fear jolted him from his bloodthirsty vendetta. He dropped Avenor, letting the senseless man fall with a graceless thud, and spun around in search of Calya.

He found her at the top of the broken stairs. He didn't remember moving, but somehow, he crossed the distance. Reached the bottom of the stairway as she faced the burning office. And was shocked momentarily speechless when she appeared to be readying to go *in* to the fiery room.

"Calya." Nocren's voice cracked, his throat gone dry. He coughed, sucking in a lungful of air to shout, "Calya!"

The Eternal Wind was with him. She stopped. Looked down at him with haunted eyes.

"Calya, don't. Whatever it is—"

"I have to," she mumbled. "I have to get them, Lowe. I have—"

"Whatever it is, I'll help you. We'll get it."

"The wind—your wind—it showed me..." Calya glanced back at the burning room. She didn't flinch when several of the bricks comprising the wall cracked, then crumbled, veins in the rockwork blazing white before extinguishing, lost in the smoke.

"They're just possibilities, Calya, not fate. You get to choose your own ending. Always have."

She stared down at him, limned by fire.

"Calya. I'm not leaving without you. Not again." Nocren held out his arms. "Jump."

Calya hesitated, shrinking back from the broken railing. His heart sank, desperate pleas rising up and jamming in his throat as he floundered for the right words.

Then a small leather bag dangled over the edge. She pushed it with her foot, letting it fall to the side. She followed it. Flew through the air toward him, not with a careful drop but a leap.

She hadn't been backing away with indecision but gathering herself. To go on faith. To jump... for him.

Nocren caught her, crushing her against his chest, his nose dropping to her hair. He ignored the ash and debris and smoke, squeezing her tight so he could feel her draw breath. To know she was alive and safe and with him.

Calya stirred, wriggling until he finally, reluctantly, let her down. He motioned that they should move toward the far wall, so they could be clear of the fire while still keeping an eye on Brint's motionless form. Calya stooped to grab the leather bag, grunting as she lifted it. Nocren moved to help, but recoiled with a pained hiss when he reached for the glazed ice brick sticking out and received a burn for his troubles.

"What *is* that?"

Calya held up her hand. A jagged scar ran across her palm. "It's kind of mine now."

"Explain," he said, carefully ushering her and her dangerous cargo to the wall. There, he sank down, and Calya tucked in beside him. Up above, what was left of Avenor's office collapsed on itself, the burning rubble spitting a plume of smoke and embers.

They watched in silence.

Then Calya's shoulders began to shake. Alarmed, Nocren slid his arm tighter around her, his head bending lower to hear—

Hoarse laughter.

"Sorry, sorry. I'll get over it," she wheezed. "I'm not used to so much... excitement."

With a wry chuckle, Nocren leaned back.

Calya lay her head on his shoulder. After a moment of quiet, she murmured, "You called your wind. For me."

He nodded. "I asked it to help you. I'm sorry if it was... abrupt."

"You said you wouldn't do that anymore. Not for your family. Not for anyone."

Nocren slid his hand gently over her hair. "I did say that. But you're more than anyone." He brushed the crown of her head with his lips. "You are to me."

Chapter Twenty-Five

Time ceased to flow in a meaningful way after Calya decided to forsake her life's goal and leap into Lowe's arms.

Perhaps that way of putting it was a touch dramatic, but she figured she'd earned a bit of melodrama. It was a short-lived wallow, pleasantly interrupted by the arrival of reinforcements.

Not long after Calya dozed off on Lowe's shoulder, she woke to find a dozen people in the pit, Orren, her sister, and her friends from the Valley amongst them. She was lying on the floor, Lowe's cloak under her head like a pillow while he stood by the glass sphere, conferring with Ezzyn and Matthias.

Their eyes met. But he didn't come over, and she didn't call out. Orren said something, drawing Lowe's attention away again.

"You're awake," Anadae said from where she sat beside Calya.

Calya pushed herself up and was promptly swept into a hug.

"Ana...dae," Calya grumbled, but without any bite. "You made it."

"In time to save my little sister. Actually, you did a pretty good job of that on your own, from what the others have said."

"I had help. Your ice thing worked," she rasped, throat dry. "Instructions need some work, though."

Anadae produced a waterskin. "I'll keep that in mind. As for your other question, we got here at dawn. Froley's courier found us yesterday, but the storm slowed us down."

Calya nodded toward the glass bubble and the two mages still trapped inside. "What is that?"

"A conduit, of a sort. And a cage," Ezzyn said, lip curling in disdain as he joined them. "A way to forcibly collect the arcane runoff from the Valley and feed it into the poison they made."

"You mean they really did it?" Calya slowly stood up, glancing between her sister and her partner as she leaned against the wall. "They made a wellspring. *Here*?"

"No," Ezzyn said, "only a poor imitation. One these fools don't have an inkling of how to control, at that. As it feeds the poison, the corruption grows and *does* generate a significant amount of power, but it takes more than it gives, and what it does produce is more volatile than useful."

Calya looked at her sister. "Help me."

Anadae smiled. "It's not a real wellspring, and the magic it makes, no one really knows how to use."

"How long will the bubble last?"

Matthias joined them. "As long as it has magic to keep it stable."

Calya glanced at Lowe, noting how he also kept looking her way, as if reassuring himself she was okay.

Anadae noticed her sister's split focus. Before she could follow the direction of her look, Calya hurried to ask, "You're leaving Treen and Aylton in?"

Matthias sighed and shook his head. "No, we won't be like them. Your friends worked out an amendment to their healing tea that works for the poison here. Better. The blight isn't as concentrated as what Rhell is dealing with. Once our team is recovered, we'll work out a rotation until we can shut the orb down safely."

"You can do that?"

"If we have enough people. But once ours started to get sick, we fell behind. When Avenor's scam to get more grovetenders over here blew up, and then Song couldn't steal the remedy from the university, the Coalition ran out of time to trick other mages with the same ruse." Matthias spat on the ground. "They'd have preferred to run and let this break down. Let it get out."

Calya watched Treen and Aylton as they floated silently within the bubble, the murky yellow mist curling around them. "So, you'll do for them what they wouldn't have done for you?" she said quietly.

Matthias frowned at the glass. At the people who had been colleagues only to turn oppressors. Captors. "They went in on their own. Avenor couldn't have forced them, not both. He doesn't have the strength," he finally said, shaking his head. "They stepped up. It doesn't change their hand in all this, but at the end, they went in rather than let it fail."

"People are full of surprises when it matters," Anadae said.

Tepid solace for those who'd had to deal with them before. Calya started to say as much, but when she opened her mouth, all that came out was a yawn.

"I'm taking you out of here," Anadae announced.

"Not without my pet rock." Calya nudged the leather bag with her foot. "I kind of—"

"Sentinel Lowe mentioned it," Anadae said. "I want Eunny to look at your hand."

Ezzyn nodded at the bag. "Leave it for now. It's not going anywhere. I won't destroy it," he added, though the comment was aimed more at Anadae than Calya.

Leaning against her sister, Calya started to limp away, every muscle protesting, but Lowe stopped her. He scooped her up with a gruff, "You shouldn't stress your... ribs."

"I'm perfectly capable of walking," she protested. But not too much. His arms and chest were a refreshing change from the ground, even if it had been cushioned by his cloak. She'd take him over some clothes any day.

"You are," he agreed, his step never slowing.

"As long as that's settled." She relaxed into his grip—only to stiffen as a firm object in her cloak pocket poked her side. She pulled her cloak up, digging in the pocket to find the small, damaged notebook she'd saved from the brazier in Brint's office.

"Here." She held it out to Anadae, who walked in step with them. "It's... magey stuff. I think."

Calya thought she heard a muffled snort, but Anadae took the notebook without comment as they exited the cave. A string of horses waited in the clearing, some saddled and others still hitched to plain carriages.

"I'll see if we can use one of the carts," Anadae said before walking away, leaving Calya alone with Lowe.

Carefully, he set her on her feet, then moved to take a respectful step back. Calya tightened her fist in his shirt, holding him close. His hand jumped as if to touch her cheek before he stopped himself. Instead, he settled for brushing his knuckles against her arm.

"Calya," he murmured, face solemn. Not his usual frown, but moody in its own way.

"I—" She swallowed, emotions rising. It had to be left over from the stress, of course. She cleared her throat. "Thank you. For coming back. You didn't have—"

"I never should've left." He huffed, raked his fingers through his hair, and shook his head ruefully. "I never should've left you."

"Yes, well..." Calya forced herself to release his shirt, patting it back into place. "I wasn't very nice to you."

His lips curved with a faint smile. "You had me all figured out from the start, too. I don't care much for a nice woman."

Calya preened. "I'm certainly not that." Seeing a horse-drawn cart coming their way, she murmured, "Where does that leave us?"

Lowe's gaze went to the mark still burned into her hand.

"We'll revisit once I get this removed," Calya said, turning toward the cart. "I haven't finished enjoying my time with you."

Then she looked back over her shoulder, adding in a quieter voice, "I'll see you at the inn?"

He inclined his head. "I promise."

She hummed softly, gaze lingering on him for a moment before she let her sister help her into the cart.

After five glorious days of being waited on hand and foot—and having drunk what felt like a barrel's worth of healing infusions Eunny insisted upon—Calya was a new woman. Though her sister and friends weren't around for much of her recovery, called away to assist in getting the false wellspring safely closed down, Froley came by often. They delivered updates and the freshest bake of the day Roxana had whipped up.

"The mayor tried to run for it," was delivered with a breakfast of cheese toast and apples. "Dockmaster rolled on him, and the young lieutenant found him trying to hide under the catch on a fishing boat. Threw him in with Avenor. Without a wash."

Spiced, fruit-stuffed hand pies accompanied, "The last member of Matthias's team is up. Weak, but no poison."

Amazingly, Brint had been telling the truth: none of the Sylveren mages had died. Over a dozen had been locked away in the bowels of the cavern, some in dire condition. But for what it was worth, Eren Galwynd had been true to his word. He'd informed the king of Rhell of the failure at the Landing, and King Jeron had sent three ships out immediately to aid his youngest brother. Between the healing tea and a pair of strong menders who'd arrived on one of Jeron's ships, the desperately ill pulled through.

Still, surviving the cursed point didn't come without cost. More than half of the afflicted mages' magic had burned out, among other lingering side effects, and not even the miracle tea could restore that which had fully been lost. Calya quietly kept a record of names and conditions, of the losses the Coalition had caused. She *would* prove her past self wrong, prove that people could be evidence. If she had to present them as numbers and damages, then so be it, but the Coalition would pay.

The fifth day dawned cold but bright, a bite of frost in the air. Winterfest was around the corner. Froley greeted Calya with a fresh-from-the-oven muffin the size of her face and a wicked grin.

"Might want to eat this down at the dock," they said. "The Rhellians are taking Avenor back today. To the Valley. Guess your Sentinel claimed authority."

"With entertainment like this, the Landing is bound to be discovered," Calya teased.

She wandered down to the water, her good humor waning a touch as troublesome thoughts arose. *Her Sentinel.* If the Rhellians were leaving, would Lowe go with them? Given all that had transpired, her forced convalescence, and his Sentinel obligations in the cleanup efforts, they'd hardly had a moment of privacy. Not that it should've mattered; they were both returning to the Valley, so it wasn't as if she'd never see him again.

Still, the notion of him sailing separately—sailing without her—caused a tightness in her chest. It was a feeling too close to sentimentality for her liking, yet Calya couldn't shake it. *Focus. HNE. You came here for HNE.*

She spotted Anadae standing with Eunny and Ollas and waved, making her way toward them. Anadae hugged her, then held her at arm's length, eyes sweeping over her with concern. "Are you feeling all right? Do you need another mending? Eun, you should—"

Calya fended them off, batting Eunny away when she reached for Calya's forehead with a glowing hand. "I'm *fine*. Goddess break, I already have one mother, and I'm not looking to add any more to the roster."

Anadae snorted. "She hasn't any nurturing instincts left."

Calya gasped, hands pressing to her chest in dramatic fashion. "Are you, Anadae the Eldest Daughter, The Perfect One, casting aspersions on our mother's name? Will wonders never cease."

She smirked. "Still a brat, I see."

Ollas whistled softly. "They're bringing him out."

A group emerged from one of the small dockside storage huts that had been used as a temporary holding cell. Rhellians flanked Brint on one side, while members of Orren's Avenor Guard contingent strode on the other.

When he saw Calya and her friends, he stopped in front of them and took a few shuffling steps closer, intent not on Calya but Anadae. He ignored the prodding of the Rhellian behind him, raising his hands and clasping them together as he implored her. "Ana, it was never supposed to go this far. You know me, you have to believe that," he said. "I-I fucked up, but I was never—"

"Was that before or after you tried to put the blame on my sister? Before or after you tried to *entrap her* in your treason?" Anadae held up Calya's branded palm, her voice hard.

Brint winced. "I panicked! I panicked, okay, but I wouldn't have left her—"

Anadae took a step closer. Tiny ice crystals gathered in the air around her, popping and re-forming with menacing crackles. "I warned you what would happen if you came after her. Consider yourself lucky the Sentinels need your testimony."

Eunny nudged Calya. "I love it when my baby gets mad."

Calya's shoulders jerked with smothered laughter. "I'm never fighting my own battles again."

"We've known each other forever, Ana," Brint pleaded. "We cared for each other once. We were engaged. We were *friends*. That still means something to you, I know it does."

Ezzyn joined them, coming to stand behind Anadae. He wrapped his arms around her, and she leaned back into his embrace, shivering as he pressed an open-mouthed kiss against the side of her neck.

Calya scoffed. "Pee on her leg while you're at it, Sor'vahl, I don't think your intent was clear enough."

Anadae flicked her wrist. "You should've thought of that, Brint. Many times over."

This time, he didn't resist when a Guardsman propelled him on.

Lieutenant Orren approached Calya next. "We were only able to intercept the Coalition's ship because of you. I'll be sure my captain knows."

"I appreciate that," Calya said. "We got our answer in the end, Orren. About your loyalties. Though I am sorry it ended this way."

"He made his choice." Orren bowed. "If I can ever be of assistance to Helm Naval, I'm yours."

Calya murmured her thanks, swatting at Eunny when the other woman tried to nudge her again.

"You are a menace." Putting Anadae between them, Calya asked, "Does this mean we're leaving soon, too?"

"Almost." Anadae hooked her arm through Calya's. "Come see what Zhen's managed with that journal you saved. Plus, we still need to get your rock."

The cavern had been transformed. It was almost... nice? The earth mages had done most of the work, opening holes in the upper parts of the walls and ceiling to let in light. Air mages kept the atmosphere less stagnant. The glass sphere was still in the crater, but even that looked less oppressive. Six mages occupied the sphere now, and though they still floated motionless, as Calya got closer she saw that furrows of dirt filled neat, sculpted rows tracing across the floor of the sphere. Small plants sprouted from the ground. Grassy clumps, their green blades edged in gold light, waved gently within the enclosure. Even the mist swirling within seemed friendlier, a warmer gold than murky yellow, and the creepy white splotches were replaced by motes of glowing light.

Zhenya and several other mages stood around the glass ball. She had a fine chisel and small hammer in her hands, carving a rune into the top of a ward embedded into the sphere's surface. A familiar looking ward—one of Anadae and Ezzyn's design. The Grae U mage from the dungeon held open the small, battered notebook from Brint's office for Zhenya to use as reference as she carefully made her marks. Golden light glowed around her hands as she worked, and it lingered in the engraved lines even after she'd finished.

"You're just in time," she called out. "I'm about to apply the ink."

Calya eyed the glass bubble, then glanced at Ezzyn, who'd entered alongside her and Anadae. "Truth. If this had popped, would it have been as bad as what's happened in Rhell?"

His jaw worked, gaze going skyward as he mulled over an answer. It was Zhenya who spoke up.

"Probably not," she said, "since Graelynd doesn't have a wellspring. However it was made, the source poison has... it has an intrinsic purpose built into it. It *wants* to destroy a wellspring, and the fake one here wouldn't satisfy that."

"How can you tell?"

Zhenya indicated the small notebook Calya had recovered from Brint's office. It was incomprehensible scribbles to her, but Zhenya handled it with reverence. "This talks about it. A little. I can't actually read most of it, but once we get back to Sylveren, I've got some people to ask."

"Super secret notes?" Calya asked.

"I think it's from an Eyllic mage. From the time they figured out how to make their wellspring."

"Regardless," Ezzyn cut in. "If this monstrosity broke, it would've destroyed the ley lines in Graelynd all the way up to the Valley."

Zhenya nodded grimly in agreement.

Calya mulled over the implications, her mind tired despite her rest but equally incapable of letting go. "Think your word will be enough to convince the Upper Council to axe the Coalition? I'm filing a complaint."

"I'll be your cosigner," Ezzyn said. "I imagine we can find quite a few interested parties to join."

Zhenya went to a side table that had been set up in the cave, then returned to the sphere clutching an inkpot and a brush. She dipped her finger in the ink, adding a few drops of her magic to the vessel. Then, wetting the tip of her brush, she filled in the runes carved into each of the five wards embedded around the sphere.

"So," Calya said, eyeing the old notebook where the Grae U mage had left it on the table, "you can read Eyllic?"

"Parts. Mostly just words that relate to inkmaking, some plant biology, that sort of thing. The writing in that isn't modern Eyllic as far as I can tell, but some of the runes and sequences are things we still use," Zhenya replied. "After studying the process used for the fake wellspring, and with the source poison available to us, we should have everything we need now."

Calya looked between her friend and Anadae, who was smiling and nodding along with excitement in her eyes.

"Since we have you here, could you bring the culture closer?" Zhenya indicated a stool she'd been using to reach higher on the sphere.

Calya retrieved the poison brick from where she'd left it days ago, though it had been removed from the leather bag. It was still heavy as shit, but either the brick had lost some of its will or rest had restored a sizable amount of her strength, for Calya was able to carry it over with minimal huffing and puffing.

"You were able to touch it?" she asked, looking around at the gathering as she set it on the stool.

"Enough to access it," Zhenya said.

"Self-preservation's a foreign concept for Zhen if there's

research to be done," Anadae muttered. The white-haired inkmaker blushed, but she didn't refute the comment.

Lowe joined them in the cave, coming to stand beside Calya. "The Rhellians want me to go back with them," he murmured.

Calya ignored the twinge in her chest, keeping her voice as soft as his. "Then you should."

"You're... okay, with that?" Confusion flickered across his face before his expression went back to a careful sort of neutral.

"Why wouldn't I be?" she said, her opaque tone giving way to a tiny, sly smile. "I'm all out of Scarlett Kisses, at any rate."

He snorted but was kept from answering as Zhenya inked the final line on the sphere.

"There!" She stepped back and added a dot of ink to the brick. One by one, the runes on the wards began to glow a brilliant yellow-white, filling the air with a soft, pleasant buzz. The mages within the sphere reacted, fingers twitching even though their eyes remained closed. Their magic, which previously had been floating freely around the sphere, now came together. Lines of light flowed from their hands down to the quartz stone in the floor, concentrating into a single, braided cord.

The dot on the block went from matte black to shimmering gold, and the poison cube within shuddered.

"Calya," Zhenya said, "can you press the source against the glass?"

She complied, having to grip the block with both hands when it suddenly vibrated upon touching the sphere. "Whoa!"

A small spot the size and color of a grain of sand detached from the poisonous cube encased in the block and floated toward the edge of its ice-like containment. It touched the surface with a flash of light far bigger and brighter than its size suggested, causing a series of answering flares from the embedded wards.

Calya stumbled back, dropping the brick back onto the stool. Lowe's arm went around her shoulders, steadying her. Slowly, he let his arm fall back to his side, but didn't step away. Calya glanced sidelong up at him, her lips tensing with a tiny smile before she looked back at the sphere. She stayed where she was, close enough to subtly lean into him.

The plants within the sphere began to sway more vigorously, as if a gust of wind blew through the glass. Then, just as abruptly, they stilled. A single droplet of light formed at the tip of a blade of grass like a bead of magic-laced dew. It swelled to the size of a grape before it finally detached, floating up, bouncing gently on invisible currents in the sphere. With painstaking slowness, it wound down to the quartz set into the center of the floor, which was still surrounded by a ring of blighted ground. The golden bubble touched down at the edge of the corruption, not bursting but slowly sinking in as if sucked into the rock—absorbed like a water drop into paper, but instead of a splash it left behind a perfect circle of unblemished stone.

The murky green veins of corruption continued to pulse around the quartz focus, licking at the edges of the small dot of cleansed ground. But it didn't penetrate.

Somewhere off to the side, Calya heard Ezzyn's hoarse curse. An oath murmured not in fury but *wonder*. Zhenya turned around, eyes alight.

Eunny stepped up and clapped the younger woman on the shoulder. "Guess the Empire kept up at least one part of their deal."

"But the wellspring didn't work," Calya said. "The Coalition sold out the Valley, sacrificed their own people, for a lie."

"I'm not denying that part." Eunny indicated the glass sphere, the wards set into the walls, and the plants growing inside with a slow sweep of her hand. "They gave us everything to make a poison just like what they unleashed in Rhell."

"So we have everything to make a cure," Anadae said, taking up Calya's branded hand. "Ready to have this off?"

"Goddess, yes." Calya glanced at Lowe, a question in her eyes.

Lowe nodded once. "I'll be there."

Calya turned back to her sister. "How soon can we leave?"

Chapter Twenty-Six

Winterfest festivities were over by the time Calya returned to the Valley of Sylveren, though the decorations were still up. The zenith of the holiday had occurred the day they set sail, and Froley had given them a grand sendoff at the Pelf. Some kind of celebration was also held on the ship as the final days of the ten-day holiday passed, though Calya missed whatever they were.

Without a big, gruff... attentive ranger to keep her engaged during the trip, Calya saw no reason to decline Eunny's potent anti-nausea brew. The ship made good time without any storms to slow it down, arriving just as the sleepiness worked its way out of Calya's system.

She spent a week in Renstown, meeting with the Order of Sylveren and ranking members of the Sentinels to provide an initial report of all that had transpired in Desmond's Landing. They outlined the next steps in their plan to bring charges of treason against the Coalition, and Calya left the whirlwind of meetings feeling cautiously optimistic.

The trade organization had always loomed so large in her world—a world so narrowly confined to Graelynd, she would admit, that she'd never given the protectors of the Valley much credit. The Valley tended to keep to itself, and she'd foolishly viewed that reluctance to get involved in petty dramas as a bent toward pacifism and weakness. And maybe some of that was true, but clearly, the Valley didn't fuck around when it came to Eylle's poison. The Coalition would soon find that out, much to their detriment.

When Calya wasn't up at the university, the rest of her time was spent on penning a lengthy report to her father. But at least she had the Helm Naval office all to herself. Wembly had somehow gotten wind of her exploits and run before she returned. He'd had enough morals to not involve himself fully in Brint's treason, as it turned out. But to stymie Calya in ways that suited Brint's needs? No problem. Calya didn't know which angered her more, his betrayal or that all it had cost was a few thousand gold crowns and a promise of Coalition favor.

After spending several days drafting letters and catching up on all she'd missed, she was ready for a break. When the chance to escape to Sylveren for a reason other than meetings was offered, Calya jumped on it.

The block of poison was positively light in the Valley. If anything, the glazed, ice-like substance encasing the blob had shrunk, no longer an even rectangle but misshapen as though it had begun to thaw.

Whatever remained of the Child, aspect of the Valley of Sylveren, it was not pleased by Calya's return. It had never liked her, and her bringing a physical manifestation of Eylle's hate went over poorly. The spirit of the Valley vented its displeasure, sending freezing rain into Calya's face as she disembarked in the small town of Sylvan.

She pulled her cloak's hood farther over her head, giving her sister an exasperated look as they met on the dock. "I'm doing this place a *favor*. Could you please convince it to calm down?"

Anadae put her arm around Calya's shoulders. "I've got a carriage waiting."

They were dropped off outside of the Grove, the giant maple tree that served as home to the Sylveren earth mages. The foliage maintained its autumnal coloration year-round, though a single crimson leaf drifted down as Calya walked beneath its canopy. She caught it in her hand, admiring the fine veins and how they glimmered even on a dreary, gray day. She gasped softly as the leaf disintegrated and turned into a handful of golden motes of light that floated up to join the others always drifting around the tree.

"This gets my vote as nicest place in the Valley," Calya said.

Anadae laughed. "We'll make a believer of you yet."

They continued on to the greenhouse complex, where a small audience awaited them. The greenhouse was one of the larger structures, with a long wall broken up into multiple workstations comprising the front half of the room. The back half was compartmentalized into half a dozen antechambers, which Calya presumed were reserved for higher-level mages. Everything was clean and fancy, the gardening equipment neatly organized, with handles and blades polished. Not new, but clearly well maintained and of quality. A blooming vine climbed throughout the building, present but never in the way. Its oblong leaves were a glossy green, and white flowers filled the air with a delicate citrus scent.

Ollas and Eunny stood near the vine's anchor pot, chatting quietly with a tall, older Hanyeok man Calya vaguely remembered as one of the department heads. Zhenya stood at a counter, grinding pigment, a few dried plant stems with blade-shaped leaves next to her. Occasional gold sparks flew up as she worked. Inside one of the antechambers, Ezzyn was putting finishing touches on the wards surrounding a large tub of corrupted soil with a glass row cover over the top. Even at Calya's distance, the oiliness of the poisoned bits was visible through the clear panes, at odds with the crumbly, dull gray of the dirt.

Movement at the far end of the greenhouse caught her eye. Lowe came forward. Her first time seeing him since they'd left the Landing.

Calya dumped the leather bag on the counter, not hearing whatever her sister said as she went to meet him. "You're here."

"I promised I would be," he replied. "Are you sure you're ready for this so soon? Your ship—"

"Slept most of the way. Alone," she added with a smirk. "Nothing worth staying awake for."

"Careful. You're beginning to sound sentimental."

"I meant wares from House Oleander. None aboard."

Lowe's mouth formed a wry smile. "Were you looking?"

Eunny interrupted before Calya could reply. "Hey, lovebirds, big stakes here. Caly, come unbind yourself from the evil rock. Nev and I are due in Talihn."

Rolling her eyes, Calya turned back to her friends, willing her blush away. "What do you need me to do?"

Ezzyn stuck his head out of the antechamber. "Would you bring it in here, please?"

At his instruction, Calya withdrew the brick, the poison source within looking particularly sad and withered. She set it in the center of the corrupted-dirt-filled tub, in between a pair of grassy clumps similar to those she'd seen inside the sphere in the cave.

Ezzyn closed the glass cover, and Zhenya painted fresh ink onto the lines engraved in the heads of each ward. Then she gently took Calya's palm, her inkbrush poised above it.

"Ready?"

"Will it hurt?" Calya asked, her fingers tense with anticipation. "Last time hurt."

"I... don't think so?" Zhenya frowned in thought. "Though I'm still pretty new to working with Eyllic imprinting spells."

"Great," Calya muttered.

Eunny gave her a small prod in the back. "You'll be fine. They only hurt going in."

Lowe didn't say anything, but he stood beside her, his arm

brushing against her in silent support. Uncaring of who saw, Calya leaned into him.

Finally, she nodded at Zhenya. "Do it."

The ink was cold to the touch as it spread across the jagged line on Calya's palm. When Zhenya followed it up with a drop of her own magic, the wet line instantly turned warm. Not burning, but the swift change made Calya startle. She closed her hand by reflex, only to have it pushed open again.

The scar seemed to peel itself off as if it had never been a part of her skin to begin with, leaving her hand unmarked. It curled inward and became a molten ball of light.

Gold flared at the corner of Calya's eye, as Anadae transformed the glowing scar-turned-mote into a shard of ice. She snapped her fingers, and it blew apart, raining tiny flakes of ice onto the ground, where they melted into plain, unmagicked water.

Within the warded tub, the source poison reacted the same. Instead of a flat white, it morphed more into a glowing gold color. The ice brick protecting it dissolved, letting the golden ball of former poison fall onto the blighted ground. It flowed apart, thin veins seeping through the desiccated dirt as the roots of the two clumps of grass wicked it up. Their long, flat leaves swayed, orbs of gold-tinged dew gathering at the tips. They struggled more than the plants in the glass sphere in the Landing, managing to shed only a few dewdrops no larger than pinheads. But the droplets drew in and landed in a small circle. Where they touched the ground, those small dots of light flared, and the crumbs of dirt they'd landed upon swelled up, turning a healthy deep brown.

Slowly, a single blade of new, green grass poked through the spot of rejuvenated soil.

Ezzyn lifted the lid, touching a glowing fingertip to the ground at the base of the baby plant. The dirt illuminated as his magic coursed through it. He looked up, taking in all of the faces intent upon him.

His mouth opened, but in the end all he could do was form a

small smile, shaking his head as a weak laugh came out. "It... worked."

The room erupted with cheers and exclamations of delight. Calya felt a strange disconnect, as if she observed the others' jubilation from the outside. Motion flurried around her as Zhenya and her mentor, Professor Rai, immediately began preparing the tub for transport to Rhell. Anadae and Ezzyn were busy refreshing their protective wards on the container; Eunny and Ollas dashed off to another greenhouse for... something. Calya watched as if in slow motion, unsure of her part, if she had one at all.

A tug at her elbow pulled her back to the present. Lowe guided her outside.

"I told them we'd alert the harbormaster to have the fastest ship cleared for Rhell," he said.

"Good thinking."

The carriage ride passed in a blur, and they were mostly quiet for the duration. Once on the dock, with a fresh spray of icy rain to the face, Calya's thoughts evened themselves out.

"It's strange," she said when Lowe rejoined her. "My head knows that this is momentous. Historic, even. But it's strange to witness it and feel so... apart."

"You were instrumental," he said.

"I suppose. But it's their victory, not mine. Not that I'm not happy for them. I guess I just thought I'd feel different." Perhaps she was as heartless as she joked she was. Still struggling to find joy in the little things, much less something as significant as a potential cure for Eylle's poison.

"I imagine the king of Rhell will want a word with you," Lowe said. "And I come with a message from Captain Malek'ko on behalf of the Sentinels. We are in your debt."

Calya perked up, her gloom blown away like a puff of smoke. "Avenor Guard, the Sentinels, and a king." She ticked the names off on her fingers, grinning at Lowe. "I love being owed favors. They're worth so much more than money."

Lowe laughed quietly, but his eyes remained serious. Slowly, he reached up, brushing her cheek. "Powerful men on your dance card. The Coalition brought to their knees. There are no barriers left—Helm Naval will be yours," he said. "What more could a woman ask for?"

Calya's heartbeat pounded in her ears. His words, and the unspoken question hidden between them, rang loud in her mind.

She tore her gaze away, blinking rapidly as she tried to collect her thoughts, any thoughts, something beyond the dull roar in her head and the ache in her chest.

"I—" She faltered, her gaze picking out a familiar figure approaching her on the dock. The *Sylvan* side of the lake. "Father?"

Andrin Helm nodded stiffly at her. "Come, Calya. We have business to discuss."

Chapter Twenty-Seven

ANDRIN SUGGESTED he and Calya find a place to talk, and they managed to get a quieter booth in the Mighty Leaf. Though the tearoom had a decent crowd leftover from Winterfest activities, it wasn't packed like a few weeks back during the reopening of Eunny's repair café.

Gods. Only a few weeks ago. The span of time was incomprehensible. So short, yet it felt like it had been years. A lifetime. How could so much change in a handful of weeks?

While her father ordered tea for them both, she gazed out the window, wondering where Lowe had gone. He'd bowed out of Calya's meeting with Andrin with diplomatic grace, his expression unreadable. No parting words of revisiting interrupted moments this time. But would she have had an answer for him if they did?

"Calya?"

Shaken from her musing, she turned her attention back to Andrin. She blinked several times, still trying to make sense of him, *Andrin Helm*, in the Mighty Leaf, of all places. Judging by his expression and how two small pots of tea and a tray of snacks had arrived, she'd been lost in thought for longer than she'd intended.

"My apologies, Father." Calya poured herself a cup, annoyed that her hands shook. "You said we have business to discuss?"

"Wembly." Her father pushed a set of papers toward her across the table. "He'll be dealt with, I assure you. His betrayal is an embarrassment to me and the company, of course, so we have to act quickly to mitigate damage."

Calya picked up the papers, pausing as she noted the Helm family crest her father preferred for personal use—a flowing 'H' over a stylized ship—embossed at the top. Her gaze flicked up, but Father's face remained impassive as he sipped his tea. He nodded once, encouraging her to read.

The top paper was a draft for a formal announcement. She speed-read it once, eyebrows rising. Another glance at her father, but he pointedly looked out over the rest of the tearoom. Calya read the letter again, slower this time. Glancing at the rest of the papers, she found Helm Naval's standard boilerplate contract for employment.

"Assistant deputy to the director," she murmured. A three-year position answering to Andrin himself, who would be stepping away from his position on the Transportation Board for the duration. All the better to prepare Calya for the full role, according to the statement.

Andrin nodded slowly. "We can make the formal announcement after Winterfest. You'll have shared oversight for six of the Districts. A small staff of your own. It's a significant promotion."

Calya hummed in response. Then, more pointedly she added, "The districts and staff provided by you, I take it."

He dismissed her concern with a snort. "You may submit your choices. I'll only reserve final approval."

It wasn't the promotion she'd always wanted, but it was something. Mostly. Looked at another way, it was essentially an apprenticeship. With a set duration, and no verbiage promising further mobility. The wording of it nagged at her.

I formally name my youngest daughter, Calya Helm, as my Assistant Deputy, in a three-year term. It will give her time and experience to learn the senior managerial duties required at such a level at Helm Naval Engineering. Under my guidance, she will be prepared to eventually continue the legacy our family has built.

At least it was written in his hand rather than dictated to a secretary. It certainly had Andrin's fingerprints all over it. His chains.

"I'm surprised you're stepping down from your government work, Father," Calya said. "There's no guarantee you'll be given your spot back once I'm named director at HNE. Three years is a long time in that world, isn't it?"

"Helm Naval is more important," he said loftily. "We need to get out in front of this Wembly business before the *Grae Port News* catches—"

"You haven't been more than a name on the masthead for years," Calya said quietly. "I've been at HNE every day. I've been steering it. Not just *continuing its legacy,* Father, but preparing us to be even greater."

"Calya."

"I've *earned* this," she said. "Haven't I proved it to you enough?"

Either her father didn't see the vulnerability in her eyes, or he didn't care. Perhaps he was incapable of looking beyond his child to see the woman she'd become. Calya had never understood her parents' reluctance when it came to her, but she'd been patient. She'd waited.

And yet.

"You don't have the experience—"

"The trustee you hired to mind me turned out to be a gods-damned crook!" Calya snapped. "And all you can think about is, is..."

She stared at her father, whose cheeks were now reddened with barely contained temper.

"You wouldn't promote me at all, but the case against the Coalition is too public," she said. "My name will be all over it. Which is it, Father? Do you want to capitalize on my success, or are you trying to save face? All that media attention, someone's bound to find out about Wembly—"

"That vindictive tone is proof of why you're not ready to have my company, Calya. You're still too impulsive."

She glared at him. "You're a fool."

"Don't test me. You know how fast Central moves. We need to stay on top of this." Andrin stood. "We return to Grae Port on the first windrunner tomorrow morning. Don't be late."

He stalked out, leaving Calya alone with the paperwork. She finished her cup, but the cozy, *happy* atmosphere of the Mighty Leaf was too at odds with her mood. She wandered down to the lake, gazing out over the gently lapping waves. The rain had softened, more of a mist than a drizzle as it pattered the lake's surface.

She felt more than heard Lowe come up behind her.

"Good news?" he asked.

Calya held the drafted announcement out. For a moment, it seemed that he wouldn't take it. His hand moved slowly, fingers gripping the paper like it was a weapon.

Maybe it was. Her father had traded magic and a workshop for a politician's sash, wielded words now rather than runes. The promotion was written like an offer, but only one response would be accepted.

Lowe handed the paper back. "When do you leave?"

His tone was carefully neutral, and when she faced him, his expression remained mask-like. No glimmer of his own feelings.

No sentiment.

Calya faced the water again. "A ship leaves tomorrow."

A series of inhales, the beginnings of words on the cusp of sound, reached her ears, followed by sighs. Sharp puffs of frustration, as if Lowe struggled to speak. Or forced himself to stop.

Finally, hoarsely, he managed, "Will you be on it?"

Anadae spoke often of how she found the lake soothing. A good place to think and find clarity. Perhaps it was a mage thing, because for Calya, it held no answers. Not the ones she sought.

"We've never talked about what a future between us would look like. If it's even possible," Calya said. "What does the wind tell you?"

"I don't know. I won't ask," he said. Softly, almost like he was afraid she would blow away. He let his fingers graze her arm. "I want to hear it from you."

"Long distance would never work. It's not who I am."

"Graelynd is your home," he murmured. "I'd never ask you to leave it. I'll—I would go with you. If you'd have me."

Calya still considered her father's words. His promise, his ultimatum. She could have it, her lukewarm promotion and her ranger. It wasn't everything she'd hoped for, yet, at the same time, it was more of a future than she'd ever known she wanted. It could be hers.

Everything she wanted. *Thought* she wanted. It wasn't really everything, after all. What good was a weak promotion that put her under the yoke of her father's expectations? *Continue the legacy our family has built.* Continue the company according to Andrin's vision. Continue to be a puppet, only now with a fancier title. Upgraded to golden strings, and even that was only because he cared more about his image than rewarding her as she deserved. The stipulated three years meant nothing. Could be continued in an endless loop, even after he returned to politics. Which he'd likely only left to avoid more scrutiny when the bungle with Wembly came out.

Helm Naval. She'd wanted it for so long. Seen it as her path. But what good was a company that could never be hers? How did putting her hope in Andrin one day changing his mind enable her to make her mark on the world? To be the best? To *matter*?

Lowe was still next to her, tense. Waiting for her—not just for a time, but maybe forever if she were to ask it.

But what good was a ranger without a forest? Without mountains. Without, Goddess help her, this rain-sodden Valley.

"No," she said.

Lowe remained stiff—until she tore the paperwork in half. Into quarters. Ripped it again and again and cast the fragments into the air, letting the lake have them. He stared at her, eyes wide.

"I won't have that life. Graelynd would make you a shadow of the man I've wanted. It would have me wearing a muzzle to appease my father and his archaic vision." Calya still faced the water, but she gripped his hand, held him close against her arm.

"Are—are you sure?" he asked, voice so soft she almost couldn't hear. "Helm Naval... it's what you've always wanted."

"My identity. What drove me to be ambitious and reckless and—"

"No. Do not trust, that was always for me," Lowe said. "A warning, because I was afraid of change."

"It's all you've ever known of me, and now that's gone," she whispered. She turned to him, palm cupping his cheek. "I don't know what the wind said, but if you would have me, I will build us something new. Something greater than anyone could ever dream."

Lowe kissed her, deeply. Resting his forehead against hers, he murmured, "You'll conquer the world."

Calya smirked. "Baby steps. Andrin thought it would take three years to mold me into a proper businesswoman." She bared her teeth in a smile. "In three years, Helm Naval will face acquisitions, or fold."

Lowe kissed her again. "You scare the fuck out of me." Then he leaned back, worry in his eyes when he said, hesitantly, "You're sure about this? Living here... you could be happy? With me?"

Calya bit her lip and took a step back, shoulders hunching. He was the first man she'd felt any real attachment toward, any sentimentality. She had it and believed it to be true, but she knew she was not suddenly changed. Lady Heartless might have a few shards left in her chest, but was that enough? Was *she*, she who had only so much in her to give?

"I lied to you before," she said softly, finally meeting his gaze. "I'll never love you back."

Lowe froze, face going pale.

"Not the way you deserve." She caressed his face again, her lips forming a sad smile. "I am still ambitious. Reckless, or ruthless. More than anything, I am *selfish*. In whatever is left in me that resembles a heart, I will struggle to keep you first, as you should be."

She pressed her lips to his. "I will never love you back. Not the way you deserve," she repeated. "But I will want you, every day. You can trust in that."

Lowe stared at her. Closed his eyes in a long, slow blink. Then he wrapped his arms around her, crushing her against his chest as his entire body shook with a laugh, one full of relief.

"I'll love you enough for the both of us," he vowed before his mouth was upon hers. Calya's lips parted, and it was all the encouragement he needed. His tongue swept in, and a shiver of delight ran up her spine at the taste of him. Of this ranger who wanted her, embraced her with all her thorns.

They might have stood there at the lakeside forever, oblivious to the world... until the world pushed back in. A scattered shower of heavier, concentrated rain slanted sideways at them.

Lowe raised his hand, a gust of wind saving them from the worst of the drenching.

Calya waved in exasperation at the sky. "I did *you* a favor! I'm staying. Get used to it."

The lake surged, a low wave splashing them both up to the knees. In only the spot where they stood on the rocky beach.

Calya glared at Lowe, who raised his hands in a helpless gesture. "It's not too late to go for a water mage instead of a diviner."

"Don't tempt me," she muttered. She started away from the lake, then turned to him. "So, where do you live?"

He laughed, the sound rich and joyous. It sent a warmth through Calya that filled her chest and settled, that sense of rightness becoming a background presence in her head.

He held out his hand. Taken aback, she blinked at it. At him. Then, feeling just a touch charmed by the novelty, she slid her palm into his and let him guide her back to town.

Epilogue
SIX MONTHS LATER

THE SUN WAS SETTING as Nocren's ship approached the harbor in Talihn, the capital of the kingdom of Rhell. He leaned against the ship's railing, watching as the grand city grew larger. A steady churn of movement along the docks resolved from mere specks on the horizon into identifiable shapes of people going about their business. Clean streets led away from the harbor, disappearing amongst the city's buildings. Though the palace was a bit farther inland, the dockside homes and businesses were made in the same vein of white and gray stone with shingle roofs and trim in red or dark gold that seemed more stately than outright colorful.

The architecture gave the impression of age, not unlike the Valley of Sylveren's Renstown or the University, but with an added sense of elegance. Of *legacy*. In Nocren's head, Talihn had an air of busyness that felt gilded in formality, where Renstown felt busy like work. And whether the implied fussiness was real or Nocren's own bias, who could say? Neither had the comfort of Sylvan, nor the sense of wisdom surrounding the school.

But they were a damn sight better than the clamor that was Grae Port, and Nocren would much rather be chasing after Calya here, surrounded by a people who at least knew they were mildly elitist by default. Better than the Graelynders, who knew they were brash to an aggravating degree and leaned into it. Somehow, he'd let his heart be caught by one of them.

Let. Nocren huffed softly to himself, letting his eyes close as he lifted his face to catch the wind whirling around him. There was no *letting* when it came to Calya. Those brief, bitter moments when he'd tried to deny the hold she had on him... at least they were in the past. He knew better now, and thankfully hadn't fucked it all up in the process. Thank the Eternal Wind for that.

Nocren opened his eyes, gaze automatically going to the figures moving about the docks, alert for a particular brunette head or a familiar dark red tunic. She wouldn't be there, of course; she didn't even know he was here already, two days earlier than planned, with her coveted documents in hand. He pressed a hand against the small bag lashed to his shoulder holster, reassuring himself that it —and its contents—were still there: an official copy of the contract granting access along Valley waterways in an exclusive partnership between the Sentinels and Calya's new company. Her as yet unnamed company. He wondered if she'd made any progress on that front.

The wind swirled around his head, a phantom caress against his face, before reverting back to the dull roar and haphazard buffeting that characterized the element. No impressions pressed against his mind; his magic remained quiet beneath his skin.

It had been doing that lately. Growing quieter. Not weakening, but being more... selective, asserting a sense of autonomy and opinion that had only made itself known in small doses until now. Before Calya had come into his life. Barged in, more like. Staked her claim and dared him—dared anyone—to resist. To question her decision.

As if he would ever do such a thing. Which was a disquieting thought for a man who'd intentionally been alone for so long, beholden to no one. Solitude wasn't something he'd had to grow accustomed to, either; he'd chosen it. Had felt most comfortable and at ease without any of the anchors that came with relationships. The camaraderie Nocren had through his Sentinel work had been enough. He'd wanted for nothing.

Perhaps it was fitting, then—was almost like fate—that he'd stumbled into a woman who had been the same. In her, Nocren found he could want more in his life and would rearrange anything to make space for it to work.

Yet, when he thought about it, he'd changed so little in the preceding months. Certainly, his life *had* changed. Though he kept a room in the Sentinels' barracks, he'd moved into a suite of rooms Calya had found in Renstown and more often than not commuted daily via windrunner rather than staying at the barracks—even when Calya was away on business, as she'd been often in the first few months since their adventures at Desmond's Landing. Sometimes, he accompanied her, such as when they'd done the final assessment for the Sentinels' patrol route and established an official headquarters in the Landing. But he despised the hectic compaction that was Grae Port, so aside from when his testimony was required in the trial against the Coalition and Avenor, Nocren happily stayed home.

He didn't think he slept any less soundly when they were apart. Didn't lie awake at night. No anxiety. But on the evenings she came in late, having adjusted her schedule to return a few hours earlier than planned so she could slide into their bed? Always, he felt a quiet relief.

Perhaps Nocren had changed more than he realized. Perhaps he possessed certain depths he'd never known, or that only Calya could bring about. After all, he'd sworn—boasted, even—that he'd love her enough for the both of them.

Hardly a feat when she made it so easy. For if Calya had changed him, Nocren didn't feel those shifts. Not so overtly. They were more the kind of thing he noticed in subtle reflections. That the transition had been mostly seamless felt... perfect. An affirmation that Calya was right for him. And if he'd made any such impact on her, well...

He put the thought on hold as he disembarked and made the short trip to the set of rooms Ezzyn Sor'vahl had offered up on his private estate. The wind swirled around Nocren's hand as he reached for the polished brass door handle. It imparted just a hint of excitement before dissipating.

It did that rather a lot now, giving him no more than a glimpse when it came to Calya, regardless of whether the feeling was good or bad. She had remained steadfast in her disinterest for his magic. That brought its own sense of relief. Although Calya had said it with her usual bluntness. Being told, "I refuse to let myself become reliant on fickle tools," had a way of making one feel indignant despite it being a favorable outcome.

His magic didn't share any such contradictory feelings. When it came to Calya, the wind's loyalty was abundantly clear. A whisper of a thrill was all it gave. Otherwise, it was simply a light breeze. Not that he had ever asked it for more, never tried to analyze Calya or their future. He had a sneaking suspicion that if he attempted to, the wind wouldn't answer anyway.

Quietly, he let himself into the foyer. Sor'vahl might live more modestly than other royalty, but he *was* still a prince, and the "set of rooms" was more like an entire wing of a mansion. It was smaller than the royal palace but still left Nocren vaguely unsettled by all the space. Even more so because Sor'vahl and Anadae were away, deploying their updated wards across as much of the kingdom as they could manage.

Despite the late hour, few of the lamps were turned up on the lower level, early summer providing enough light for Nocren to easily make his way up the stairs. It was quiet, suggesting the staff had already retired for the evening, but it wasn't so late that Calya would be in bed. Maybe, if she'd known he was coming tonight. He'd been greeted in such a manner when they'd traveled separately.

Many times. He lamented his lack of foresight to send a message ahead that he'd arrive a day earlier than expected. At the time, it had seemed like his arrival would make for a welcome surprise.

The bedroom was empty, the lamps on either side of the bed pleasantly dim. The magicked lightstones present in so many Rhellian buildings didn't flicker, their illumination accompanied by a soft hum audible only if one stood very close. It was a sound easily overridden by the gentle splash drifting from the adjoining washroom's open door.

Nocren's pulse sped up as he walked toward the door, but he forced himself to keep a deliberate pace, neither sneaking nor hurried. Which took some discipline after being away from her for the better part of a week.

Gods. A *week*. He'd been well and thoroughly ruined by Calya Helm.

He wouldn't want it any other way.

Tapping softly on the washroom door, Nocren pushed it fully open and stuck his head in. Warm air brushed his face.

Calya lounged in the tub, perusing a sheaf of papers. Though a pair of lamps provided ample light, a smattering of candles arranged on the window ledge added their own glow to the room.

"Hello ranger," she said, smiling and setting the papers down on a low stool next to the tub. "You're early."

She reached for the towel on the stool, but Nocren motioned for her to stay. He commandeered the stool for himself, shrugging out of his cloak and shoulder harness.

"Wanted to surprise you," he said.

Calya leaned against the side of the tub, her arms resting on the edge. "Consider me pleasantly surprised."

The heated water gave her skin a rosy tinge. A hint of petrichor filled his nose as he bent for a kiss, but she turned her face away, a wickedness to her smile. "Toll. Did you bring me anything with your speedy arrival?"

"Only want me so long as you get something, eh?" Nocren fetched the documents from his bag.

"I've never pretended to be coy."

"Or patient." He handed her the paperwork. "Malek'ko sends his regards."

Calya made a delighted sound as she took hold of the exclusivity contract.

Nocren settled back on the stool, kicking off his boots as he eyed the papers she had abandoned. "What were you working on?"

A vague fluttering of fingers accompanied her distracted, "Just some new terms for the armament side of the deal with Froley. Putting a few sweeteners in for Orren if he stays on the full two years."

Nocren glanced at the figures she'd scrawled onto the page. "Sweetheart, are you trying to poach the good lieutenant from Avenor Guard? Not very business partnery of you, is it?"

"It's very businessy, though perhaps less on the partnership side," she said mildly. "But that all presumes I want to *stay* business partners a few years from now." She turned to the next page in her contract, not looking up as she added, "*Captain* Orren has a nice ring to it, don't you think?"

Nocren shook his head. He flipped the paperwork over and moved to set it down when he noticed a jagged list of names on the back, several of which were scratched out.

"What is this?" he asked. "V-L-E-N."

"Some ideas for my new business name. I circled the leading candidate."

"Valley Logistics, Exchange, and Navigation," Nocren recited. "V-L-E-N. *Villain*, Calya? You can't be—"

"What? Everyone's going to be thinking as much anyway, so why not embrace it?" She laughed. "I couldn't think of anything with 'Helm' that I liked."

He pinched the bridge of his nose, then, exhaling dramatically, reached for her. "I paid the toll," he muttered before claiming her mouth.

The contract papers hit the floor as Calya tossed them—carefully—to the side and wrapped her arms around his neck. "You did," she agreed, returning his kiss. "Overpaid. Such expediency deserves a reward."

The front of Nocren's shirt clung where it was soaked through by Calya's damp skin. He ignored it, letting the water creep up his sleeve as he reached to cup her breast. She leaned into his hand, sighing with pleasure as his thumb circled her nipple.

"What strings are attached to this prize?" he asked.

"None." Calya drew back enough to meet his eyes. There was a mischievous, *hungry* glint in her gaze as she waited for his reaction.

"An unconditional reward?" Nocren shrugged out of his wet shirt. "How unlike you."

"Well, if you don't want it…" she said in mock indignation. She moved to get out of the tub. "I'll be—"

Nocren gently pushed her back, smirking when she hardly put up a fight. He kissed her again, slower this time, savoring the taste of her.

With one hand keeping her mouth tilted up toward him, he let his other roam freely across her chest. Her nipples had already begun to harden, and she shivered when he rolled each one between his fingers. Made a pouty sound when he tweaked them and made her jump.

He kissed the frown from her brow, then moved down, his lips feathering over her neck, trailing lower until he could replace the teasing of his fingers with his mouth.

Calya leaned back, letting her head rest on the tub's rim with her legs splayed open. Nocren's cock throbbed against the confinement of his trousers. He didn't let it, or Calya's restless shifting, hurry him along, as much as he'd like to toss her onto the bed and not surface until morning. There was plenty of time for all of that.

Eager as he was, nothing instilled a wicked brand of patience in him than an *im*patient Calya. She liked being a challenge, but as he grew bolder, as they became more familiar with each other's desires, he suspected she enjoyed pressing him simply so he would take her in hand. She let him. Trusted him enough to do it. Wanted it, at least with him.

Now, to be gifted so much discretion, so many fantasies clamored in his head. Being spoiled for choice made his hands shake as excitement and indecision clashed.

Best not to think ahead at all, but only of the moment.

Nocren laved her nipple with his tongue, eliciting another shiver and appreciative moan. Calya's back arched away from the tub as he increased his pressure, alternating between sucking and flicking with the tip of his tongue. Her hands came up to grasp his head, her fingers tangling in his hair. She held him close in one instant and tried to pull him away at the next, moans growing more insistent.

When Nocren swiped his thumb over her clit, a small gasp had her perfect tits bumping against his face. His mouth released her with a wet pop, and he nipped at her exposed throat before returning to her chest. Calya squirmed as he latched on to her other breast and gave it equal treatment.

"L-Lowe." Calya's voice had a breathless quality to it. Her hips canted up as she sought more of his touch.

"Hmm?"

His mouth never left her nipple. He settled on sucking the hardened point between his lips and massaging it with his tongue. Tonight, that combination had her wound especially tight. Had her chest already beginning to heave as her breaths turned to soft pants and her pelvis chased his teasing fingers. Even her hands were beginning to tremble, still clutched around his head.

A warm, pleased hum ran through Nocren's mind. He could have a lifetime of exploring her body and it wouldn't be enough.

To learn the whole of Calya and her preferences required constant study. An eternal craft he could dedicate himself to and still be surprised every day.

Thank the wind for its prescience.

Nocren let a single fingertip slide through her folds. Delved in only to his first knuckle, resisting when Calya tried to bear down.

"You're very needy tonight," he said, raising his head. He traced his tongue along the column of her throat, letting his finger rub over her clit before toying with her pussy again.

Calya tried to spear herself on him, a frustrated exhale ruffling his hair when he eluded her efforts. "Lowe."

"Did you not take care of yourself while I was gone?" he asked, tone innocent as he tapped her clit.

"I thought you liked it when I put you to work."

Nocren pressed his thumb against her sensitive nub, chuckling softly when her head tipped farther back, her eyes squeezing shut with anticipation.

"I do," he murmured into her ear. "Though it hardly feels like work when you're so willing."

Another exasperated huff left her mouth when Nocren ignored her attempts to coax his finger deeper. "Don't make me regret it."

"I would never." He let a second finger join the first. Let them slide slowly in until he couldn't go any farther. He crooked his fingers, satisfaction streaking through his chest when Calya's inner walls gripped him, her inhale sounding more like a long hiss.

She was already so close. So primed for him.

So mistaken, if she thought giving Nocren free rein would mean a nice, quick release and then some passionate lovemaking.

Impassioned, yes. As for the rest, that was where the similarities ended.

"But tonight, Calya, love," Nocren rumbled, "I will make you beg for it."

Her questioning sound turned into a yelp as he withdrew

abruptly and gathered Calya into his arms. Ignoring the bathwater cascading down, he carried her to the bed and tossed her onto it.

He ditched the rest of his clothes in record time as she perched on the edge of the bed. She leaned over to drag the nightstand's top drawer open. Gods all bless his woman for always being prepared. No sooner had Calya finished swallowing a contraceptive potion than Nocren had spun her around and bent her over the bed.

Fingers slick with lubricant, his fingers penetrated her without any further warning. No hesitation or leisurely strokes. Nocren set an immediate, rapid pace. One might even have called it punishing.

But not Calya. She gasped, her thighs twitching closed by reflex as her pussy clenched. When she started to rise, he leaned forward, his fist wrapping around her hair to keep her head still. Down. She growled at him, shaking her head to test his grip.

He could have sworn that she clenched even harder when his hand tightened in her hair. Or maybe it was caused by the slight angle of his wrist so his thumb could join the assault on her most sensitive parts.

Caged between him and the edge of the bed, Calya could only shift restlessly from foot to foot. Hoarse gasps mingled with short, stifled cries as Nocren's thrusting fingers ratcheted up the tension in her.

"You spoke of being earned once, do you remember?" he asked, the hand in her hair not letting Calya bury her face in the mattress. "But you don't want that. You want to be taken, don't you, sweetheart? Taken by me. No one else."

Her legs shook as she came. She trembled in his grip, her desire dripping down his hand as he gave her a final stroke.

She moaned when he pulled his fingers out. It was a plaintive, low sound. One that went abruptly high and indignant when he gave her pussy a slap. And then it became a cry as he replaced his fingers with his cock.

Nocren released her head so he could grip her by the waist. Better leverage. Better for him to watch his cock as it disappeared into her beckoning heat. He allowed himself a few long, measured thrusts, reveling in the way Calya grabbed fistfuls of the sheets. She cried out, her legs shaking. Her inner walls fluttered weakly around him, already swollen from the vigorous finger fuck he'd given her. His skin still glistened with the evidence of her enjoyment.

She turned her face to the side, enough so he could glimpse one of her eyes. Catch the slight curl of her smile, the dare in her arched brow as she met his next thrust and squeezed when he was buried balls deep.

Nocren picked up his pace.

There were many things he loved about Calya, and when not in the throes of lust, he could name several at the top that didn't have to do with her body. But here and now, the sound of her cries filling the air, the sight of her body jerking with every impact as he bucked into her, the twitching of her shoulders and jiggle of her perfect ass, all of it took over. He could hardly think beyond the smugness that came with each *plap-plap-plap* as his balls slapped against her pussy. That he was fucking her hard enough to hear it, and she strained for more even though she had to be feeling tender so soon after coming.

He thanked the wind for pushing him toward her. This fierce woman who never wanted him to be gentle. Never wanted him to be *nice*. Let go of herself enough to have that with him and trust that he would know how to take care of her.

He did. Already had her back arching, her heels lifting as she tried to fit as much of his cock as she could.

It gave him a feral pleasure to have her wanting him so. To see her take his rough handling and want more. To take her wrists in each hand, pull her arms behind her back, and use them to hold her in place as his hips pumped against her.

Nocren was wound as tight as she was, balancing on the edge. He wanted to feel her come apart all over him, have the rapid pulsing of her core jerk him into oblivion. But not yet. Not like this. He wanted more. Of her, and of the submission she'd teased him with all those months ago.

Tonight, he'd prove that she was already his.

His hips snapped flush with her, kept him buried as he released her arms and leaned over her back to take her chin in his hand. A possessive joy rolled through him when her lips sought his. They parted so easily for him, a whimper muffled by his tongue as it swept into her mouth. He swallowed down her moan as his free hand reached to find her clit. His thrusts were shorter now, but no less deep. No less forceful, even as his weight made her feet slip against the slick wooden floor.

He rolled her clit between his fingers. Timed his next thrust in with a light pinch. Calya shuddered beneath him, her climax so close it was all but a physical thing held in his hand.

"Do you want to come?" he rasped out.

She nodded. Another whimper escaped when he squeezed her sensitive nub again.

"I can't hear you."

A frustrated whine came from the back of her throat. Then, softly, "Please." She swallowed hard. "Please, I'm so close."

He pressed his lips to her temple. "My name, Calya. Say it."

"Lo—"

"My *name.*" His pelvis stilled, fingers hovering away from her skin. Pinned against the bed by his hips, Calya couldn't chase her own pleasure.

"N-Nocren. Nocren, please," she managed. He got a brief glimpse of her eyes, her pupils blown wide, before her lashes lowered and she sought his mouth again. "Please make me come," she whispered.

The plea hadn't fully left her mouth before he was surging forward again. He gripped her by the hips, pushed her up onto her tiptoes. A few more thrusts and he stiffened against her, hand reaching for her clit again to work her over until she writhed. Her pussy contracted around him, coming so hard she practically pulled his release from him.

Nocren collapsed against Calya, his entire frame rising and falling with his panting breaths.

They lay like that for several moments before Calya finally elbowed him. "Lowe, you're squashing me."

He grunted in response, pushing up enough to drag them onto a drier spot on the bed. They lay on their sides, and Calya slotted into place, curling against his chest as she let her leg drape over the top of his hip.

"I love you," he mumbled into her hair.

Calya preened and hummed in response. "Oh, do you?"

"Everything about you."

"Name them, then. All of my lovable qualities."

"Ruthless and ambitious, you already know."

Calya nodded, forehead thumping against his chest. "You need new material."

Nocren snorted. "Vicious. Wicked. But my new favorite might be..." Smirking, he moved to cover her with his body, propping himself up on his elbows to spare her some of his weight. "How obedient you are for me."

He smothered her feigned outrage with a deep kiss. When she nipped at him, he groaned—kissed her even more thoroughly until she was reciprocating with a hunger to match his own.

"And you call me wicked," Calya pouted when they finally came up for air.

"I've only just begun, sweetheart." He kissed the tip of her nose. "Now that I have your submission," he teased.

She rolled her eyes.

"Think of all the sweet, torturous things I could do to you, and they're yours." He nuzzled her cheek. "Didn't I promise you edging all night with the Kiss in your veins?"

Calya let out a bark of laughter. She pushed him over, rolling on top so she could straddle him. "Perhaps it'll be you, ranger, burning for me. Begging for it."

Nocren rubbed along her legs. "Would you like that? More than the other way around?"

One of her shoulders lifted in a careless shrug. "Who could possibly say? We'll just have to try both."

It was his turn to laugh. "Not sure where you're going to find the time. *Villain* won't establish itself."

There was a roguish gleam in her eye as she leaned forward. "It's a good thing we have forever to exact such revenge on each other, then, hmm?"

Dodging his mouth, Calya kissed his neck, sucking hard enough Nocren imagined he'd have a mark to hide in the morning. Another laugh rumbled up from deep in his throat, and he crushed her against his chest, kissing away her squawk of protest.

After her grumbling subsided, Calya softened. Slowly, her arms crept around him so she could hug him, and she tucked her head beneath his chin.

He did love her. Though he knew Calya would probably never have it in her to say those same words, it didn't matter. If they had forever, he'd simply have to become fluent in Calya's many ways of showing how she loved him back.

THE END

Thank you for reading *Mistral Hearts*! I hope you enjoyed your time in the world of Sylveren as much as I've enjoyed writing it. If you have a moment, please consider leaving a review on the retailer and/or review site of your choice. Reviews are the gift that keeps on giving. *Your* thoughts are key to books finding their way to readers who will enjoy them the most, long after the release day buzz has worn off.

NOT QUITE READY TO LEAVE CALYA AND NOCREN? With Nocren still hung up on the Storage Shed Debacle, Calya's determined to help him move on. Best way to get over a bad experience is to replace it with a better one, right? Join my monthly newsletter to see how her spicy plan unfolds!

Sign up for my newsletter here!

Acknowledgments

Here we are again. The Acks, and this time for the end of a trilogy. It's a weird mix of satisfying and bittersweet to be closing out this particular phase of my life. I'm happy and proud to have these books out in the world. Though I'm feeling a little misty at the thought of not writing them anymore, I think we've all seen by now that I also love to have characters keep showing up, regardless of whether or not they're the main attraction. Got to love that found family.

Family, found and otherwise, are the reason I've been able to write. Firstly, many thanks to my family and friends, for always being supportive and excited about my books. Thank you to my husband Steven, for being my first reader, my biggest fan, my rock. Thank you for always encouraging me to do this, for always being willing to listen, and always valuing my work—and reminding me to do the same.

Cara. I don't know how, but for some reason, the universe decided to bring us together and I am forever grateful for it. Platonic fated mates—it's a thing. Thank you for being you, my #1 hype guy, twelve years strong.

If my books are enjoyable, it's by the grace of my wonderful critique partners. Steven M., Cara M., S.A. H., and Marit H., thank you for giving me so much of your time, and exemplifying that honesty need not be brutal to be effective.

Huge thanks to Isla and Adie, not only for your eagle eyes and ruthless hands in correcting my apparent misunderstanding of... a lot of basic grammar and punctuation. I joke (kind of), but truly, I've been fortunate to work with two amazing editors who are not just excellent at their craft, but also incredibly understanding people. Thank you for being so accommodating with your schedules.

The writing community has a way of being vast and yet small at the same time. To try and name everyone would make this way too long, and I'd inevitably forget someone, so I give blanket thanks and am hugely grateful to everyone in the FaRo Society and Wide Author Resources communities for being so generous with their time and knowledge. Anyone who underestimates the indie romance community does so at their own peril.

Thank you to everyone in the book community who has helped me along the way. Whether you've shared my covers or were part of the ARC team. Whether you've written reviews or told a friend about my books. Or whether you've left a kind word, maybe a heart emoji, on one of my posts, I am truly grateful. There are so many books out there vying for your attention, and it means so much that you took a chance on me. Thank you to Sarah C., for being awesome and keeping me wrangled into some form of order. Thank you to Roxana O., and Scarlett K., for lending me your names!

To Jin, so many thanks. If the nicest thing that is ever said about my books is that they have pretty covers, I'll make peace with that. I'm biased but I think I've got absolute stunners for covers. I'm still pinching myself that I got not one but *three* beautiful pieces that are each individual and yet flow together so perfectly. To think, this all started with elves and egg tarts.

And of course, lastly, thank you, dear reader, for picking up this book and letting me share my words with you.

Jaime Ryanne, January 2026

Also by Jaime Ryanne

The Valley of Sylveren

Elemental Affections

Growing Memories

Mistral Hearts

The World of Sylveren

A New Leaf

About the Author

JAIME RYANNE writes fantasy romance featuring competent heroines of color, secondary world settings with modern touches, and plenty of spice. There's usually angst involved, but it always comes with a happy ending.

She is a Korean American adoptee living in the Pacific Northwest with her husband and two cats. When she isn't writing, if she's sitting then she's probably knitting (or spinning yarn. Actual yarn, not tales). She loves fountain pens, collecting notebooks, and wishes her enthusiasm for gardening was reflected in the actual results.

www.jaimeryanne.com
Instagram: @jaimeryanne_writes

www.ingramcontent.com/pod-product-compliance
Lightning Source LLC
LaVergne TN
LVHW040041080526
838202LV00045B/3441